"Mark Graham is a writer to watch."
Oregonian

HOW DID SHE DIE?

"What makes you think she was a whore?" I asked, lifting up the canvas a little bit more.

She wore a cheap dress which clung to her bloated figure like a ready-made shroud. I picked up her thick hand. There was a tiny scar on her right index finger. And something on the wrist.

"See that?" I said. "Cuts or burns, maybe."

"Well that's mighty interestin'," Brown said. "Course that still don't counter-dict my theory about her drownin'."

"Maybe she slit her wrists before she jumped in," Herbert said.

"That's what I call hedgin' a bet," Brown said.

I shook my head. "No. They're not deep enough."

I unwrapped a pathetic looking bow tied around her collar. Then I saw her neck. It was covered with thick welts, spaced apart just right. Impressions from a human hand.

Other Mysteries of Old Philadelphia by
Mark Graham
from Avon Books

THE KILLING BREED
THE BLACK MARIA

THE RESURRECTIONIST

A Mystery
of Old
Philadelphia

MARK GRAHAM

AVON BOOKS
An Imprint of HarperCollinsPublishers

AVON BOOKS
An Imprint of HarperCollins*Publishers*
10 East 53rd Street
New York, New York 10022-5299

Copyright © 1999 by Mark Graham
Inside cover author photo by Fauzia N. Graham
Published by arrangement with the author
Library of Congress Catalog Card Number: 99-94792
ISBN: 0-380-80067-5
www.avonbooks.com

First Avon Printing: August 2000
First Avon Twilight Printing: August 1999

Avon Trademark Reg. U.S. Pat. Off. and in Other Countries, Marca Registrada, Hecho en U.S.A.
HarperCollins® is a trademark of HarperCollins Publishers Inc.

Printed in the U.S.A.

WCD 10 9 8 7 6 5 4 3 2

To Aaron Ramson White

Prologue

I SPENT THE last day of 1875 in prayer with ten thousand two hundred other people. That was how many seats there were in the Grand Depot on Thirteenth and Market. John Wannamaker, Philadelphia's merchant prince, had recently bought the whole depot for his new store. He generously donated it to house the Moody-Sankey revival as long as it lasted.

Dwight L. Moody handled the preaching and Ira D. Sankey the singing, along with a choir of three hundred. Despite what some of the papers said about Moody being a theological charlatan, I found the nation's most famous evangelist inspiring. I attended whenever I could.

Moody's sermons hit on the same theme over and over. No matter how far you fell you could still save yourself. It was a message that I liked to hear, though I didn't quite believe it.

Every now and then I would think on Eddie Munroe and the kidnapping—my first case as a detective. It had almost been my last, too. I nearly quit police work for good after that one. My reasons for wanting to quit were as complex as my reasons for staying. Perhaps they were the same reasons.

I kept going into the wilderness of streets to test myself. I failed test after test but I kept going back. Even if I

1

couldn't save myself, I wanted to keep trying.

That afternoon we sang a hymn and then Moody read from the 28th chapter of St. Matthew, the story of the resurrection.

It got me thinking on the new year coming up, the Centennial year. America was turning a hundred and it felt like a second birth was coming. After the war, the country needed it.

The city was planning a huge celebration of industry, art, and agriculture that would be the greatest exhibition the world had ever seen. In Fairmount Park they were already at work constructing the enormous halls that would house exhibits from all over the civilized and uncivilized world.

A new age was coming, everyone could feel it. And it was starting in Philadelphia just like the last one had.

I hoped the new age would be better than the one we'd buried in the war.

After the reading Moody preached on the evils of intemperance. The services closed after the benediction. Then I went home and fed my fox terrier Jocko. The two of us fell asleep in front of the stove.

That night I was on duty. The New Year's Eve festivities were the loudest ever. The city wanted to bring in the Centennial year on an incendiary note. In front of the red, white, and blue–festooned State House a crowd of several thousand was gathered to witness the fireworks display, despite the muddy streets.

Right before midnight Mayor Stokley showed up. A replica of the flag unfurled by George Washington over the camps of the Continental Army in 1776 now appeared over Independence Hall. Crackers and cheers accompanied it. For a while I watched the crackers being set off right beside the statue of Washington. The fireworks looked beautiful against the misty night sky.

We were waving our hats, joyfully. It was one of those moments when you knew without a doubt that the United

States of America was the greatest nation in the history of the human race.

A few moments later I had to disperse a crowd of thugs who were beating up a deaf-mute boy. It took some doing. There were three of them and one of me. I got knocked down and shook up a bit. At one point I was on the ground, in the mud, getting kicks in the head and the body. Eventually I got in a few nut-crackers with my club and put the bracelets on one of them. I made sure he lost a few more teeth before we got to the station-house.

In the early hours of the morning I made it back home. Before I went to bed I read some Scripture, like I always did. I found a passage in the Gospel of John, the one about being born again.

Remembering the events of the night, I wondered if a whole nation could be born again. When I thought of the drunks beating a cripple during our glorious Centennial New Year's celebration, I knew the time wasn't right. I wondered if the time would ever come.

Thinking that made me go to my closet and withdraw an old segar box. There was an envelope inside it. I sat down on my bed and took out the contents. There was only one thing there, something I hadn't looked at in a long time.

I held the thing in my hand, running my fingers over it again and again.

I stayed there on my bed with the lock of dark hair. I was thinking on the future.

The thinking got too painful. So I brought up memories to fight the pain. I held her hair to my lips and remembered the first time I saw her.

THERE WERE ONLY five days left before the election. That would make it Friday, October 6, 1871. I'd spent that morning in court, testifying against a sneak I'd collared a few days before. His specialty was hair goods. When I pinched him he had a crate full of Fluffy Fedora Hair Curlers which he'd just appropriated from a parked dray. The sneak was no greenhorn when it came to the penitentiary. So he had a long bit coming to him. Turned out to be a two-spot.

The owner of the hair goods shop was overjoyed. He wanted to give me a token of his appreciation. I waited until we were out of court. Then I let him give me five cans. Getting a reward for the recovery of stolen merchandise was standard back then.

The day was glorious, with gleaming clouds whisking past a deep blue sky. The sun, now hidden, now revealed, shone on us with a soft luster. In its light, the whole world was suddenly transformed into something mysterious and somber, yet still beautiful. That was how autumn always made me feel.

I was in no hurry to get back to City Hall. Things were very tense at the Central Office. Fox was on the way out. Anyone could see that. Ever since the negroes got the right to vote the Democrats had the shakes. Colored men knew which side to vote for: the party of the man who freed the slaves. With their help it looked like Fox and his boys might get the boot. That meant a lot of coppers would lose their politically appointed jobs. And all the fat scale they squeezed out of grafters on their beat.

I wasn't worried, being a Republican.

On the way back from court I took the old green Chestnut and Walnut Street car. The horse team waited at the corner for a long time after I got on. They'd been working hard all day like everybody else. In no time the car was packed. There was usually room for about twenty people to sit down. All those seats were taken now as we neared Fifth and Chestnut. I jostled my way to the window behind the driver, facing the back platform where the ticket taker stood.

As the team started sliding the car along the rails, a gust of autumn wind knocked off my new soft hat. When I stooped for it, I caught sight of someone at the back of the car. I stood up with my hat held to my breast, brushing dust from the black felt. Then I looked through the car again. That was the first time I really saw her.

The first thing I noticed was how beautiful she was.

Even in that crowded car she seemed alone, set apart. Her eyes were cast downward at a book in her lap. I wondered what the book was about. Then I shifted my gaze to the window.

After a few moments I looked at her again, this time noticing her clothes. She wore a mourning bonnet, trimmed and crowned with dull black crepe. Her suit was also black, and elegant. But not too flashy. The skirt was kilt-plaited with folds of velvet. A cutaway basque with velvet collar and cuffs did a lot for the corset she wore underneath.

Thinking on the corset made me turn away again, ashamed of myself.

This hadn't happened in a long time. And now like this. With someone like her.

I tried to stop myself from watching her. I tried concentrating on the floorboards of the car. That didn't work too well.

I noticed she was tapping those same floorboards with her slippered foot. It was surprising to see her without boots. Of course the slippers would be more comfortable, but ladies usually didn't concern themselves with comfort if it got in the way of style. Still, her hands were covered with jersey gloves. If that wasn't the sign of a lady, I didn't know what was.

She kept tapping away as we rode toward the State House. I wondered what the rhythm was in her head. I watched her face, trying to see if she mouthed any words.

It was a handsome face. Dark and serious eyes, a shapely nose, and full lips which now and then parted in a lovely smile, responding to a private joke.

As the car came to a stop again I closed my eyes. I tried to hide in the darkness there, but her face kept coming back to me. At first I felt guilty. Then I asked myself why. There were plenty of answers to that question.

I might as well have kept my eyes open. I would have seen the same thing with them open or closed: all the details of her dress and her figure and her face.

And the brown color of her skin.

She was the handsomest negress I'd ever laid eyes on.

The car stopped and I watched as the new passengers packed themselves in. As we got started again I noticed three of them crowding around the colored young lady. Two wore cheap ready-made suits with vests fit to burst from their bellies. The other looked like a wiry sport with plaid trousers and a silk neck tie. They were crossmen from the look of them. That is, criminals.

Their lidded eyes were full of malice. What they said to each other was not for polite ears. From the way they swaggered and pushed people out of their way, I got the feeling they were small-time strong-arm men. I knew their type well. They were the kind of robbers who slam bricks into peoples' faces when a simple biff in the jaw might do.

All three took turns spitting long gobs in the cuspidor right by the colored girl. I averted my eyes a fourth or fifth time. Then I heard the men talking.

From the profanity they used I figured their back teeth were afloat. A few of the other passengers resented the strong language. They gave the men withering looks. But when they saw to whom the language was directed they turned away.

I tried to do that too, like the coward I sometimes am.

But I still heard the words.

The sport stroked his long side whiskers and said, "Looks like we don't have no room to sit down, Uriah."

"Yeah," said the fat one with a long thick mustache, "ain't no room. We gotta stand up."

"Imagine. We folks gotta stand and a nigger gets a seat. Now that don't make no sense to me. What about you, Brode?"

"They got a nerve, that's no joke," said the clean-shaven fat man. "I think they should get their ass on the front platform when a man wants a seat."

"What about it, darling?" the sport said, leaning toward the colored girl. "You gonna move like a good little gal? Or are we gonna have to kick you out?"

"Listen, you men," said an old fellow next to me. "You know the rail company lets niggers ride inside same as everybody else. Been that way for three years."

The old fellow was correct. A battle had been fought for that right for years after the war. Before it was won, the negroes had to stand on the crowded front platform, exposed to the elements every day and night of the year, no matter what the weather.

The sport turned to the old man and said, "But we ain't talkin' to you, you stupid bastard."

At this point the ticket taker walked up to the men and said, "What's all this about?"

The clean-shaven fat man said, "Our pal wants the nigger's seat."

The ticket taker rubbed his chin and shook his head. Then he turned to the colored girl and said, "Why don't you just stand up and stop causin' all this trouble?"

I'd been watching her for some time now. She kept reading her book as if they were speaking a foreign language. Ever since they started she had betrayed no expression. No tear of outrage, or flush of anger. Just that cold look of detachment.

The bruisers didn't care for that look. They wanted some reaction. So the sport knocked the book out of her hand.

"You mind me when I speak to you!" he shouted for the whole car to hear.

She stared at the floorboards like the book was still in her gloved hands.

I remembered my feelings from a few moments before. And I still tried to snuff them out.

Then I saw her lower lip quiver, for just a moment.

I pushed my way over to where she was sitting.

Ignoring the three thugs I said to her, "Miss?"

My tone was different from the others. I put a little gentleness in it. Her dark brown eyes gave me a hesitant, wary look.

I said, "You want them to leave you alone?"

The brown eyes searched mine for not so long a time. Then she nodded.

I turned to the three men who by that time were surrounding me.

The ticket taker told me not to make any trouble. At the same time the sport put his hands on her.

I ripped his hand off her arm and sent my fist into his face. His teeth cut into my knuckles.

Then I kicked his knee. He fell down on the floorboards, crying and cursing.

Before I had a chance to make any other move Uriah and Brode pinned me against the side of the car. I struggled but their meaty arms must have had some muscle in them. The clean-shaven one put his hand around my neck while his pal slugged my kidneys. I cried out with pain, feeling them twist my arms behind my back in a firm hold.

Uriah said to the sport, "Take him, Tommy boy! Take him out!"

My arms felt like they were about to burst from their sockets. I lashed out with my boots but wound up kicking air.

Tommy was pulling at the leather strap used to signal the driver when your stop was coming. I heard the bell clamoring on the other end as Tommy tore the leather apart.

I kept watching as he wound one half of the strap around my neck.

He squeezed. The leather bit into my skin, choking out any air I had left.

My head felt like it was going to explode. My tongue oozed out of my mouth.

The inside of the car grew hazy, like I was watching it from behind a curtain.

Then Tommy screamed. I didn't know why or care. For a moment I collapsed to the floorboards, my eyes watering with pain. I heaved air into me and looked up. The colored girl was gripping the handle of a knife now. The business end was imbedded in Tommy's right hand.

Uriah took the girl and wrenched her from his pal. His fat leg swung up as high as he could get it and kicked her over to me. All the passengers looked ready to scramble out the windows.

Then the car halted, quite suddenly. The passengers, the strong-arm men, and the two of us tumbled all over each other. About two or three people landed on top of me. I felt their hot breaths in my face.

There was plenty of air but somehow I couldn't breathe with those people scrambling all over me. It made me angry and scared.

Panic got me to my feet. I hauled some passengers off the colored girl, and wasn't too gentle about it. I used to have that suffocating feeling sometimes in prison, cooped up with thirty thousand other men. I'd look up at the guards and want to tear their hearts out. That hate was coming back to me now.

This time I had a new focus for my rage: the three thugs piling out the rear.

A sane man might have left them there and gone about his business. All I wanted was to thrash them to my heart's content.

I sprang at Uriah as he tried squeezing himself down the stairs to the curb. My elbow rammed into the back of his skull and we both spilled onto the cobbles. For a second I rolled with him until we landed in a rather filthy gutter. Uriah's head bumped against the curb. He lay where he was as I stood up, brushing the ash and horse manure from my jacket.

I turned around to the other two who watched me with horror.

"Which one of you nancy boys wants to take a crack now?"

The sport cradled his lame hand. He wasn't in the mood.

Brode was game. He came at me like an artillery barrage.

It was so fast I didn't have time to get out of the way. The fat man slammed me back a few feet. My back ran up against a metal pole supporting an awning. The pole came loose from the sidewalk and clattered to my side. He was on top of me by then, driving fists into me that could have been steel girders for all I knew. Before he could crack a rib I had the pole in my hands. I lifted it from the asphalt and into a few of his chins. Brode sunk against the vendor's stand of tomatoes. As he slid to the pavement the little red tomatoes bounced from the stand and onto his prone body.

I stumbled to my feet, running my tongue over my teeth. One felt a little loose but not enough to worry me.

Something was wrong with my eye. At first it felt like a gnat got caught in it. Then I realized it was just a twitch of the lower lid. I hoped no one could see it.

I turned to walk back to the streetcar and clean up. I was going to arrest all three of them for mayhem. They belonged in a cage.

Just as I turned from Brode's tomato-covered body, a fist hit me square in the bread basket. I dropped to my knees. I guess I didn't kneel close enough to the pavement for his liking. Something hard crunched the back of my head and sent me sprawling.

Trying to see who did it was a little hard. A wound must've opened on my scalp. The blood got into my eyes, almost blinding me. I took my handkerchief out. Or I tried to. Before I even got to my pocket, he slammed a boot on my fingers. I howled and said, "Just a wipe!"

A big hand tore through my pocket and dropped the handkerchief in front of my face. I pressed the cloth on a small gash on my scalp. Then I wiped the blood off my eyes.

The first thing I saw, being stretched on the pavement, was a pair of incredibly shiny boots. The leather seemed to sparkle over the India rubber soles.

Above the gleaming jet black shoes were pant cuffs. The material and cut were quite familiar. Then I saw a wooden club dangling in front of me like a pendulum.

When I tried to lift my eyeballs heavenward they protested with a sharp jolt of pain. But I'd seen enough to have an idea of who brained me. At least I knew his occupation.

"Put the mace away," I said. "I'm a police officer."

He let me pick myself up. I held the handkerchief in place with one hand. The other brushed dust off my vest and necktie. My watch chain had snapped. That made me swear a little.

A guttural voice, full of malice, said, "Well, well, well. If it isn't Special Officer McCleary."

"Sergeant Duffy," I said. Then after hesitating for a moment, I added, "Sir."

For a moment I forgot about the pain erupting in my limbs, spine, and skull. When Sergeant Duffy was talking to you, you didn't think on much else.

If I hadn't hated him so much I might have been afraid of him.

Duffy was an ox of a man. His body bristled with muscles just beginning to go to seed. At five feet ten I was a little taller than most. But the sergeant towered over me.

I watched his thick, meaty hand curl around the mace in his fist. The knuckles had a lot of scars on them. They'd collided with plenty of teeth.

The copper's uniform was barely large enough to contain his solid, dangerous bulk. Straining from the collar, his neck was like a tree trunk. Perched on top was that ugly mug of his. A long, well-oiled mustache stretched from cheek to cheek. Absurd freckles covered his broken nose.

And then there were his peepers. Always with the lids half-covering them, like he was coming out of an opium-induced swoon.

Duffy's intoxicant of choice was pain.

"Why don't you tell me what this is all about, Wilton?"

He made my name sound like a synonym for sodomite.

I spat a defiant gob of blood on the pavement. My eyelid kept twitching. The last thing I wanted to do was answer to him. But I didn't have a choice.

Sergeant Walter Duffy was one of the most powerful policemen in the city of Philadelphia. His rank didn't fool anybody. He liked being a sergeant and getting juicy details like breaking up riots. The desk and inkwell weren't his fancy.

Since I joined the force in '66 I'd heard rumors about Duffy. Vaux was the one who appointed him to the force.

That was before the war, when the Rangers and the Killers had their names painted all over the waterfront. Mayor Vaux got a body of men together to get rid of the gangs. Those men were selected for their ability to hurt and nothing else. Duffy was one of them. The gangs didn't last long.

When I joined the force Duffy was the house sergeant in my district station-house. That was the Nineteenth district, which took up the whole Seventh Ward. Of all the wards in the city the Seventh was and still is the worst.

Duffy and I first brushed up against each other when I refused to collect his scale for him. A few days later I got my beat: Seventh, Eighth, and Lombard streets by day, and Walnut, Sansom, Eighth, and Ninth by night. That was the colored slum, the home to the lowest scamps in the city.

I used to think Duffy kept me on that beat in the hopes I'd get croaked. He didn't know what I was used to in the war.

After McMichael's term as mayor expired in '68, I became a special officer at City Hall. Duffy became the sergeant of the Reserve Corps. The reserves were hand-picked men whom the mayor kept on hand in case of emergency—that is, when a lot of heads needed to be cracked, like in a riot or an election.

The corps also patrolled the Reserve District. From Chestnut to the Delaware lay the city's mother lode—banks, trust and safe deposit companies, shops of all kinds, jewelry stores, diamond stores, large hotels, the Post Office, and the Mint. A robbery never happened without Walter Duffy knowing about it. And profiting from it.

Ever since I discovered Sergeant Duffy at the Central Office I'd kept my distance. He was too powerful a man to have as your enemy.

Now all my months of hard work were ruined. I got the feeling the crack on the head was just an appetizer.

Duffy's gnarled hand grabbed my lapel and pulled me

into his face. I was close enough to smell the oil on his whiskers and the tobacco in his mouth.

"Let's have it, Wilton."

"I'm arresting those three scamps for mayhem."

"And which three scamps might you be referrin' to?"

"That bloke in the gutter, this fellow here sitting in tomato juice, and the sport holding his hand right behind you."

Duffy didn't even look where I gestured.

"Is that so, Officer Wilton? Now try this on. I'm arresting *you* for mayhem."

"Are you out of your bloody mind?" I bared my teeth like an angry dog. My mustache poked over my lip like hackles.

"Wilton, you were always such a joker." With a gesture of mock affection his hand patted me on the head, right where my wound was.

"I want you to take a look at Uriah Strunk there. He's still unconscious. You could've killed him. Now is that a way to treat a brother officer?"

I stared at the fat man in the gutter. My mouth stayed open.

"And what about Reserve Officer Tommy Murphy? What did you do to his hand? If he's not crippled for life it won't be on account of you, will it?"

"Listen, Duffy . . ."

"I ain't finished. Last but not least we have Reserve Officer Brode. It's a fucking disgrace. No. I take that back. You're the fucking disgrace, McCleary."

His using my surname wasn't a good sign.

"See," Duffy said, "I had those officers on special duty. We've been havin' some trouble on the streetcars. Some color trouble. The mayor don't want that kind of thing. Respectable folks don't either."

"So you detail your Reserve Corps thugs to the cars to start a little trouble, right?"

"I don't know what you're talkin' about," he said. But his half-smile said otherwise.

"Let me guess. Those two yesterday. That was your affair, wasn't it?"

"You mean the two niggers who got on the streetcar smelling like shit? Caused a whole lot of ruckus. Complainin', a little fisticuffs. No reason why respectable folks gotta ride with men who smell like shit."

"Course not," I said. "And shame on the men who paid those two negroes five dollars each to ride a streetcar after they'd worked in a cess pool all day. Did you dip into your own savings for those ten dollars?"

"Well, now. Someone made a donation, Wilton. You know how it goes. That's one thing I always admired about you, if you can believe it. You keep those ears open."

With a sigh he said, "Maybe I'll have to nail you right now. Hell, the Central Office is only half a square away. I bet Mulholland'll have your star within a minute."

I jerked myself out of his grasp and smoothed my lapel. Looking over his shoulder I noticed the colored woman for the first time since we'd hit the cobbles. The sport had his good hand clamped to the ribbon of the bonnet wound around her chin. He yanked it like you would a stubborn dog's leash.

"We got the little darky who started it. How'd you like to join her? You like dark meat? That why you gave my boys grief?"

I stared at his cold eyes with undisguised hate. The funny thing was, I wanted to argue with him, to deny it. And I did deny it. To myself.

"Looks like I hit the nail on the head. No wonder you liked the Nineteenth so much."

Duffy never laughed. He just pursed his lips in a half-smile. Then his eyes grew big and round like an imbecile's.

"You know, when I look at you in this light you're sure as ugly as a nigger."

The insults were invitations I didn't accept.

He must've seen my knuckles growing white. Maybe

he didn't like something he saw in my eyes. At any rate, he stopped jeering and said, "All right, let's get you to the Central Office. You're under arrest."

From his belt he pulled a pair of bracelets.

"You're actually going to put those on me? In front of all these people?"

"Chains and niggers go well together, don't they, Wilton?"

Go for his eyes. That's what I was thinking. Go straight for his eyes and don't stop till you've reached the back of his skull.

Then he relented again and said, "I got a better idea. Special Officer Wilton can take the young lady to the station-house and have her booked for mayhem. We have plenty of witnesses who saw her cut up poor Tommy Murphy. But who needs witnesses when old Duff gives his say so, huh? You collar her and we'll forget the whole thing. Just make sure the police intelligence column gets wind of it by to-morrow, hear?"

My body, still tense, made no move. The sergeant said, "You got two choices. Pinch the bitch or lose your star. Can you do that arithmetic?"

I brushed past him and walked over to Murphy and the colored woman. I stopped to pick up my new soft hat from the gutter, where Strunk was coming out of his nap. Duffy said to the crowd, "All right, get movin'. Nothin' to see here. Get movin', you."

Murphy whispered something in the girl's ear. Then he pushed her into me and said, "I'll be seein' you, pal."

It was nothing I looked forward to.

I took the girl firmly by the arm and headed for the Central Office. As I headed down Chestnut Street, I looked over my shoulder. Duffy was watching me, twirling his mace with an expert's nonchalance.

2

CITY HALL WAS next to the State House in those days. As we passed the most venerable building in the city, I wondered what the fellows who assembled there to write the Constitution would've made of our city government, or lack thereof. I wondered if that was a war fought in vain. I also wondered if the war I fought was in vain. The colored girl at my side had no answers for me.

We kept our mouths shut the whole way to City Hall. Most of that time I spent making a decision. By the time we reached the State House my mind was made up.

The colored girl and I stepped through the portals of the squat brick building we Central Office coppers called home. From the quaint antique atmosphere of Independence Hall we emerged into the spartan, ugly chambers of the present.

It was like the waiting room at a railway depot. There was an air of anonymity and near-decay. The scents of hair oil, dust, tobacco, old wood, and human sweat lingered in the air like a wraith.

The Central Office was a thoroughly masculine world. Even if the young woman weren't colored she would have attracted attention. This was a private club and intrusions from the fairer sex were resented.

I saw that resentment on the face of the house sergeant

17

when I approached his worn desk. He looked at the woman and then at me. Then he said, "You lookin' for a place to sleep to-night I'd advise one of the other station-houses."

Evidently we looked dirty enough to be penniless tramps who were too poor to pay seven cents for a bunk for the night. In the basement of the station-house, such wretches could sleep in relative comfort. As long as they didn't mind sleeping on the cold floor with only a puny stove to heat them and the other two dozen lodgers. It was a charity provided by every district I knew about.

"Ha ha," I said, straightening my necktie. "As a matter of fact this young woman here's been assaulted. She wants to make a complaint."

The colored girl gripped my arm. She said to me, "What did you say?"

"I said," talking to the sergeant and not to her, "that this young lady was assaulted on a streetcar. I was a witness."

"And what would you like us to do about it, friend?"

"I want an officer to take this woman's complaint."

The house sergeant gave the girl a look and said, "Assaulted, huh?"

"You heard me, damn it. Now get the book out and log us in."

He was about to say something smart to me when the girl started crying. She covered her face with her gloved hands, which muffled her sobs. I saw the house sergeant's mouth wrinkle in embarrassment.

"All right, control yourself. Enough of that. Why don't you sit down?" he told her.

I walked her over to a nearby bench. She looked at me, the bonnet encircling her delicate face like a dark halo. I saw something in that face that looked like trust. It didn't feel like something she gave to just anyone.

"You're not going to arrest me, then?"

"Of course I'm not. I'm going to sign a complaint with you. Against those officers."

"Officers?"

"Yes. Those thugs were police officers. Like me."

"Why would you do that for me? Cause trouble for them and especially for yourself?"

She looked at her lap, as if to avoid some inevitable disappointment.

I couldn't answer her question the way I wanted to. If I did that I would have to tell her about how I felt when I first saw her on the streetcar. And how I'd turned away, not once but many times.

So I let it go, for the present. Instead I asked her name.

"Cole."

"Is that spelled like the fuel?"

"No. Like the king."

"What?"

"Old King Cole was a merry old soul . . . You never heard that one?"

The crisp, clean way she pronounced her words was pleasant-sounding, but a little daunting. I wasn't used to dealing with educated negroes.

"Oh yeah. The nursery rhyme. What about your Christian name?"

"Arabella."

"Miss Arabella Cole." I repeated the words slowly, deliberately. I wasn't going to forget them.

"Do I get to know your name, officer?"

"Excuse me. I'm Special Officer Wilton McCleary. At your service."

I wasn't used to formal introductions. There weren't many opportunities for me to mingle with society. For a moment I thought it strange to be embarassed in front of a colored woman. But she wasn't like most I'd known. I twigged that when I first saw her.

"Thank you, Mr. McCleary."

Her hand reached out to mine. The gesture was very brazen. Some would say unladylike. But I wouldn't.

I clasped it, feeling funny. For some reason I was a little warm.

The sergeant was hollering at me from his desk. Before I went back I told her, "Just stay put and we'll get this thing started. I have a little bit of pull around here."

When I approached the desk, the sergeant said, "Look, I gotta have your name before anything else happens."

"Special Officer Wilton McCleary."

"You a police officer?"

"That's right. I work here six days a week, same as you."

"Wait a minute. You're McCleary."

"I'm glad we agree on my identity."

"You're the one the chief wants to see."

"What? The chief? Since when?"

"Right before you walked in with the nigger woman he sent word to have you brought up as soon as you stepped inside. Sorry. I don't got such a good memory for faces."

"You're a credit to the force, Sergeant. I'm wanted now?"

The sergeant nodded his head.

"Well," I said, "see to that young lady over there while I'm upstairs. Okay?"

Without looking at me the house sergeant nodded. He was engrossed in picking tobacco bits from his stained teeth.

As I walked past Miss Cole I held up my forefinger and said, "I'll be right back." Then I added, over my shoulder, "I hope."

The chief's clerk peered from his desk when I entered the office.

"Oh, it's you, McCleary. He's been waiting for you."

When I walked through the oak doors I saw the chief sitting with his back to me, his feet propped up on the windowsill. He had a large tablet in his lap.

"That you, McCleary? Give me just a minute. I need to put the finishing touch."

I stood where I was while he continued to draw. The

tall windows cast long rays of light. Dust drifted through them like snow.

I looked at the gray-papered walls. There were paintings hung on them. They were mostly street scenes of Philadelphia. One portrait looked like the chief's wife. It was happily idealized. A few of the portraits were more realistic. They were of certain scamps who'd been arrested since Mulholland took over three years ago. Whenever he saw an interesting face brought in he'd sit the prisoner on his velvet-upholstered chair and do a sketch. Some of his more absurd works seemed to be imitations of French paintings. Scenes of Christians being thrown to the lions, Napoleon on horseback, that sort of thing. What made them absurd was the faces. They were all culled from our rogues' gallery.

There was nothing Mulholland wanted more than to go to Paris and study art from a master. He told me this many times. We struck up a friendship when I actually criticized one of his paintings. I hadn't known it was his. It showed three Greek goddesses taking a bath. All three of the goddesses were in fact high-class parlor-house whores from a brothel we pulled one night. Mulholland let them off when they promised to model for him. I gave him my honest opinion of the painting, something he was not used to getting from his cronies. He wound up selling it to a saloon for a hefty sum.

"How do you like that, McCleary? I think I'll call it *Afternoon on Chestnut Street.*"

The sketch was well done. Two men were struggling. One a huge creature, with shadows for a face. The other was fair-haired, mustached, and had a sort of haggard look around the eyes. It was a good portrait of me.

"Who do you think will win the fight?" the chief asked.

"Who's my opponent?"

"Oh, I don't know. I don't think you do either."

He tore the paper off his tablet and slid it across his expansive desk.

"A present. And a warning. I want no more amateur pugilism in front of the State House. If you have a problem with one of the reserve boys, you settle it on your own time, not on the city's. I'm docking you a day's pay for that jackass stunt."

I started to explain but Mulholland gestured for me to keep quiet.

"I imagine your five-dollar gratuity in court to-day should see you through till to-morrow."

"It's nice to have a fly cop for a chief."

"I figured you'd get the customary bounty for a scamp well-collared. Well, I have to do something to make you look bad for a little while. Duffy'll be breathing down my neck. I saw the whole thing, by the way."

"Even what happened on the streetcar? With a colored woman?"

"Ah! I see. The Reserve boys are causing trouble again, huh?"

"That's the straight goods. And I . . . I got tired of standing around and letting them do it."

"Well, that's their job."

He waved for me to take a seat but I shook my head. I thought better standing up. My eyelid was still giving me grief. I turned away from the chief's desk and looked at his portrait gallery.

"I don't mind intimidating grafters looking for a touch. Or even tramps if they're causing respectable people trouble. But I've had enough of pushing citizens around."

"Well, they're not really citizens, McCleary. They're negroes."

I turned to look at him. Our eyes met. And they spoke volumes.

"I think you need to be reminded about the nature of police work, my friend. We are not on the streets to cause trouble. We're there to prevent it."

"Prevent trouble by harassing harmless negro girls on streetcars?"

"Prevent trouble by making sure everyone does what

they're supposed to. And stays where they're supposed to stay. If people lost sight of that who knows what could happen?''

The chief stood up and hooked his fingers around his suspenders. He went to the window. Gazing on Chestnut Street like a good-natured god, he said, ''Take a look at the grafting. Now no matter how much I pretend to have it on the run you and I both know it's not on the run. Hell, it's not even crawling. Nope. It's standing on its own two feet and not moving a damn inch. Because you and I let it. But we make sure we know exactly where it's standing. And we don't let it stand too close to a crowd of respectable people if we can help it.''

My response was a harsh laugh.

''It isn't funny, McCleary. We're doing picket duty for civilization. If we don't apply the club in the right places . . . well, the barbarians are always waiting at the gates.''

He gestured to a painting of his showing the sack of Rome. The barbarians in this case were based on a gang of copper pickers the Harbor Police pinned about a year ago. I don't know what we ever did with the recovered metal. Probably sold it and raised money for a new station-house somewhere.

''Who says our civilization is worth defending?''

My eye was twitching double time. Mullholland pressed his oiled hair, smoothing the thin strands over his pink scalp. While he did that he looked at me, as if for the first time.

''You got an awful lot of anger in you, boy. I wonder where it all comes from.''

There was an uncomfortable silence in which I felt a lot of things, most of all disappointment.

''Sorry. I guess that whole affair on the streetcar got me thinking on things.''

''Things you got no business thinking on, Officer. You were a soldier, remember? Just like me. Remember what it was like to not think? Just to follow orders? That's what you should be doing out there. We're all fighting the same war, McCleary. We just got different ways. Different jobs to do. Even Duffy. Understand?''

"Yes, sir."

I was tired of thinking anyway.

The chief sighed and pulled out a segar box. Selecting one, he rolled it under his nostrils and closed his eyes. Then he said, "You got work to do now. I want you to walk over to the Delaware waterfront by Old Swede's Church, near the Washington Street Grain Elevator."

"What for?"

"A roundsman found an innocent washed up down there."

"Why should I go?"

"Because it happened to be a nigger woman."

"Ah, I see."

"That's right. I thought you would. I want you to see if you can identify it. Then maybe we can settle this whole disappearance business once and for all."

"I'm surprised you even have me looking after it."

"Well, my friend, let's be real frank. You haven't done much to make friends around here. But you make a lot of champion collars. I can't just toss you out on your ass. Right? So I give you something to occupy your time and keep you away from fellows like Duffy who'd like to give you your balls for supper. I'm trying to be a good friend to you."

"That's awful generous of you, Chief."

"Think nothing of it. Now get your tail over to Southwark. And report what you find. Let's hope it's one of them. I'm tired of getting lambasted in the colored papers. They're voting now, after all. All right, get going."

I rolled up the chief's drawing and took my leave.

As I walked outside I searched around for Miss Cole. She was nowhere to be seen. I hoped an officer was taking down her complaint. Then I put her out of my mind. I had another colored woman to think on.

Once outside I headed straight for the Delaware.

I TRUSTED MULHOLLAND just a little bit more than I'd trust any Democrat. Which wasn't a whole lot. I don't say the Republicans were any better. But I still had some loyalty left to the party of our late President.

I wasn't assigned to this case out of charity. Somebody, maybe Duffy or the chief himself, decided I was making too many arrests. The detectives were looking bad. The city was lucky if they pinched a third-rate shoplifter a week. There was too much money to be made with all the touches going on. Meanwhile I was pinching queer shovers, horse thieves, fences, bunco steerers, what have you. The more arrests I made the happier I was. Each one of them thought a little scale would keep the bracelets off. But I didn't want their money. I marched them to the station-house instead.

Like any other human being, I want more. But not more money. I want something else. Every once in a while when I think on the war, the one I didn't fight and the one I did fight, I feel I'm getting close to what that something is.

That's why I didn't fuss over this case. Mulholland and Duffy and all my other good friends thought this was a cul-de-sac. That if I pursued it I'd wind up with no arrests worth speaking of. Then they'd have their chance to give me the boot. Maybe even allege I was horsing around, just like Duffy had done that morning.

I had a feeling Mulholland was dead wrong. But other than my intuition, I had nothing. Nothing except this:

For several months there had been murmurs in the Seventh Ward. Colored women were disappearing. Nobody knew just how many. I had a few mouth-pieces in the Seventh Ward who told me it was getting folks plenty scared. No bodies had turned up yet. Since most of the disappeared were low characters no one at the Central Office gave a damn. The negro leaders told me their delegation was met with scorn.

"Nigger men and women live in sin right and left," the Central Office told them. "And you think it's strange when one of them ups and leaves for another fresh fish?"

But it wasn't as easy as that. After about a month I compiled a list of the disappeared. It ran to eight. All of them were women. Their ages varied. Most of them were from the almshouse. Some worked in trades, such as dressmaking or as public cooks. All took part in what we call the "social evil."

I beat a path from Spruce to South, from Tenth to the Schuylkill, looking for someone who might know where any of them had gone. I turned up nothing.

When I stumbled into my bedroom after a long night of canvassing I'd ask myself what I was wasting my time for. I came up with two answers before I passed out on my bed.

One was it felt like detective work. I was still only a special officer with little chance of getting promoted while Fox and his pals were in charge of the hall. When I was younger I used to daydream about all the big collars I'd make if I were a detective. Collars that would make the Pinkerton Agency, the Big Man, look like nickel-and-dime thief catchers.

This was my aspiration.

And another thing. The disappeared women were all

low negresses. White Philadelphia cared about two cents' worth for any of them.

They reminded me of those days when I was forgotten and damned like them. When my legs and gums ached from scurvy and my flesh was covered with bedsores. When I did my bunk in the same water I drank from. Each day and night at Andersonville I breathed in the stench of death, for months and months. And the government whose tattered uniform I wore didn't give a damn about me or the other thirty thousand of us.

Those memories or nightmares kept me searching.

Then, just a week before, a new girl had disappeared. And this one was no laborer or fallen woman. She was the daughter of a prominent African Methodist minister. The Martins were a ''representative'' family—as respectable as colored people could get. The daughter, Josephine, had graduated the Institute for Colored Youth and went to school some place out West where they let colored people, even women, attend. She'd been back in the Quaker City on a holiday. One night in the last week of September she went calling on a friend. It was right around her father's house on Delancey Place. That was just on the border of the Seventh Ward and their house was in a mostly white neighborhood. I found no one who'd seen her after she left her house. She never paid that call.

Josephine's father, Reverend Augustus Martin, had just enough pull to force Mullholland into assigning an officer to the case. Of course it wasn't worth a detective. So Special Officer Wilton McCleary got to work it.

The reverend thought his daughter had eloped or had run off with some rascal. So did I, until I started canvassing. Then I realized the minister's girl was only one of many. Too many for it to be a coincidence.

But I still had nothing but suspicions.

The car was half-way to the Delaware when a voice disturbed my revery.

"Wilton McCleary, isn't it? I thought I recognized you."

Sitting next to me was a portly, gray-haired and whiskered man in a fine new suit. A Masonic pin decorated his lapel. I knew him from the Lodge and the Republican Club. His name was William R. "Cap" Heins. Before Fox became mayor, Heins was a division captain.

We shook hands in our peculiar way and then I said, "What do you say, Cap?"

"I saw your frolic in front of the State House. Nice work."

"They were reserve officers."

"I know. We've been keeping an eye on the Central Office muscle. Especially your friend Duffy. I heard how you two used to get along so well in the Seventh Ward."

Heins pulled one end of his watch chain from his vest pocket. It had a tiny pocket knife attached to it. He started to clean his fingernails with the extended blade.

The car stopped abruptly, bumping us against each other. I heard the driver shout a volley of oaths at someone. Leaning out my window I saw it was two newsboys whose tattered clothes stuck to them like a cake of dirt. One had knocked the other on the tracks. When we got under way again I could hear them arguing over which one had the right to sell the *Star* on that street corner.

I turned to Heins and said, "What do you boys at Eleventh and Chestnut have on your mind?"

That was the location of the headquarters of the Republican Party.

Heins curled his lips under his gray mustache and said, "You got a brain in that nob of yours, I'll tell ya. See, we all know it's time for a change in the city. We gotta get these Fox boys out of the hall, plain and simple. Stokley's been counting on those nigger—I mean Negro voters on Tuesday. We can't let someone stop them from getting to the polls."

"What does that have to do with me?"

"We have it on good authority that Fox's coppers, especially the reserves, are going to make trouble during the election.''

''Trouble for the negroes?''

''You got it. Now we can't have the blue bellies horsing around the polls, can we?''

''Why not? They've always done it in the past. *We* both have.''

I had a part in keeping Democrats from the polls during the last election. My club got some use. But I wasn't proud of it.

''Ah, you mean back in '68? Well, of course. We were only protecting our livelihoods. You were just damn lucky Fox needed you.''

''Yeah, to help break up the volunteer fire companies. They had a lot of pull, remember? But I dug up the dirt on them. I happened to have a few of their rank for mouth-pieces. I gave Fox the information and my muscle. That helped to ease them out quietly. He let me keep my beat in the Seventh Ward. We both got what we wanted.''

''No need to get defensive, Mack. I never held it against you that you didn't resign like most of the other boys.''

''Don't give me that, Heins. You didn't resign. You were booted with every other Republican they didn't need. Just like we're going to do to them when Stokley takes office.''

''And that's just what I wanted to talk to you about. Now, I guess you don't plan to take part in any ruckus with the colored folk?''

''Why don't you get down to business, Heins? You trying to tell me Stokley'll kick me off the force just because I served with the Democrats? I've been a regular Republican since before the war. In fact, I got plenty of votes for our pal Sweets the last time he ran.''

''I'm not denying your integrity, Mack. I'm just saying that it might rub people the wrong way to see a fella keep his job while they had to go through three lean years.''

''What are you telling me?''

''I'm telling you that you have to prove yourself, Mack. Prove to us that you're still our boy.''

''By staying off-duty during the election? You think I'd go strong-arm colored men at the polls?''

My voice almost cracked with anger. The insult hit me harder than I was prepared for. I liked to think I was different from uniformed thugs like Duffy.

Then I remembered the cracked skull of a repeater I clubbed in the last election. He was voting with a bogus name, and I got him dead to rights. After he pushed me I got angry and used the club. Used it hard. I almost killed him. My hands didn't stop shaking that day.

They were shaking now as I thought on Duffy. And myself.

''You've always been square with the niggers, Mack. I know that. We got other plans.''

''Like what? Look, it's almost my stop. You better make your pitch.''

Heins finished picking his nails and moved on to his teeth, a few of which were missing. A hazard of our profession.

''It's no secret who's going to be at the forefront of all this trouble. The reserves.''

''And Duffy.''

''That's it. We want you to take care of him.''

I looked down at my dusty boots and said, ''You mean kill him?''

Heins took the Lord's name in vain and said, ''Of course not. We just want you to do what you're good at. Get information.''

''What sort of information?''

I had an idea but I wanted to see how much he knew.

''Don't play games with me, boy. I know you used to have that beat in the Seventh Ward. Someone like you couldn't help but notice who was running the show down there. Especially after what happened to you.''

''How'd you hear about that?'' I asked, a little wary.

"Word gets around. You're an honest copper, Mc-Cleary. That's nothing to be ashamed of. I heard you wouldn't collect his scale for him. But you probably figured out that scale was just a small piece of the pot."

"He had his hand dipped in every kind of game in town. From policy to panel cribs."

"Still does. He runs that district like a fief, even though he's a reserve bull now. Half the coppers at the Nineteenth District station-house are nothing more than his tax collectors."

"Yeah," I said. "The only time they make a pinch is when the money doesn't come in on time or a negro gets too drunk in front of a white person."

"I see you understand the situation. So you see what sort of information might interest us. We wanna know about all the golden calves he's got in the Seventh Ward. If we can get evidence that he's behind the policy, bunco, prostitution, and every other game there it'll make Fox look mighty bad. We can squeeze him then. Squeeze him good."

"What difference will that make now? We only have a few days before the election!"

"I know that. Let's just say if we can convince Fox and Duffy to play square with us by letting the niggers vote then maybe we won't have to let any information you acquire become public. That would ruin Fox even if he wasn't in the hall. And Duffy."

It was a tall tale, I was sure of that. If they had wanted to discredit Fox and Duffy it would have made sense to rake up the filth long before now. Nothing I did was going to stop Fox and Duffy from trying to fix the election.

What Heins really wanted was for me to get information on Duffy's business ventures so the new Republican police force could assume control when they mustered in that winter.

It was ugly all around. No matter what I did I figured it was going to happen anyway. So I said to Heins, "And me?"

"You get a promise from me. And that means something because Stokley has me picked for Chief of Detectives. The promise is, one more year of being a special officer. That makes sense. You're still a young fella."

"And then what?"

"Detective."

I tugged the leather strap for my stop. Heins was still picking his teeth when I walked off the car. On the street I saw him lean out the window, his eyebrows raised questioningly.

He watched me nod as the car slid away.

SOUTHWARK WAS QUIET that day. A few little shavers, too young to be in school, pushed their toy hoops over the dirt-encrusted cobbles. Women in wrappers stood above the streets, stringing laundry across the narrow spaces between the row homes. They didn't care if anyone saw them in just a wrapper rather than a dress. They probably didn't even own a corset. There were no husbands around for them to impress anyway. Their men were scattered over the city, working in mills or at the Navy Yards just a few squares off.

It was a neighborhood of brick and smoke and a half-dozen trees. The homes were three-storied, with a different family on each floor. Some had shutters painted black on one story and white on another. Or none at all. That seemed to be the one bit of exterior decoration the different boarders allowed themselves. Mostly mechanics and laborers kept their diggings here. But it was respectable enough.

Walking past a Lehigh Coal Yard I saw a woman sitting on a basket, selling some apples off a broken dray. I bought two for a nickel and headed toward Old Swede's Church. Before I stuck one in my mouth I made sure to wipe the dust off it. Horse dumpings on the street had a way of drying up and blowing here and there. It was a windy day.

33

I had no problem finding the church. Its white spire perched like a beacon over the largest cluster of trees in all of Southwark. The Delaware used to lick at its foundations. As I approached, the church bell tolled mid-day.

I'd decided to go to the church before meeting up with the coroner. From what Mulholland told me the body wasn't far off. I knew my way around, since I'd been to the services here a few times.

Before the entrance was a churchyard bisected by a walkway. For a few moments I gazed at the church, feeling rather than seeing the river beyond. Around it were warehouses and boardinghouses. I felt like I was in a fort, the last outpost before an infinite wilderness. The tombstones and monuments on either side of me were like silent guardians. I stopped to read an inscription from one or two of them.

A memory came to me then of a happy time when my family used to pic-nic in a cemetery near our home in Troy, New York. It never occurred to me back then that the names on those stones were the last traces of living people. I just liked the quiet and the sense of something old and mysterious about the place. It made me feel like I was on the edge of something far beyond me. I was never scared or lonely in those moments.

The little cemetery was peaceful and full of shade. Song sparrows were raising a racket in the tall maples. I stopped where I was and breathed in the autumn air. There was something else mixed in with the usual kerosene stench from the mills and the pleasant odor of damp leaves. It wasn't quite a smell. It was a feeling that went into me. Maybe it was from standing in front of the oldest building in the city, almost two hundred years old. Maybe it was being in the bone orchard, also the oldest one in the city.

I bowed my head and listened to the wind shake the leaves above me. The sounds were like words. I tried hard to listen, wondering what the message was.

I didn't decipher any words. I didn't need to. All I was supposed to do was listen.

I left the cemetery and headed for the river. The masts of tall ships appeared over the trees to guide me. I navigated my way along a bunch of railway cars and waterfront warehouses till I reached a particular dry dock. From the back of the church I'd seen a wagon parked there, one I recognized. It belonged to the man the coroner hired to haul bodies to the morgue.

A few sailors and stevedores ogled the thing on the weathered planks. Someone had put a bit of canvas over part of the body. The spectators were jawing and smoking pipes and staring at the corpse like they were expecting it to do more than just lie there.

One roundsman was present, talking with some of the sailors. He was sharing the contents of a smoky brown bottle with them. The flush on their faces told me it didn't contain spring water.

There was a puddle around the body so it hadn't been that long since they drew it out. The water leaked between the planks like blood rejoining the gigantic artery of the Delaware.

I walked past the wagon, giving the horse a pat on its thick neck. The animal ignored me and burrowed deeper into its nose bag.

The owner was still in the seat. His name was Irish but I forgot what it was exactly. A shapeless broad brim topped his squat face, barely visible under a thick growth of beard. He wore an old sweater with pockets that drooped down to his waist. Spots of various kinds covered his work-pants and ancient boots. He welcomed me by spitting a big gob of tobacco juice not too far from my feet.

My first sight of the coroner was his posterior, bent over the half-enshrouded innocent. His arms were stretching toward the canvas like it was the lid of a cookie jar.

I resisted the urge to kick him, stepped right up behind him and said, "Coroner Brown?"

The words jolted him out of his concentration. He nearly lost his balance. Turning around clumsily he said, "Coroner John Gilbert L. Brown at your service, young man."

He pronounced his name like it was something sacred. Brown took his job very seriously. Since the previous coroner's untimely death Brown had been enjoying his status. In his earlier years he'd been the operator of a cooperage. Now he was a big bug and he acted the part. The coroner wore his six thousand a year salary well. The clothes hung on his burgeoning figure in a perfect fit. His silk striped cravat had loosened, showing a puffy red neck.

Brown ran his stubby fingers through well-oiled black hair. It looked like he applied some sort of tonic that colored it that way. His whiskers were gray. They fluffed down his jaw and over his lip. As he chewed tobacco the burnsides rolled in waves over his plump face.

"Don't I know you from somewheres?" he said to me.

A short thin man beside him said, "He's a policeman." From his official-looking expression I twigged he was Deputy Coroner Herbert Sees.

"Herbert. How about callin' me sir every now and then? Or would that be askin' too much?"

Deputy Sees smirked and said, "He's a policeman. *Sir.*"

"I can see that, Herbert. The man has a star in his hand."

I introduced myself and said, "I met you about two months ago in Kensington."

Brown thought a moment and said, "Mick mechanic hanged himself in his parlor. You cut him down."

I nodded my head and said, "What do you have here?"

"Another floater. Colored gal."

Impatiently I said, "What happened to her?"

The coroner looked at his deputy and said, "She croaked."

That tickled his ribs. The other men guffawed. I said, "That's your professional observation? Did you examine her?"

"I didn't have to examine her. Doc Shapleigh's the one with the know-how."

That was the coroner's physician. I wondered why the city appointed a man as coroner who had no medical knowledge to speak of. Of course that was nothing new. Since the office was created in '39 there had been eighteen coroners. Only four of them were doctors. One had been a lawyer. The rest were shopkeepers.

Which was all right since his main job was to organize the inquests. The coroner's physician did the dirty work. Two men for one job. That was the way city government liked it. The more jobs they doled out the more votes they got.

"Where'd that fella get to?" Brown asked the sailors who were watching us with intense curiosity.

"Here I am, Brown."

Shapleigh pushed himself through the crowd from the edge of the dock. His shirt sleeves were rolled to the elbows, revealing thick and muscular arms. I bet he was capital at sawing off limbs during the war.

"What do you make of the floater, Doc?" the coroner said.

"She drowned. Hasn't been in the water long or she'd be more eaten up. My guess is she fell in last night. Probably a whore from one of the waterfront dives."

"That's what I make of it too, Doc," Brown said, turning to me. "Probably a catfish death. These unfortunates kill themselves off plenty. Get tired of living the sinful life and take a swim. I see it all the time."

"Can I take a look at her?" I asked.

"Sure, Officer. Hey, friend," the coroner said to the red-faced bull, "how about making a little space for the fella?"

The copper bounced into some sailors and threw his

club around with lackadaisical swings. He was pretty relaxed by now.

I stepped over to the heap under the canvas. Lifting the flap up I stared at the dead woman's face.

Wet, half-straightened hair clung to her dark brown skin like a wilted flower. She'd never been handsome and death didn't improve her looks. Her fat face looked warped and distorted from the river. Between her large lips I saw something shining. Reaching my finger there I pried them further apart. The skin was cold and damp. It made my hand shake when I touched it. Then I saw where the gleam came from.

"See that?" I said. "She's got a gold tooth."

The coroner, his deputy, and the physician all squatted to admire the dental work.

"Now what's a colored whore like her doin' with a gold tooth?" Sees asked.

"What makes you think she was a whore?" I asked, lifting up the canvas a little bit more.

She wore a cheap dress which clung to her bloated figure like a ready-made shroud. I picked up her thick hand. There was a tiny scar on her right index finger. And something on the wrist.

"See that?" I said. "Cuts or burns, maybe."

"Well that's mighty interestin'," Brown said. "Course that still don't counter-dict my theory about her drownin'."

"Maybe she slit her wrists before she jumped in," Herbert said.

"That's what I call hedgin' a bet," Brown said.

I shook my head. "No. They're not deep enough."

I unwrapped a pathetic-looking bow tied around her collar. Then I saw her neck. It was covered with thick welts, spaced apart just right. Impressions from a human hand.

"Would you care to alter your professional opinion, Coroner?" I asked.

Deputy Sees giggled and said, "Maybe those are love marks."

Brown huffed and said, "That don't prove nothin'. Maybe her bully smacked her around some and that's what made her drown herself."

"How's she gonna do that with a broken neck?"

"There ain't no broken neck!" Brown said.

"There surely is," I told him.

"Shapleigh, what's all this about?"

"Nothing, Coroner. The officer is jumping to conclusions. The corpse might have been tossed against a dock postmortem. It happens quite frequently that bones are broken against rocks and such."

I stood up and said to Shapleigh, "So you're telling me the Delaware strangled her after she drowned?"

The physician shook his head and looked defensively to his colleagues.

"Did you even notice the broken neck? Doctor?"

The coroner intervened and said, "It don't matter whether he looked or not. He didn't have to anyway. Anybody can see she drowned herself."

"How?" I asked.

"Well, we pulled her out of the water, didn't we? She's dead, isn't she? What more do you want?"

I stared across the river at Camden and watched the Federal Street and Gloucester ferries ease their way toward Jersey. I took several deep breaths.

When I had calmed down I said, "She's a floater. But she wasn't drowned. Look at those bruises on her broken neck. And the rope burns on her wrists. She was tied up and strangled, Coroner. And then pushed in."

"Why you makin' trouble here, son? Listen, let me explain somethin' to you."

Coroner Brown put a well-tailored arm around my back and walked me away from the crowd. Ferry whistles moaned in the distance.

"McNamee," the coroner said to his wagon driver. "Take a walk."

The driver mashed the tobacco in his mouth with a vengeance. Then he stumbled off toward the copper and the bottle.

"This might surprise you," Brown told me in a half-whisper, "but I ain't exactly unacquainted with death. I seen it in all shapes and sizes. We did eighty-six inquests last month."

"I know. I read the list in the *Ledger*."

"Then you know what I see every day. Death from burns, catarrh, congestion of lungs, dropsy of brain, pneumonia, spasms, apoplexy . . ."

"And drowning. There were twenty of them last month."

"You got a good memory, boy. By the way you left out the two suicides by drowning."

"Don't you think it's a little funny that a quarter of your suspicious deaths last month were drownings? Are Philadelphians such bad swimmers?"

"If we find a floater we're going to say it's drowned. That's our policy unless some real evidence presents itself."

"Like a gold dagger sticking out of their neck?"

"No need to get cheeky. You just don't seem to understand the circumstances of our job here."

"Why don't you explain them to me?"

"Now, I'll make this simple for you to understand, you bein' a copper and all."

That didn't offend me. I knew for a fact that the coroner had never made it past McGuffey's First Reader.

Brown led me behind his wagon, resting his bulk against the backboard. He stroked the lapels of his suit like they were pet cats. Then he looked back at the assembly on the dock. "I'll let you in on a little secret. We don't like to have murder victims."

I stroked my mustache and said, "What's that supposed to mean?"

"Each time we find a body we gotta dispose of that body, right? We gotta put it in the ground, in the potter's field. That costs money. For the box and the digger. Now the city pays a nice fat fee for suicides and accidents. But with murders the city don't pay burial expenses. It comes out of our pot instead. So if we find a floater with a gold dagger stuck in its throat we're gonna say 'found drowned,' understand?''

Twenty were "found drowned" just last month. I wondered how many had cuts in their throats, or caved-in skulls. And what about the ones on dry land? A strangling could be written up as asphyxiation. Or that vaguest of categories I'd read in the *Ledger*: "violence."

"That's the way the system works," Brown said. "You don't whine about it. You play along with it. You know that, being a copper."

I sure did. I'd just wanted to hear him say it. But it didn't make me any less disgusted with him or myself for going along with it.

Brown looked left and then right, nodding his head up and down. Then he pulled something out of his vest pocket. He held the greenback in my direction without looking at me.

"Look, we all got debts to pay, right? Go back to the Central Office and tell 'em we found a nigger floater and leave it at that? Okay?"

I held it in my hand for a while like I didn't know what it was. My eyes were drawn to a salt warehouse not far off. A wooden hovel leaned against the rear of the building. In the doorway was a filthy-looking man with clay and ash-covered clothes. He kept in the shadow of the murky interior. He was watching us intently but I was the only one who saw him.

I transferred the greenback to my vest pocket, folding it neatly so it wouldn't show.

"Attaboy. I knew you was square."

As I left the dock I heard the coroner say, "Herbert, you help him put the stiff on the wagon. McNamee, don't just stand there! What am I payin' you six dollars for? Let's get movin'! We're off to the morgue."

My eye was drawn to the wooden shack nestled against the back of the warehouse. There was no one there this time. But the image of the tattered man I saw stayed in my mind. He had seemed interested in the goings-on at the dock. And even more interested in not being seen.

I headed back to the Central Office at a brisk pace. I wanted to check on Miss Cole and see if she got any satisfaction. At least I could do one thing that didn't make me feel like dirt.

5

THE STREETCAR RIDE took about twenty minutes. There
was a lot of traffic around the waterfront. The streets
themselves were crowded with grocers and their customers. Women bumped into each other's new-style bustles
under awnings stretched from corner to corner. Packs of
kids, street arabs, mingled around them, their eyes on the
leathers and handbags. The swell ladies were perfect tar-
gets for what pickpockets called a "touch."

Business as usual on fair Chestnut Street, all the way
back to the Central Office. When I leaped up the marble
stairs and through the portal I saw Arabella Cole, still
occupying the same bench.

She was reading her book, her gloved hand making
notations on the pages with a tiny pencil. Beneath her
sable bustle skirt a leg moved nervously up and down.

"Miss Cole?" I said, walking up to her and removing
my hat.

Her lips formed a halfhearted smile. "Officer Mc-
Cleary."

"Is everything all right here? The sergeant take your
complaint? Put it on the blotter?"

"I spoke to the sergeant, all right. That was about an
hour ago. Then he told me to wait for the next available
officer. I've been waiting since then, watching people

come and go after an officer took care of them. White people, I might add.''

I cleared my throat, a little embarassed. "I'm sorry about that, Miss Cole. Look, why don't I write up the report for you? You've waited long enough.''

She passed a hand over her smooth brown forehead and said, "Let's forget the whole affair. I'm tired of this place. I just want to go home.''

"What were you doing sitting here then for so long?''

The girl adjusted her hat and brushed a strand of hair from her brow. She said, "I don't really know why. After I saw how they were going to treat me I decided to just sit here and never leave until they took notice of me. It was all I could think of doing.''

"Well, I'm glad that you did stay," I said and hoped that feeling in my face didn't mean I was blushing. "Because it gives me the chance to escort you home.''

She stood up, clasping the book to her bosom. "You don't have to do that, sir.''

"There's no problem. It's the least I can do considering all you've gone through to-day.''

Her eyes met mine. They held a question. I was afraid to answer. Motioning toward the door, I ushered her outside.

An omnibus clattered to the curb, depositing a family of tourists. They gaped at the State House. The father lectured his brood on it from a guidebook:

"They call this place Independence Hall. Built 1729. Cost five thousand six hundred pounds to build the thing. Hmm. Could have done more with that I think . . .''

Their accent sounded English. The little boy, still young enough to be dressed in a suit with a plaited skirt, was more interested in me and my companion. His expression was one of utter fascination.

I wondered for a moment what the child was staring at. Then I noticed how close I was standing to Miss Cole. Too close for a respectable gentleman to be standing to a girl like . . . like the way she was.

Miss Cole noticed the staring too. She made a face at the boy and walked off. I had to run to catch up with her.

When we were walking astride I said, "Don't mind the brat. He's probably never seen a colored woman before in his life."

"Not with a white gentleman, that's for sure."

I chuckled and said, "I'm no gentleman. I'm a copper."

"The most singular policeman I've ever met."

I tipped my hat to her and said, "Miss Cole, do you mind if I ask you a question?"

"Do you mind if I answer?"

"Where exactly are we going?"

I hadn't given our destination too much thought before now. It felt nice to walk along Chestnut with someone who wasn't a copper or a grafter. Someone with a little polish.

I wasn't sure if that meant I wasn't noticing her color or the exact opposite. At any rate I kept myself at a distance so people wouldn't get the wrong idea. I still let her have the inside of the walkway. There was enough of the gentleman in me to extend that courtesy.

Miss Cole laughed. It was a luxuriant sound, simmering from a place where a lot of other emotions were hiding.

"I can make it home on my own from here. It's not that far away. Please don't trouble yourself."

Her tone was a little cold. But I didn't feel like she wanted me to leave.

"It's no trouble at all."

The last few words came out in a stutter. I got the feeling she was testing me. When her brown eyes looked at me I saw the same thing in them I felt in myself. An interest. And an apprehension.

She sighed and said, "I live on Twelfth and Pine. I board at a friend of the family's house there."

"Good for you. That's a nice neighborhood," I said. I must've sounded condescending.

"As nice a neighborhood as a negro can get into."

Wincing, I said, "I didn't mean it like that."

She smiled and said, "I know. I'm just feeling bitter to-day."

"You've got a right."

"Let's stop talking about it. Please?"

"Okay by me. Hey listen, how's about a little snack? I'm famished. Haven't had a bite since court this morning."

"What do you have in mind?"

A nice restaurant was out. I knew that. And so did she, probably. For a second I imagined what it would be like to whisk her into the Union League. That would ruffle a few feathers.

I said, "How about some ice cream?"

"Perfect!" I caught sight of her ivories again in a wide smile.

Twelfth and Pine wasn't exactly around the square from where we were. But I didn't mind the extra walking. It wasn't every day I strolled with a lovely girl down the fashionable promenade of Chestnut Street.

It was only when I looked at the dudettes prancing about in their tassled and ribboned bustles and coquettish hats that my bubble burst. They were all staring at me or trying not to stare. As we walked past I could hear them whisper or giggle to their companions. When we went by a window I looked at myself and the girl beside me. The picture didn't look right. For a second I felt myself stiffen. Then I thought on the talks I had that day with Mulholland and the coroner. I hated feeling like a hypocrite. I kept walking and tried to ignore my discomfort.

There was an ice cream saloon on the way to her boardinghouse. Whenever I was in the neighborhood I paid a call to nurse my sweet tooth.

The door was closed to ward off the autumn chill. I opened it, upsetting the bell perched on the inside. Nobody noticed the jingle.

Around the wooden counter there were three couples enjoying sweetmeats and some ice cream. All three of the young men wore checkered suits and freshly-shined shoes. They were respectable-looking. One couple was even colored. The owner didn't mind. That was why I'd taken Miss Cole here in the first place.

Next to the colored couple was a doorway with a cloth draped over it. Smoke leaked out from under the curtain. Men were in there. It sounded like they were playing cards. I heard glass strike glass and knew they were doing something else too.

The owner wasn't there. A kid was behind the counter, a stained apron covering his lanky body. Perched on his head was a paper hat he was probably ashamed to wear.

I scanned the slate on the wall to our right and noticed the flavors for that evening: Strawberry, vanilla, and lemon. A chalk smudge beneath the last told me chocolate had just sold out.

"Anything there you fancy?" I asked Miss Cole.

"All three," she said.

I approached the counter. That's when the customers and the kid noticed us. Or more to the point noticed who I was with.

Their looks ranged from mild curiosity to disapprobation, the last being from the colored couple. Whether they disapproved of her being with me or the other way around was anyone's guess.

The boy made a smirk and said, "Sorry, mister. This is a respectable place."

Miss Cole stared at the wooden floor, biting her lip.

"What was that you said?" I asked.

I must not have looked that intimidating. Either that or the kid was especially stupid. He told me, "Take your colored whore and get out or I'll call the boys in back."

I lost my patience with him. I took my star and tossed it on the counter.

"This currency good enough?"

It took him a while to twig I was a copper. He was so sure I was just a low character out for a frolic with my colored pick of the night. After all, white men only associated with one kind of colored woman.

When it hit the kid he started wiping his hands against the stained apron. He said, "I didn't know you was a policeman."

I walked to the curtained doorway. The voices had gotten quiet.

"I wonder what's goin' on behind here?" I said. Tearing the cloth down, I saw three mechanics, their clothes covered with oil and metal filings. On the table where they sat were a couple bottles of what looked like whiskey.

"How'd you boys like to spend a night in the chokey?"

They stuffed the cards and money into their pockets and dusted off.

I turned back and found only the kid and Miss Cole still in the saloon.

I said, "How'd you like me to nail you for runnin' an illegal sample room in the back of this saloon? With card-playing yet!"

"It's the boss's place! Not mine!"

"That makes no difference to me."

I took my bracelets off my belt to scare him. He started whining, begging. After I'd humiliated him completely I said, "I'll tell you what. You can make it up to the lady and me by giving me two bricks of vanilla. And . . ."

I looked at Miss Cole who was trying to control her smile.

She said, "A brick of strawberry, please."

"A brick of strawberry."

The kid opened the little wooden ice-box behind the counter and deposited our ice creams before us, shaped like squares on pieces of butcher paper. Sweating, he handed me a spoon, his hand shaking.

Then I said, "Now go back to the room there and stay out of our way. And turn the gas up, the sun's goin' down."

When he was gone I said, "Miss Cole, I'm sorry you . . ."

"Mr. McCleary, please stop calling me that. I have a Christian name. You've been chivalrous enough to deserve the informality."

"I thank you kindly. Arabella." I knew plenty of colored women by their first names. But Arabella was different. It felt strange to be this familiar with her.

I said, "Where'd you learn to talk so . . ."

"So white, you mean?"

"Well, I wouldn't put it like that."

"Why not? My own people do."

"What do you mean?"

"Plenty of children said the same thing when I taught school a few years back."

"You mean colored kids?"

"Yes. I was an instructor at the Institute for Colored Youth."

"I know it well."

"Perhaps you're a graduate?"

We laughed. I said, "When I was a roundsman my beat was in the Seventh Ward. Took me right past it."

Our conversation came to a momentary halt. It was something different and refreshing, just sitting there with her and not caring what anyone might be thinking.

She put her book on the counter next to her melting brick of strawberry. The spine was facing me and I read the words *Forbes's Elementary Treatise on Human Anatomy*.

"That your hobby?" I asked, pointing to the book. "Or are you thinking of being one of those female nurses like Clara Barton?"

"It's more than a hobby, I assure you. I'm a student at the Women's Medical College."

My face must've telegraphed my surprise.

"I know. It's not every day you hear about a colored female medical student."

"I should say not."

I felt compelled to tell her, "I never went to college."

It came out sounding wistful. So I said, "But you don't need a diploma to carry the club."

"But you might have gone?"

"No. College is for the swell mob."

"Did you want to go?"

"Not to college." I was almost embarrassed to admit it to her, I don't know why. Then, surprising myself, I said it.

"I was planning on going to seminary."

"Why didn't you?"

"Things happened."

Arabella was looking at me intently now. Even with my eyes averted I could tell. A warmth was growing between us. It manifested itself in the tone of our voices and our casual positions at the counter. I wanted to tell her things I'd told no one for a long time. She had the kind of face that inspired those feelings. A beautiful face. For a split second I had this picture of my hand against her cheek, light and dark. I liked the picture very well, but it scared me.

After scouring my expression, the premature wrinkles around my eyes and the tautness of my lips, she said, "You were in the war."

Then I knew I would tell her those things.

"Yes."

"You were wounded?"

"No. Just captured."

"You were a prisoner of war?" Her voice was interested, curious. But the interest didn't feel casual. She wanted me to tell her all about it.

"I started out with the 125th New York Regiment, in Colonel Willard's Brigade. I joined up with them after they'd been captured at Harper's Ferry in '62 and paroled, when they were wintering in Virginia. All the boys came from Troy or thereabouts and one of my best friends from home, James O'Connor, was their sergeant. After they got taken prisoner by the Rebels I decided I would join up with them, first chance I got. I figured they needed the help.

"We didn't see any action until the next summer when the Rebels invaded Pennsylvania. Our division became a part of Hancock's Corps on the way to Gettysburg.

"We got there after the battle started. The closer we got the more I was shaking. I could feel my spine jar with every artillery shot. Maybe I imagined it, but I thought I could smell the blood. I could certainly hear the cries of wounded, dying men all through the night. The next morning we wound up on a place called Cemetery Ridge."

I took a few hurried gulps of my vanilla ice cream, tasting the paper it rested on. Then I said, "That morning we got caught in some skirmishing around a brick barn in the middle of this farmyard. The Rebels must've been about forty rods away. Mississippians I think they were. But I didn't think of them as people. All I knew was they were death incarnate.

"The Rebels gave us a good pounding, I'll give them that. James and I and the rest of the boys weren't used to heavy fighting or anything. But the 125th had a lot to prove, having once surrendered. We weren't about to give ground. The Rebels finally started falling back. I was so happy, Arabella! I thought it was over. I'd barely gotten a half dozen shots out, most of which probably went over their heads.

"Then the colonel ordered us to advance, with bayonets fixed. I was so afraid . . ."

My hands were trembling, just like they had back then.

"See that? See them shake? Now multiply that times ten. Balls were shooting past us every which way the closer we got. The smoke was so thick I couldn't even see where I was going. James and I got lost after a dozen rods or so. My ears were ringing so loud I couldn't hear a thing. James saw I was crying and made some joke. I pretended it was just smoke in my eyes."

There went my eyelid, twitching. I was back on the field, far from Arabella and myself.

"Some Rebels started firing and I let one off myself. Just afterward I twigged I'd left the damn rod in the barrel. It fired out like a harpoon. I didn't have any way to load my gun anymore. James was prying a rifle loose from a dead man's hand to give to me . . . when I heard this roar. The next thing I knew James didn't have a head. Something flew into my neck, cutting my cheek to pieces. I . . . think it was his teeth.

"That's when I started running. I didn't care where I went. Just so long as I was moving, as if death couldn't catch up with me. The further I could get away from my regiment and James and the noise and the death, the better. Eventually I found my way out of the smoke and into the middle of a Rebel regiment. They did me the disservice of taking me prisoner."

I laughed then. It sounded like a choking sob.

"Our colonel was killed that day. So were some other boys I knew, friends of mine. If I'd stayed I would've been a hero like them, dead or alive. It was several weeks before I found out that we'd won the battle. By that time I was in Belle Isle. After rotting there for half a year I was loaded on a cattle car and taken to Andersonville. I suppose I deserved worse."

Andersonville seemed to be familiar to her. She said, "I'm sorry. It must've been horrible."

I tried to ignore the pain welling up in me by saying, "But you don't want to listen to my old war tales. I'd rather hear your stories. It's not often I get to talk to a lady with a college education."

Arabella's mouth contorted in a grimace, then a smile. Laughter came with it. She reached toward my face and I drew back just a shade.

"Don't be scared," she said. "You have vanilla ice cream all over your mustache. It's been bothering me."

Tearing a piece of paper from her ice cream she wiped my upper lip. I was too embarrassed to feel anything else.

"I'm sorry," the girl said. "I don't mean to be uncouth. Or too familiar. I can't help it, though. My upbringing."

"What kind of upbringing did you have to come out the way you are?"

"I hope that means I came out well. I was raised in an environment where I and my family didn't have to feel, be, so inhibited."

"California?"

"Close. France."

"Europe, you mean? You're a singular girl."

"Perhaps," she chuckled. "My father was a music tutor employed by a very wealthy man outside of Paris. He became interested in my father after his singing group toured the country. It didn't take much to persuade my father to leave the States. People were less concerned with . . . the way we were there. We lived in isolation and I was educated along with the other children in the town. I grew up with our benefactor's children. I never had a playmate of my own race. Maybe that's why I don't feel queer talking to a white man like this."

"Even with a copper."

"You're a singular copper." The slang word sounded funny coming from her. She said, "I've seen how your brethren deport themselves."

"Don't take the scamps this morning as your example. We're not all bad eggs."

"At least one isn't. You're very sensitive for a policeman. You seem to be sympathetic."

"What's that mean?"

"You feel other peoples' pain or joy."

"I've seen a lot more of the first kind."

"That's why I think you could understand why I wanted to be a doctor. When I came back to America after the war I couldn't believe the state my people were in here. My father had told me stories but they hadn't quite prepared me. Shoving us off streetcars was legal back then. Walking down Lombard Street and seeing all the miserable wretches crammed in foul-smelling back courts made my heart ache. I realized I had to do something with the gifts I'd been given. I wanted to give something back. Do you understand? So I worked for a year and saved money to begin my studies at the Medical College. And two years ago I became the second negro student in its history.'' She said the last with real pride.

''So this is your final year?''

''Yes,'' she said, looking at her book. ''I passed the anatomy examination the very first year. But I enjoy this book. It was written by my preceptor.''

''Oh. Forbes is his name?''

''Yes. William Forbes. He holds the chair in anatomy at our school and also does clinical lectures at the Pennsylvania Hospital.'' Then she added with admiration, ''He's a brilliant man. That very first year he decided to take me on. I've been his protegee for the past two years. And learned so much. I attend his lectures in anatomy at the college and the hospital even though my examination's finished. I just like to see him at work.'' Her hands were tapping nervously against the leather-bound volume.

I said, ''That's your primary interest? Anatomy?''

''Oh no. I'm more interested in what we call psychology. The study of the mind and intelligence itself.''

Although Arabella seemed eager to talk, she held herself in check. Probably because she knew I wouldn't understand anything she said.

I looked down at the dark finished counter and noticed my brick had melted into a sticky white puddle.

Thinking out loud I said, ''They could use you at the coroner's office.''

''It's interesting that you should say that. I know the coroner somewhat.''

When I made a questioning face she said, ''Through my preceptor, Dr. Forbes. We get most of our cadavers from the morgue.''

''Well,'' I said with a tone of disgust, ''you might be getting a new one for your dissecting room.''

It was Arabella's turn to look puzzled.

I said, "That's where I was while you were at the Central Office. Fishing a floater out of the Delaware."

"What's a floater?"

"A drowned corpse. A colored woman, as a matter of fact."

"How terrible," the girl said. But she wanted me to go on.

"It wasn't pretty. She wasn't, I mean. That tooth of hers was hard to miss."

"Tooth?" Arabella leaned forward, taking her hand from her book, and gripped the counter.

"Yeah. She had a gold tooth. Right up in front." I bared my teeth and pointed to the position.

"What did this woman look like, Wilton?" It sounded like she already knew.

"Fat, thirty years old or so. But she looked older. Those kind of women age fast. About your height."

"How was she colored?"

"She was no high yellow girl. Not your color either. This one was real dark."

"Did she have a scar on her index finger, right hand?"

When I nodded, surprised, she said "Goldie. Goldie Collins. I know her, Wilton."

I repeated the name and said, "That moniker sounds familiar."

"She was a low character. The kind you'd make a business acquaintance, as it were."

"Oh. Prostitute?"

The girl didn't blush at the blunt term.

"I think she used to be. But she told me she'd been in the penitentiary for assault."

Now it was my turn to get excited.

"Yeah!" I said, snapping my fingers. "I remember now. Goldie the Bludget."

"Bludget?"

"What they call a female garroter. Preys on drunks and slummers out chasing the elephant. Lures them into a doorway with the promise of . . . you can guess what. And then clobbers them. Next morning they wake up with a bump on the nob and their pockets empty.''

I knew Goldie all right. Or her reputation at least. And I knew one other thing.

She was one of the nine on my disappeared list.

Then I asked, ''By the way, how did you know this, uh, woman?''

''Volunteer work I did at the Magdalen Society.''

A refuge for ''fallen women'' at Twenty-first and Race.

''Why there?''

''They seemed to need it most.''

I was beginning to really admire this girl.

Arabella put her fingers to her mouth as if to bite her nails. The gloves must've tasted funny. She made two fists and held them in her lap.

''Well,'' I said. ''You can show up to her funeral at potter's field. She'll be buried at city expense. Thanks to our dutiful coroner.''

''Doesn't the woman deserve a funeral at least?''

''I don't mean that.''

Then I told her about the coroner's opinion of cause of death. And a little of our private conversation behind the wagon.

Arabella was genuinely shocked.

''How can they do that? It's insidious!''

''They can do it because no one gives a damn. Pardon my language.''

''Oh, stop that. I've heard it before.''

''Okay. That's the way the game works. And that's why we only have a half-dozen detectives in Philadelphia. Murders don't have any rewards attached to them like stolen property does. Especially murders of poor colored women. So it makes sense to pretend the killing never happened. It makes the citizens feel safer. And gives us less work to do.''

Then an idea came to me.

"How would you like to come with me to the morgue?"

It was not the usual invitation a man extends to a young lady.

"You can identify the body. I'll pay for the cab fare."

She cleared her throat and stepped off the stool.

"Of course I'll go. The poor wretch."

That made me think of the kid in the closet at the end of the store. I hollered, "You can come out now, sonny."

We stepped up to the street and hailed a cab. The sun had gone down and I hadn't even noticed.

THE HANSOM CAB was cramped quarters. Our legs pressed against each other the whole way. Just that touch was enough to distract me. When the wheels hit a chuckhole in the cobbles she was thrown forward. Her hand landed on my knee, bracing herself. Quickly she drew it away and said, "Sorry."

"Don't be," I said. When the light of a street lamp crossed her face I noticed a curious smile.

About halfway she said to me, "Why are you going out of your way for a creature like Goldie? What is she to you?"

"Goldie's been missing for some weeks. Along with a bunch of other colored women. Most of them streetwalkers and almshouse inmates. Then an A.M.E. minister's daughter disappeared. From the same general area."

"Do you think the disappearances might be somehow connected?"

"Could be."

"What proof do you have?"

"None. Yet. All I know is nine women are missing and no one knows where they went. And nobody much cares either."

"So why do you?"

I paused, listening to the gay-sounding jingle of the

horse's harness. My own thoughts seemed discordant.

I didn't have an answer for her.

Arabella turned her head to look out the tiny celluloid rear window. Then she said, "Well, why do you even bother talking like this to me? To someone like me?"

I waited for her to turn around and look at me. I was glad she didn't. It made it easier for me to tell her, "I don't care what you are. I want to talk to you. Other things don't matter to me."

That much, I wanted to add.

Instead I told her, "Here we are."

The City Morgue was located on Beach and Noble streets. It was only a few years old and had all the charm of a well-used water closet. The one lone gas lamp over the entrance gave off a weak flare. It reminded me of those votive candles you see in a Catholic church.

Arabella walked through the doors and headed down the empty hall like she knew where she was going. The sound of our footfalls seemed sacrilegious.

We walked past a door with an opaque glass window. Stencilled in fine script were the words *John L. Gilbert Brown, Coroner*. There was no light behind the glass.

"You seem to know your way around, Arabella."

"Dr. Forbes sometimes asks me to come down here and arrange a delivery."

"How does he find out about them?"

"Oh, he scours the *Ledger*, *Press*, *Bulletin*, and *Star* for any accidents and deaths. I come periodically just to see if any strangers to the city have been found dead."

The coroner must have been only too happy to get rid of those. No fee acrued for their burial, after all.

At the end of the hall was a set of two well-polished metallic doors.

We pushed them aside and entered the death-house.

The first thing I noticed was how cold it was. I could see our breaths.

It was a long room with a sickly-looking green tile

floor. Gas lamps poked out of the ceiling at intervals. Only two were burning.

The rest of the room was submerged in shadow. There was just enough gas on for us to see the tables and the draped bodies resting on them. It was amazing how well aware I was of things so carefully concealed.

There were voices coming from the opposite end of the room. An attendant in a white smock was conversing with a colored man. I took a few steps to see them better. Then I noticed that Arabella was lagging behind.

"What's the matter?" I said, turning back to her.

The girl shook her head while keeping her eyes firmly fixed on the two men. She moved back slightly, into deeper shadow.

The place was getting to her. And to me too. I wanted to conduct our business and leave as soon as possible.

I hailed the attendant.

"Hey, can you give us a hand here?"

The colored man took his leave when I'd made it half-way across. I was only able to get a brief glimpse of his features and clothes: bristly hair in need of a trim, low brow and deep-set eyes, clean-shaven, with denim overalls and a green, collarless shirt. There was something strange about his hands. I couldn't see too well in the dim light, but I thought I saw patches of white on his dark skin.

I asked the attendant, "Who was that man?"

The middle-aged attendant, as sallow-faced as the less lively occupants of the room, said to me, "More importantly, who are you?"

I pulled my star out and introduced myself.

"It's a little late to hold a viewing. All the big bugs have gone home for supper."

It was a good change of subject. He sounded lonely, and more importantly, venal. I decided to see what I could do with him.

"Well, seeing as how it's official police business, how about you show me where the body of the large colored woman with a gold tooth is stretched out? They brought her in to-day."

Arabella was at my side by then. I could smell the toilet water she used in her hair. Lavender and Violet I think it was. It helped to drive out the other odors in the air—some medicinal and others more corporeal.

"What's this?" the attendant asked, looking at Arabella.

"This," she said to him, "is a young woman who would like to see you do what the officer told you to do."

The rotund man huffed and said, "Can't."

"What do you mean?" I said, taking a threatening step toward him.

His hands came up in gesture of defense.

"They took the body already. Just now."

Arabella and I exchanged glances. I said, "Explain that."

"That nig—colored fella. He just hauled it off."

"Where?" Arabella asked him.

"Do I care? Maybe he was a relative."

"What about an inquest?" I said.

That would take at least a day.

"Inquest? Coroner had one when he came back with the stiff."

Suddenly I remembered the coroner saying something to the men on the dock as I left him. Something like, "Who wants to make $1.50?"

The fee paid to coroner's jurors.

"Are you tellin' me he had a jury assembled and everything?"

"Sure. Looked like a bunch of sailors. Smelled like 'em too."

"Were you present?"

"No. I came in just as the inquest concluded."

"What does this mean, Wilton?" Arabella asked. It was only then I noticed her hand around my arm, squeezing. I left it there and said, "It means the coroner held his kangaroo court and got rid of the body on the double.

Paid a bunch of waterfront scamps to be the jurors at the inquest. Didn't even waste the time to assemble a legitimate jury. I think he wanted that body out of sight and mind. I wonder why? What do you think, friend?''

"The coroner doesn't tell me what's going on in his head," the attendant whined. I looked at his hands. He was rubbing the tips of his fingers together. I remembered thinking he had a potential for greed. I decided to test my theory.

"Arabella, could you leave us alone for a few moments?"

"Certainly, Wilton. I'll wait in the hallway."

"I'll be right there."

The two of us waited for the metallic doors to slam behind her.

Then I began to walk around him, sizing him up. I was a big man. He wasn't. Like a dog, I could smell his fear.

"Not too easy, working around here. Being an attendant and all. Brown can give you the boot whenever he wants, can't he?"

"That's right," he stuttered.

"So why are you looking out for him?"

"I ain't lookin' out for nobody. I told you. I don't know a thing about that nigger whore."

"Now you're fibbing," I said, standing right behind him.

His spine was arched so stiff I thought it'd crack.

"Whatta ya mean?" he whispered.

"You said she was a nigger whore. Now how would you know about her occupation?"

"I musta heard them say somethin' about it."

"How much else did you hear?"

"What's it to you, pal?"

"I don't like Brown. Don't like the way he lords it over everybody, you know what I mean?"

"Yeah," the attendant said with conviction.

"Makes you feel small, like a peasant. And he pays peanuts."

"You can say that again."

He was pretty buttered up. I took the five Coroner Brown had given me out of my pocket.

"He gave this greenback to me to-day. He thought he could keep my mouth shut about something I saw at Southwark. For a lousy five-dollar note. What do you think of that, friend? Me worth only five dollars?"

The attendant was cagey and said nothing.

I put my face in his and said, "How much did they buy you for, friend?"

His lower lip pushed against the upper one. Looking askance he said, "A couple of good segars."

"Well, how'd you like to spit in his eye for that? For thinking he can buy you for a couple of segars? A man's got some dignity after all, right?"

"That's right, by damn!" he said, clenching his fist. Beneath his smock his chest swelled, no doubt with the memory of past indignities.

Inwardly I smiled.

The attendant said, "Well, he tried to shut me up this time all right. Just like he's done some other times."

Hopeful, I asked, "With other colored stiffs?"

"No, this is the first one. But I only been here for three weeks."

"What about this one? Why the bogus inquest?"

"I don't know. I think Brown had to get rid of the body. Somebody made him."

"Who?"

"I don't know. All I know is when I show up for work the inquest's breaking up. Brown comes in without saying a word to me. He's with this copper and—"

"Hold it. What copper?" I described the roundsman I'd seen at the waterfront.

"No it wasn't him. Bigger. Taller."

"Describe him."

In about five words I knew who it was. The accompanying chill felt like someone holding a blade to my spine, running it up and down.

"You ever see this man around here before?"

"No, this is the first time."

"What did Brown and the copper say?"

"Nothing. Brown just showed the copper the body. The copper slipped him some green goods, right in front of me," the attendant said, making a feeble and hypocritical attempt at outrage.

"And then what?"

"The copper said, 'I'll send my man for her.' That was it."

"The colored man?"

"I guess so."

"You didn't get his name?"

"No. I didn't hear him say it or ask it."

I stuffed the five dollars Coroner Brown had given me into the attendant's smock. I said as I turned away, "You didn't see me to-night, understand?"

He nodded his head vigorously, looking at the greenback. As I took my leave of him, a gloating smirk creased his face.

Arabella was leaning against a wall, reading her anatomy book for want of anything else to do. She only looked up when the doors slammed shut.

"Well?" she said.

"I'm getting you a cab. You need to go home."

"That's it? You're not going to tell me what happened?"

"Not right now."

She looked hurt, like I'd just betrayed her confidence.

"I can't, Arabella. It's better for you if you don't know."

We walked out in silence and stood on the streetcorner for a few minutes, waiting for a cab to trot by.

Wanting to heal the rift between us I said, "Did classes start for you already?"

"Yes," she said, a little coldly. "In fact I have a lecture at the hospital to-morrow morning. Dr. Forbes actually."

"That's good. Maybe it'll take your mind off to-night. I'm sorry I dragged you all over town."

"I wanted to help. I still do."

"I know."

Down the street I saw the twin lamps of a cab heading our way. I stood out in the street and waved. The driver pulled in the reins and the horse stopped right in front of us.

"Good night to you, Arabella."

She put her hand in mine. I held it longer than I had to.

"Good night, Wilton. And goodbye."

I watched her cab recede into the shadowy distance.

Then I turned and headed for Southwark again.

I walked the whole way. It took me an hour but I didn't mind. The autumn wind rushed into my lungs and stung them with its chill. I listened to the sound of church bells ringing the ninth hour. For a while my mind drifted with their mournful music.

I kept thinking on Arabella and how much I wanted to see her again. But I couldn't involve her any more in my investigation. For her own good.

Because I didn't think the copper who was at the morgue was playing games. Sergeant Walter Duffy wasn't like that.

I wanted very much to know why he'd been there that night. And where the body ended up.

Something told me I might be able to answer both questions by visiting Southwark again. Maybe someone there could help me figure it out. Someone I'd seen that afternoon at the waterfront. The man who hadn't wanted to be seen.

I quickened my pace, thinking on that little shack behind the salt warehouse.

I STOOD ON the dock where the body was stretched out that afternoon. Watching the river gave me a peaceful feeling. I needed some of that. So many things had happened to me since court that morning that only now, after a nice long walk, did I realize how I felt about them.

Anxious, bewildered, and scared.

Then I looked up to the night sky. You couldn't see too much of the stars. It was a cloudy night. The gray wisps glowed red, reflecting the fires of the oil works and the scores of street lamps scattered across the sleeping city. The crimson haze reminded me of the apocalypse, just waiting for the right moment.

I made my way past the salt wharves and the stately wooden crafts moored there. Across the way was the salt warehouse and the hovel I'd seen that afternoon.

It was the size of a shed. No windows or any other decoration marred the claptrap wooden exterior. The frame looked about ready to implode from the weight of years.

Locating a door with at least three coats of paint stripping off it, I felt around for a knob. There wasn't any. Nor was there any lock. The door came open with the pressure of my hand.

Inside was nothing but darkness. The cool night air was

at my back and rushed into the stuffy chamber, fumigating it. That didn't bother me because the place stank to high heaven.

The meager starlight did little to illuminate the interior. I stepped away from the doorway to try to accustom my eyes to the deeper darkness. It didn't do much but let more of a draft in.

After a particularly vigorous gust of wind, I heard someone say, "Close that damn door. You want me to freeze my ass off?"

Trying to get closer to the sound I stepped forward. That was a mistake. My foot struck something hard and metallic. The thing was heavy and didn't budge. I did instead.

I reached out to keep myself from falling, my left hand closing on something solid. It turned out to be the edge of a wooden bed frame. At least that's what I assumed it was. It was hard to tell. The person on it had lit a lantern. The light momentarily blinded me.

I could smell the smoke from the lantern. The scent it gave off was very distinctive.

"You're still burning whale oil, friend?" I said as my eyes got used to the brightness. I took my hand off the bed frame and stood up.

There on the bed was the dirtiest creature I'd ever seen. At first I wasn't sure if he was a white man or not. Every pore of his face and hands was covered with a fine gray dust. He wore a moth-eaten hat with a deflated brim. The lesser degree of filth above the brim was the only trace left of the ribbon. Beneath that a stocking cap was wound around his head, covering his ears. A corduroy jacket draped his meager frame, the outermost of many layers of shabby and stained clothing. Striped trousers poked out from under a host of tattered, noisome blankets.

It smelled like the last time he took a bath was during his baptism. The whole tiny shed, his living quarters, got that much smaller with the overwhelming stink. It was hard to master it. I'd smelled worse in prison but at least that had been in the open air.

For a minute or so this creature had been regarding me silently. When I took my eyes off him for the first time and started looking around his diggings he said, "I seen you before."

Now it was my turn to be silent while I completed my inventory. On the wall beside his bed were three nails. From the first hung a pair of thoroughly cracked leather boots. From the second a dented coffeepot. And from the third a florist's calendar for 1871 depicting a garden scene in ancient Greece, the only unsullied color in the room.

The rest of the walls were covered with bags of varying size. On the floor were three old and soot-covered trunks. Finally I noticed the large metal pail I had tripped over. The contents looked to me like those of any ash barrel: garbage, tattered clothes, broken bottles, and the like.

It was enough to tell me this man was the lowest of the low, a ragpicker. Worse, a ragpicker who didn't even have the heart to scrounge anymore.

Looking at his wretched little shack made me think of my own row home on Porter Street—the tall ceilings and windows, and the good air, if you didn't mind the oil works fumes. Then there was the plumbing and the coal heat.

I'd been wondering if I have to push this man around. Now I didn't think I'd have the heart to do that.

As if detecting this change of mood, from hardhearted copper to human being, the ragpicker said, "I knew you'd come back."

I set my rear on a flat-topped trunk. Lightly, just in case it would break. I didn't want to touch the contents if I could help it. Then I said, "How'd you know that?"

The man lit a clay pipe he produced from under his garments and said, "'Cause I saw you to-day. I could tell you didn't like what you saw."

"Well, you seem to know a lot about me. But who are you?"

"Me?" He choked on that, like it was a question he hadn't heard in a long time. It seemed to almost flatter him. "My name's August Drimmer. Gus for short."

"How'd you come to live here, Gus? I mean, behind a salt warehouse?"

"Oh, well I used to know a fella that worked in the office over there. He was my brother-in-law."

"But he's not working there anymore?"

"No. He died before the war. So did my wife. But they keep letting me live here. I don't cause trouble. I even saved the salt wharves once, when a fire got started. Used that pail there and held the flames back till the engine came. So they leave me be."

"What were you doing watching us on the dock to-day?"

Gus puffed on his pipe, sending bursts of cheap tobacco my way.

"I got nothing else to do. Been a year since I gave up peddling. Can't do nothin' much anymore. I got a nasty case of gout."

"You know they can take care of that for you at the almshouse?"

"I know. I been there years ago. But I don't want to feel better. I just wanna stay here in this bed and never get out. Ever. That'd be nice."

He spoke like someone in a half-sleep. His eyes peered through the fog of his pipe smoke into the past. It was hard to believe that there had been better times for a creature like this. However it was, the past flitted across his eyes and made them cloudy.

Rising very slowly from the bed, he put both of his feet on the stone floor. Part of the contents of the metal pail lay around them like shoddy tribute.

I said, "You know why I'm here?"

"You saw me watching you to-day."

"And?"

"You want to know why."

I nodded and said, "I got the feeling you didn't want me to see you this afternoon, Gus."

"Nah. I didn't. Not at first. Then I heard you arguin'. I wasn't sure what to think. I was afraid."

"Afraid of what?"

"Nothing. When you came to-night I wasn't afraid. I was almost looking forward to it."

"To what?"

"To getting killed, of course."

I leaned back and hit the flimsy wall. "You think I came here to kill you?"

"Not anymore. I saw the way you were lookin' just now. You don't look like a killer to me."

"Have you seen one before?"

"Oh yeah. I've seen killers. And killin'."

"When?"

"Plenty of times. But you'd be wantin' to know about last night."

His feverish gaze fixed on me, like he was trying to anticipate my next move. From the corner of my eye I noticed his left foot pawing at the floor like a nervous animal.

"Yeah," I said. "Why don't you tell me about that?"

"I was just lyin' in bed smokin', with the lamp off."

"When?"

"How the hell do I know? Look like I got a clock around here? Nighttime."

"Okay. So then what?"

"I hear a woman's voice. Nigger woman, sounds like. Not hollering, you understand. But loud enough for me to hear it."

"Who was she talking to?"

"I couldn't tell. At first. But I could hear her givin' him a lot of sass. Mighty sassy that one."

As if my head needed more air to think, I took a deep breath. The fetid air did nothing for my mental powers. Nearly gagging, I said, "What were they saying?"

Gus took a puff and grinned. The interview was a welcome respite from his lonely squalor.

"She said something like, Did he bring what she told him to? And he said he did. And this woman started cussin' him out, sayin' he better. 'Cause she don't want to have to take it up with him."

"Him, who? The one there?"

"Nah. She was talkin' about somebody else that warn't there."

"Did you get his name?"

"No. She didn't say. But the other one knew who she meant. He said, 'You ain't goin' to him 'cause I'm givin' you more than you deserve.' Then she laughed and said she'd see about that. She seen a lot and she had a mind to peach on him. What he did to her and the others."

"What? What did he do?"

This might be it, I thought. Just a little bit more and I'd have something to smear in the chief's face.

"I don't know! They didn't explain it to me! All he said after that was, 'Gimme them things of hers.' Then she said, 'Oh no, pet. First the pay-off. Then the swag.' "

My palms were moist with sweat. I rubbed them against my trousers and said, "What'd he do then?"

Gus shifted the pipe stem from one corner of his mouth to the other. Then he warmed his hands over the lantern's open fire.

Gus said, "He killed her."

"You saw him do it?"

"Oh yeah. I had the door open just a crack. Beat her in the head and then strangled her."

"Did he tie her up then?"

"No. Why would he do that? She was dead already."

After a second or two I decided I might have made a mistake about the rope burns. They didn't seem to fit with what Gus was telling me. And what he was telling me was what I wanted to hear. So I forgot about the burns.

"Did he toss the body over the dock?"

"Yeah. Sort of rolled her over. She was a big gal."

"Okay, Gus. Important. Think. Who was he?"

"I didn't see him all that well."

"White? Black?"

"Oh he was white, all right. All you coppers are."

The words were barely out of his mouth when I snapped back, "Say that again."

"All you coppers are white, ain't ya? This one was a copper."

"You saw the uniform?"

"That and his nightstick turning her head to mashed potatoes."

It was too much to take. I stood up, nearly banging my head against the low, grimy ceiling.

"Let me guess," I said. "He was a big fella. Taller than me. With a mustache from ear to ear."

Gus nodded.

"Did she call him anything?"

"I don't know. She might've. It was hard to make everything out."

I thought of the copper the attendant had seen at the morgue. The one who arranged for the swift release of a corpse to parts unknown.

For some reason I had a hard time saying his name.

"How about Duffy? Did she call him that?"

The ragpicker made a wincing face and said, "It coulda been something like that. I don't know for certain."

It was close enough for me.

Sergeant Duffy was a murderer. He killed Goldie Collins and made sure no one got around to identifying her and possibly linking the two of them.

All I had to figure out was why Duffy would want to kill a colored bludget. And if he'd killed some others. Eight to be exact.

I felt my pulse quicken, my whole body tensing with excitement. I could give Heins what he wanted on a silver platter. And see Duffy get taken down.

Somehow that didn't make me feel as good as it should have. It wasn't that I had any sympathy for Duffy, him being a fellow copper and all. My loyalty had its limits, and Duffy was well beyond them. He'd get his deserts and then some.

The problem was with me. I wanted Duffy to fall. I wanted to be the one to collar and drag him into the magistrate's. Maybe this would be my final climb and I'd reach the top, be a detective.

It would do a lot of good things to me. But somehow that made me feel more like a scavenger. A parasite.

I wondered if that was how everybody felt who made the same sort of climb I was making. Perhaps it was a necessary condition of the climb.

I stood up, about to say some parting words to the ragpicker. Urge him to stick around and say nothing to anybody else. That sort of thing.

My head bowed as I thought on Duffy and what I would do. I felt burdened with weariness, anxiety, or shame, I don't know which. Maybe all three. My eyes were drawn to the pail I'd tripped over. My clumsiness had skimmed off the top layer of garbage, some of which I now noticed was spilled around the ragpicker's feet.

One of those soiled, stockinged feet was placed right on top of what looked like a cheap change purse. There was nothing remarkable about that. Except that Gus seemed to be moving it slowly under his bed, where I wouldn't be able to see it.

I didn't like the implications.

"What's in the change purse, Gus?"

The foot froze. Like a mesmerist, he stared straight at me, as if to avert my eyes from the floor.

With one step I was at the bedside. Reaching down to pick up the change purse I almost had my nose pushed in by his foot. I grabbed an ankle with one hand and the foot with another. Then I gave a twist.

Gus yelped with pain. It gave me enough time to snatch up the purse. Then I gave his shin a good kick. That got another yelp from him.

"Sit tight," I said. "And leave that lantern where it is.

You don't want to ignite the oil by tossing it at me do you? It might just fry you too.''

The ragpicker leaned back on his bed, holding his bruised leg like it might run away from him.

It was the kind of situation where a barker was useful. My fingers grazed my belt for a second before I remembered the revolver was sitting on my dresser at home. One doesn't usually appear in court with a fire-arm.

Keeping my eyes on the ragpicker, I fumbled for the clasp on the purse. It was a relatively new one. French kid with leather inside, worth not more than fifteen cents.

I found just three things inside: an earring, shaped like a star with Brazilian pebbles in it. Looked like solid gold. A lace pin, which might have been solid or rolled gold. It had a cute little cat holding a Brazilian pebble in her paw. The kitty was perched on a wedge like a crescent moon. The last item was a gold ring, engraved with a tiny pendant from which hung a crescent moon and star, like the Muhammedan religious symbol. The moon and star were set with what looked like real diamond chips.

Stars and moons.

Not a huge treasure. All three probably would go for not more than fifteen dollars.

But it was a king's ransom for a ragpicker like Gus.

"You didn't want me to see these things. Now tell me why.''

Gus didn't have to open his half-toothless mouth.

I was rolling the jewelry around in my hands, like I was going to shoot some craps.

In the dim light I saw what looked like deep scratches on the back side of the ring. When I held it closer to the lantern I saw they weren't deep scratches at all.

They were initials.

"J.M.''

I thought of the moon and stars. Of the kind of murky night where thick clouds swirl across the heavens, cloaking them. Beneath the sky a shadowy curtain coats everything around you in darkness. Then, through a momentary parting of clouds, the moon peers through, gently drawing back the dark curtain.

The curtain had just been drawn for me.

J.M.

Josephine Martin.

Reverend Martin's daughter. The last of my disappeared women.

I had a feeling Gus didn't find her jewelry while casually picking through an ash barrel.

The clouds passed across the moon again and I was left in darkness. I wanted some more illumination.

I knocked off the man's shabby hat with a hard slap. Then I shook him frantically, shouting, "What're you doing with this stuff?"

I had to have the answer now, as if the girl's life depended on it. For all I knew it did.

Gus was crying. "I earned it fair and square. You can't take it from me."

"How? How'd you get it?"

My hand cracked across his face again, ripping the clay pipe from his lips. His mouth quivered like a baby's would, deprived of its bottle.

"You can tell me right here or I'll sweat it out of you at the hall. *Bleed* it out of you."

I might not have meant it, but I wasn't exactly in control of myself. Gus decided not to take any chances with his life's fluid.

"I helped him get rid of the body. You think I'd let a guy do a croaking right in my backyard without taking a percentage? He gave me the nigger gal's change purse. Told me if anyone came around I should tell 'em what I told you. Or I'd be the one takin' a swim."

"What else did Duffy say?"

My hands kneaded his collar, trying to squeeze the truth out of him.

He spoke one more time, shaking his head.

"That's what the nigger . . ."

I waited for more. Nothing came out except a gasp.

That was when I felt cold air on my back. I whirled around and ran straight into something heavy and hard. It landed on my head, where I'd taken too many whacks that day. There was a black blossom of darkness. I don't remember hitting the floor.

I WOKE UP to a familiar smell.

The smell of blood.

From the feeling in my head I thought it was my own.

I reached toward my scalp and felt around for any open wounds. A finger brushed over a cut. It stung but not enough to account for all the blood.

When I brought my hand back down to my side, my palm brushed against something cold and metallic on the floor. A small object. I thought perhaps it was one of the pieces of jewelry belonging to Josephine Martin.

It took me a few moments to find it. I knew I had it because I felt something sharp poke into my fingertip. I was too groggy to curse or shout with pain. Although I couldn't see it I figured it for the lace pin of the cat and moon.

Then the door to the shack flew open with a crash and splinter of wood. A bright orange light shone on me. I shielded my eyes with my punctured hand and for the second time that night wished I had a barker on me.

A harsh voice bellowed from behind the light. It said, "Two of 'em. One of 'em thrashed pretty bad. The other . . . Well, look who it is. The Chestnut Street Pugilist."

My eyes adjusted to the light just in time for me to match the face with the voice I already recognized.

Sergeant Walter Duffy's face, half-obscured by shadow, was now transfigured by the lamp into a leering jack o' lantern.

Although my brain was just starting to warm up, I had a little bit of sense. I knew I had to be very, very careful.

The pin disappeared into my coat pocket. Then I stumbled to my feet. The sergeant didn't assist me.

"How 'bout tellin' me what you're doin' here, Mr. McCleary?"

Half my face was caked with dried blood. When I tried to wince I felt it stretch my skin.

"You sure are a messy worker," Duffy said.

Brushing my hair gingerly to avoid the cuts and bruises, I said, "What the hell is that supposed to mean?"

Instead of answering me, Duffy said to someone behind him, "You boys stay outside. I want to have a private chat."

The door shut halfheartedly. Duffy propped his lantern on the trunk where I'd sat listening to Gus.

We both looked at what was left of the ragpicker, lying on the cold floor. With his arms folded across his chest, he looked like a supplicant at a holy shrine.

"They don't get much deader than that," the sergeant said. "How about telling me how you made him that way?"

"Listen," I said, "I didn't kill him. Do you think I'd brain him and then stretch out and take a nap in his blood? Nobody can be that dumb."

I looked at the dead man again. Remembering how I'd roughed him up made me feel guilty.

Gus was no angel I admitted to myself. But his death could have been a little less ugly than his life. Except it wasn't. He seemed to want it that way.

Somebody had given him a great deal of help. I had a feeling that party was standing right in front of me.

"Let's start with what you were doing here."

The sergeant was poking through the garbage on the floor. If there had been a pile of junk before my collision with a blunt instrument, there was a mountain now. It looked like all the trunks had exploded and jettisoned their contents every which way. The chance of finding the earrings and ring were pretty slim now. I swore under my breath, knowing that ring was the only real proof I had that Goldie had something to do with Josephine. Whoever had killed her wanted to kill that secret as well.

I was tempted to ask the sergeant about it right now. But I decided not to push my luck. It looked bad enough for me as it was. He could pinch me for the killing if he wanted to. He could also push my face in for a little while to figure out what I knew. Or use that gun on his belt to shoot me while I supposedly resisted arrest.

Duffy leveled his eyes at mine and fired all the menace he had at me. To emphasize the point, he rested his meaty hand on the club at his belt and said, "Out with it. This place stinks."

I had to act stupid or he might twig how much I learned from the ragpicker and the coroner's attendant. The stupider I was the easier it would be for him to let me continue breathing.

I started out with the truth, omitting a plethora of facts along the way.

"I thought the ragpicker might have something to do with the drowning of this colored woman."

"What colored woman?" Duffy asked, bewildered. His incredulous mouth was open just a little bit too much and too long. It was a good charade. I almost cracked a smile in admiration.

"The chief sent me over here this afternoon to look at a colored floater. There didn't seem to be any witnesses. But I noticed this shack near the dock. This man was watching us, a little too interested, you know? So I came back here to see if he knew anything about it."

"And? What did he tell you?"

"Not much. That he heard her arguing with someone."

"About what?"

"He couldn't hear it too well. Then he heard a splash. He stayed right where he was."

The sergeant leaned closer to me and said, "That's it? Pretty weak, if you ask me. How do you know he didn't do it himself? He looks like the type who'd do his own grandmother up for a three-penny change purse."

Involuntarily, I felt for the lace pin in my pocket. Had Duffy flattened me, grabbed the change purse, and then killed Gus? That was the only explanation. Then he'd come over here with his pals on some phony pretext to see what I knew. And whether or not I had to go the same way as the ragpicker.

"From what I saw of the colored woman," I said, "it looked like she could have had Gus for breakfast."

"Just who was this nigger gal?"

"A bludget from the Seventh Ward. Name of Goldie Collins."

The name made him adjust his shoulders and neck, very slightly. Like the words were an unpleasant breeze that had just blown right in his face. I knew the two of them were acquainted then.

"Now, maybe you can explain this to me. What's a special officer doing on the waterfront in the middle of the night investigating the murder of some nigger bludget?"

I couldn't resist saying, "Did you say murder, Sergeant? I don't recollect mentioning she was murdered."

That caught him off-guard. His mouth hung open again but the lips were drawn taut over his yellow choppers.

Duffy stumbled for some words, finding them only after a bit of a struggle.

"Well, this scamp told you he heard someone pushin' her in, didn't he?"

"That's what he told me," I said, my eyes on Duffy's hand, still resting on the club.

The sergeant moved over to the body and tapped a limp shoulder with his boot.

"Musta been like that then. Except this fella saw more

than he told you. Probably saw the killing and the killer. Got himself killed for what he saw.''

''I'll go along with that.''

''And you came mighty close yourself.''

Since Duffy's face was turned from me to the dead man, I couldn't read the expression that went along with those words. I was left to draw my own implications. One of those, the foremost in my mind at that moment, was that the words sounded like a warning.

The sergeant tore one of the filthy blankets from Gus's bed and draped it over him. ''Let Brown take care of him now.''

Then he turned to look at me again. His bulk seemed to take up the whole room.

''Sort of a mess for a simple killing. Looks like he was looking for something. You got any ideas about that, McCleary?''

The lace pin in my pocket felt like a dead weight. My hand crept toward the side of my coat. I thought of arresting the motion, then realized it would look queer. So I pretended to brush dust from my pantaloons, making sure the pin was secure in its hiding place.

''I don't know anything about that,'' I said. ''We didn't have too much time to go into the particulars.''

''Well, I'm gonna have the boys take a look while we go to the Central Office.''

My body tensed. I didn't like the idea of going anywhere with him alone.

Duffy pulled open the door and said, ''You fellas take a look around in there. You know the kind of thing we're looking for.''

It was another innocuous comment that could also mean other things.

I recognized one of the other bulls who squeezed into the rank-smelling shack. Uriah Strunk, the fat reserve officer I left in a gutter that morning. He stayed out of my way.

Outside the dawn was making it easy for me to see our

frosty breaths. For the first time I noticed the ache in my limbs from lying in the cold air all night. In terms of restfulness it hadn't been up to snuff. All I wanted to do was go back to Porter Street and stretch myself out on a nice bed. Maybe shovel some coal in the stove and bake myself to sleep.

The last thing I wanted to do was go to the Central Office. Especially in the shape I was in. The ragpicker's blood had covered the top of my coat and the back of my head and the right side of my face. My collar and right cuff were stained an ugly brown color. I looked like a casualty of a particularly vicious war. And felt like one too.

A prison van was parked next to the salt wharves. The dull black color of its body and gear gave it the common name of Black Maria. It was about the size of a milk wagon with a row of windows at the top. In anticipation of the passengers' future lodgings, the tiny slits were barred. It was a grim-looking vehicle, the panels devoid of any embellishment. Hitched to it was a horse, snorting frosty puffs of air like a lethargic locomotive.

"What's the Maria doing here?" I asked Duffy.

"It's all we could find this early in the morning. You can ride in the back. That'll be a switch, won't it?"

Duffy climbed into the narrow seat while I crawled into the compartment for prisoners. I heard the sergeant ring the bell dangling from the top in front of him. We pulled away from the salt wharves as the sun broke over the hills of Jersey.

There were no benches inside and the whole interior was lined with sheet iron. It didn't make for a comfortable ride. I kept the rear door slightly ajar, just in case Duffy decided I should go somewhere other than Fifth and Chestnut. Somewhere like the bottom of a backhouse privy—with a few pills in me to keep me there.

The ride made my bones ache even more than they did already. The horse wasn't allowed to take its time. The iron surface compounded my aching with a nasty chill.

But I wasn't complaining. I had a little bit of time to organize the shreds of evidence I'd collected.

My thoughts swirled in my head like ghostly fingers. The fingers seemed to be writing words on the iron walls around me. I'd been reading the book of Daniel that week and knew what the words meant.

Someone had been judged and found wanting. Their days were numbered.

I got no heaven-sent inspiration to tell me who that someone was. That person's identity haunted me the rest of the way back. I wasn't so much of a fool to think that it couldn't be me.

BEFORE WE GOT to the Central Office I decided to disembark, nearly breaking my leg in the process. I wasn't interested in talking to Mulholland. Especially not with Duffy there. I needed time to clean up and to think.

I must have made quite a sight. Half-caked with blood, clothes torn to pieces, stumbling through the streets. My breath trailed after me like smoke from a smoldering ruin.

It was still early. My pocket watch had luckily survived the tussle at the waterfront. The time was seven minutes to seven. I headed for my barber, Elwood George. His shop was next door to the Continental Hotel, on Ninth and Sansom.

The distance I walked felt like nothing. I was beyond exhaustion and distracted by my aching head. My body felt like a machine that kept going without any steam to power it. The only thing that kept the wheels turning was inertia. I thought of a smooth chair at Woody's, just waiting for me to collapse into it.

Curtains were still down in the blocks of row homes. I could smell bread coming right out of the oven and it made my mouth water. Morning papers, twisted in damp rolls, rested on front steps next to bottles of milk and cream.

Street merchants were out cleaning their sidewalks,

hurling buckets of warm water onto the filthy pavement. The accumulated dust from horse dumpings, segar butts, spittle, and shreds of paper flowed into the narrow gutters. I stepped in puddle after puddle but I hardly cared. I couldn't get any filthier than I was.

Work whistles were blowing all over the city, signalling the start of the mechanics' ten-hour day of labor. Huge gusts of steam puffed into the dawn. Somewhere far off a church bell tolled for an early mass.

A couple streetcars passed me. The conductors were leaning out the sides, wiping the windows and metalwork in preparation for the first batch of passengers. A horse pulling a dray filled with lumber halted in the middle of the street. While the driver cursed and implored it to move, the beast calmly urinated.

It was as normal a morning as could be. Somehow that lifted my spirits.

I made it to Woody's about ten minutes after seven. There was only one other customer, with a hot towel sizzling on his face.

The barber was a short, bald man with white wisps of hair combed slick against his head. A white beard like the late President's curved around his jaw. He stood there in his usual uniform of blue striped shirt, arm bands tightly secured, a long green apron, and shapeless, ageless pantaloons. His shoes already waded in a small pond of human hair.

Woody was Pennsylvania Dutch, from the counties to the north of the city. When he got excited sometimes he broke into a dialect that even the German immigrants puzzled over. The rest of the time he spoke English like he was trying to whistle it instead of talk it.

He was running a razor up and down a cracked leather strop. When the bell rang he gave a quick look to the door and said, "Hiya, Mack."

"Hiya Woody."

"Cold enough for ya?"

I closed the door behind me and sat down. The cane-seated chair moaned when I sat in it. Next to the chair was a flimsy table that looked like it was lifted from a parlor. A water stain marred the top where a plant had probably stood. Lying on it now were various magazines. The sort you didn't keep on your parlor table.

Right on the top of the stack was a copy of the *National Police Gazette*. On the cover was a scene of a policeman arresting two fast girls or "dashing Providence damsels" as the caption put it. They were "imitating the Lords of Creation" that is, us men, by smoking segars. The artist made sure we got the point they were fast by showing their hitched-up skirts, revealing not only their ankles but a little bit of their calves.

That gives you an idea of the general emphasis of the magazine. Most of the stories were illustrated with similar scenes. One was about a hydrophobiac killing his wife on their wedding night by biting her neck. I wondered how I could become a staff writer. I had better yarns than that.

My eyes wandered to the wall at the end of the shop. At first you'd think it was a rogues' gallery like we have at the Central Office. Instead this was a framed case enshrining Woody's collection of cartes de visite. He was very proud of this collection and his customers always made sure to give it a perusal.

Where else could one see a dozen lovelies dressed in nothing but tights and sleeveless shirts that reached just below their waist? Whether or not the women in the photographs were really actresses wasn't important. The thing was to get a look at their rather plump limbs and ample bosoms. Woody's cartes were tame compared to some others I'd seen during the war, when the boys hadn't been in the mood for subtlety.

Somehow I got to thinking on Arabella. I wondered why I'd been so interested in a colored woman. It could have been the fancy way she talked, or that pleasant smile of hers. I still wasn't afraid to admit she was beautiful. I didn't have to jump on a rooftop and shout it though.

It must have been nice in France, I thought.

Woody startled me out of my musing.

"Take a sheat, Mack, I'll get a hot towel for ya."

I went to the second chair and sat down. It felt like a throne. Woody tilted it back and got a good look at my face.

He broke the second commandment and said, "What the hell did you do? Shtand under a streetcar?"

I didn't have to explain. Woody was used to seeing me in various stages of disfigurement.

"A pair of knuckle dusters must've given me a love tap or something."

"You don't remember?"

"No."

"You shee who did it?"

"No. But I think I know who did it anyway."

"You're queer, Mack. Other coppers don't get roughed up like you do. You're like a moth that gets too close to the candle, huh?"

"I guess so. Makes me feel useful. Better than standing around directing traffic."

"That sounds like someone I know," said the man next to me with the towel on his face. "Woody, take this thing off."

Beneath the steaming cloth was William Heins. He came in for a shave about the same time every morning. It was here that I'd first met him and some of the other boys at the Republican Club.

"How goes it, Mack? Ah . . . a few bruises. Hope that blood ain't all your own."

"No, the lion's share was the other fella's."

"He have any left after you got through with him?"

"I didn't touch him. He looked a little drained when they pulled the cloth over his face."

"Ah. I see. It was like that. Hell of a way to break in the day, huh?"

"And how," Woody said, meaninglessly.

I stared at myself in the mirror. It wasn't a pretty sight. My blond hair was greasy and needed a wash. My mustache needed a touch of wax. Besides having dark stubble all over my mug I had some nasty cuts that were settling in for the long haul. My collar was ruined. I'd have to buy a new one. Same with my shirt cuffs. My suit jacket was dark enough that the stain wasn't showing. At least I couldn't see it.

In the corner of my eye I saw Cap watching me. Woody was puttering around with some hair oils.

I decided to tell him what happened. It was okay to talk around Woody. He was aware of what was going on, what we coppers would call fly.

"I've been working on what we talked about yesterday," I said to Heins.

The older man narrowed his eyes and nodded.

"Let's say I think he had a hand in this." I leveled a finger at my face.

"And the other fella? The killing?"

Without meeting his eyes I kept looking into the mirror.

"That's what I think."

Then I told the whole story. Heins stopped me a few times. He wanted to know why I cared about colored women disappearing from the Seventh Ward.

"It was a case no one was interested in. That very fact made me interested in it."

Not much, but it was all I could come up with at the moment. And it was pretty close to the truth.

I went on and detailed the rigmarole at the waterfront. Leaving out Arabella I told him about the trip to the morgue and the vanishing body. And who was the one who made it vanish.

"Certainly sounds like our man has a hand in the business, doesn't it?"

"I'd say he's got both hands in."

"What about last night?"

I told him about the ragpicker, and what he'd had on him.

"His story got a little confusing right before we were

attacked. But I don't think there's any question that Duffy was the one who killed Goldie.''

"Why would he do that?"

"If I knew that Duffy would be in the chokey right now."

"You say you got some evidence that this nigger woman had some jewelry on her? From the other one? The minister's daughter?"

"That's right. Here. I'll show you."

I hadn't bothered to look at the lace pin since I picked it off the floor that morning. When I opened the palm of my hand I got a shock.

It wasn't any lace pin.

I'd picked up the wrong thing. Maybe even picked up the lace pin at first and then when it pricked me I'd closed my hand around something else.

"Oh . . ." What came next was a juicy four-letter word, suitable only for a barber shop.

"What's the matter?" Heins asked.

"I picked up the wrong damn thing! The killer, I mean Duffy, must've grabbed all the stuff when he knocked me on the nob. Oh capital. Absolutely capital."

I stared at my palm again wishing the metal object would dissolve away.

From the looks of it, it was a worthless brass badge. Much tarnished, it bore a shield with the stars and stripes and an eagle. Below the shield were four letters. D.S.O.L.

"Well, whatta ya have there, Mack?"

"Looks like a worthless engine company badge. I don't know. What the hell difference does it make? I needed that lace pin. It was the only bit of evidence I had."

I felt Josephine, who'd been so close to me that morning, slip away into the murkiness of the ragpicker's shack.

Heins was leaning over by this time and scrutinizing the badge.

"Hold your horses, boy. Lemme see that gewgaw."

He snatched it out of my hand and held it toward the

window, where direct sunlight was just beginning to stream through.

"Oh yes. Well that is *mighty* interestin'."

"What?" I said, nearly getting out of my seat.

Heins said to Woody, "Woody, do us a favor, will ya? Could you go over to the hotel and tell 'em to bring some oysters and coffee over? I feel like some breakfast."

Woody accepted a greenback. He wouldn't go run errands for just anybody. But Heins was different. He had a lot of pull. Woody knew it was handy to have that pull on his side. So he said, "I'll be right back."

"Get somethin' for yourself," Heins called after him.

Then, turning to me, he said, "Listen, you know what these four letters here stand for?"

I shook my head.

"This is a membership badge for the Democratic Sons of Liberty Club."

"Don't think I heard of them."

"Their hall's in the Seventh Ward. Not too far from the hospital. On Keble Street. You know where I mean?"

"Sure. My beat used to be around there. Below Pine, between Eighth and Ninth?"

"That's it. You find that interesting?"

"Maybe. It's a white neighborhood right near the lowest colored slum."

"Right near a mighty bad neighborhood. And I don't mean bad just because there's niggers there. This one's where the bad niggers live."

"St. Mary's Street. Seventh and Lombard."

"Yeah. Just about a stone's throw."

"So what? What's the difference? There are neighborhoods like that all over the city."

"Let me tell you somethin' I know about the Democratic Sons of Liberty. First off, they hate niggers. A lot of boys in there come from the Killer and Ranger gangs. Used to pound the niggers back before the war. They caused a lot of trouble in last year's election. Remember?"

I did. It was hard to forget an election where federal troops were sent into the city to keep the peace.

"Lot of rioting that time. Mostly over the colored voters," I said.

"Precisely. They don't call themselves Republican Sons of Liberty, do they?"

"We all know what friends of the colored man we Republicans are, right?"

Heins cut the air with his hand impatiently. "Don't muddy up the issue. What I'm tryin' to tell you is that these boys on Keble Street are making trouble this time around too. Some beatings and stabbings. It's gonna be real ugly and that's the way they want it."

"I know. That's the way half the coppers want it too."

"Well, speaking of coppers, guess who's Grand Master of the Democratic Sons of Liberty?"

I nodded, casting my eyes from left to right, like I was reading those words on the wall again.

"Walter Duffy."

"Yep. Still disappointed with your find from last night?"

The tighter that invisible noose got around Duffy's neck the more I felt like a carrion eater. But I wanted the bait Heins had dangled before me. Being a detective in a year or so sounded good to me.

The only way I could get rid of the guilt or whatever was bothering me was to convince myself that Duffy was as bad as Heins said and then some. Whenever I thought of Duffy as a person I got kind of cagey. So I let the evidence pile up on him until he wasn't human anymore. He was a big, ugly shadow I could hate.

I said, "Tell me more about this D.S.O.L."

"Don't know much about it, really. They're a secret society like a hundred of the other clubs in town. But it's no secret what they do. They make trouble for the niggers. At the club they drink lager beer and play billiards. Every once in a while they have some rat pits set up. That's all I can tell you."

"Most of the fellas are plug-uglies from the old fire-house gangs?"

"Yeah. They're human bludgeons just waiting for someone to give 'em a head to beat in."

"Who pulls their strings?"

"This time I don't know."

Woody came back in with the oysters then. I tossed some in my mouth and felt my jaws bounce. Then I washed the salty mess down with steaming coffee. Meanwhile Woody was starting to shave Heins. Some other customers had wandered in and were looking through the magazines. Heins and I didn't say anything more to each other.

When Woody put the hot towel on my face I felt the steam rip through my pores and into my brain. It seemed to clean it out inside there. I floated in that state where you're about to fall asleep but not quite there yet. As if he were a mile away I could hear Woody lecturing Heins on his system for craps. Woody loved the ivories.

"Thash the only game where ya got control of yer money. Not like faro. Thash a shucker's game."

I blotted out the words and concentrated on Duffy. And the disappeared women.

It read like a story in ciphers. Except there were whole words missing. The message wasn't clear.

Woody lifted the towel off and wiped some of the blood from my face. I heard the razor scrape against the leather. Something cold and scented splashed against my cheeks and chin. Then there were two nimble fingers on my jaw. Woody applied the razor to my face in quick economical strokes.

"Shorry if thish hurtsh a little, Mack. Did I ever tell you about the time I shaw Jenny Lind back in '51? It was the last concert she gave for a long shpell. I took my wife. The dropsy hadn't affected her then and that evening we . . ."

I let Woody's story, which I'd heard at least a dozen times, fade away. With my eyes closed I focused my thoughts on what I knew about Duffy and Goldie and Josephine.

I needed to know more.

Why did Goldie have some jewelry of Josephine's? Why did Duffy kill to get that jewelry back? Why was it so important to get rid of Goldie's body?

The answer was like the wind shaking the trees. You didn't know where the wind came from. Invisible, it still left a thick pile of crimson leaves in its wake. The blood of Goldie and the ragpicker scattered like those leaves, obscuring the pattern in their descent.

But there was just enough of a trail left.

Fifteen minutes after I'd had the hot towel on my face I was getting out of the chair and paying Woody a quarter.

Then I started out on that trail of blood. There was a person I didn't want it to reach. Someone I had tried to stop thinking about. And failed.

All the events of the past day swirled through my head. One thought overrode them all. I wanted to see Arabella again.

The trail led me to the Pennsylvania Hospital.

I WALKED STRAIGHT down Ninth till I got to Pine. I made a left and walked half a square till I was standing right in front of the hospital. A bronze leaden statue of William Penn gestured with his right hand as if he were beckoning me.

The stately center building was composed of red brick and white-washed Corinthian columns, topped off by the Circular Room, the oldest medical amphitheatre in the United States. The building looked more like a Greek temple than a hospital. Now a hundred and sixteen years old, it seemed out of place in a modern city where gilded ornamentation was all the go.

Somehow I liked the fact that it made you feel out of place, like you were in the wrong time. Like the State House, it had an aura of majesty that made everything else around it look decayed.

I circled around Pine and up Eighth. There I entered through the gate and saw Captain George Taylor, the old gatekeeper. He had a pet parrot named Crockie sitting on his tiny desk. I'd never heard the bird speak in all the years I'd passed through those gates. But every time I tried getting it to talk just the same.

Taylor knew me well from all the time I'd spent as a roundsman in the Seventh Ward. When I passed by him

94

he saluted me and went on feeding Crockie some sun-flower seeds. For a moment I watched the green bird shift its plumed head, chewing its breakfast. The captain and I chatted about the weather and the poor condition of the streets. Then I headed inside.

A clerk directed me to a recently erected octagonal building next door. This was where the new Clinical Amphitheatre was, built just three years before.

When I walked in I asked an older gentleman where the amphitheatre was. He smoothed his cravat, fidgeting with the gold stick pin. Then he told me, "I'm afraid you have got your schedule confused, young man. To-day is the ladies' clinical lecture. The students from the Women's Medical College."

His lips curled up in disapprobation.

I said, "I'm no physician, sir. I'm a policeman. I want to look in on one of the students there."

"Not to make any more unpleasantness? I hope there hasn't been any more problems with the females." It sounded like what he really hoped was the exact opposite.

"What do you mean by that?"

"Well, you of course heard what happened when the male and female students attended a lecture together for the first time."

I shook my head.

"Ah, I see." He was pleased to have the opportunity to tell me all about it. Adjusting his pince-nez he said, "Well, back in November of '69 I was giving a lecture when thirty women entered the amphitheatre and took their seats among the male students. The men, I'm afraid to say, behaved somewhat indecorously."

Suddenly I remembered the fracas. The men had hissed and shouted what the papers would call prurient remarks.

"I fought having women in my clinical lectures with some of my other colleagues at the university. We issued a remonstrance against the admission of women. But the public had their way. Such is the rule of the mob. We were forced to admit women once a week. I've been waiting for trouble to show ever since. And now a policeman shows up. I always said that women had no place in the medical profession. Why, if my . . .''

I cut his harangue short.

"Listen, is there a Dr. Forbes giving a lecture in there?''

"Oh yes. Fine young fellow, Forbes. A luminary in the field of anatomy. He was Morton's brightest pupil, you know.''

That was supposed to impress me. But I had no idea who Morton was. I raised my eyebrows in mock admiration.

"You still haven't told me where the amphitheatre is.''

"Oh, how remiss of me. Right through that arched doorway there. But you'll want to wait till the lecture concludes in forty-five minutes.''

"I probably won't. Thank you, Doctor.''

I blundered through the doors and nearly walked right into a large slate with some scribbling on it. Twenty young women gave me the eye. The evil eye, that is. From their expressions I got the feeling I was disturbing a temple sacrifice.

Slipping over the oilcloth laid on the floor to catch up fluids, I climbed a set of ascending stairs and took a seat behind the back row of students.

The physician and his assistants hadn't even looked at me when I came in. The two young ladies sitting just below me turned to stare. Like matrons in a free library they narrowed their eyes and pursed their lips, daring me to break the silence. When they saw the cuts and bruises on my face, they exchanged looks of surprise and turned around abruptly.

The Clinical Amphitheatre was the most modern of facilities but like the rest of the hospital it had a venerable air to it. A skylight cast steady illumination on the operating table below. The table was wooden and covered with zinc. A gutter ran to one side. It was filling up with fluid already. The human being beneath the bloody cloth was barely visible. Above the operating table, over the door-way, was Benjamin West's painting *Christ Healing the Sick in the Temple*. I thought we needed more of His kind of healing.

Five men surrounded the patient. They were dressed like gentlemen in long, dark frock coats. Their cuffs and collars were the only bit of white showing and most of the cuffs were stained by now. From what I could see they appeared to be performing surgery on the man's stomach. One stood at the head of the table holding a cloth soaked in something stronger than the whiskey we had to dull the pain of surgery in the war.

Two other doctors were working on the abdomen. One had clamped some metal retractors to keep the incision open. Another was probing the slivered flesh with some-thing that looked like a lithographer's stylus. A young man fetched their tools from a set of boxes propped on a moveable table nearby. An older woman in a severe-looking bonnet and tasseled wrap was seated by the doc-tors' instrument boxes. She must've been a relative of the patient. At least one relative was required to attend. From the look on her face she appeared ready for medical as-sistance herself.

Dr. William Forbes stood by these men, lecturing to the class. He was attired in a black Prince Albert suit, with no color on his person except a diamond stick pin in his necktie and a coating of very red blood on his right hand. He held a knife with which he'd probably just made the first cut.

Around the doctor, in the dark-finished wooden benches, were the female students. They were rapt with attention. Not one chin was propped up by a hand.

Dr. Forbes was a strapping fellow. His hair was long and mostly brown, with a few streaks of gray. He had a beard which he trimmed close and his mustache was nice and oiled. I could see why the ladies were so attentive.

"This great cavity occupies more than half of the space enclosed by the ribs, and all the interior of the trunk of the body below the thorax. It is formed by the diaphragm, supported by the lower ribs; by a portion of the spine by the various muscles which occur between the lower margin of the thorax and the upper margin of the ossa innominata; and the ossa innominata, which contribute, for the purpose, the costae of the ossa ilia, as well as the pelvis.

"Now this largest viscus of the abdomen, when in a healthy condition is of a reddish-brown color. But as you can see . . ."

The girls stared in rapt silence. My head started to ache from where I got knocked.

Dr. Forbes took his bloody knife and stropped it on his shoe. Then he made another incision with the cleaned blade. The gesture reminded me of a surgeon I'd seen during the war. He had huge white whiskers. When he operated he held the instruments in his mouth, the blade of a knife sticking in one whisker and the handle in another.

The physicians seemed to be doing their best to keep their hands clean. The bowls as well as the wooden sink were filled with bloody water.

The smells of the anesthetic chemicals and the blood were a little overpowering but I was used to them. If the morgue didn't cut me up this sure wouldn't. But I noticed a few of the ladies trying hard not to turn away from the gory enterprise.

It didn't take me long to notice one particular lady. Hers was the only dark face in the gang. She'd seen me walk in of course, and was staring at me. Her expression could have meant a dozen things. I wasn't sure that she was happy to see me. I gestured that I wanted to talk to her. She gestured that I would have to wait.

So I settled back in my uncomfortable bench and watched the operation. And Arabella.

Her bonnet was off now and I noticed her fine dark hair, done up in curls with long tresses flowing down both sides of her neck. She was still dressed in mourning. I realized that I'd never asked her why. It was hardly a proper topic for a first meeting anyway.

I watched her as she followed Dr. Forbes's every move. She had a front row seat. Her hands were folded as if in prayer with her index fingers touching her lips. I wondered what I could do to command that kind of interest from her.

Briefly my eyes scanned the other females of my own color. Somehow I kept going back to Arabella. There was something about her that made me want to pay attention.

I closed my eyes and tried to picture her at the ice cream saloon. Vaguely I remembered our knees touching in the hack.

The whispering of the two young ladies in front of me startled me out of my daydreaming.

"Jenny?"

"What?"

"Do you have anatomy this afternoon?"

"Yes."

"Oh good! We are classmates again! Are you excited?"

"About what?"

"You know . . . This afternoon. Our first chance to get our hands dirty."

"Yes! I hear we're starting out right away in the dissecting room."

"Really? From whom did you hear this?"

"Dr. Forbes himself. I caught him on his way here. He was eating a peach in Washington Square."

"Oh! You talked to him! Well. You shall have to tell me all about that . . ."

"Later. Anyway there's not much to tell. The colored girl was with him."

"Oh. The Cole girl. I wonder why the doctor lets her hang on him so."

"Probably feels sorry for her. I hear she's an orphan."

Now I understood why she wore the mourning dress.

"Do you know how she ever got into the college?"

"She has a bit of money. Don't ask me how that's possible. I didn't hear this from her of course."

"You've never talked to her?"

"No. Most of the other girls don't either. She seems a pleasant enough creature. But you know . . ."

I knew. Whether their conversation was making me angry or depressed I couldn't tell. Probably both.

"Of course. Well, what about the anatomy class?"

"The doctor told me we'll have a subject we can start working on to-day! Can you believe that?"

"That's capital! I wonder what . . ."

"What kind of person? I did too. I asked the doctor about it, just to hear him talk. He told me it wasn't proper to ask about such things. But later the Cole girl told me it was the body of a colored woman."

"I was hoping somehow it would be a man."

"Well, she said this was a rare opportunity for us. I hate it when she lords it over us. Just because she's a second year student doesn't give her the right to put on airs. At any rate they'd just received the subject. Quite fresh from what I gather."

Suddenly I felt my teeth bite into my lip.

A fresh cadaver of a colored woman.

That would be a class I'd like to attend.

The surgery didn't look anywhere near completed. I decided it was a good time to take a nap.

I was wrong.

When I woke up an hour and a half later the amphitheatre was empty. Even the oilcloth was rolled up. Cursing, I clambered down the stairs.

I tried to recall when the anatomy class was to be held. I seemed to remember the girl saying it was in the afternoon.

That left me with a few hours. I would put them to good use.

Exiting the hospital I made my way toward the Magdalen Society, wondering why Arabella hadn't woken me up.

THE MAGDALEN SOCIETY was near Logan Square, at Twenty-first and Race. I took a seven-square walk to Dock Street, navigating my way through teeming crowds of late morning shoppers. I caught the Race and Vine Street car and rode it all the way to Twenty-first and Vine. A few squares and I was there.

The society itself was a drab, anonymous building next door to the Blind Asylum. High brick walls surrounded it. Otherwise the curious public would've been surrounding it themselves to get a look at the "unfortunates." Thankfully the place didn't admit tourists like the penitentiary, morgue, and insane asylums did.

A plaque near the door stated the society's purpose was "to rescue from vice and degradation that class of women who have forfeited their claims to the respect of the virtuous." From my experience I knew they didn't always forfeit those claims willingly.

I rapped on the door and was admitted by a severe-looking woman in a tassel and ribbon-free hoop skirt that was just a bit out of fashion. Her hair was parted in the center and clung smoothly to the sides of her head in the old style. The gas-light that dimly lit the interior cast a wan glow on her harried features. I twigged she was an old inmate who'd never left, preferring to stay behind the protective brick walls.

She was polite enough.

"May I help you, sir?"

I showed her my star and told her my name and title. For an instant her ancient revulsion for coppers showed plain.

I said, "Don't worry. I'm not here to make a collar. I've got a murdered woman on my blotter. She used to live here."

"I don't see how we can help you in any way."

"You probably can't. But her girlfriends might."

She said nothing. But I felt her wanting to ask me the old question: Why do you care?

I didn't bother answering. I wasn't sure what I'd come up with this time. Instead I asked, "Can you show me to the colored section?"

The matron walked ahead of me and said, "All the girls are in chapel now. I can bring you to the room but you'll have to wait until the service is over."

"How long will that be?"

"The reverend should be finishing his exhortations about now."

We headed through a long hallway and into a large open space where chairs were set up. A few dozen women were sitting in them listening to a man recite the story of the woman caught in adultery from the Gospel of John. They probably heard it every day. As far as I knew from my reading, the woman was never identified as Mary Magdalen. Nor as a prostitute. But that didn't matter. There was something to be said for tradition.

Most of the colored girls were seated toward the back. They were a mixed lot. A few miserable-looking ones had probably just checked in for the victuals. Others were nursing bruises. They'd be back to their bullies in a week. Then there were a few who seemed actually sincere and punctuated the reverend's sentences with amens.

Some of the faces in each category were familiar to me.

One of the hungry ones looked like an old acquaintance of mine, Rose Laws. She was a bludget like Goldie. They frequented the same dark alleys and courts.

When the service broke up I took Rosie aside from the crowd heading toward their breakfast.

"Hi, Rosie. Remember me?"

"You was the pig near my crib a few years back."

"You always had a way with words, Rosie. I was also the pig who collared you for streetwalking. Those were the good old days, huh? When you didn't have to hide in the shadows to rope a sucker."

"Do I have to stand here all day listenin' to yo' trash?"

"No. You can tell me about Goldie Collins and I'll disappear."

"Don't know no Goldie. So long, copper."

I put a hand around her arm as she stepped away. There was muscle there, lean and hard. The kind of arm that could make it hurt. Especially with a brick or cobble, her weapon of choice.

"Not so fast, Rose. You can do better than that."

"Take your fucking hands off me now, you piece of white trash."

My hand tightened out of involuntary anger.

"Sit your fat ass down and listen to me."

I pulled up a chair and shoved her into it.

As she sat down she managed to get a big gob of spit on my necktie.

She said, "You white bastard. You the one pinched my man and sent him inside. Where he got himself dead. And left me with nothin'. You think I be *wantin'* to work with the likes of Goldie? *Wantin'* to live in a shit-hole like this? Shit. I used to turn heads."

Her lips crunched together in self-pity and grief. She was about to spew another insult at me. I cut it off by saying, "You can curse me all you want, Rose. Your bully nearly beat you to death. That's why I pinched him. I'm glad they did the bastard up at Cherry Hill. But I'm not here to talk history. I want to know who killed Goldie Collins."

The old bludget blinked a few times. Her lips went slack.

"You say, killed?"

"Mmm hmm. She took a swim. After getting strangled. We fished her out yesterday afternoon."

This one was too far gone for tears. She just shook her head and mumbled something that sounded like, "Poor Goldie. I tole her he warn't no good."

"Who? Who wasn't any good?"

Suddenly the bludget went through a transformation, erasing any residue of grief or anger. Now something else was there instead. From her narrowed eyes and the way she snickered I figured it was greed.

Rose sighed and crossed her hands over an expansive bosom. She said, "We gots to arrive at an understandin', copper. I mean, you expectin' somethin' fo' nothin'. And I never give somethin' fo' nothin'. You know?"

"Yeah. I sure do. How's about a buzzard dollar?"

"What you take me fo'? Some penny ante draggle-tail?"

I said, "You know what I take you for."

I gave her the dollar coin.

She hiked up her skirt to her knees and shoved the coin down a torn, striped stocking. Rose was used to being indecent.

She began her story like she'd been waiting eagerly to tell it.

"I tole her he was a no good nigguh. But she don' lissen ta me. We was livin' here for a few weeks when he first came in. Goldie'd had some kinda disease and this nigguh gal was treatin' her. I thought, this gal fo' real? A nigguh doctor? And a gal, at that? But she talked so white and dressed so fancy I just shut my mouth. Anyway she was nice to me and Goldie. Brought us a whole bag of honey-roasted peanuts one day."

I thought on my talk with Arabella the previous night.

My admiration for her increased. Anyone who volun-
teered to care for creatures like Goldie and Rose would
have to have a lot of courage. And compassion. The more
I thought on her the more I wanted to see her again. Just
to see what would happen. I already knew what I *wanted*
to happen.

"So this nigguh gal fixed Goldie up mighty fine. She
don't complain no mo' 'bout nothin'. Fact, she gettin'
randy, you know? And along comes this boy one day
when she come home from work . . ."

"What do you mean, from work? Was she gone from
here by then?"

"No. See, they let us go out fo' work in the mills and
such. So's we can pay fo' our board soon as we's able.
Goldie got to be a janitress at the hospital up the road."

"Which one?"

"How'm I s'posed to know that? One where the doctor
gal's from."

She must mean the Women's Hospital, I decided. The
one they ran the Women's Medical College out of. It was
right up Twenty-first Street.

"Then one day when she's comin' back for suppah,
she meets this boy who starts sweet talkin' her and such.
She tell me all about what he say."

"Like what?"

"Like he want a piece of a gal fine as she is. You
know."

"Who was he?"

"She tell me his name. It was somethin' funny. I
laughed and the ol' gal nearly smacked me. Lemme think
on it now."

Rose paused for a moment, pouting in concentration.
Then she said, "Thassright. She say he call himself
Levi."

"That's it?"

"No. He got a last name too. I 'member cause we
laughed about that one. His last name be Chew. Goldie
say he could chew her anytime."

I smiled halfheartedly at the obscene joke.

Behind the smile I was repeating the name over and over.

I said, "Did you ever see him?"

"Sho' I did. One day when Goldie and I both went to work I seen him talkin' with her."

Again, I said the name to myself.

Levi Chew.

It meant nothing to me.

Not until I asked her, "What did he look like?"

She said, "He had these long fingers . . ."

"No. How dark was he? Facial hair? Height? Weight?"

"Awright! Shit. Not so dark like Goldie. His hair was on the long side. And he was lookin' like this . . ."

She described at least half the Negro population in Philadelphia. Medium height. Clean-shaven. Brown eyes. Weight somewhere between one hundred seventy-five and two hundred pounds.

But there was one thing worth mentioning. Rose said his face was pitted with scars. Probably smallpox.

That triggered something.

A memory of a face. I closed my eyes and took aim in the darkness.

"Did you notice something else about him? His hands?"

"Thas what I was tryin' to say if you'da let me finish! Shit. He had these long fingers and they woulda been pretty 'cept he had some kinda rash on them. Patches where there warn't no color. Like his hands be half-white and half-colored. You know?"

I knew exactly.

She'd just described, I was sure, the colored man I saw at the morgue the night before. The one who'd taken Goldie's body.

I felt tension shoot through every vein, every sinew, every muscle.

"How long did his mash go on?" I asked her.

" 'Bout a week. Then she say she's leavin'. Goin' ta move in with him."

"She say what he did for a living?"

"She didn't have to. I already knew."

I had the feeling I was about to get my dollar's worth.

"I know this boy from the Seventh Ward. That is, I heard o' him. He the Boss's man."

"What boss?"

"*The* Boss. The one what runs the whole damn ward."

"The name, Rose."

"You a copper and you tellin' me you don't know who run that ward? Shit."

Suddenly I felt a little short of breath. The vein in my neck was pounding. I rammed my hands into my coat pockets so the shaking wouldn't show.

"You mean Walter Duffy."

"See? You ain't as stupid as you look. Now she tell me this Levi's gonna take care o' her."

"You mean be her new bruiser?"

"No. I mean he work and give her the money. That sounds good to her."

"I'll bet. Then what?"

"Then nothin'. She up and leave. That was a month ago."

"And you didn't see her again?"

"Now, I didn't say that, did I? Goldie come back . . ."

I cut her off and said, sharply, "When?"

"Just two days ago. When was that?"

"Thursday morning," I answered.

The day Goldie had been killed.

"She caught me on my way to work. I'd been doin' some stitchin' at a mill. I can do some skilled labor when I has to. Which is more than I can say for the other sorry bitches around here."

I interrupted her again, raising my voice. "What did she say to you, Rose?"

"She just popped out of nowhere and dragged me into

an alleyway. I said, 'Take your hands off me, bitch, I gots to get to work.' But she said, 'You gotta help me.' I axed her, 'What'm I s'posed to do when I's livin' at the society?' So she say, 'Well, do you got some change for ol' Goldie?' And I gave what I had to her 'cause she looked gone. Shit. I mean she had cuts on her wrists like she tried to kill herself or somethin'. There was these dark circles 'round her eyes like she dint get no sleep for a week. And she warn't so big no more. Look like she'd been starvin' herself.''

Rose stopped for a moment. She looked like she was making a decision within herself.

''Then she said somethin'. I don't know what the bitch be talkin' 'bout. Somethin' like they was tryin' to kill her. But she got away from them when they warn't watchin' her. And she went and hid herself fo' a day till she got her head together.''

''Who's they?''

I waited for Rose to tell me the name on my mind.

But she disappointed me.

''Goldie dint tell me who 'they' was. Just that they was tryin' to kill her. Like the others.''

''What!'' I was out of my seat now. Almost frantic, I paced around Rose's chair. For the first time the bludget lost her cool pose and looked worried.

''Say that again!'' I said.

The bludget whispered, ''She say, They was tryin' to kill her. Like the others.''

The fog was lifting, little by little.

It was about to clear some more.

''Then she, she tell me to hold on to somethin' fo' her.''

The woman reached behind her dress to the pocket there. Her dark hand extended toward me and opened. There was something made of gold in it.

Something familiar.

An earring in the shape of a star with Brazilian pebbles in it.

The missing one in the pair.

Josephine's pair.

Barely able to contain my excitement I asked her, "Why do you still have it?"

"Don't think I dint try to sell it! Look like gold to me. I ain't stupid. Shit. But the sheeny pawnbroker tell me he can't be sellin' it without th'other one. So I just held on to it. Just in case Goldie need it agin."

I took the earring from her thick hand and deposited it in my coat pocket.

"She won't be needing anything anymore. Did she tell you where she got it, Rose?"

"All she say was she found it. It was goin' to help her. She say she had him by the cods now. And she was goin' ta *squeeze*."

"Whoever it was squeezed back. On her neck."

"It was that nigguh Chew, fo' sure! I warned Goldie 'bout him! Tole her he was in the toils. You can't trust no bastard what peaches. Shit."

Rose's story was over. She slumped back in her chair as the other girls came back for midday chapel service. When I left her she was grumbling about sitting through a sermon and getting no breakfast out of it.

I HAD TO wander through the Women's Hospital a little while before I found the area alloted to the Medical College. A few very serious-looking young girls were swishing their crinoline through the halls, clasping satchels filled with books. They were darting in and out of various rooms. Classes must've been commencing after the luncheon hour.

My nose followed a peculiar medicinal smell that reminded me of rotten pickle juice. It led me to the dissecting room. Before I stepped in I heard some nervous giggling.

Right beside the entrance was a rack for the ladies to hang up their wraps and bonnets. Next to the gay-looking clothes were some well-soiled oilcloth aprons.

I declined to put my own hat on the rack. I looked more businesslike with it on.

The dissecting room was long and narrow, with a tall ceiling and white-washed floor. The walls were a similar color and brightly reflected the sunlight pouring through two sets of very large windows.

The room had all the personality of a station-house basement. The regular occupants didn't seem to mind, I guess.

Ten oblong tables stood between the windows on either

side. What lay on them was positioned right where the sun was brightest.

Around each table the girls stood with their lace and ribbons covered by the blood-absorbing aprons. They also wore false sleeves made of coarse muslin. It was a good thing they were wearing some protection. They were making a mess.

Their faces were a sight. The live ones, I mean. All the girls had their nostrils flared and lips tightly clamped together. There was so much tension I had a notion to holler out "Boo!" and see how many would faint on the spot.

A few were getting into the spirit of things. Two girls were gripping the hand of a severed forearm, exclaiming, "He must've had quite a handshake!"

Some others, with their backs to me, had a corpse propped up in a chair. They yelled at their classmates across the room.

"Yoo hoo! Hannah! Rebecca!"

When those girls turned from their work their classmates, crouched behind the chair, raised the corpse's arm up and down in a mock wave. The entire assembly burst into frantic, nervous giggling.

"Enough!"

It was a holler to shatter windows. Like Moses coming off Mount Sinai and shouting at the wayward Hebrews.

Dr. William Forbes stood at the entrance to an office directly opposite the door I entered. His black frock coat, vest, and pantaloons stood out like an exclamation point against the white-washed walls and floor.

"These are not playthings, young ladies. These are your teachers. And your tools. Moreover they are human remains that deserve your respect."

The girls were almost sobbing with remorse. The doctor glared at each one of them during their awestruck silence. Then he said, "I demand a professional demeanor from each and every one of you. If you wish to be taken seriously by the medical profession, by the *men* of the medical profession, then you had best start acting seriously. Now carry on.''

Behind the doctor, seated by his desk, I saw the edge of a crepe-lined gown. It did not stir while the doctor delivered his tirade. Only a few moments later when the doctor asked me, ''May I help you, sir?'' did I see Arabella rise from her seat. She stood in the doorway, partially blocked by Forbes.

I walked across the hall while many of the girls glared at me askance. I ignored the cadavers on the tables, keeping my eyes straight ahead.

When I reached him I touched the brim of my hat in salutation. Then I said, ''You're Dr. William Forbes?''

The slightly bored, official-sounding tone I used got his attention.

''Yes. What can I do for you?''

''He's a policeman, William.''

It was nice to hear that voice again.

''He's the one I told you about. The one who helped me.''

''Ah! The gallant knight who rescued Miss Cole! Splendid! Pleased to make your acquaintance, sir!''

His hand gripped mine in a firm clasp. There was no extra pressure in it to test me or assert his manliness.

''Why don't you come in the office, Mr. . . . ?''

''McCleary. Thanks. Don't mind if I do.''

The office itself was as bland as the rest of the dissecting room. Some books were piled at the corners, their spines looking threadbare. A human skull stood before the blotter. It kept smiling at me during the whole interview.

Arabella was the first to speak.

''I am so sorry about this morning, Wilton.''

I was watching the doctor's eyes at that moment. They shifted to Arabella and back to me again, quite quickly, when she said my Christian name.

I shrugged my shoulders. ''My fault for falling asleep on the job.''

''You looked in need of a rest, quite frankly. And Dr.

Forbes and I needed to come here right away to prepare everything for the girls."

"It's okay. Like you say, I needed the rest. Last night wasn't so restful for me."

Misunderstanding me, Arabella said, "I'm sorry we parted so abruptly."

"Me too. Well, here we are again." I looked behind me and said, "Quite a way to pass an afternoon."

The doctor asked me impatiently, "You have not yet told us why you are here, Officer McCleary."

"Sorry about that. I wanted to check up on Miss Cole. We had quite a time last night."

I guess the words could have meant many things. One such thing came to my mind. I tried to fight what happened next but it did no good. My cheeks were blushing.

Arabella laughed, though she pretended to cough.

Nearly stuttering I said, "I mean, at the morgue and all."

The doctor's smirk didn't do much for my self-confidence.

I did what a lot of people do when they say things that make them look stupid. I changed the subject.

"But I didn't hike over here just to check up on Miss Cole."

"Oh?" the doctor said, getting a little bored.

"Actually I'm interested in what you'd call a subject, Dr. Forbes. One that you received yesterday night or today."

"Well, I'm sorry you wasted your time, sir. We received no new subjects within the past twenty-four hours."

Forbes was leaning back in his chair. He didn't seem to be too interested in me. His attention was focused on a box of pen nibs.

Arabella took in a breath, about to speak. I cut her off.

"That's funny, Doctor. Because I was sitting behind two girls this morning at the hospital who said they heard otherwise."

Suddenly the pen nibs weren't so fascinating. Arabella moved closer to the doctor's desk, almost defensively.

"Are you calling Dr. Forbes a liar?" she asked me. The hostility in her voice was new to me.

She seemed very protective of her preceptor.

"What do you mean?" the doctor said to me.

"I heard two girls mention seeing you and Miss Cole in Washington Square this morning. You told them a new subject had been brought in."

I looked straight at Arabella and said, "A colored woman. Found drowned."

The last part I threw in for the hell of it. The girls hadn't mentioned anything about cause of death.

"You're mistaken, Wilton. I'm the one who told them about the subject, who was certainly not drowned."

"*You* told them?" I said. "I don't understand."

But my memory was clearing up. All I remembered the girls saying about the doctor was that he reprimanded their curiosity.

Dr. Forbes knotted his handsome brow in concentration. Then he whipped a pair of spectacles out of his vest pocket and said, "Arabella, get me the record of subjects received."

The girl walked over to a bookshelf by the desk and withdrew a shabbily bound ledger. Its warped covers were tied together by a piece of faded ribbon.

Taking it from the girl, Dr. Forbes leafed through the pages. They were full of names and dates and payments.

"Eh? What's this?"

I stepped closer to look myself.

The last line stated: "Colored female age approx. 35 yrs. Recvd. 6 Oct. Payment $8."

"Arabella! This looks like your writing!"

The girl was worrying one of her dark tresses with her delicate hand. The doctor's scolding tone made her flinch.

"Why didn't you say something to me, Arabella?" I said, feeling hurt and somehow suspicious.

"I'm sorry, Dr. Forbes. You too, Wilton. I never mentioned it to you because I entered this yesterday before I took the streetcar home. They brought it from the alms-house.''

The doctor's features relaxed a little.

''After I left for my clinical lecture?''

The girl nodded.

Forbes turned to me and said, ''I'm sorry for the confusion, Mr. McCleary. Miss Cole assists me in receiving the subjects.''

That was quite a way of saying she helped him haul in dead bodies.

''But never in paying for them. However there's been a dearth of good subjects lately. You were quite right in not waiting to consult me this one time, Arabella.''

The girl's face lit up with the praise. She said to me, ''I'm sorry for the obfuscation, Wilton. But I'm quite sure it wasn't Goldie Collins. I received the body early yesterday morning, before I even met you. And paid the eight dollars we pay for cadavers from the almshouse.''

''They're usually in the best shape,'' the doctor explained.

I suddenly remembered that the two girls hadn't said exactly when the body was received.

It was I who assumed it had been last night. Because that was how I wanted it to be.

Even though I knew I'd made a mistake, I wasn't quite satisfied. Arabella looked nervous. Which, to be fair, is how most people get when policemen ask them a lot of questions. I didn't want to upset her any more. Or to make her dislike me. But I had to say, ''I don't suppose I could look at this cadaver?''

I was a little surprised, and relieved when the doctor said, ''Of course. Follow me.''

The three of us went back into the dissecting room. I tried not to look Arabella in the eye, already upset with myself for calling her honesty into question.

This time around I noticed what the girls were working on. By no means did they have a body per table. Instead

I saw a trunk here, an arm there. One girl was working very intently on a leg, which made me shudder. I was remembering the sight of pile upon pile of sawed-off limbs by the surgeon's tent during the war.

The only intact corpse had been taken out of the chair and put on the table. I saw now it was the corpse of a woman. My eyes flashed to the pathetic white globes beneath a neck bearing a fresh incision. The blue taint of decay coated the body like a fine patina. I quickly turned away. Dead men I was used to. But seeing women that way still gave me the shakes.

Toward the back of the room I noticed part of a body on a table. The shade of the skin was dark brown and looked free of corruption.

"This one, Arabella?" Forbes asked.

The girls working on it halted their probing. I saw the head, propped up by a wooden support.

It wasn't Goldie. Just another poor soul as tormented in death as she was in life.

I cleared my throat and turned toward the office.

Forbes said, "Is that the woman you were inquiring about?"

I shook my head.

"Well, I'm sorry. From what Arabella told me of your investigation, I gather you have very few . . . what do you call them?"

"Pointers. Clues. Yes. Very few."

I turned to Arabella, who'd been steadily regarding the white-washed floor for the past minute.

"My apologies, Miss Cole. I didn't mean to imply that you were being dishonest. But, you see, I have to ask questions. It's my job."

"It's all right, Mr. McCleary. I understand."

I winced at her use of my surname.

Why should it have mattered? I asked myself. I would probably never see this woman again. Even if I did, what would possibly happen?

Perhaps I was interested in her because she was so dif-

ferent from any girl I'd known before. We were both out-
siders, in a way.

And I could feel an invisible hand hovering around us.
Sometimes it pushed us together. At other times it pulled
us apart. I wished it would make up its mind one way or
the other.

Dr. Forbes eased the tension a bit by saying, "Arabella,
I need some plaster casts from the museum for my lecture
this afternoon. Would you go and arrange it with them?"

With a glance at me that revealed nothing, the girl said,
"Certainly, William."

The familiarity between them amazed me. I had never
seen a colored girl so sure of herself before.

"If it's corpses you're interested in, sir, I think I can
render you more assistance."

"Why not?" I said.

Forbes put a hand behind my shoulders and ushered me
back to his office.

The skull was still perched on the desk, laughing at me.

13

"MEMENTO MORI," FORBES said.

I stopped staring at the empty sockets of his macabre paperweight and grunted, "Huh?"

"Remember that thou must die," the doctor said, caressing the yellowed cranium. "Latin." For a moment he looked at me, unsure of what to say next.

"The language of the Romans, you know."

"Yes. I know. Veni, vidi, vici."

"Ah! I see. You're very erudite for a policeman."

"It's not the first time somebody's assumed I was ignorant just because I had a star on my lapel."

"I beg your pardon, sir. I had no wish to offend you. It's just that your colleagues are not known for their . . . cerebral faculties, shall we say?"

"How many of them have you met, Doctor?"

"Oh, none. Not personally of course. I've seen a few wielding their clubs."

"I use one too. But only when I have to. Believe it or not, when I'm not kicking streetwalkers around I have been known to read a book. In fact, I even made it into the high school."

Suddenly we were butting antlers like two young bucks, something we'd avoided while Arabella was around. It was foolish and I quickly put an end to it.

118

"Sorry, Doctor. Don't mind me. I've had a long day and it's not even time for my luncheon yet."

The doctor relaxed into his chair and smiled.

"My apologies as well. I had no right to make assumptions about you. Please sit down, Mr. McCleary."

I did, watching the skull again.

Forbes noticed my interest and said, "Fascinating, isn't it? To think that that shell once housed a living, thinking, dreaming brain. An individual who loved, hated, hungered just as we."

"I was just thinking it made a clumsy paperweight."

The doctor chuckled.

"I keep it for sentimental reasons. It was a gift from my mentor, Samuel George Morton. Perhaps you've heard of him?"

It was the second time somebody had asked me that this morning. This time I could answer yes.

Forbes inhaled deeply, like he was gathering in the dust of memories.

"There was a great man, sir. A brilliant man. He wrote *Crania Americana* and *Crania Aegyptiaca*. Classics in their field."

"Wait a minute," I said, remembering something I'd read in the paper a number of years ago. "Is this the fella who had the 'American Golgotha'?"

"The very one," Forbes said, smiling. "The greatest collection of skulls and crania in the New World. Perhaps the entire world. I'm proud to say this very skull is from an Egyptian catacomb from the time of the pharaohs. It was used by Dr. Morton himself in his research. I've been adding to that research myself though my experiments will take years and years to conduct. And the results may never see publication."

Our conversation was entertaining. I didn't usually go for lectures but this was like having one all to myself. I decided I had a few moments to spend listening to Forbes. I needed some mental relaxation. Maybe I would even learn something to impress my friends at the lodge. It took my mind off Goldie Collins and Josephine Martin. And Arabella Cole, for a while.

Like a captivated pupil, I asked, "What exactly was Morton's research about? Why collect all these skulls?"

"Ah!" Forbes said, as if addressing a student who'd spoken a question that would lead him perfectly into the next topic on his lecture notes. "Morton was interested in the theory of polygeny. That is, the theory that the various 'races' of humanity are in fact separate species. Do you follow me?"

"Yes. You and I are one species. And colored people another. And red indians another."

"Precisely! Furthermore, Morton hypothesized that physical characteristics of the brain, particularly cranial capacity, determined intelligence and that these same characteristics were determined by race. Morton had a curious way of measuring skulls."

The handsome doctor flushed with excitement. His eyes no longer focused on me or the room but something beyond.

"We filled the cranial cavities with one-eighth-inch-diameter lead shot. The size they call BB. Then we read the skull's volume in cubic inches."

"Ingenious."

"Quite. Well, the results showed that the Anglo-Saxon race in particular and whites in general had a higher cranial capacity than all other races. The indians were next."

"And the negroes at the bottom?"

"Precisely."

"Well, that comes as quite a surprise," I said, sardonically.

Forbes laughed and said, "Yes! Well, nevertheless it was an objective, scientific study. His data are still used to-day."

I couldn't resist saying, "I wonder how Miss Cole feels about Morton's data?"

"There's no question, from a scientific viewpoint, that negroes have an inferior mental capacity compared to whites. By nature they are joyous, flexible, and indolent. Much too undisciplined for any rigorous mental activity. Any phrenological measurement of negroes plainly shows their prognathous nature. Which we all know is associated with low intelligence.''

"But Arabella's not quite the same as most negroes.''

"You're quite right. Her intelligence is so pronounced it seems to contradict most of Morton's conclusions. I've theorized she has some white blood in her. That could explain it.''

Dissatisfied with that, Forbes shook his head. "But she's no quadroon. Her case has fascinated me, quite frankly.''

Then the doctor shook his head again and said, as if in confidence, "You know, sometimes I don't even think of her as a negress. I reach past her physical deficiencies and see her as an intellect, on a level with my own. It's rather . . . refreshing.''

A strange feeling rose up in me like bile. I swallowed it back down. The taste was unpleasant.

I didn't like to think of Arabella as deficient in any way. Yet she was a negress. Even the scientists said they were deficient. Why argue with them? They knew what they were talking about. They had cold statistics on their side.

"You certainly trust her,'' I said.

"Oh, yes. I trust her implicitly.'' Then, as if noticing me sitting there for the first time since we'd come in, he said, "I'm sorry there was any confusion concerning the cadaver she received yesterday morning. Naturally I'm the one who usually deals with such affairs.''

I pulled my pocket watch out and flipped the lid open. It was thirty-four minutes past noon. I snapped the lid shut and wound it a few times. Our conversation had changed direction. It was one I wanted to pursue. I had to get back to work.

So I said, "And you pay the ones who deliver the bodies to the college?''

"Yes. That's right."

"Well maybe you could help me then. I don't know how much Arabella told you about last night at the morgue."

"She gave me a fairly detailed account of your adventures."

"Did she mention the colored man who carted off Gold—I mean, the drowned woman's body?"

"She said someone took the body away. And that she couldn't see him too well."

"I did. An average-size negro male with longish hair, smallpox scars, and hands that had patches of white on them."

"Are you referring to an abnormal skin coloration? Vitiligo?"

"You'd know better than me, Doctor. His hands were half-black, half-white."

"Yes, yes. That's it. Pray continue."

"He's got a name, which I found out this morning."

I paused to see what effect the name would have on him.

"Levi Chew?"

Nothing. Not a flicker or blink or twitch or clearing of the throat.

"Does that sound like anyone who's ever delivered cadavers to the college?"

Carefully, Forbes shook his head.

"We've accepted cadavers from . . . a variety of sources but this fellow doesn't sound familiar. I'd have remembered someone with such peculiar characteristics."

"Well, perhaps some of your colleagues might remember."

Forbes smiled almost paternally and said, "Mr. McCleary, there's something you should know about medical men, particulary anatomists. They aren't too discriminating about where they get their subjects. And they prefer their sources to remain confidential as often as possible."

"What's the need for secrecy? Everybody knows where

the bodies come from. The morgue, the penitentiaries, and the almshouses.''

''Ah, yes. Most of the time. But when there is a great influx of students who require more cadavers than are available the professor might pursue other less . . . savory means.''

''You mean grave robbing?'' I said, repulsed.

''I prefer to call it resurrectionist work. A term that's gone out of fashion along with the practice itself.''

I'd suspected this went on. But I was stunned to hear an eminent physician admit it so blatantly.

''Mr. McCleary, you must understand that the science of medicine is like a machine. Just as steam or oil is required to move a machine's monstrous gears and levers, so too does medicine require a constant supply of fuel to propel it forward. This fuel is knowledge. When a student dissects a cadaver he or she is gaining knowledge of vital importance to the progress of medicine. And when medicine progresses the human race goes with it.''

''That's a pretty speech, Doctor. I'll bet the youngsters eat it up in the lecture hall. But try it on the family of someone you ripped out of a grave to pick apart in the laboratory.''

''Please don't misunderstand me. I'm not implying that this practice is conducted habitually. It certainly was in the past but in the modern age there is too much disapprobation. Anatomists do what they must. I myself have willed my body to science. I am honored to do so. I see no desecration in the pursuit of knowledge that may one day cure diseases like smallpox, and consumption, and cholera. And even cancer.''

''I'm old-fashioned. I like to think my body'll be all in one place for the *real* resurrection.''

''I respect your religious convictions, sir. But didn't the Lord say to leave the dead to bury the dead? I seem to remember Him also saying that God was the God of the living, not the dead.''

"Your knowledge of Scripture is impressive, Doctor. But I'm still not satisfied."

"I applaud your convictions. Please don't think I'm working with any resurrectionist gang. We have too few students to need their services."

"But such gangs exist?"

"Perhaps. They used to, years ago."

"Do you think this man Chew could be a . . . what did you call it . . . a resurrectionist?"

"If he was carting bodies from the morgue he might ply his trade elsewhere. Who knows? Most people aren't worried with the disposition of criminal corpses. Especially those of negroes."

That was the straight goods. Neither Mulholland nor anyone else at the Central Office seemed to care about my nine.

"Chew might be doing more than carting off bodies. He might be helping someone kill them."

A smile creased the doctor's handsome face. I squinted at him, wondering what was so funny.

Forbes recited a poem in answer.

"Burke's the butcher, Hare's the thief, Knox the boy that buys the beef."

Then he laughed.

Dumbfounded, I said, "What's that supposed to mean?"

Forbes picked up his Egyptian skull and turned it to him, like the two were having their own private conversation.

"About fifty years ago in Edinburgh, Scotland there were two rascals named Burke and Hare. The lowest kind of shanty Irish. They lived in the poorest slums of the city. One day a boarder in the building where they lived died suddenly and they hit on the bright idea of selling his body to a medical university. They made a good deal of money doing this but people didn't seem to die quick enough. So they decided to hasten the process. Usually their victims were the poorest and the weakest of their downtrodden class. Burke found the best way of killing was suffocation with a pillow. That way there were no signs of violent death. A word was coined during his trial to describe this form of manslaughter. They called it 'burking'. Rather droll, eh?''

I nodded and said, "What about this Knox fellow?''

The doctor faced me again, putting down the skull. It kept up with the smiling. I noticed the old Aegyptian's teeth were crooked.

"Knox was an eminent though rather unscrupulous anatomist. He was their client and just respectable enough to avoid being hanged himself. Of course his reputation suffered. I think he ended his life writing textbooks.''

Behind us I heard the girls begin to clean up. The class was drawing to a close.

"It's funny,'' Forbes said. "Whenever people think of something as outré as resurrectionist work they always think of Burke and Hare. Yet they weren't resurrectionists in the strict sense of the word. They never actually robbed graves.''

"It's the strangest way to make a profit from a killing I've ever heard of. Do you think, Doctor, that such an operation could exist in our city?''

"Body snatching? Frankly I doubt it. The laws are much stricter about it these days, you know.''

"But it could . . .''

"Perhaps. But you'd have your work cut out for you, my dear fellow. There are a host of physicians in this city who habitually use cadavers in their instruction. And enough cemeteries to fill a city directory.''

He didn't have to tell me that. Philadelphia was well known as the center of medical education in the United States. If I tried to interview every anatomist in the city it would take me weeks.

I stared at the skull again and thought on Forbes's interesting story.

I would never have come up with such a wild yarn. Or believed it was possible. Yet now it seemed to fit like a ready-made suit. Not perfectly. But well enough.

"You don't seriously believe a resurrectionist gang could work in Philadelphia, do you? I only meant to entertain you, McCleary."

"I don't know, Doctor. It is pretty fantastic, isn't it?"

"Yes, I think so."

It occurred to me that Arabella hadn't returned. I wondered if she'd left the college entirely or was just waiting for my audience with her preceptor to end.

I got up and said, "Thank you very much for your time, sir. You've given me quite a bit to think about."

"Oh! I think not. Just a lot of silly old stories. I really wish I could have given you more useful information. Well! The best of success in your investigation."

We shook hands and bowed, very formally.

"Good day, sir," I said.

The girls had draped their oilcloths on the pegs by the door. Their feminine scents departed the room with them. I was left with the faint smell of corruption and half-hearted preservatives. The last thing I saw when I closed the door was Forbes's desk. The skull was perched on the end of it, leering at me.

14

BURKE AND HARE.

I couldn't get that story out of my head. I knew the doctor had just brought it up to be entertaining. But he didn't know what I knew.

I remembered him saying that Burke and Hare had preyed on the poorest of the poor. The kind respectable people would never talk to. The kind they'd avert their eyes from, pretending they didn't even have to share the street with them.

I couldn't come up with anyone lower than a poor negro prostitute. They were as invisible to the respectable class as the wind itself.

The perfect victims for . . . what did Forbes call it?

Burking.

The old ditty about the Irish killers went through my brain. It was very insistent.

Except that now I was substituting my own names.

Duffy and Chew.

And the boy who bought the beef?

It took me a few moments before I remembered what the morgue attendant told me. A man had been talking with Duffy there, right before Chew arrived to pick up the body.

Coroner Brown.

127

Duffy's the butcher, Chew's the thief, Brown the boy who buys the beef.

By the time I exited the Women's Hospital I'd made up my mind where to go next.

Brown was going to have some explaining to do.

I cursed myself for not taking the time to go back to Porter Street. My club was there. And my barker. I had the feeling I would need them before the end of the day.

Back out on Twenty-first Street I looked left and right for an oncoming streetcar. My eyes had to squint in the brightness of the afternoon. For a moment I stood there and let the sunlight seep into me. I needed a little bit of that after a morning like this. Turning up the street I admired the leaves of an elm that were just beginning to lose their vibrant green color.

Looking south I noticed something more interesting. A half-square away a figure in mourning was looking in the window of a glove shop.

I had some more apologizing I needed to do. Now seemed like a good time to do it.

Arabella kept staring at the gloves while I crossed the street. I was two shops down from where she was.

My gaze turned casually to the opposite side of the street. There were large signs on the upper stories of the buildings there, like all over the rest of the city. Black letters on a huge white board.

Then my eyes dropped down to the street. A sound drew them there.

It was music, of a sort. The plaintive notes came from a shabby-looking hurdy gurdy. I think the tune was "I Cannot Sing the Old Songs."

I could hum the words to that tune. There were a lot of memories that came with the music. Some bad, some good. Most of all they were sad.

It was no surprise the organ grinder was playing such a mournful song. All you had to do was look at him and you could see he had a reason.

An old, tattered Union Army wrap protected him from

the cold October air. That was the only piece of clothing that gave a clue to his former occupation. Even though most anyone could buy a Union greatcoat, I knew he was a soldier. I knew it because he wore his wound like a medal. The kind of medal that has no flash or glory in it. He was missing a leg.

The old soldier stood on the streetcorner, propped up by a crutch. His two upper limbs grasped and operated the organ. He probably rented the instrument, paying a large portion of his meager profits to the owner.

There were many, many veterans like him. Amputees had no chance of getting jobs in mills or works of any kind. They were forced to beg or eke out a pathetic living as organ grinders.

For the second time that morning I remembered the reek of gangrene in the surgical tents, the sight of piles and piles of amputated limbs. I could hear again the cries and see the tears of men who woke up from their whiskey-induced stupor to find themselves crippled forever.

Automatically, I felt inside my pockets for loose change. I was about to go over and dump it all in the fellow's basket. Then I got back on the curb and turned quickly away.

I stopped where I was and pretended to be very interested in the shop display of a bookseller specializing in medical texts.

A man was standing a few feet from the organ grinder. A negro.

In the glass I got a good look at him. He was average height, with his curly hair in need of the shears. His brow projected over deep-set eyes like a cliff face. But his hands were the interesting part. He was rubbing them together, like he was impatient to get moving again.

They were very curious hands for a negro. Their piebald shades were distinct even from across the street.

I had to smile with my luck.

Then I noticed where Levi Chew was staring. He

wasn't trying to be subtle. I didn't think it was the glove shop that interested him.

A bell rang from behind me. A streetcar driver was getting impatient and taking it out on our ears with his gong. I turned to look at the car and saw it at the corner. The team was turning slowly while the driver urged them to move faster.

When I turned back to Arabella I saw her watching the driver ring his gong. I don't know if it was anything I did—a movement or whatever—but our eyes met. When I turned to the other side of the street she turned with me.

Chew was already dusting out of there. In that split second he'd recognized me.

I hollered, "Stay there!" at the girl and tore off after Chew.

My hand went to my waist and hit my suspender strap. There was no holster where it should have been. If I'd had the revolver I could have winged Chew from where I stood. Now there was nothing to do but outrun him.

I dashed across the street, right in front of a delivery wagon. The driver hurled a few oaths at me as he pulled on his brake. Chew was turning the next corner. I made it across the tracks in the street and onto the curb. The gong of the streetcar driver echoed my footfalls.

I was a few steps from rounding the corner when I heard a woman scream.

With a quick glance over my shoulder, I saw an elderly woman cry out, "Help! The poor man!"

Then I peered past the curb she was standing on to the street. A form was sprawled on the cobbles. A Union coat covered it. The organ was lying in the gutter.

There was no one else around the veteran but the old woman.

The shrill gong sounded again.

The streetcar was moving along the tracks, very quickly now. The driver was shouting something to the conductor, his head turned from the road. Right across the path of the team was the veteran, still not moving.

I had a few seconds before the horses trampled him.

My heels pushed me forward, past the old woman. At the curb I sprang into the street. The team's harness rang in my ears. The iron-capped wheels whirred over the tracks. And above all was that damn gong.

The leap from the curb took me over the veteran's body. My foot caught on the track and I plunked my hand on a cobble to steady myself. Then I turned and grabbed him by the shoulders. He was no featherweight. The horses' hooves were a rod off when I finished dragging him across the tracks and into the middle of the street.

By this time the driver had his eyes on the street and was busy cursing at us left and right. Luckily his gong drowned him out. His hand was on the brake. The wheels squealed like yelping dogs.

The noise seemed a little too much for one car. Something felt rather than heard made me look to my left. That was when I saw a truck about to smash right into us.

There was nowhere to move. The streetcar was blocking us to the right and the truck to the left. We were about to be pulverized. The veteran would lose his only leg. And I'd lose both of mine.

I could've saved myself by dropping the veteran. But I stayed where I was. The teamster was screaming at me to get out of the way. He wouldn't be able to stop in time.

A second later the end of the streetcar rushed past me, the brakes only slowing the momentum a little. I saw the conductor leaning over the rear entrance, grabbing a handrail on the outside of the car. There was a step there to assist passengers getting on or off. It was within a few feet of me. So was the truck team, neighing with fright when they saw I wasn't moving.

In an instant I reached out and grabbed the hand rail and, heaving the veteran with me, clambered up the step. I felt the rush of the horses as they galloped past us. The streetcar had come to a halt by then.

The driver was off the front platform and heading

straight for me. He was calling me all the names they don't put in any book.

I was in a bad mood. I'd lost Chew and almost gotten myself a free amputation.

The driver kept moving toward me. When he came within a few feet of me I stopped his progress with four of my knuckles.

The passengers screamed with fright. The conductor tried to wrap his arms around me in a bear hug. That was when I lost my patience altogether.

I tilted my head back sharply. My skull butted him in the face and he let go, groaning.

Then I pushed him down in a seat and said for the benefit of the passengers, "Police! Everybody off the car!"

The two workers weren't going anywhere. The crumpled heap beneath the Union coat was beginning to stir.

A blue belly stumbled into the car, waving a club at me.

"Come here, you!" he hollered.

I sat down on one of the seats and plunged my hand into my vest. The club was a few inches from my crown when I brought the star out.

"Why didn't ya tell me you was a copper? Christ, I almost brained ya!"

The patrolman listened to my story. We decided he should fine the driver for recklessness. I convinced him not to arrest the fellow. Then I'd have to waste time in front of a magistrate.

When I got off the car the veteran was slumped against a money loan office. Before I could reach him the old lady who'd been screaming from the curb jumped in front of me.

"I seen the whole thing, Officer! That nigger pushed the man right in the street! Coulda killed him!"

I didn't know Chew too well but I got the feeling he didn't do it by accident.

The veteran was staring at his only leg and weeping. I

stood in front of him and said, "Say, you all right?"

He nodded at first and then shook his head.

"My organ got mashed up. The colored fella kicked it in the street with me. I think that truck ran over it."

"You got any bones broken? Any bruises?"

"No, no. I'm all right, I tell ya. But it don't matter now. How'm I gonna pay for that squeeze box? I got a family. That organ's gonna cost me two weeks' pay, I know it. And my change got grabbed while I was in the street. What'm I gonna do?"

I took out my leather and handed him a ten-dollar bill. There went all of my pay for the week.

"Here you go."

"No, no. I can't take that from you. You saved my life. You owe me nothin'."

The veteran bit into his lip to keep back his tears.

"Listen," I said. "You take it. From one soldier to another."

I took his hand and put the greenback in it. Then I said to him, "You take care."

Arabella was nowhere to be seen by the glove shop. Or anywhere else.

A woman, walking by with her daughter, gave me a wicked stare. It was then that I realized how much I was cursing.

I said to the woman, "My apologies, madam."

Then I headed south, toward Arabella Cole's residence on Twelfth and Pine.

15

I COULDN'T SAY how long it'd been since I was at the
theatre. Probably close to a year before, when I saw *Uncle
Tom's Cabin* at the Eleventh Street Opera House. The
northeast corner of Twelfth and Pine was at least as interesting as any production I'd ever seen. I was poised on
the brink of the colored part of the Seventh Ward. The
next street down was Lombard, the main artery of negro
Philadelphia.

I leaned against a lamppost and watched the street. For
a few moments I felt like the lone audience for the every-
day spectacle going on around me.

Beside me was a stationery store. Peering through the
window I saw the white shopkeeper helping a colored
woman. From the looks of her purchase I figured there
was a death in the family. She selected stationery edged
in black. I'd received a few letters like that myself, informing me that an uncle or aunt I'd never seen had died.
You knew as soon as you saw the black trim around the
envelope that it bore grim news.

Across the street was a vendor of Venetian blinds and
shades. He had an ornately carved wooden eagle perched
over the entrance to his shop. What the eagle had to do
with Venetian blinds is beyond me but it caught my attention. My eyes wandered to the upper stories of the

134

shops, looking for shades or blinds. I saw a few but most were drawn to let in the sunlight. No one in this neighborhood could afford to waste kerosene.

Next door to the shade vendor was a colored barber. A shoe shiner, probably related to the barber, stood outside whipping his soiled cloth across a man's boots. From his uniform I twigged he was a domestic. There wasn't much call for colored domestics in Philadelphia. The swell mob preferred the Irish for those situations. In fact, there wasn't much call for colored men or women in any profession. This man was lucky and he knew it. When he walked away from the shine boy he pulled a pocket watch out and snapped down the lid. I could tell he hadn't looked at the time. He was simply proud to bear such a badge of respectability and success.

On the corner by the barber was a negro woman shouting at the top of her lungs. She wore a shapeless sable wrapper with no corset on—dressed for her kitchen rather than public. No one expected negroes to look respectable anyway.

There was a wild gleam in her eye. In her hand was a leather-bound volume that was probably a Bible.

"Hear, O women, the word of the Lord," she proclaimed. "And let your ear receive the word of his mouth! Teach to your daughters a lament, and each to her neighbor a dirge! For death has come up into our windows, it has entered our palaces, cutting off the children from the streets and the young men from the squares! Thus says the Lord, the dead bodies of men shall fall like dung upon the open field, like sheaves after the reaper, and none shall gather them!"

From inside the barber shop came hoots and whistles.

I recognized the words from the prophet Jeremiah. Every now and then I got the feeling the Lord was trying to send me a message. This one was edged in black.

One door down from the woman was a plain brick row home with shutters painted dark green. Like most houses in Philadelphia, it had a marble front step. On that step was Arabella Cole. She was talking to a top-hatted man, half-obscured by a pile of overflowing ash cans. The city hadn't been too conscientious about collecting coal ash lately.

I made a left onto Pine and got closer to her doorstep, trying to see the man she was talking to.

There was an alley directly across from her that would serve my purpose. From there I could watch them in the shadows. And I could attend to, well, a call of nature that was getting urgent.

I slipped up the narrow alley named Grayson Place. Now I could see her companion's face quite well. It was a familiar one. Dr. William Forbes.

For a few moments I watched the two of them, Arabella on her front step, Forbes in the street. It looked like a sentimental chromo of a lady and her suitor. Their expressions were hard to read at this distance. I wasn't sure I wanted to anyway.

That a respectable physician like Forbes would have an interest in Arabella was hard to swallow. I was choking on it.

Why I kept watching them for so long I can't say. There were new kinds of feelings inside me, conflicting and painful. I realized that I wanted to be the one she was talking to. And I felt embarrassed and ashamed for wanting that.

Through the narrow slit of vision I had of the street beyond I could see no other people, no sign of the nineteenth century and its realities. Just the two of them standing there, together. For an instant I imagined a time and a place where it would be perfectly natural and normal for me to be the one talking to her, to perhaps entwine my arm around hers and escort her proudly through the streets like a gentleman would his lady.

But it was the nineteenth century. In the modern world there were boundaries one couldn't cross. This was one of them.

I felt that invisible hand again. Except it wasn't pushing

or pulling me this time. Now its steel grip was choking the life out of me.

She stood above him regally, the marble step her pedestal. Forbes was stooping to the ground to pick something up. It was a black bag, what we call a keister. Arabella was reached into her change purse, extracting a tiny bundle wrapped in butcher paper. She placed the bundle in Forbes's hands. The doctor tipped his hat and Arabella bowed slightly. Then he took his leave of her, placing the bundle in his keister. The girl disappeared into the doorway of her boardinghouse.

By this time I was in a little bit of distress. A few feet behind me was, what we Philadelphians call a backhouse. I headed for it, hoping the owners didn't keep it locked.

I didn't get to make my stop. When I was a few feet from the backhouse someone stepped in front of it. The light in the alley was dim. But I could see who it was well enough.

Sergeant Walter Duffy.

"What brings you down here, Officer McCleary?"

"A call of nature, Sergeant," I said, careful not to let my voice quaver.

"I can think of a hundred and one better places to take a bunk in."

"Just happened to be passing through."

The sergeant's club wasn't out yet. Nevertheless his arms hung ready at his side, his gristly hands already curling into fists. The thick arms had to curve around his expansive torso. His whole body rippled with violence. It seemed to focus on me like a beam of light through a magnifying glass. I could feel it burning already.

"Let's dispense with the horseshit, McCleary. I know why you're here. Checkin' up on the Cole gal. You have quite an interest in that piece of muslin, eh?"

"And you, Sergeant? What's your interest in her?"

"I'm conductin' a little investigation. I got a black memorandum book full of names and addresses. Guess who's in there, Wilton? 1634 Porter Street, ain't it? And I got whoever talks to you, too.''

Duffy leaned toward me. I felt my back go against the alley wall.

''You know what? It ain't good to have your name in that book. Next time I see you I might not be so friendly.''

Then, like I wasn't even there, he muttered, ''They're gonna find out who's boss in the Seventh. They're gonna learn their place again.''

Just another white man raving against negro suffrage.

''You gonna rewrite the Constitution, Duffy?''

That made him laugh. ''You ain't so fly after all. Get lost, McCleary.''

Wondering what he meant I headed down the alley, unsure whether I could get out or not. Above my head linen was stretched from one side of the alley to the other, blotting out the sunlight.

After I walked a dozen yards I came to a brick wall, blocking my way. To my right or left were more back-houses. A tiny alley paved with wooden cobbles extended past them. I made a left. Just as I was doing that, I saw Duffy at the alley's mouth, still staring at me.

Then I walked inside a backhouse, holding my breath.

About ten seconds later I was outside, buttoning up. A narrow back court ran behind the row of backhouses, parallel to Grayson Place where I hoped Duffy was still standing.

I didn't run. My boot heels would've sounded on the wooden blocks they used in place of cobbles. It was an ancient back alley and the smells made it seem not only ancient but dead, buried, and corrupted.

I held a handkerchief to my mouth and nostrils. That way I wouldn't catch any diseases from the rank miasmas. When I was directly behind the backhouse where Duffy'd been standing I stepped inside and nearly tossed my cookies.

The stink emanating from the hole in the ground was almost unbearable. I put my face against the rotting frame boards and saw just enough of Grayson Place to see that Duffy was still there. Someone else was with him now.

Biting into my lips to keep from vomiting, I did a little eavesdropping.

"... gone," Duffy was saying. "Scared the little runt off."

"He the one at the river yesterday, boss?"

"You tell me! I wasn't there! Did you get a good look at him from the street?"

"Sure, sure. Blond fella with whiskers like that. And a mustache. I remember that black hat of his. Like a sport's."

"That's him all right."

"He gonna be a problem?"

"Not if I can help it. If he pokes his nose around anymore we're gonna find out. And punch his ticket mighty quick."

"Who's watchin' the girl?"

"I got some of the boys stickin' around. And there's Chew. Who nearly got his ass nailed to-day by our blondie."

"You talked to him?"

"Course I did, stupid! We gotta get some of the swag to-day. I gotta make some payments to the reserve boys for Tuesday. Chew set up an appointment with the ikey mo for me. Without mentioning my name of course."

"Whatta ya want *me* to do?"

"Go over to Brown's and get the swag. Then drop it off with Chew at the fencing crib."

"Why don't ya just give it to Chew?"

"Who's in charge here? You or me, McNamee?"

The name meant something to me. I remembered it from Friday afternoon at the Delaware waterfront. The coroner's wagon driver.

To anyone unaccustomed to flash language their conversation would've sounded like a lot of nonsense. Swag, ikey mo, fencing crib. But I had his number now. Brown had some stolen booty to sell to a Hebrew receiver of stolen goods.

The swag would go toward paying off reserve officers for services rendered election day. Strong-arm stuff, I bet. The negroes were in for some bruises and broken limbs. Or worse.

McNamee was whining. "Okay, okay. I dint mean nothin' by it."

"No one's supposed to put the two of us together, see? Or the three of us. Brown doesn't know about Chew and me. I wanna keep it that way. I like our understanding the way it is. So we do things my way, understand? Now git. Meet me back at the club when you're done."

"Ya think they'll let me in? I musta lost my membership badge. Don't know what became of it."

"Of course they'll let you in! You're one of the officers!"

"Yeah, I guess you're right. What about the job tonight?"

"What about it? You and Chew work it out. How many you think you can get?"

"At least three or four."

"How many in the warehouse?"

"A half-dozen more. But they won't keep long, even with this chill."

"Take care of it soon. To-night. You got the keys to the colleges, don't ya?"

"Yeah. I'll make some deliveries, to-night."

My body shivered. I ran over the words again and knew there wasn't any other answer.

McNamee was a resurrectionist. To-night he was going to snatch three or four freshly buried corpses. He and Chew.

And Duffy would sit back behind a roll-top desk somewhere and count the greenbacks.

The only thing I didn't understand was why Duffy said the coroner didn't know about him and Levi Chew. The negro had been there last night, when Duffy had bribed

Brown into releasing the corpse to him. I'd even seen Chew with the morgue attendant.

But I didn't have time to puzzle it out. All I could think of was the grave-robbing they had just discussed so business-like.

I had to stop them, had to find out where . . .

Suddenly all the tension and disgust combined with the reeking stench of the backhouse. I could stand the smell no longer. My oyster breakfast and my stomach parted ways.

The retching sound put a stop to Duffy's conversation. For a moment I was afraid the two men might rip open the door. If they found me I'd be the next corpse on a doctor's dissecting table.

There was a rap at the backhouse door. I tensed my body, ready to fight for my life.

Duffy laughed and said, "What's the matter, fella? Pig's feet and grease gettin' to ya?"

He laughed again and said to McNamee, "Amazin' what these niggers put in their mouths. C'mon. Let's make tracks."

I counted to twenty and then burst out of the backhouse door. Then I dashed up the narrow alley and around to Grayson Place. Huffing and puffing I reached the mouth of the alley and was in time to see Frank McNamee unhitching his horse from a wooden post. Duffy was nowhere to be seen. I kept where I was, just in case he was watching for me. When McNamee rode away I could wait no longer. Stepping out onto Pine, I followed him east.

16

EVEN THOUGH MCNAMEE was in a wagon and I was on foot, I didn't have any trouble keeping up with him. The streets were full of traffic of all kinds: streetcars, omnibuses, drays, trucks, delivery wagons, hearses. The stables must've been empty that day.

I knew he didn't see me tailing. Looking around me from time to time, I knew no one else was watching either. It made me feel invisible. I liked that feeling.

Sometimes I was afraid I'd lose him. The crowds on the sidewalks were thick. Women were exploring their favorite vegetable carts and butchers. Fresh fish and oysters lay in barrels of ice, blocking movement. Once I had to shove a woman out of my way who refused to budge. She was too busy arguing about the price of some shad.

Gentlemen hurried from corner to corner, consulting their pocket watches. They snapped the lids shut with a smile. They liked the sound of gold scraping gold. A horde of them poured into the Reading Railroad Passenger Depot, right on Pennsylvania Avenue, which eventually turned into Noble Street, where the morgue was.

As I walked eastward, locomotives roared out of the depot, throwing clouds of steam into the air. The beautiful sleek engines sailing through the streets were something I never failed to remark. People looked at us from the passenger cars like we were a lower species of animal. Over the din of the whistle I could hear the fireman and the engineer shouting at each other. Then like a black thunderbolt the train would flash and be gone, the great symbol of our city's power, its idol of iron.

Kids too young or too poor to be in school raced through the streets hawking newspapers or chasing hoops. They rolled those little hoops straight ahead of them, and bad luck for you if you were in their way. One little boy in britches banged my knee with one. The little brat laughed in my face. I nearly picked him up and dumped him in an ash can.

By the time Frank McNamee got to the morgue I was pooped. I'd been going for the whole day on the oysters I'd had at Woody's and the nap in the hospital. It wasn't enough. My stomach began to growl.

McNamee was waiting for an express wagon to pass. It was piled high with barrels and the driver was being careful, going slowly. While he was held up, I managed to grab a couple pretzels from a German vendor, tossing him a nickel. It was too much to pay but I was in a hurry.

After I'd stuffed one pretzel into my mouth the jam cleared up. McNamee hitched his horse behind an ambulance that stood right out front. A pair of men were unloading a body on a stretcher. My man followed them in.

I figured he wouldn't be going anywhere without his horse and wheels so I stayed put. Then I noticed a fruit stand propped up against the building on the opposite corner. I went over and bought myself a few apples, careful to wipe them before I ate them. After a rub they tasted plenty good.

For twenty minutes I stood on the corner, waiting for McNamee to come back out. When he did I noticed he had a black keister with him, the kind doctors carry their instruments in. It was bulging at the sides and looked heavy.

The swag. Whatever it was.

Now all I had to do was follow him to the Jewish fence, or as Duffy put it, the ikey mo.

Lucky for me we didn't have far to go.

Just a square to the north he turned left onto Dana Street. It was more an alley than a street, with rows of decrepit brick row homes on either side. Half the street was uncobbled, the pile of stones resting in a dusty, muddy heap by the corner. The Public Works people had probably forgotten Dana Street existed.

It would be hard to stay invisible in a place like this, with no one around except McNamee, myself, and his horse.

I walked back out onto Beach Street and waited. The few mechanics and stevedores on the streets at this time of day were too tired to care what I was doing. Half of their ten-hour workday was just over. They were looking for a free lunch at the local saloon most likely. I would've welcomed one too. But victuals weren't important now. Not when I had a chance to get Chew in my sights again.

When I'd counted to ten I turned back into Dana and saw McNamee hauling the keister down to a cellar door. The cellar belonged to a nondescript building wedged between a broom-maker and a cooper.

While I waited for Chew to show up I tried to draw myself a picture. It was what Chief Mulholland would call a thumbnail sketch. The painting would be one of those epic history paintings like the one I saw at the hospital that morning. There were a lot of characters to include. First I had Coroner Brown and his wagon driver McNamee. Then I had Sergeant Walter Duffy and his mouthpiece Levi Chew. Then there was Goldie Collins and the ragpicker. And finally eight other colored girls.

I stopped drawing my picture and took a step back to look at it. From this distance I wasn't too impressed. The figures weren't distinct. They were as vague and shapeless as the marbleized designs on a book's endpapers. I had a lot more work to do before I could exhibit the thing downtown at the Central Office.

The biggest flaw was in the composition. I still wasn't sure what the figures had to do with one another.

I had a motive behind the killings: to generate fresh cadavers for the medical colleges. But something seemed wrong about it. If Duffy was indeed the boss of the Seventh Ward, would he waste his time with such a trifling game as body snatching? And then why switch from that to burking? Was the demand for cadavers so great? I didn't think so.

There might be another reason why the girls were disappearing, and probably dying. I had a feeling the contents of the keister might help me figure it out.

Then I heard the cellar door slam. Frank McNamee walked up the stairs. He wasn't holding the keister anymore.

As he unhitched his horse and rode slowly down the street, I dashed to the cellar door. The clip-clop sound of the mare was fading when I pushed the door open and went inside. My fists were clenched and ready for swinging.

What I walked into was no fencing crib but a long passageway. At the other end, at the rear of the house it opened up into a back court. There was no one there now. Chew must've been waiting here, grabbed the keister from McNamee and then dusted off.

I'd failed completely. The keister was gone, Chew was gone, and I had no idea where the fencing crib was.

Dragging my feet back out the door I stepped up to street level. I was just in time to see McNamee's backboard pass out of sight, heading south.

Hissing a four-letter word or two I took off after him, as fast as my heels would carry me.

McNamee was heading south on Second. I wasn't sure how long he'd be going this time. I had no inclination to walk across half the city again. It had been a long day and I was exhausted. I'd slept only briefly in a pool of blood and a very uncomfortable lecture hall seat. I'd eaten nothing in twenty-four hours except a brick of ice cream, oysters, some pretzels, and a couple of apples.

I chastised myself for complaining. During the war I'd done my share of arduous marching. But I was older now and didn't have an officer screaming at me.

I decided to take a gurney cab I saw parked a square away from the Freight Depots. It was sharp-looking, mostly covered by sheet iron painted black and olive. I entered through a rear door, like on an omnibus. There was room inside for four people so I stretched my legs.

Sticking my head through the window I said, "Follow that delivery wagon going down Second. When it stops you stop, okay?"

"You bet," the driver said, tipping his top hat to me. I heard him put a switch to the horse's rump. We got moving then.

The interior of the cab teetered like a ship at sea, but I didn't mind. I let my back sink into the new cushions.

I must've dozed off. The cab came to a halt and I heard the driver say, "Here you are, sir."

Rubbing my eyes I stumbled out the rear door onto Keble Street. We were parked a few doors away from a building I'd heard of but never seen. Beneath the third floor cornice a sign read Democratic Sons of Liberty Club.

My pocketwatch said it was four thirty and twenty-six seconds. I had a few hours before Duffy would meet McNamee there.

I had a feeling I would need a little more strength than I had to get through this night. I would need my new Smith and Wesson revolver too.

Going back through the rear door I said to the driver, "Take me to Porter Street." At the very least I could get into a new suit of clothes. Maybe I'd be lucky and get no blood on them this time.

Then again, maybe not.

A CLATTERING SOUND coming from outside woke me up a few hours later. I'd fallen asleep in my wooden tub. I got out quickly, trying not to drip on the freshly varnished floors. Looking out my window, I saw it was the coal man, shoveling anthracite down my chute. I was thankful for the noise. There wasn't much time before Duffy would meet McNamee at the club. I had to get ready.

I put on a clean pair of unmentionables. Then I got a freshly laundered shirt and slid on the arm bands. I needed them because the sleeves were a little too long. From the closet I took a black suit. It wasn't a frock cut, the style I usually preferred. This one was a sack suit, with the coat reaching only a tad past my nether portions. I could get to my barker better this way.

The revolver was still in its box. I took it out, admiring the blue finish and rosewood stock. For a killing machine it was pretty.

It was Smith and Wesson's newest invention. A revolver with a cylinder in which metallic cartridges were loaded from the breach. Quite different from the front-loading, percussion ones I was used to. There were seven chambers and no more balls or powder involved.

The cartridges seemed insubstantial by comparison. But I was willing to give the new barker a try. Thinking of

Chew I felt in the mood for experimentation.

After I put on some new cuffs and a collar I grabbed my hat and headed for the street. I'd already supped before my bath. I was ready for business.

A couple squares from my door I caught a streetcar and headed toward Pine Street. I was there in about twenty minutes.

On the way over I tried to empty my brain by staring at the sunset over the red brick row houses. The dull orange haze in the sky looked like tongues of flame licking the horizon. As the streetcar slid along the tracks I watched the light slowly ebb like embers on a fire.

By the time I got to the D.S.O.L. club the gaslights were flaring inside. Right past the door there were two men dressed in shabby suits, probably the only ones they owned. Their hands were thick and dirty under the nails. They smelled like kerosene. I twigged they were laborers at one of the oil works. They formed a wall in front of me. One of them said, "Evening, friend."

It occurred to me that there might be some secret sign or word. A lot of the clubs had things like that. If I said the wrong thing I'd be tossed out on my rump.

When the one talking held out his hand I knew he wanted to see something. My dues from last month? A membership card?

Ah! The badge! The one I'd found at the ragpicker's shack.

Quickly I fished it out of my pocket. He seemed satisfied. The human wall separated and let me pass into the saloon.

The club was no Union League. To me it looked like a blind pig, an illicit liquor saloon. The only bit of color in the place was the cream-colored iron stove in the middle of the room. So far it was doing its best to asphyxiate the burly mechanics and laborers drinking around it. The men were helping it along. Each one had a segar or pipe stuffed in his mouth. I had to wade through several puddles of tobacco juice. While cuspidors were at every table the men were too drunk to bother with aiming.

Next to the bar was a marble statue decidedly not modeled on anything Grecian. The name of the sculpture was *Diving Girl*. Her hands were joined over her head like she was about to take a dive right onto the floor, which was covered with a thin coating of damp sawdust. This diving girl was dressed in her lace unmentionables, showing more leg than swells even dreamed of. Her arms were practically bare and the bosom was . . . very anatomically correct.

The bartender was busy refilling lager beer mugs. Except the stuff in the mugs wasn't lager beer. It was whiskey. The men poured it down like human drains. Profanity poured out their mouths with equal rapidity. Above the glass behind the bartender was a large sign proclaiming, "Ladies Not Invited." But they'd take females who weren't ladies, I was pretty sure of that.

A familiar green felt cloth with a suit of cards stitched into it was laid out on a table. It was a faro bank, the most popular card game in the country. Men leaned over the players' shoulders to get a peek at the action. In an adjoining room I saw some sports throwing money across a billiard table. The players fingered their cue sticks with more gravity than pallbearers.

There were too many men for any to take notice of or care about me. I took my hat off, ordered some whiskey which I didn't drink, and kept my eyes open.

A roar of applause came from the billiards room. One of the sports was getting slapped on the back. Someone turned to spit in the cuspidor by the entrance. For an instant the gaslight caught his face. It was Frank McNamee. His sour expression probably meant he'd bet on the wrong fellow.

Just as the billiards players were about to commence another match, a thunderous noise sounded behind me. Everyone turned his head to its source. It was the bartender with two cymbals in his hands. Shouting above the oath-laden patter of fifty to a hundred men he cried, "All right, boys, the meetin' is about to begin."

The gamblers shuffled out of the billiards room. The man in charge of the faro bank rolled up the green felt cloth. "Just one more, Johnny," a few of the card-players said, but Johnny shook his head. Serious matters needed to be attended to.

At every table in the long narrow hall there were a dozen men swilling whiskey. I didn't recognize too many mugs. A few looked like volunteer firehouse gang members I'd run up against when I was a roundsman. They were plug-uglies, with enough brains to make a fist and aim it somewhere. Anything else would overtax them.

There were some reserve coppers in uniform. They weren't taking to heart the rules against smoking and drinking on the job.

Everybody else looked like he'd just come from a mill. Their faces were hard and hostile. Drinking and fighting were their only pastimes.

Laughter started up as I moved toward the back of the room. The closer I was to the entrance the better. That way I'd see Duffy coming in before he saw me.

Things felt a little tense. Violence simmered beneath the cloud of segar and furnace smoke.

A beaten-up lectern was placed where the bartender stood. Now a fellow approached it wearing a paper hat, the kind mechanics wear in pictures. Everyone else in the room promptly donned his paper hat with the letters of the club emblazoned on it.

My hands got a little moist. Very soon I was the only one with a bare head. The bartender said, "Hey fella, where's your hat?"

"I think it musta fallen out in the streetcar."

The whiskey slinger reached behind the bar and tossed a paper hat at me. "You can use this one to-night. But don't forget to bring it next time, understand?"

I nodded gratefully.

The assembled audience eyed the podium and waited

in expectant silence, interrupted by a few coughs and one man's snoring.

The fellow at the lectern combed his long burnsides with his fingers. They stuck straight off his jowls like a mangy dog's whiskers. Clearing his throat, he began to speak.

"This meeting of the Democratic Sons of Liberty is hereby called to order."

The men cheered and tipped their glasses back.

"I'd like to call the Grand Master to the podium."

Everyone looked toward the billiards room.

From out of the crowd stepped Sergeant Walter Duffy. He'd been there all along, probably talking to McNamee. I turned my face to the door just in case they looked in my direction. I clapped along with everybody else.

When Duffy got to the podium, paper hat perched on his large head, he made a sign by sticking his index and little finger out. The group quieted down.

Then Duffy began his speech.

"With the election only four days away, we got our work cut out for us. Stokley's men are already out organizing the nigger vote."

Boos from the audience nearly drowned out the speaker.

Holding up his hand, he said, "We've been doin' our level best to make trouble for the Sons of Ham. There've been some incidents on the streetcars that got into the papers . . ."

Some men laughed. I remembered the fracas yesterday morning with Arabella. I wondered how many more negroes all over the city had been pushed around and humiliated by these men.

"But that's just a start. We gotta see to it that the niggers don't reach the polls on Tuesday. (Cheers) Because we all know what's gonna happen if they do. Now I ask you, shall niggers stand beside us on election day, upon the rostrum, in our places of amusement, in places of public worship, ride in the same coaches? Never! Never!

Never! Nor is it natural or just that this kinda equality should exist. God never intended it anyhow. He sure as hell didn't intend for darkies to go chasin' after our white women, by damn!''

The crowd laughed again but there was nothing comical about it. I saw a few men display some knuckle dusters and others some knives. White knights dead set on protecting the virtue of their womenfolk. Somehow it didn't seem too heroic.

"You and I have both seen the hordes of coons pouring out of the South and into our city since the war. Like some plague out of the Good Book. Now with this goddamn Thirteenth Amendment from that bastard traitor Lincoln the niggers are threatening the entire white race!''

The room roared with applause and foot stomping. My blood started boiling. I didn't like these scamps talking about our late President that way.

"Is this going to be a country for the people or for the niggers? You tell me!''

"Kill 'em all, by damn!'' screamed one man. "String 'em from a tree!'' cried another.

"In the South a few courageous men tried to stop the outrages perpetrated by the niggers. But these men were unjustly harassed by our own Republican government. The Ku Klux are martyrs, boys. They are sounding the bugle call for a war we all gotta fight. A war against these damn monkeys who want to take our jobs and rape our wives!''

The reserve copper pulled a poster from behind the lectern. The picture showed a colored man's face with exaggerated lips. Next to it was a picture of some ape. The way the artist drew the pictures made you think the two were similar.

My teeth were biting into my cheek. I was thinking on Arabella, wanting to hold her, to touch her hair and cheek. Now more than ever.

Pointing to the picture, Duffy said, "You see any difference between a pickaninny and a monkey? I sure don't

But the Republicans do. They see more votes for themselves. And hang the working man. The decent fella who has a family to support. Well, I ask you, are you gonna give up your job to one of these? You gonna let them run wild in our streets? No, by damn! They got a place sure enough. The boys down South had a better idea of what that was than some other people we know. (Laughs, jeers.) Well, I say we gotta learn 'em their place right here in the Quaker City. And Tuesday we're gonna learn 'em, all right. Ain't we, boys?''

The audience hooted their agreement, sounding like gorillas themselves.

Duffy cracked a smile, or a facsimile of one. A couple teeth were gone. I wanted to lose a few more for him.

Then the copper continued. ''We got some of our boys from the station-house here to-night. Yeah, I seen you. We're gonna be stationed at the polls early and the first sign of a nigger we're gonna beat 'em off. Now that leaves it up to you other fellas to run 'em out. You do whatever you gotta do. The niggers'll have razors like usual cause they're always spoilin' for a fight. So I suggest every man comes armed with somethin'. If by some chance,'' and he smiled again, ''some brawlin' occurs you can bet the coppers'll have somethin' else to do at the time, ain't that right, boys?''

The reserve bulls nodded their smug heads.

''We gotta give special attention to the nigger leaders like that bastard Catto and his cronies.''

He was talking about Octavius Catto, the principal at the Institute for Colored Youth. Catto was also the shortstop of a ball team, the Pythians, who were a damn sight better than the white Athletics or the Phillies. I'd been to a few of his games. He was an educated, religious man, a real representative negro. That qualified him for Duffy's black memorandum book.

I couldn't believe what I was hearing. The D.S.O.L. club was planning a riot and beatings and maybe a murder. They did it like they were organizing a pic-nic in Fairmount Park.

It was too much for me to handle. I wanted to put a pill through Duffy's fat neck right there.

But I wasn't just angry. I was scared. Not for myself. For the innocent people who were going to get their heads caved in by these thugs.

Worst of all, I was afraid that one of those people would be Arabella. If any of these bastards did anything to her . . .

Something told me Duffy would have that pleasure all to himself. Why else would he have been watching her, writing her name and address in his book?

I had to save her from him. I'd do what I could about the others. Tell Mulholland and Heins. Maybe the Republicans could get their own muscle to beat off these copperhead bastards.

I would stay with her the whole day if I had to. I wanted a chance to apologize to her, talk to her a little more. Why hadn't she waited around for me after I helped out that veteran and lost Chew? Did I offend her that much? I hoped not.

Duffy ranted on, and the more he preached his hate, the more I recoiled from it. There was just a tiny part of me that was like everybody else in that crowd. A part that was taught since a child to treat colored folk like niggers. A part that believed they *deserved* to be treated like that.

When I felt that inside me now I hated it. And myself. But it was there, every time I thought on Arabella, every time I talked to her. It was there.

God, I wanted to get rid of it. Because it made me no different from the men in the club.

I wanted to be different. I wanted to be better.

Duffy was still waxing poetic when I decided to get out. I'd heard enough and I knew I couldn't do anything else till I saw Arabella. I needed something from her. Exoneration maybe.

As I walked out the door I bumped into one of the

human walls. His pal was nowhere to be seen.

"Where ya goin'?" he asked me. "The Grand Master ain't done yet."

I turned around and made sure no one was looking. Then I socked him in the bread basket as hard as I could. He was down on the floor sucking air as I walked out the door. I took one more look around and noticed McNamee by the billiards room. He was staring straight at me. A second later he looked toward the lectern. If I stayed around any longer they'd probably be using my face for a floormat.

I took my paper hat and stuffed it into the wall's mouth, patting him on the head. My hand ached but I felt good anyway. I'd needed to hit something. By the end of the night I'd have some more chances for pugilism. I'd see to that.

Before Frank McNamee could summon help for his comrade I dusted out of there. When I was on the street I headed toward Twelfth and Pine. The whole way there I tried to figure out what I'd say to her. It scared me, some of the things I came up with.

18

BY THE TIME I got to the boardinghouse the sun was already going down. The door to the place was slightly ajar and I could hear someone in the vestibule taking off his coat. Stepping in myself I nearly walked right into a colored man putting his hat on the wall rack. He got one look at my face and said, "Think you got the wrong address, sir."

"I don't think so. I'm looking for Miss Arabella Cole."

"You from that Medical College?"

"No. I'm a friend of hers."

"I don't recollect her mentioning she got any white men for friends."

"That's her business. Isn't it?"

I nudged past him and walked toward a pleasant aroma of fried chicken. The kitchen was set in the back of the house. The first thing I saw when I stepped in was a woman's rump sticking out of the oven. The person backed up and out came a head.

"Damn! Nearly burned my hand agin!"

It was an elderly colored lady with a frowsy wrapper on. Instead of mittens she had a cloth wrapped around her hands. When she saw me there staring at her she began to absently stroke her glisteningly white hair.

"What can I do for you, young man?"

156

"You should take care, ma'am. Use mittens instead of those cloths."

"Can't stand them things. Make it hard for my hands to breathe."

I smiled and said, "My name's Wilton McCleary. I'm a friend of Miss Arabella Cole. I take it you're her land-lady?"

"Scales. Mrs. Artemis Scales. Yes, I run this establish-ment."

"Could you tell me whether or not Miss Cole is in?"

"Well, I can't rightly say. I been in the kitchen getting supper ready for . . . seems like an hour. I got a lot of boarders and I swear they got bottomless pits for their stomachs. I wouldn't know if she came or went."

"I saw she was here a few hours before."

"Seems I recollect her coming home. But . . . hmm. Al-bert! Albert!"

A voice answered from upstairs, "Coming!"

Bare feet clambered down the set of stairs next to the kitchen. A colored boy poked his head around the jamb.

"Yes'm?"

"Albert, this gentleman here's calling on Miss Cole. Have you seen her since you got back?"

"I seen her . . ."

"Saw her," Mrs. Scales corrected.

"I . . . saw her on my way back home. She was leavin'."

"Did she say where she was going?" I asked the boy.

"Well, sir. Not exactly. I said, 'Afternoon miss.' And she say . . ."

"Said!" the old woman hollered at him.

"She *said*," Albert repeated, his lips curling up in a pout. " 'Hello to you, Albert.' I saw she had a bag with her. So's I said, 'You want me to deliver this for you, miss?' 'Cause I saw this new card for my stereoscope that I wanted and was five cents! You remember the one I was tellin' you about? The one with the picture of the bear on it?"

The old woman nodded her head.

"So I was hopin' to make enough to go and buy it down the street. But Miss Cole said, 'No I won't ask you to deliver this for me. The likes of you got no place goin' where I am.' "

Suddenly the boy winced and bit down on his bottom lip, like he'd said something he wasn't supposed to.

"Where was she going, Albert?" I asked gently.

The boy looked left and right like he was trying to find a way to escape my question.

Mrs. Scales picked up a wooden spoon and hollered, "Albert! You answer the man!"

"Albert, I'm a friend of hers. She wouldn't mind if you told me."

"She say I shouldn't tell nobody."

The old woman didn't bother correcting his grammar now. She gripped the wooden spoon with a livid look.

One glance at her toppled the boy's wall of silence. We needed someone with her interrogation techniques at the Central Office.

"I asked her where she was goin' and she said she gotta meet someone in St. Mary's Street."

I grabbed the boy by his lanky shoulders and said, "When did she leave?"

"Not more than twenty minutes before."

"Bless my soul!" Mrs. Scales said. "What's our little Arabella doin' in that awful place!"

"She dint tell me, Grandma. I swear."

"You git up and wash for supper, boy."

The youth was glad to get away from us.

"Well! What would that girl be doin' in a place like that?"

"Don't worry, Mrs. Scales. I'll go and see."

"I wouldn't if I were you, mister! That's a plum nasty place! Some real nasty niggers over there!"

"I can be nasty too," I said, patting my side where the barker was.

I thanked the old woman and got back on the street.

Dusk was transforming the sky into a phantasmagoria of color. Shadows were lengthening everywhere. St. Mary's Street was where they were the longest. And darkest.

St. Mary's was the kind of place you went if you were looking for a craps game with the most unsavory negroes in the ward. Or a streetwalker who'd lean against a wall and lift her skirt for, and I'm using their term, a fast fuck. If you were interested in getting beaten and robbed there were always bludgets like Goldie Collins.

It was the lowest of the city's negro slums, the kind of place even coppers avoided during the day. Any man, white or colored, didn't stray there at night without taking his life into his hands.

The thought of Arabella Cole going there made me tremble with worry. I decided she must be working on finding Goldie's killer. Because St. Mary's was the kind of place Goldie would call home. Had she discovered some information that led her there? Something that she didn't want to tell me?

It was just possible. And it was the only explanation that I wanted. Any others were too disturbing.

It explained why Duffy and Chew were taking an interest in her. She'd been so eager to help me, so distraught when I told her to stay out of it. A woman as strong, as compassionate as I knew Arabella was wouldn't give up like that.

I felt like a fool. All the time she'd been trying to find Goldie's killer the same as I had. That morning at the college she'd lingered around Forbes's office, probably waiting for a chance to talk to me. Then I messed up the whole thing by calling her a liar. No wonder she hadn't wanted to talk to me on the street. To hear me accuse her like that must've been too much for her. Especially after she'd been trying so hard to find the truth.

A truth that was waiting for me in St. Mary's. I just hoped that I could get there in time. To make sure that dirt she was digging up wasn't used to bury her.

From out of my vest pocket I took my star, pinning it

to my lapel. I hoped it might save me some unnecessary trouble.

I headed east on Pine. The hospital was on this street and most of the neighborhoods were "good," that is, without negroes. When I got to Eighth and headed south I entered a different world. I went right past Keble Street where, from the sound of it, the D.S.O.L. meeting had turned into a drunken debauch. Men were outside in the street singing, off-key to a man, "Aura Lea." A square down and I saw St. Mary's on my right.

It was another of those alleys dignified as a street. Except this was more like a sewer. At the opposite end was where all the offal and filth got chaneled: Seventh and Lombard, perhaps the most dangerous street corner in Philadelphia. Colored corner loungers would do you up for a nickel. The whores' fancy men paraded around in plaid suits looking for a craps game. Or a neck ripe for slicing with their razors. The female predators were even more deadly.

From what I remembered there were about eighty families crammed into a street a square long. Close to three hundred people lived in the thirty-five houses there. The only sewer around was the human sewer of the street itself. A few squares past the end of the alley were Hurst and St. Giles, more of the same.

It was smack-dab in the middle of my old beat. I was in no ways anxious to walk again the golden pastures of my youth.

A few men and women huddled together on the pavement, passing bottles around and hoping the liquor would stave off the chill October air. They had nowhere else to go.

As I took my first steps down St. Mary's Street I noticed the queer wooden shacks built behind the more substantial brick row homes. They reminded me of slave dwellings I'd seen in Georgia. The only thing holding them together was the inertia of age. They were about eight feet long by six feet wide, with no windows or fire-

places. Just a hole about a foot square alongside the front
door to let the air in and out. Heaven help you if you
stuck your nose there for a whiff.

I'd seen better living quarters for hogs. It was in such
a place that I'd found a dead man one night. He was
curled up on the wet floor beneath a soiled blanket. It
looked to me like he'd choked on something. Probably
his own vomit. His drunken wife was snoring away in an
adjoining box with some dirty hay for bedding.

That was St. Mary's Street for you. Philadelphia's
greatest shame.

And it was here that Arabella Cole had ventured.

It was going to take me a long time to check into thirty-
five homes.

At first, I wasn't sure I'd get the chance.

I'd taken not more than a half-dozen steps into the alley
before three young men stepped out of one of those
wooden shacks and barred my way.

They were dressed with as much style as low-class stable boys. No fancy men these fellows. Probably gang
members. There were plenty of colored gangs in the city
in those days.

"Hey, you. Where do ya think you're goin'?"

I put my hand on my right hip, on the rosewood stock
I'd been admiring that morning.

"You know where the hell you are, you white bastard?"

"How many guesses do I get?" I said.

"You steppin' on our territory, you prick. Don't you
got any fuckin' eyes?"

Then he pointed to a wall nearby. Paint was splattered
across it. Barely legible were the words "The Killers."
A particularly vicious colored gang, named after an even
more vicious white gang the illustrious Sergeant Duffy
had helped dissolve.

One of his pals said, "Hey, this one's wearin' a star. I
don't wanna make no trouble with the coppers, man. The
boss wouldn't like it . . ."

"Shut up, fool! There's one o' him and three o' us. What're ya afraid of?"

"You've got it wrong, boy."

He didn't like being called a boy. I figured on that. I wanted to get him a little fired up.

Taking a menacing step toward me he asked me to repeat what I'd said.

I crooked my left arm around his neck and drove his face right into the muzzle of my barker. Then I said, "You still game?"

My thumb pushed down the hammer as I rammed the barrel up one of his nostrils.

The other two dusted off. The one with the revolver in his face began apologizing, asking me not to kill him. For a moment I seriously considered it. I mean, killing him. I'd probably just be saving someone else the trouble.

Then the coldness and anger faded from me. I pushed him away and said, "Go home before I kick your ass, *Killer.*"

The Killer did just that.

The revolver stayed in my hand as I walked down the street. I guess the star was too subtle for them. I wasn't worried about a negro challenging me with a fire-arm. In those days next to nobody had a revolver. Especially negroes. I couldn't even remember the last time a fire-arm was used during a street robbery. The weapons of choice back then were still knives, garrottes, and knuckle dusters. Those were the good old days.

While I put the hammer back in place a sound came to me. It wasn't an unusual noise in a place like this. Someone was crying.

Whoever it was, they weren't far from me. I had a sudden fear it was Arabella. Maybe she'd been attacked and . . . I didn't want to imagine the rest of it. I ran toward the sound. It was coming from behind an ash can stuffed to the brim with coal ash and garbage. The miasma was so bad it could've put a whole neighborhood of respectable swells in the hospital.

The girl there didn't even notice the stink. All she did was weep.

She was a little colored girl about eight or nine. Her dress had a few holes in it that needed mending. A button was missing from the back. On her feet were a pair of cracked shoes, something of a luxury in these parts.

Her tiny hands held her closely cropped hair while she cried. Next to her was a much-dented tin pail, lying on its side. A thin trickle of liquid leaked out of it.

For a moment I forgot about Arabella. All I wanted to do was see if I could get the little girl to stop crying.

"What's the matter, honey?" I asked.

My voice startled her. She looked up and saw the color of my skin. Then she started wailing again, this time out of fright.

I stood in front of her, stooping. I wondered why she was so scared. Then the weight of the revolver in my hand reminded me. In no time the barker was in its holster. I said to her, "You afraid of a poor old policeman? Huh?"

The girl summoned up some courage and said, "You ain't gonna take my daddy away agin, are ya?"

"I don't even know your daddy, honey. I'm lookin' for someone else. Now why don't you tell me what's all this fussin' about?"

My tone was quiet and gentle. Not what she was used to, especially from a white policeman. Or her own parents, most likely. Child-rearing in a place like St. Mary's Street was not given the same kind of reverence as in other parts.

She still wasn't answering. I said, "You lost? You can't find your home?"

She shook her head. My gentleness was having an effect on her.

"Here," I said, picking her up and brushing the dust from her dress. "This is no place for a little lady to be at night. Why don't you show me where you live and I'll walk you there. That okay with you?"

Again she shook her head. Tears leaked from her eyes. She gave me a quick glance to see if she could trust me.

I must've passed the test. She said, "If I go home Daddy's gonna belt me agin."

"What for?"

"I done dropped his pail on my way home from the saloon."

"So?" I said, sniffing the pail. It had been full of lager beer. Now I realized why the child was terrified. In places like this children were a common sight in saloons. Parents would send them down to fill up pails of beer to bring back home. The beer slingers didn't mind doling out liquor to babies. If they drank the whole pail themselves that wasn't the saloon keeper's look-out.

This girl was in for a beating if she didn't bring back any beer. I'd seen children covered with bruises for less. But I wouldn't let it happen to-night.

Then I thought of Arabella being somewhere in this alley, in one of the seventeen buildings that stretched on either side. She might be in trouble, might need me.

But this little one needed me too. I wouldn't turn my back on her.

"C'mon," I told her. "Let's get him his beer."

I said a silent prayer for Arabella and let the girl direct me to the saloon.

We passed a white boy carrying out two pails. Inside the beer slinger cracked a joke when he saw the girl. "Couldn't resist a few sips, huh?"

Then he noticed me and the star on my coat. It didn't impress him. I told him to fill up the girl's pail again. He did so and I tossed a nickel on the counter.

As I walked the girl out the beer slinger said, "Hey copper, I got ones younger than that upstairs." The saloon burst out laughing. I got the impression he wasn't kidding. Just thinking of that stoked the rage in me to a fever pitch.

I waited until we were outside. Then I picked up a half-full ash can that stank worse than any others near it. Grunting with the effort, I heaved it through the window of the saloon. Hearing the glass shatter put a smile on my face. The girl started giggling. Inside I saw a heap of ash, offal, and chamber pot dumpings spread all over the floor.

The beer slinger rushed outside with a baseball bat. A crowd burst out behind him, eager to watch. Before he took a swing at me I took a chance and said, "Put the fucking bat down. Duffy wouldn't like it."

I don't usually use such language but I was a little agitated.

The words worked like a charm. Duffy's name put the fear of God in the beerslinger. He dropped his bat and said, "He's gonna hear about this, you son of a bitch."

"Yeah. And some pals of mine at the hall will too. They'll be comin' in a few days to pull your house. Try and have it clean by then."

The little girl and I walked away without anyone laying a hand on us.

"What's that mean, pull their house?" she asked, gazing at me admiringly.

I said, "It means some coppers and I will go arrest him and shut down his place for a while."

"But if he knows you're gonna do it then . . ."

"He can clean it up real good, you mean? Move the girls away? He won't do that. Not if he thinks he has any pull with Duffy."

The girl nodded her head like she understood what I was saying.

That's what would happen, I thought. He'd think Duffy would protect him. But he didn't know that I was going to take Duffy out of the picture. Right now there was nothing I wanted more. Because he was the one who was pulling in the pieces and making the wheels spin. He was the one who benefited more than any other from the illicit gambling and the prostitution. And from saloons that served liquor to babies and sold childrens' bodies.

I didn't know how involved he was in the case of the disappeared women. At this point I didn't care anymore. He was the heart of all this misery and filth. I wanted to rip that heart out and chew it to pieces.

My hatred for Duffy was overwhelming. It crowded out

all my other thoughts. All I wanted to do was get him.
But, when we emerged back into St. Mary's, I realized I
needed to do something before that.

I needed to find Arabella Cole.

At the front step of the girl's home I asked her, "How
long were you sitting out there on the street?"

"A long time," she said. "I was too afraid to go back
home and I didn't have no money left to get mo' beer."

"Listen," I said, "you didn't happen to see a lady walk
by? Dressed all in black?"

"The one wif the nice clothes?"

I described Arabella's outfit.

The girl nodded her head.

"Yeah. I seen her when I brung the pail back the fust
time. Not ev'ry day I see a lady as purty as she was. But
the man she was wif . . . he the one who knocked me over
and spilled my pail. He cussed at me 'cause I got in his
way."

It took a supreme effort not to shout a volley of excited
questions at her. I said, slowly and calmly, "What man?
Did you see what he looked like?"

"Sho' did. He was colored like she was. But mean-
lookin'. And not dressed half so nice."

She put in a few more details. Enough to convince me
the man who'd been with Arabella was Levi Chew.

I was really excited now.

"Where, honey? Where did they go? Can you show
me?"

She pointed to a row home toward the mouth of the
alley. "That one there. With the boards in the windows."

My hands were shaking when I gave the little girl a
two-dollar bill. I said to her, "Now you promise me to
hide this from your parents and buy yourself something
nice?"

The girl took the bill, awed. Then she nodded her head
vigorously.

"You want me to come up to make sure everything's
all right with your daddy?"

I was surprised when she shook her head. "He's passed out by now. He'd already drank two pails when I left last time. By mornin' he won't remember nothin'."

She skipped up the stairs and said, "Bye bye, mister. You're a nice white man."

It was the best thing anybody had said about me in a long time.

Fortified with her praise, I walked across the street and headed toward the building where Arabella had gone with Levi Chew.

It was the same building the gang members pointed out to me. Across each board in the windows they'd painted their gang name "The Killers."

Those words meant something different to me now.

I tried the door with one hand. The Smith and Wesson barker was in the other. To my surprise the door was unlocked.

I walked into the darkness of the hallway.

Then I tasted fear for the first time that night.

19

IN THE DARKNESS I had a rank stench to keep me company. Cribs like this didn't offer much ventilation. It was a typical mixture of city smells: the stable, soot, and vapors from the works and backhouses. The air was stagnant and I could feel the solid particles in it crawling into my lungs. I took out a handkerchief and wrapped it around my nose and mouth. I knew enough about medicine to know bad smells were the cause of most diseases.

Gradually my eyes became accustomed to the darkened interior. I listened for human sounds but heard only the vermin scattering as I approached. After making a quick scan of the first floor I climbed the stairs leading up.

When I was about halfway there, I heard something that wasn't a rat. It sounded like a chair or table being moved across a room. Abruptly, the scraping sound stopped. So did I, poised at the top of the stairs. I didn't want to take another step for fear of being discovered.

Leaning against the wall, I slowly peered beyond. There were four doors in the hall. Beneath the one furthest from me came a faint, mellow glow. Someone was in there. They were moving things around again.

Carefully, without putting too much pressure on the half-rotten floorboards, I crept closer to that door. I held the revolver in front of me, the hammer pulled back. I was taking no chances.

With my ear pressed to the door I could hear muffled voices. It was impossible to determine what they said, or who they were.

But I wanted to know and I wanted to know right now.

If the door was like the rest of the building I figured one well-planted boot would break it in two.

I was wrong. The damn thing wouldn't budge. I heard someone say, quite clearly, "Shit!" from behind the door.

I tried to ram my way in with my left arm and shoulder. That did nothing but rattle my teeth. Pain surged up my arm. I lost my patience then and barked the thing. The shot in the cramped hallway was so loud it made my ears ring. The bullet blew off the door knob and made a sizeable hole where the lock had been. With another sharp kick the door gave in and I stumbled through.

My eyes were drawn immediately to the lantern propped on a roll-top desk. There was a cold draft, coming from an open window. A few steps and I was there, leaning over the sash. Below, a dark form scurried down a back court. My fist slammed into the wall next to me and I took the time to curse myself. I should have just shot the door right off.

Then it occurred to me to see whose door it was I'd just broken down. The feeble lantern light didn't reach too far into the room. I didn't see the thing lying on the floor until I tripped over it. Whatever it was groaned. When I fell down on my knees beside the heap I smelled a faint, familiar scent. The smell of crepe. The kind of cloth they use in mourning clothes.

"Arabella?" I whispered.

I brought the lantern over and saw that it was indeed she. Frantically I searched for any wounds but found nothing. Her bonnet lay a few feet away. I ran my hand over her scalp, checking for a cracked skull. Then I tilted the lantern toward her face and saw the small bruise beginning to form on her jaw.

It was only then that I realized I'd touched her for the first time. I couldn't help myself from doing what I did next.

I touched her hair again. But this time my touch was soft, more like a caress. I'd never felt hair of that texture. Fascinated, I held it between my fingers. Then I smoothed it against her temple. My trembling hand ran down the curve of her cheek and jaw. Her eyelids fluttered. I wondered if she were actually awake and letting me do what I was doing. I wanted her to be.

I was thinking, Thank God she's all right. I kept saying that over and over to crowd out all the other thoughts, hoping I could make that hand stop what it was doing.

Then her eyes opened. I jerked my hand away, trembling more than ever.

"Arabella?" I said. "Are you all right?"

Her brow knotted together and her eyes closed again. When she spoke her voice was hoarse. "Where am I?"

"You tell me. I just broke down the door and found you lying here unconscious."

"Who . . . ?" Her eyes came open in a frightened stare. "Wilton? Is that you?"

"Yes, it's me. You're all right now. Here, why don't you try to get up?"

I was glad for the feeble light. My blushing would be invisible. But my trembling limbs weren't. When I helped her sit up my arms were shaking. My whole body throbbed with so many conflicting emotions and fears that they made me light-headed.

"Are you all right, Wilton?"

"Yes, yes. All the excitement got to me, I guess. I had to break the door down. Listen, are you hurt in any way?"

I was afraid of what Levi Chew might've done to her. Maybe he'd hurt her in a way that wasn't readily visible.

Arabella shook her head and then asked, "What are you doing here?"

"Me? What're *you* doing here? And where the hell are

we anyway?'' I grabbed her by the shoulders and said, ''How did you meet up with Chew?''

She got up off the floor. I guided her over to a thread-bare couch propped against the unpapered wall.

I stood in front of her with my arms crossed, waiting.

Looking up at me fearfully she said, ''You're going to be angry with me. I've done some stupid things but this . . .''

''Takes the cake?''

''I'm afraid so. I was only trying to help you. You see, I found out some things about Goldie Collins's murder.''

So I was right about her. Any suspicion or anger I'd felt toward her seeped out of me, gone for good.

Tilting her head back, she gave a deep sigh. I watched the muscles in her lovely neck tense and relax.

Then she said, ''Ever since we were at the morgue I've been followed. At first I thought I was just being hysterical. But this morning on the way to the hospital with William . . . I mean, Dr. Forbes, I noticed a policeman walking on the other side of the street.''

''What did he look like?''

''Wilton, it was the same one from Friday morning, when I met you. The same one you had some words with.''

''I know.''

''What do you mean?''

''I know Duffy's been watching you. I caught him doing it this afternoon. Or rather, he caught me.''

''Did he hurt you?'' the girl asked, worried more for me than for herself.

''No, but I managed to hear him talking to a pal of his. What they had to say wasn't pretty.''

Arabella waited for me to continue but I didn't want to repeat Duffy's conversation with McNamee or with me. I didn't want her to know she was in his memorandum book. I softened the blow by saying, ''He's a very dangerous man, Arabella. I don't like this interest he's taken in you.''

"Nor do I, rest assured."

"Do you know that Levi Chew is his mouth-piece?"

"What's that?"

"It's what coppers call a criminal who informs on his brethren."

"Now I understand. Yes, I knew that Chew was Duffy's informant."

"How could you know that?"

"He told me."

"Chew? Why would he have told you that? And how do you know him, anyway?"

Arabella sighed again, leaning over. She cradled her arms around her knees and said, looking at the floor, "You remember when we went to the morgue?"

I nodded my head.

"And there was a colored man taking a body away? Well, that was Chew. I recognized him. The body he was taking away was Goldie's."

"How did you know him? Why didn't you tell me?" I said, sounding betrayed and hurt.

"Oh, Wilton. I wanted to tell you. This morning at the college. But you were so interested in Dr. Forbes and then you . . . well, you implied I was . . ."

"I know. I wanted to tell you how sorry I am for that, Arabella. I've been waiting all day to say that to you. A woman like you doesn't deserve that kind of treatment. I am sorry."

Her hand reached out to touch mine. The flesh of her palm was warm. For a moment we stood there like that and something passed between us. I felt it in my spine. Withdrawing her hand, she said, "I know, Wilton. I'm sorry I acted like such a stupid little child. I should have told you this morning. It would have saved us both so much trouble. But I'll make it up to you. I'll tell you what I know and maybe you can make some sense of it all."

I sat down on the couch, angling my body toward her.

"This summer last I was assisting Dr. Forbes with some research he was conducting. He'd fixed it with the

college that I could have my second year paid for if I
aided him on this project. It was around the beginning of
August that we received a call from Levi Chew one evening. He delivered a cadaver, one that he said was from
the morgue. We were both a little surprised because usually a white man makes the deliveries, one who is known
to us. An Irish man.''

"A fellow named Frank McNamee?"

"Yes, that's him. Well, this time the doctor inquired of
Chew what he was doing there. Chew replied that he had
a cadaver for the doctor if he was willing to pay for it.
The doctor replied that he would have to see it first. I
examined the cadaver with him. It was an elderly negro
male. When I saw the face I cried out in terror. Because
I knew him, Wilton! He'd been boarding with us on Pine
Street just a few days before when apoplexy took him.
And now here he was!''

"He didn't go to the morgue?"

"No! That's why I was so horrified! He was buried in
Lebanon Cemetery on Passyunk Avenue.''

"The colored cemetery?"

"Yes! Just a few days before Chew came to us.''

"What did the two of you do then?"

"Dr. Forbes told the villain at once that he wouldn't
participate in any body-snatching gang. Then he told me
to summon the police.''

"Did you?"

"No. Because Chew told us that would be a mistake,
since one of them, a very important one, was a friend of
his. He made it very clear that we had better accept the
cadaver or this policeman would make a lot of trouble for
us.''

"What trouble could he make?"

She hid her face for an instant and said, "Chew told
us some rumors might get spread. About the doctor and
me.''

I could feel my face coloring.

"I see. So the doctor backed off. He was too worried about what people might say."

"Oh no, Wilton! You don't understand him. He's a good man, truly. He was more concerned about me. I had so many opportunities ahead of me. The doctor was afraid the taint of scandal, no matter how unfounded, would ruin those opportunities."

"So the doctor took the body?"

"Yes. Since then he's had to accept a few more. All from Chew."

I cracked my knuckles and said, a little harshly, "Why didn't he tell me about this to-day?"

"Because, Wilton. He was afraid for me. But he told you just enough, didn't he? That's what he said to me this afternoon. He said he'd given you a few hints that might lead you to the right trail."

That was the straight goods. It was the doctor who'd put the idea of resurrectionist work in my mind. And the idea of burking. When I thought on it now it all made sense. That intellectual fencing match must've been a test To see if he could trust me and rely on my powers of deduction.

I said to Arabella, "Thanks to him I began putting the pieces together."

"You see? He was trying to help you as best he could Of course he couldn't tell you the whole truth."

"But why would Duffy force your doctor into accepting cadavers snatched from their graves?"

"It doesn't make sense to me either, Wilton."

I stared into the lantern light and remembered Duffy standing at the D.S.O.L. lectern, words of hatred spewing from his mouth. It was ugly and simple.

"Arabella, Duffy hates negroes with a passion. I heard him talking about the election to-day at a club stuffed with other men who think your race are nothing but animals. He talked about warring on the negroes. Well, maybe this is a way for him to make war on them, by desecrating their remains. Sort of like the savages do out West. Fo a sick mind like his it almost *does* make sense."

"Oh, Wilton," Arabella said, squeezing her temples, "It's too horrible. Too deranged."

"Yes. But what I heard at that club was real."

Then I thought of Josephine Martin and the other disappeared women. Now that began to make sense too. Maybe that was another way to war on negroes. Kill the helpless ones who couldn't defend themselves and sell their bodies to the surgeon's knife like the rest. I pictured Duffy stabbing or strangling the life out of them himself. The picture was so clear, so real. I could even see the look of pleasure on his face. It turned my stomach.

"Tell me the rest of it, Arabella. What were you doing here with Chew to-night?"

"Remember this morning when I went to the college museum for Dr. Forbes?"

"Yes. I was surprised at how much time you spent there."

"Usually it wouldn't have taken me so long. Except that Levi Chew was waiting for me by the front desk. I recognized him at once, of course, and asked him what it was all about. He asked if I was interested in who killed Goldie Collins. I said I was. He told me to meet him at St. Mary's Street this evening and he would furnish me with some pertinent information."

Probably not in those words, I thought. Then I said, "Were you out of your mind? Don't you know how dangerous this place is?"

Her brown eyes stared deeply into mine. "I was well aware of that, Wilton. But you see, I didn't care. I wanted to find out what he had to say."

"Why didn't you find me and have me go instead?"

"Because I wanted to prove to you that I wasn't a liar. That I cared. I wanted to help you."

She was barely able to speak the last few words. Then she went to staring at her lap.

"You little fool! He could have killed you!"

It wasn't much of reprimand. My voice was quavering

with emotion. I stopped speaking then for probably the same reason she had. We didn't want each other to detect the feelings that lay beneath our words.

We waited in silence for a few moments. Then Arabella spoke up, still looking away from me.

"I told you it was probably the stupidest thing I've ever done. But I was afraid of being followed. So I tried to face my fear by confronting Chew. I wanted to know what it was all about. If it was just because he'd seen me with you at the morgue or if it was about . . . something else."

"What else?"

"I wasn't sure. But I found out, Wilton. I found out a lot."

"Tell me everything."

"Chew met me a square away from my boardinghouse. Evidently he was worried that we might be seen. So we took a circuitous route and walked hurriedly. Along the way he began to open up to me about his part in the whole affair."

"Why would he do that to you?"

"I'm not sure. He seemed frightened, very frightened. And he had no one else to turn to. You see, he wanted to escape from Duffy's control."

"It's not too easy for someone in the toils to get out of it."

The girl nodded and said, "He told me the same thing. But he had to now. Because he wasn't going to play Duffy's games anymore. Not when they included murder."

"So Chew said Duffy killed Goldie?"

"Wait. I'll get to that. *First* I have to tell you all he said to me. He asked me if he could trust me. I summoned up my most sincere air and said he could. He told me he'd been watching me for Duffy, for the past day. The more he thought on it the more he knew that he couldn't let Duffy do what he was going to do."

"Kill you?" I whispered.

She nodded again, shivering. "Chew told me that

Duffy wanted me out of the way, as he put it. And you too, Wilton. Just for looking into Goldie's death. He doesn't want certain questions to be asked."

"Like what kinds of questions?"

"Why Duffy wanted her body. Why the coroner let him have it. Why the coroner didn't list her death as a homicide."

"How about this one? Why Goldie and some other negro girls have been disappearing?"

"Yes, Wilton. Duffy has your answers. He's going to try to kill us to keep them secret."

"Why does Chew care? Did he have anything to do with Goldie's death?"

"This is the way he told it to me, Wilton. It wasn't easy for him. I think he was in love with Goldie."

I tried restraining my laughter.

"I'm serious!" Arabella said, annoyed. "That's what he told me. They'd been living together for some time."

"Yes, I heard about that."

"You did? From whom?"

"It's not important now. What else did he say?"

"Sergeant Duffy found out about Goldie. It seems they had a history. From what Chew told me the sergeant had . . . used Goldie in the past. Once she learned that Chew was Duffy's informant she used whatever powers of persuasion she had to learn about Duffy and his criminal activities in the Seventh Ward. Chew was stupid enough to confide these things to her. Once she had enough dirt on the sergeant she decided to blackmail him. They arranged to meet at a quiet place along the Delaware."

"Where he killed her."

Arabella wiped an errant tress from her face and nodded, grimly.

"Chew didn't doubt it for one second. I don't either. But Duffy had to go back the next night. It seems there was a witness . . ."

"Was is the correct tense."

This made more sense in light of what McNamee had

said in the alleyway. He must've been in the ragpicker's shack with Duffy. That would account for his lost badge, the one I found.

But it didn't account for Josephine Martin's jewelry. I wondered why.

"Chew was very upset, just talking about it. The man was practically in tears, knowing he was the cause . . ."

"I can't say I'm all compassion."

"He's a victim, Wilton. Just a creature of that vile man. At least he had the courage to try to fight back."

The story was possible. Chew knew her and might have trusted her just because she was a negro. Certainly a white policeman wouldn't have inspired the same kind of confidence. Especially since most of the policemen would help rather than hinder a man like Sergeant Duffy.

"What about the other girls? What did he say about them?"

"Nothing. He told me the answers were all right here." She looked up from her lap and gazed about the room.

It was like coming out of a spell. Suddenly I realized I had no idea where we were or why. I thought it might be a good idea to find out both things.

"Do you know where we are, Arabella?"

"Oh yes. This is Duffy's secret office."

"What!" I exclaimed a little loudly.

Arabella shushed me and said, "That's where Chew was bringing me. He was one of the few people who knew where it was."

"Wait a minute. You walked right into Duffy's hideout with a known criminal? Knowing what you already knew?"

"Yes, Wilton. I trusted Levi Chew. I knew he wouldn't hurt me."

"Well, from the looks of it I'd say you were taken for a sucker."

"No! It's not what you think. We were both searching the room when you banged on the door. He thought I betrayed him. What he did he did out of fear. And it didn't hurt when he rapped me. The only ill effect is a slight headache."

"How would Chew know about a place like this?"

"He told me Duffy liked to entertain ladies here. The kind Chew could acquire in the alley outside, or on Hurst Street."

"Duffy brought colored whores up here?"

"Not necessarily whores. But always colored women."

"I've got the bastard now. I've got him!"

I could barely contain my excitement. I wanted to take her in my arms and share my joy. It was a queer sort of joy, stemming from the uncovering of so much filth. But I was too dizzy with the thrill of having Duffy nailed. I wasn't thinking on the consequences.

If I'd only known what it would take to make things right I might've wiped the smile from my face and walked out of the room right there.

I'm glad I didn't. There are a few things I like to hold on to. My dignity, my pride, my spirit. I don't have much else. If I'd dusted out then I'd have sacrificed all three.

Even Arabella was smiling now. Then we became aware of how inappropriate gaiety was in a place like this. An evil place.

"Let's search the davenport," I said. "And get out of here as fast as we can. Duffy might be coming back here from the D.S.O.L. meeting. Might already be on his way. I don't think he'd appreciate a call this late at night."

"Especially from us," Arabella said.

The davenport seemed absurdly small when I considered how huge Duffy was. It was about the size of a schoolhouse desk. The top was propped up to reveal the innards. Two dozen tiny pigeonholes were stuffed with papers. A couple of ledgers and envelopes filled with cash were on the blotter. Arabella searched the side drawers.

Then she gasped.

From one of the drawers I saw her pull some items that weren't paper. She held them in the light, so I could take a look at them.

"These belonged to Goldie Collins, didn't they?"

Her voice was an excited whisper.

I pulled her palm closer to me. There were three items in it: a ring, an earring in the shape of a star and a lace pin with a cat dangling from a crescent moon.

"This is the proof you needed. Isn't it, Wilton?"

"It's proof all right. Except these aren't Goldie Collins's."

Arabella's brow furrowed with confusion. Then she stared at me feverishly, her lips parted in dread.

I had enough time to say, "They belong to Jo—"

A door slammed downstairs. We both heard keys clanging together on a chain.

"Quick!" I hissed at her. "Douse the lantern!"

She blew out the kerosene flame as I stuffed a few of the papers and one ledger into the pockets of my frock coat.

Arabella closed the davenport as footfalls sounded on the rotten stairs. I whisked her over to the open window where Chew had gone.

Peering over it I saw how he'd made an escape. Directly beneath, not more than ten feet, was one of those wooden shacks I saw before. I wasn't sure if the roof would hold both of us. Or even one. But we had to try. It was that or wait to see who was coming up the stairs. I wasn't that curious right now.

I climbed over the sill and clung to the side of the building.

"Hurry, Wilton!"

As soon as I heard her voice I stopped worrying about breaking my back. My fingers let go.

In a second I was on the wooden shack. My right foot had gone through one of the boards, disturbing the occupants below. A thick miasma puffed out of the opening, enough to gag on.

"C'mon!" I nearly hollered up at the window.

I could see her leaning out, hesitating.

I held out my arms to her and said, "Just let yourself drop! I'll catch you!"

That got her over the edge. She dangled for a few moments just a few feet beyond my grasp. Her petticoats fluttered in the night air.

There was a sound even I could hear from beyond the window.

That was when Arabella let go.

My arms reached up and grabbed her sides as she slid down the wall. Only when she was on the roof of the shack did I feel my hands on her. I kept those hands where they were. Suddenly her arms were around me and her head nestled my shoulder. I let myself hold her, smelling that lavender scent. Her hair brushed against my cheek. I was about to turn her face to mine.

Before I could do that I heard the window clattering above us. I took Arabella's hand and jumped off the shack to the court below. As we ran back to the street, I didn't look behind me to see who it was. I knew well enough. He would know quite soon what I knew.

We made it out of St. Mary's Street and kept running all the way to Twelfth and Pine. Only when we got to her boardinghouse did we let go of each other's hand, reluctantly.

At the door to her place I said, "Can you stay in someone else's room until I get back?"

Out of breath, she said, "Yes . . . Mrs. Scales . . . will still be up."

"Good. Don't go anywhere else, understand?"

Before I could turn away completely I felt her hand on my arm.

"Where are you going now, Wilton?"

"I have to talk to a man at the Republican Club. A man I can trust. He might be able to help us. Or at least keep Duffy at bay. Even if he can't, I just want someone else to see these things."

I indicated the papers in my stuffed pockets.

"That way if something happens to me it won't end there."

Her hands reached behind my head and pulled me toward her. I let my lips touch hers.

She said, "Nothing better happen to you. Do you understand?"

I broke away from her and headed toward the Republican Club.

By the time I reached it I knew I was in love with Arabella Cole. I didn't give a damn about the consequences.

IT TOOK SOME doing to pull Heins away from his whist game. The first thing he said to me was, "Look, Mc-Cleary, if this is about the parade on Monday night, I don't wanna hear it. You signed up for that months ago and we need you."

"I'll be in the parade, Heins. This is about something more important."

He raised his eyebrows and waited.

"Not here," I said. "Someplace private."

Heins walked me up a luxuriantly carved staircase. We went through the first mahogany-finished door on our right. It led to a balcony that overlooked the spacious dining room. A huge flag was strung across the far wall. Twin pictures of Lincoln and Washington decorated the head table. Chairs hung on the edges of the tables. The dining room wasn't in use to-night. To-morrow there was going to be a big dinner, prior to the parade. A few men were busy sweeping the red, white, and blue carpet in preparation.

We kept our voices down.

"To-night I broke into Duffy's secret headquarters."

"Did he catch you?"

"Almost. Before I jumped out the window I managed to grab a few interesting documents."

I took some of the papers stuffed in my pockets and handed them to him.

"Read these and tell me what you think," I said.

He had to lean over the balcony to read them. The feeble gas light barely sufficed.

His hands were trembling like an old man's when he was done.

"This . . . this is incredible, Mack."

"I know."

I'd read them on my way to the club.

"These papers," Heins went on, "detail Sergeant Duffy's illegal activities in the Seventh Ward ever since Fox was inaugurated. I had no idea . . . I mean, we knew Duffy was behind a lot of the Seventh Ward demimonde. But I never imagined it was this . . . involved."

"He's into everything. Policy, prostitution, illicit liquor saloons, faro banks, bunco games, extortion, panel cribs, and buzzer mobs."

"It reads like an encyclopedia of crime."

"That's the straight goods. And he's not just taking scale from the operations. He's running them."

"Mack, you are one hell of a copper. This just bought you a ticket to the detective branch."

I should have been elated. But I knew I was buying the detective job with a man's life. It was a high price to pay.

I kept telling myself he was a bad egg. The rottenest. That I was doing nothing except my duty. Duffy belonged in the penitentiary. If I got something out of it who the hell cared? Isn't that what all the other detectives did? Make a percentage from the stolen property they returned? Or a bounty on the killers they captured?

The logic was persuasive. For the moment, I let it sway me.

"Look at this, Mack! These papers are like blueprints. All you have to do is read over these and you'd have every criminal operation in darky-ville under your thumb. They got information on every man and woman who runs every joint. And the dirt he has to keep 'em kicking back scale. Here's an account book of all the Hurst Street brothels. It lists the take for every month. It's thousands of dollars, Mack. Just on Hurst Street! And look here, at the bottom. Duffy wrote in his percentage.''

I took the papers from him. He was reluctant to let go of them. Then I read the scrawled-out figures. ''That's more than I make in six months.''

Heins smacked his lips together and said, ''Multiply that times ten. Or twenty. There's a lot of sin going on down there.''

''Duffy's got an interest in keeping it sinful.''

''Why not?'' Heins said. ''You think the respectable class cares about what the negroes do?''

''Of course not. They don't want to look at it too closely. If they did they'd see a lot of white men doing the same things the negroes do.''

''Well, that's neither here nor there. The important thing is that we got Duffy dead to rights. You understand? There's no way he can deny any allegations now.''

''Not when these books are in his handwriting.''

''You sure they are?''

''I've seen his penmanship before on daily reports at the Central Office. This is his work all right.''

Heins took a toothpick out and started working it between his teeth. He always did that when he was thinking.

''There's more,'' I said, breaking his concentration.

''Huh?'' The toothpick hung off his lip when he turned to me.

''He doesn't stop with prostitution and grafting. You can add body snatching, abduction, and murder to the list.''

I went into the whole story about the disappeared girls. I told him everything. When it was finished he was wheezing with indignation.

''The man's a degenerate! A villain! We gotta get rid of him. No doubt about it. A man like that won't just lie down and play dead when the Republicans take over. He's gonna keep on runnin' things his way. We can't let him do it. No, we gotta get rid of him somehow. You gotta get rid of him, Mack. For all of us.''

"What do you mean, get rid of him?" I asked, suspiciously.

"Mack, this fella's a mad dog. You know what's gotta be done with them."

I stood up and edged away from him like he had the cholera.

"You want me to kill him? Just like that?" I hollered, snapping my fingers.

"Sit your ass down right now and shut yer yap."

The men sweeping the floors were looking at me. I sat down.

"Now you listen to me, boy. From all accounts I'd say if any had it comin' to him it'd be Duffy. But I'm not tellin' you to kill him. You just misunderstood me, that's all.''

Heins cleared his throat again and eyed me nervously, like he'd just put on some spectacles and was really seeing me for the first time.

"All I'm sayin' to you is bring him in. But we can't have any of this comin' up," he said, pointing at the papers I still held.

"Why the hell not? Wouldn't it just discredit the Democrats even more?"

"Now that's a good thought. But it won't work. We don't want it gettin' out to the respectacle folks that percentage coppers like Duffy exist, do we? 'Cause there are and will be plenty of them. Hell, it goes with the job. A man's got a right to a gratuity now and then for protectin' people's property, don't he? Even if that property's a whorehouse or a gamblin' hell. The point is you gotta have responsible men controllin' those officers or they get too greedy. Like our friend Duffy."

"So you're saying it's okay to look the other way? When robbery and vice take place right under our nose?"

"That's the way the game is played, Mack."

"Your game. Not mine. I play by different rules."

"That's why you're still a special officer and not a detective. Let me change that for you, Mack."

"How? By pinching Duffy just so a Republican copper can take his place?"

"That's about the size of it. With one of our boys we'll keep the leash a little tighter."

My shoulders slumped as I sank into the chair.

"If you pinch him, Mack, pinch him for this nigger girl business. Juries love to punish white men who screw colored women."

My hands were gripping the arms of the chair. I wanted to hit something. Maybe Heins. Or myself.

"They'll crucify a policeman who keeps nigger whores. If you can prove he murdered them, so much the better. Can you prove that?"

"I think so."

"Then there you are. All you gotta do is take the evidence in on Monday. I'll make sure some boys from the press are there to catch wind of it. See, Mack? I'm not asking you to assassinate the man. Just his reputation. From what you say he's got it comin'."

Heins was right. Duffy was a cold-blooded killer. A rabid hater of colored men and a rapist of colored women.

But he was still a human being, though barely. To discuss his destruction like this turned my stomach. I wanted to pinch him because he was a criminal. Not because I would get anything out of it. How could I make money from scum like Duffy? I had a feeling anything I got out of his arrest would be tainted by its source.

Heins only wanted Duffy removed so he could replace him with a boss loyal to the Republican machine. That machine was almost certainly going to take control on Tuesday. I was going to help it do that. I was a part of it.

I knew they were little better than the Democrats. But

they were going to be in charge at the Central Office. And that's where I needed to stay.

I might have to play their game a little, just to hold on to the power that gave me the chance to play *my* game, by my rules.

Remembering why I played that game, and for whom, made me step back to the balcony and bow my head, ever so slightly.

I let go of the greed and the hunger and the vengeance that Heins put in my heart. I conjured up Arabella's face, and the memory of her lips on mine. Then came the faces of a colored whore and a colored young lady. I heard the words Duffy spoke at the club and remembered the beatings I'd taken for speaking up against people like him, comrades of mine, in prison.

Then I turned around and said to Heins, "Now it's your turn to listen, Heins. I don't give a damn about you or the election or the whole damn Republican Party. I'm not doing this for you or for anything you can give me. I'm pinching Duffy because he is a killer and a hatemonger. Because he's everything I thought I was fighting against in the war. And when I see men like him still around I know the war isn't over yet."

I left Heins there with that toothpick hanging on his lip.

Then I caught a streetcar on its way south, in hot haste to get to the Lebanon Colored Cemetery.

I'd found a note, attached to one of the ledgers we'd found, which read: "L.C. 10-7, 10 p.m." This appeared to be written in Duffy's hand. It was to-day's date. I twigged it meant Chew and McNamee would be ready at ten to violate some more graves.

I was going to stop them.

21

T WAS QUITE a hike to the Lebanon Colored Cemetery.
followed Passyunk Avenue all the way to Eighteenth
nd Wolf. When I got there it was half past nine. If I was
ight I had a half-hour before McNamee and Chew would
how up to do their ghoulish work.

By the light of some matches, I went over the details
n Duffy's papers. There were no diary or journal entries
o record his criminal ventures. Instead he kept accounts
nd schedules. That was enough information for me.

One column, headed "Leb. Cem." began with the date
March 1870. The number 3 was beside it. In the next
olumn was the amount of $15.

Duffy had begun grave robbing a year and a half ago.
The first haul was three corpses which netted him fifteen
ans. Not bad for one night's work. It was almost as much
s I made in a week.

The last column was the most interesting. It listed the
laces where the corpses were delivered. I noticed some
ntries read simply, "W.house." For a few moments I
vondered what a whorehouse would want with fresh
orpses. Then I remembered the conversation between
Duffy and McNamee in the alleyway. They had men-
ioned a holding place for their booty. A warehouse. I was
omehow relieved it wasn't a brothel after all.

The list of receivers of the stiffs read like a roster of the city's most respectable physicians and schools: The University of Pennsylvania, Jefferson Medical College, the Pennsylvania College of Physicians. All had at one time received bodies from Duffy's gang. The Women's Medical College and Dr. W. Forbes were listed in the last few entries. Forbes was in distinguished company. These men wouldn't enjoy the tarnish this business would put on their reputations. From the frequency that their names appeared I figured they were all regular customers, all except Forbes, who appeared last and only accepted a few corpses. Under duress, like Arabella said.

It was only the second or third time that I'd gone over the list that I noticed the penmanship. There was something a little queer about it, something too polished. When I compared it to some of the other documents I knew why it seemed queer.

The writing was not Sergeant Duffy's. I was sure of that. Duffy's writing was spare and forced. Here there was a touch of the feathery flourishes, embellishments, and shadings associated with the Spencerian school of penmanship.

I wondered what sort of educated man would Duffy take into his confidence. Who had written these records?

It was a question that I might be able to answer before the night was over.

The Lebanon Colored Cemetery sprawled across thirteen acres. The iron fence and gate were freshly painted. The owner must've been pulling in the pieces. More negroes were living in Philadelphia than ever. In fact, the Quaker City had the highest colored population in the North. Plenty of them had got around to dying.

It was no different from any of the other bone orchards reserved for whites. The occupants were all just as dead. The same mechanics made the headstones for both races, decorated with the usual motifs of a weeping willow or an urn with wilted flowers drooping over it.

Most of the stones were already begrimed with soot

from the city's industry. A few of them were toppled, but over all the place was in pretty good shape.

Scattered here and there on the grounds were some fat oak trees. Their defoliated boughs trembled in the October wind. I crept over to one of them and stood with my back against a sepulchre. Shadows hid me.

As far as I could see I was the only one there that evening. The office building windows were dark, as were those of the tool shed. The only sounds that came to my ears were the hiss of wind through the leaves above me and the far-off, mournful sigh of locomotive whistles.

I took my barker out and added a cartridge to replace the one I fired at St. Mary's. I wasn't quite used to it yet. There was no trigger guard and the trigger was set into the stock. Pulling it was like pressing a button.

I would have to get accustomed to it soon enough. Something told me Chew and McNamee wouldn't go along with me if I just asked them politely.

For a while I did nothing but wait. It didn't bother me to spend time in a place reserved for the dead. Years before, in the war, I saw friends die right in front of me. Later, in prison, I spent nights sleeping beside dead men for the warmth they offered against the winter chill. I helped drag their bodies to the dumping grounds where the deadhouse wagon picked them up. I watched men loot the corpses as they rotted under the hot Georgia sun. After a few months in Andersonville I sometimes wished I could go with them to those long burial trenches.

Nineteen men died there every day—of scurvy, gangrene, and starvation. I think by the time I got out of that stinking hole thirteen thousand of us were dead.

Death and I were well acquainted with each other.

I still believe my survival was a miracle. I was meant to live. But not so I could waste that life.

Standing there in Lebanon Cemetery, I was well aware that I was singled out to be an instrument of a will greater than mine. That will was, unfortunately, hard to discern sometimes.

But not to-night. I knew quite well I had to stop the grave robbing. I also knew I had to get the men who made those colored girls disappear.

The girls were powerless and damned, just like my comrades and I had been seven years ago.

I couldn't go back and change what happened to me and my friends in Georgia. I would still have the nightmares.

But I could change what was happening now to those who were voiceless and forgotten. Just like I had been once.

Maybe if I did that, and kept doing it, the nightmares would cease, and the hell I lived through would finally mean something.

A harsh, familiar sound jolted me out of my revery.

Peering across the night I saw where it came from.

Beside the iron fence about thirty rods away was a policeman. He was knocking his club against the pavement as a signal. Usually that was done only to summon other patrolmen.

To-night it had a different purpose.

A wagon pulled around the corner. It was the same one I'd seen at the Delaware and followed through the streets earlier that day.

Frank McNamee was driving it. Beside him was Levi Chew, who dimmed the lamps at the seat and dash.

The men slid off the wagon as it drew near the curb. McNamee pulled a blanket over his horse's back while Chew conversed with the blue belly. They were speaking in whispers so I couldn't hear what they were saying. But I got the picture when I saw the patrolman's face.

It was Uriah Strunk, the fat, whiskered reserve officer who'd nearly killed me yesterday morning.

I didn't think it was a coincidence that he was here.

Duffy probably instructed him to patrol the perimeter of the cemetery to guarantee the resurrectionists weren't interrupted. He would also keep an eye on their horse and wagon. It wouldn't do to have their means of escape wandering off.

Strunk walked down the street as the two men hopped the fence. Chew handed a bag to McNamee when he was on the other side. I could hear wooden tools clatter together in the sack.

The two body-snatchers creeped across the graveyard under the cover of a new moon. With acres of land around to insulate them from discovery, there was little chance of surprise.

They didn't waste time looking here and there. Instead they proceeded swiftly and silently, like they knew right where they were going.

After a few moments I detached myself from the shadow of the oak tree and followed them. I dashed from monument to headstone, crouching in the darkness. My progress was slow because I had to watch my feet. Half-buried tombstones could send me sprawling. That would make noise.

Ten minutes of walking and the pair had found their first fresh grave. It was covered with a green tarpaulin and stood beneath an evergreen. A statue leaned against the tree. The angelic woman was obviously white and held a garland of flowers. I wondered if there were black angels as well as white ones.

I lay flat on the cold grass, watching them unwrap their sack of tools. They weren't more than twenty feet away from me. I had a front-row seat. The production was a grisly one.

The soil was loose and dry. They worked in silence, casting aside the tarpaulin. They had two canvas sheets of their own, and these they laid on either side of the grave. Then they began plunging their wooden shovels into the earth. Metal shovels would've caused unwelcome noise. Soon the dirt was piling up on the twin pieces of canvas.

Every now and then they took swigs from a sizeable jug of spirits. I almost laughed to see Frank McNamee, a diehard member of the Democratic Sons of Liberty, sharing a bottle with the enemy, a negro. That was our great Union for you. Any prejudices could be shirked if they got in the way of making a buck.

It took about twenty minutes of digging. Dirt was piled up on both sides of the grave and all I could see were the men's heads and shoulders.

All three of us heard the sound of wood strike something other than earth.

They snickered while they tossed the shovels over their heads. McNamee scrambled up top and handed Chew something that looked like a crowbar. Then he stretched the tarpaulin over the opening.

The next thing I heard was a creaking sound like a door being ripped off its hinges.

The tarpaulin muffled the noise well enough. The only reason I heard anything was because I was so close to them. These boys knew their business.

Then McNamee uncoiled a rope from their sack and dangled it down in the grave.

I was too fascinated to be horrified. They worked with awesome speed and efficiency. I wondered how many of the corpses I'd seen at the Women's Medical College that morning had been taken like this. It was something I wasn't sure I really wanted to know.

Chew clawed his way up to McNamee and the two of them started pulling on the rope. They grunted with the effort, cursing at the body on the other end. Soon its head appeared over the mounds of earth.

The corpse was a woman. Or had been. A young woman from the looks of it. Soil spilled from her well-coiffed head. The rope was tightened around her neck like a hangman's noose. A broken neck wouldn't much matter to her.

They drew the body up out of her grave. Her cerements slid against the dirt with a sickening noise.

Chew and McNamee ripped off the clothes until she was quite naked. They chuckled the whole time. No outrage against a woman could be so vile as this. Arabella had painted Chew as a victim, a hapless pawn. That's not what I was seeing.

He was enjoying this. I had half a mind to put a pill in each of them right there. But I wanted them alive. At least for a little while.

I waited until they had the wooden shovels in their hands again, ready to fill in the grave and move on to the next.

Then I sprang from behind the headstone. The revolver was in my hand.

I said, "You better make room for two more."

McNamee, screaming, dropped his shovel.

Chew flashed their lantern at me. I saw a glimmer of recognition in his eyes. He might've smiled.

Then he raised his shovel and struck McNamee on the head with it.

Shocked, I stayed where I was while Chew ran.

It took me a second to get over my surprise. I didn't bother with shouting "Halt!" or anything like that. I just leveled the gun and shot him in the back.

With the darkness of the night and all the excitement, I guess my aim was a little off. He kept right on going.

I pulled back the hammer and got off another shot. This time I winged him. He fell to the ground, cursing up a storm.

That was when the copper grabbed me from behind.

Before I could react Uriah Strunk knocked the gun out of my hand. The next thing I knew I had a billy club biting into my neck. Strunk was lifting me off the ground with it. He was a strong brute. I was already losing any strength I had.

I tried falling to the ground but the club held me firmly in place, strangling the life out of me. Both my hands gripped the nightstick but couldn't wrest it away. Then I got an idea for doing something else with those hands. I stuck out my thumbs and jabbed them backward, toward his eyes.

One of them must have done the job. The club relaxed on my throat while the copper cried out in pain. Coughing, I landed a well-placed boot in his groin. That doubled him over. By this time Strunk was in pretty bad shape. I decided to do a little more damage to him.

Gripping his coat, I whirled him around and landed a couple of punches in his bread basket. Then, seizing his club, I cracked his skull. The blow sent him reeling backward. Strunk tripped over the freshly dug precipice and fell into the grave. His back slammed against the torn-open coffin. Peering over, I saw he was out cold. There was some bleeding but none he wouldn't get over.

I turned my attention to McNamee, who was still lying prone on the ground. My neck throbbed with pain and my eyes ached. I coughed up something and spat it next to the Irishman. Then I cursed, seeing Chew was gone. The bullet must not have hit anything crucial. I was sorry it hadn't.

McNamee was beginning to come back to life. Before he was fully conscious, I dragged the copper out of the grave and wrapped him up in the tarpaulin. Then I walked over to the wagon driver and bound his wrists and ankles.

His eyes fluttered open. McNamee groaned when he saw me. It was the sound of mortal fear. He had a reason to feel that way. I was sick and disgusted by the whole business. Somebody was going to pay for it.

Running a hand through my tousled hair, I said, "You're in for a sweating, pal. So get ready. 'Cause I'll be glad to make it hurt."

22

"Y-YER GONNA KILL me, ain't ya?"

The Smith and Wesson was back in my hand.

I spun the cylinder and said, "There are five cartridges in this beauty. You've earned all of them."

McNamee's mouth opened in a silent cry.

"Give me one reason why I shouldn't punch some holes into you."

His jaw was quavering. Petrified with fear, he said, "I can tell you about Duffy."

I pulled back the hammer, keeping the barker level with his chest.

"Start talking," I said.

The Irishman blinked, clearly bewildered. He couldn't decide whether I was going to kill him or not. I couldn't either.

He decided to take a chance.

"I seen you at the club to-day. And the day before at the waterfront. The nigger floater, right? I was wonderin' how come we kept runnin' into each other."

"Me too."

"Well, if you think I know anything about the bludget you got another think comin'. I don't know anything about that."

"You tellin' me Duffy doesn't either?"

"I don't know what the boss knows and doesn't know."

"That won't do, McNamee. That won't do at all."

I leaned over and grabbed his suspenders.

"Get up."

He got to his feet, a little shaky.

"You're gonna do better for me, McNamee. I wanna know about you and Duffy. I wanna know about Chew and the swag and ikey mo and the coroner."

His eyes widened as he whispered, "You heard us today . . ."

"You bet. But no one's around to hear you now."

Then I kicked him into the open grave. The coffin creaked when his body fell on it. He was screaming now, cursing, "Get me out of here, damn it! What the hell do you think you're doing?"

I never could stand scamps like him swearing at me. I picked up the shovel, got a bit of dirt and let it dribble below. McNamee coughed and spat as the dirt spilled on his face.

"You get the picture now, friend? I got all night."

I shoveled some more dirt on him. Then he started screaming hysterically.

"Oh my God! Help! Get me out! Sweet Jesus!"

I was playing games with him, but he didn't know that. I wanted to see how far I had to push him before he broke.

I let some more dirt spill on him. Just enough to make him even more hysterical. He made quite a spectacle of himself. I thought of the way he laughed while he was stripping the woman's corpse. The memory didn't leave me with much compassion.

"Nighty night," I said, shoveling a load onto his legs.

That's what did it. He was bawling like a newborn now. I reached down and pulled him out of the grave. He didn't respond to my voice for a few minutes. I had to pour some whiskey down his gullet. After hacking on the stuff he got a little more lucid.

"I-I'll t-tell ya anything. Anything you want. I-I'll tell ya."

"Good. Tell me about the swag and who fences it."

McNamee answered me like a soldier with battle fatigue, wide-eyed and emotionless.

"Simon, Moses Simon. The ikey mo near the morgue. Runs a broom shop."

The store right next to the court where he met Chew that afternoon. No wonder it seemed like Chew had disappeared. He'd just stepped right into the back entrance of the broom shop and done his business with the fence. While I stumbled around like a lunkhead.

"What do you bring him? Where do you get the swag from?"

"The things."

"What do you mean, things?"

He pointed to the body of the woman lying on the ground.

"That's what you call them. Things?"

I pushed him toward the corpse and said, "Put those clothes back on her. And keep talking."

His thick fingers quivered while they redressed the body in its cerements.

I said, "You scavenged booty from corpses?" I was beyond disgust by now.

"Yeah. Any time the coroner found a corpse of a stranger, see. He and I checked the pockets. Whatever we got . . . if it wasn't stolen already . . . we took. Fobs, chains, clips, pins, rings. The clothes too. We'd empty the pockets and take the clothes off at the morgue. Then I'd get sent to fence the stuff. We'd been doing that since the last election. Up until a couple months ago."

"Then what happened?"

"One night at a club meeting I started talking to Grand Master Duffy. He knew all about me. It gave me the creeps. Knew where I lived, how many kids I had, where my favorite saloon was, and where I worked. And he knew all about the business with Coroner Brown. 'Cept now he said he was . . . how'd he call it? . . . mergin' his business with the coroner's. From now on I'd be takin' the money from the swag to him. So then he says to me, 'How'd you like to make some extra money?' And I said, 'Who wouldn't?' So he says, 'I want you to meet this fella named Chew, the digger at Lebanon Cemetery at such and such a time in front of the main entrance.' He told me to bring my wagon.''

He rubbed the part of his head where Chew's shovel had landed. Then he went on.

''Course Duffy didn't tell me this Chew was a nigger. Or I'da had nothin' to do with him. I couldn't believe the Grand Master would either. But there he was waitin' for me when I pulled up. He took me to a fresh grave and showed me what to do. Chew'd been the digger at this place for years, he told me, and packed the earth real loose on purpose so we could get the things out quicker. When we got the thing out we took it to this place Duffy knew about in the Seventh Ward, this tiny warehouse, and put it on ice. Then Chew gave me some money and I went home.''

''Why'd Duffy bring you in on it if Chew was already on the job?''

''I don't know. He said we could snatch more in a night this way. He was right. But I think he also wanted me to keep an eye on Chew. Didn't trust him too good.''

''How come?''

I wasn't about to tell McNamee what I knew, that Levi Chew was Duffy's stool pigeon. Let him tell me that, I thought.

It turned out he had more interesting things to say.

''He found out Chew lost a lot of money at a craps game. One goin' on in some dive in St. Giles. Duffy knows everything that's goin' on in every inch of that ward, I tell ya. He got to wonderin' how Chew would get all that extra money. 'Cause he wasn't exactly pulling in the pieces digging at Lebanon Cemetery.''

McNamee looked over his shoulder, like he was expecting somebody to be there. The only company we had were mice scurrying beneath the thin canopy of leaves.

"How come you and Chew were at the fencing crib to-day?"

"You heard Duffy, didn't ya? He just wanted the two of us there to confuse anybody watching. That was all. He's been gettin' edgy lately. He thinks somebody's out to get him."

So he knew I was getting close to nailing him. After he discovered his headquarters had been ransacked there would be no room for doubt.

"Duffy didn't want the ikey mo getting wise either. So we alternated goin' in. That way he wouldn't get the idea we were connected or nothing."

"When was the last time you saw the fence?"

"This morning. I had some stuff the cornoner wanted me to get rid of. Something queer happened when I got to the broom shop though."

"What do you mean, queer?"

"The Jew told me I scared one of his customers off. He made such a big fuss over it. I wondered how come the darky was scared of me . . ."

"A darky?"

"Yeah. The Jew said I scared off some darky bringing around these jewels that his cat liked. He's a little loose in the head. Talks to his cat like it was a person."

I was about to interrupt McNamee's prattling when he said something that took the breath out of me.

"Simon didn't even talk to me. Just to that cat of his. About how this darky had brought in a lace pin that looked just like Bruno—that's his cat, see—and I came in and scared 'em off before Simon had a chance to buy the damn stuff. Gave me hell for something I didn't even know I done. I . . ."

"Shut up," I told him.

I had to think. It didn't take me long.

"You didn't see this negro person, did you?"

"No, sir."

"And they didn't want to be seen by you, right?"

"Uh huh."

I was pretty sure the fence's customer was Levi Chew, trying to get rid of the lace pin in the shape of a cat. Just like the one I'd found in Duffy's headquarters that evening.

Josephine Martin's lace pin.

And I'd let Chew get away.

I clenched my fists and shook them impotently.

"Tell me the rest of it," I said, through gritted teeth.

"Ain't nothin' left to tell. We were supposed to meet up with Duffy to-night at the warehouse."

"Where?"

"Plume Street."

"That back court runnin' out of Barley Street? Between Tenth and Eleventh, south of Pine?"

"That's the one."

"Where were the corpses gonna go, McNamee?"

"I don't know about that."

It was the first negative answer he'd given me in a while. I didn't like that.

"I think you do."

"No, I swear. Chew's been taking care of that."

"But I think you got an idea."

"I'm tellin' ya! I swear I don't know. I never delivered the things. That was always Chew's job."

"Why?"

"Duffy didn't think it would be a good idea, with the doctors knowin' me from the morgue and all. He was afraid Brown might find out about it and want a cut."

"I don't like that. Tell me something else."

I stayed where I was on the tombstone but got my revolver out again, just to remind him.

"I ain't lied to you yet. I ain't doin' it now. Alls I know is there's a good chance they're gonna go where most of the others went."

"Where, damnit?"

The shot went off with a thunderous noise.

McNamee fell to the ground, a gaping wound in his chest.

There was a rustling sound to my side.

A hand was creeping out from under the tarpaulin. It held a gun. Strunk must've kept the weapon concealed under his blue coat. A thin blue finger of smoke curled out of the barrel.

I wondered how long the reserve bull had been listening. Long enough to decide McNamee was better off dead.

We held our guns at each other for a few seconds.

My thumb and index finger were quicker than his.

Uriah Strunk's dead hand slumped against the mouth of the open grave. I stood staring at it for a few moments while I planned how I could extricate myself from this mess. Then I pulled Strunk out from under the tarpaulin and hauled Frank McNamee's corpse closer to the reserve bull. I arranged the bodies so it looked as if they'd both struggled for possession of the revolver and wound up shooting each other. It was a far from likely story but it was the best I could come up with at the time. Killing a man hadn't done much good to my nerves.

I was feeling sick when I hopped the fence and headed toward the nearest station-house. Before I got there I made sure to stash my barker behind a monument.

It took practically the whole night before I could go home. I had to explain why a copper was dead. Strunk, I said, must've caught the grave robber dead to rights. I'd been in the neighborhood and heard the shots. When I found them they were both dead. The coppers seemed satisfied with my story, after I told it to them about seven or eight times. They recognized Strunk and knew he was one of Duffy's pals. After that they seemed more than willing to let the matter go till the morning. Nobody wanted to look into Duffy's business too closely. I left after telling them where I lived.

I knew it wouldn't be a good idea for me to return to my house on Porter Street. It probably wouldn't be safe for a while. Not when it was in Duffy's black memorandum book.

After retrieving my barker I decided to make my way to Twelfth and Pine.

There were no lights on in the parlor when I lightly tapped against the door. She was waiting up for me. Before I knew it I was in Arabella's room.

I told her what happened while I shivered. Killing a man was not something I took lightly. After a time, when she was caressing my hair, I started to weep. I felt evil. She told me I wasn't. She told me I was everything they weren't. I wasn't so sure.

I thought on sweating McNamee. It had been more like torture. Not of the body but of the mind. It was one of the ugliest parts of policework and I'd made it ten times uglier that night. I tried to justify it by saying his crimes were the vilest kind. But I'd let their violence and their evil take me over, sweep me up. For a short time I'd been just as evil as they were, maybe worse. Because I knew better.

I kept weeping and Arabella put her lips to my eyes and kissed the tears.

Then she stepped behind some blinds. It only took her a few moments. When she emerged, we embraced. In the darkness I couldn't see her flesh, but it felt warm against mine.

23

I WOKE UP suddenly. There was a sound like a gunshot. Then I heard a voice say, "You're my prisoner now."

My eyes blinked sleepily. I saw Arabella holding a tray in front of me. She must have just slammed the door shut.

"Don't make a lot of noise. Nobody knows you're here. Mrs. Scales told me up front this wasn't the kind of place for a lady to have assignations."

I sat up in her bed. Sunlight streamed from the double windows overlooking Pine Street. It was so bright I had to squint.

Then I smelled what was on the tray. I inhaled deeply.

"What's all this?" I asked her.

"I beat Mrs. Scales to the kitchen and fixed you a real breakfast."

She deposited the tray in my lap and sat down beside me, ruffling my hair.

"A meal for the condemned man," she said with a smile.

"Condemned to what?" I said.

Her hand rested beside me on the edge of the bed. There was a slightly uncomfortable formality between us, a gulf that hadn't existed the night before. We were waiting to see how the other would react to what had happened.

205

At first I hesitated to touch her. I still had a chance to pretend that the previous night was a hallucination or a mistake.

For a moment I glanced about her small room. There were a few decorations on the vermilion-papered walls, mostly engravings of old Italian paintings. On the shelves and tabletops were several books. Most were her textbooks: *Agnew's Dissector*, *Taylor's Toxicology*, *Human Physiology*, and the like. A few were French titles by someone named Zoya. I'd never heard of him. Another large tome said *Origin of Species*. That sounded familiar but I couldn't quite remember where I'd seen it.

After a strained minute or two I took her dark hand and turned it over. I was fascinated by the contrasting shades of pigment. I tried to find the exact point at which one color changed to the other. Then I held her palm to my lips and kissed it.

She said, "You really are a condemned man, you know. Condemned to put up with me." Then she added, more softly, "If you want."

I pulled her to me. When I kissed her I wasn't thinking about her being colored.

Arabella looked melancholy as she stroked my mustache into place. Then, as if to snap herself out of it, she said, "You better eat your breakfast while it's hot!"

On the tray was the kind of breakfast a prosperous man expects in the morning: oatmeal, lamb chops, hot biscuits with marmalade, baked beans and stewed potatoes, an omelette, and coffee to wash it all down.

It took me thirty minutes to eat it all. The whole time she watched me eat with the simple joy a child takes in feeding a puppy.

After giving my mustache a last wiping, she whisked the tray away and said, "I guess you'll be wanting to wash up."

She pulled her blinds over to the wash stand and beckoned me.

In another ten minutes I stepped out of the little tub a

the base of the stand. I wiped the soapy water off me with a clean linen and put on my suit from yesterday. Fortunately the fracas in the cemetery hadn't soiled it.

When I was adjusting my necktie I asked Arabella, "What did you mean by saying I was your prisoner?"

Looking up at me from her rocker she merely smiled. Patting a chair beside her, she said, "Come sit down."

I did. Then she said, "I have a stereoscope if you want to look at some pictures. Right there on the table, behind the plant."

The stereographs were piled high on the little table. I flipped through them. They were scenes of Africa, Asia, our Western Territories, and other exotic places. But I wasn't interested in looking at pictures.

"Don't even think of getting out of that seat, Wilton. You are spending the day with this young lady. You are not going to engage in any police work. We are going to stay here, in this room, all day long and pretend that the outside world doesn't exist. How does that sound?"

"Capital." I was about to say I should report to the Central Office. Then I remembered I had this Sabbath off.

Chew would find out that McNamee was dead, but I didn't think that would change anything. They didn't realize I knew where the warehouse was. I wanted to keep them in the dark until the time was right.

The fence could wait until later.

The case was knotting my shoulders and neck with tension. I needed a day to relax and forget about it. Monday, the day before the election, I would go to Mulholland with everything I knew.

Even if it wasn't the best idea, I decided to forget about police work and do just what Arabella said. I was in a room with a beautiful woman who wanted me as much as I wanted her. The disapprobrious eyes of the outside world could not see us now. Neither could my own inner eye, the one that before last night made me feel uncomfortable with my feelings for her. I had extinguished the light of that eye. Now I was content to share this new-found darkness with Arabella.

That darkness was beautiful. Her darkness.

Recognizing and admitting that fact was a great relief.

I put those thoughts into different, more clumsy words. They were enough to make her embrace me. Her grip was strong.

We broke away from each other and I took a deep breath.

"Do you really think I'm beautiful?" she asked suddenly.

"Of course I do."

"You're quite sure?"

"Yes."

"You . . . you don't think of this when . . . you look at me? Do you?"

She opened the book she was reading. The spine said Glott and Niddon, *Types of Mankind*. On the front page I read the date: 1854.

"Don't be fooled by the date. This is still used in academic circles."

Then she showed me an illustration.

The point of the picture was to prove the similarities between negroes and different kinds of monkeys.

There was a portrait of a Hottentot with lips and brow grotesquely distorted. Above it was an animal called an ourang-outang that looked more like a gargoyle than an ape. The jaw stuck straight out from its face at an impossible angle. The two portraits were made to look similar.

"Is that what an ourang-outang really looks like?" I said.

"I've only seen one when I was in France. And I've never seen a Hottentot. But I don't think the drawings are too accurate."

Then she showed me another picture of a gorilla and an African. The two pictures didn't look alike at all. But because they were on the same page, it was easy to draw conclusions.

"Is that what you see when you look at me, Wilton?"

"This is garbage, Arabella. The same kind I heard at Duffy's club yesterday."

"This book wasn't written by a bunch of shanty Irish hooligans, Wilton. The authors were two of the most respected scientists of their day."

"You say they still use this textbook?"

"Oh yes. I'm afraid so."

"Well, to hell with them."

I slammed the book shut and flung it across the room.

"Let's forget about them," I said, gesturing to the street outside. "Like you said. Okay?"

The melancholy drained from her face as she nodded.

With a spry step the girl walked over to a trunk at the foot of her bed. Opening it, she lifted out some books and albums.

"Would you care to look at these?" she said.

Not knowing what they were, I nevertheless said, "All right."

They were several albums of pressed flowers she'd arranged into different designs.

"Quite artistic. Awful pretty, these."

"Thank you. A little hobby of mine. I see so many ugly things every day. Now and then I like to touch and see pretty things."

"I know how you feel."

"Yes. You probably do. I can imagine what it must be like for you, being surrounded by the lowest kinds of people every day. Mired in their filth. And all the time no one wants to hear about it or think about it. No one cares about the sacrifice that you're making for them."

"That's right," I said slowly, amazed at her insight. "That's exactly how it is."

"I know. My experience is somewhat similar."

She stood up and went to the window. With her back turned to me she said, "Look at them out there on Pine Street. A sea of colored humanity. Some representative ones, like they call them here. From good families with respectable careers like theology or catering."

I turned my chair around and watched her elegant form. She was holding herself too erect, bristling with tension.

"But no one thinks of them when they envision the negro race. Instead they picture the Hurst Street whores and their gambling bullies, the illiterate slum dwellers, breeding incessantly, living and dying in squalor."

It was almost frightening to see the sudden change come over her. She seethed with anger and resentment.

"When I first came to this country I wanted to help them. I saw the horrible, degrading conditions in which they lived. And I wanted to change it somehow. That's what my father had wanted me to do. I used to hear horrible stories from him about America. I wanted to alleviate the suffering of my people here. I had a lot of dreams."

She sighed and turned away from the view.

"I was here just a few months when I realized the truth. It came to me slowly. The men and women I spoke to were suspicious of me and my education. They called me a white girl in a black girl's body. I was snubbed on the street. Never invited for visits. And only approached by the kind of men who, hearing I was from France, thought I was the same sort of girl as the streetwalkers they habitually patronized."

Leaning against the sill, she regarded me fiercely.

"You know what I found out? They didn't care for my help or my compassion! They shunned me like the cholera. I couldn't understand why. I never sought to make them feel inadequate or different from me. I just tried to be the person that I was. But I was different from them, Wilton."

"How?"

Arabella looked away and said, "I knew I was no different from people like you, Wilton. White people. They"—she gestured to the crowd on the street—"think differently."

"I don't understand."

"They don't either. They've been hoodwinked for too long. All they do is concentrate on insignificant physical disparaties."

"What's all that mean?"

"It means, Wilton, that you and I understand something that is beyond the grasp of most people, white or colored. We understand that the differences between human beings do not lie in color but in the psyche."

I didn't understand that last word.

"The mind," Arabella said. She began strutting about the room in her elegant mourning dress. I felt like a college freshman at an introductory lecture. I marveled at her eloquence.

"The mind," she repeated. "That alone is the sole arbiter of human types. One intelligent mind can join with another no matter what color they are. Just like we have done."

"I never thought my mind was that intelligent."

"But it is, Wilton! I would never have been attracted to you if it weren't."

Stopping in mid-stride, she said, "Have you ever heard of Herbert Spencer?"

"No."

"He's a proponent of Darwin's theory of evolution. But he applies it to social principles."

"I think I heard of that Darwin. Isn't he the one who says we descended from monkeys? And that there was no creation by God? A bunch of hogwash, if you ask me."

Arabella shook her head impatiently and smirked.

"I won't get into an argument with you. But I think if you study human nature as I know you have to do, then you'll see that Spencer at least has a lot of valid points."

"Like what?"

I was enjoying our intellectual conversation. I couldn't remember the last time I'd had any kind of chat with a respectable person that didn't have to do with something dirty. It felt like a gag had been untied from my brain. All of a sudden it could breathe and speak again.

"We're a part of the animal kingdom. The dictum of life in the natural world is that it is, as Spencer says, a 'survival of the fittest.' "

"That's an interesting phrase. I'll have to remember that one."

It certainly seemed to apply to the streets—to America in general. Some fellows in the oil refinery and steel business could attest to that.

"Survival of the fittest," Arabella repeated, emphasizing the last word. "Who do you think they are?"

"I don't know. The strongest? Might is right and all that kind of thing?"

With a look of disappointment she said, "Not at all, Wilton. Physical strength is insignificant when weighed against intelligence and imagination. Mere strength doesn't make a man a leader, does it?"

"Sometimes."

"Are they ever true leaders? The ones with vision? Was President Lincoln a brawny Samson? Or Christ?"

"I guess not."

"The fittest, the ones who will, who must survive, are the leaders, the creators, the discoverers. The ones with the intellect to transcend savagery and attain the next evolutionary stage."

"I'm lost, Arabella. What are you talking about?"

"I'm talking about the future of the human race, Wilton. Don't you ever wonder what we will be like in a hundred or a thousand years?"

"Every once in a while. But it makes me melancholy."

"Ah! Because you don't expect good things from mankind."

She turned again to the window and said, "Why should you when that is your raw material?"

I stood up and walked to her side. Looking below I saw the typical shoppers, vendors, wagon drivers, and gangs of street arabs scampering across the slightly filthy pavements.

"The discovery I made was that though I may be the

same color as they, I am not one of them. I belong to a group of humans of all colors who alone possess the key to the future.''

Stroking her long, intricately curled hair, I let her talk, realizing how pretty her voice was. Her sincerity and intellectual passion were inspiring.

"Without people like us, men and women of the mind, the whole human race is doomed. We are the only ones who can draw mankind out of the quagmire.''

"That seems a little extreme. Surely there are folks who are less than intellectual but who have things to contribute?''

"We're talking about a survival of the fittest. With war after war mankind is doing nothing but proving its unfitness.''

"You can't take the violence out of people. I think it's our nature.''

I knew it was in my nature. I needed it to stay alive. But it was a part that I hated and feared as well.

"I disagree, Wilton. It was an evolutionary adaptation for survival that has turned on itself and become destructive. Think of the war in which you fought. I can't think of a greater, more efficient slaughter of men. Do you think warfare will stop its march of progress? I think not. Sooner or later men will invent weapons to destroy not only regiments but whole cities, maybe even whole countries. And what causes those wars? Greed and hate. Hate for those who are different from you and a need to possess what they have.''

It was a pretty accurate picture, as far as I was concerned.

"Stop talking. I'll feel less like a hero.''

"The real heroes are those who are thinking of the future of mankind. The ones with the vision to create and not destroy. Don't look that way, Wilton. I didn't mean to imply you were part of the latter. You're a creator in your own way. A person with the vision to see past racial differences and peer into the bond that unites those of us who are the future.''

"What about those of us who aren't the future?"

"When I first came to this country I wanted so much to help them make their life better. But they didn't want to help me help them, Wilton. Do you understand? They wanted it all handed to them on a silver platter. They were like cattle, looking for someone to fatten them up and provide them with shelter. They don't possess the brain-power to act, to search, to create. There they go," she said, watching the crowds below with contempt. "They remind me of parasites. Dragging down those of us who want to help them. And don't think for a moment I mean just the negroes. For every one negro like that there are twenty whites. Unimaginative brutes whose mental lives revolve around the saloon. They're a different breed from you and me. A breed on its way to extinction."

I was a little shocked by her spite toward these plain old people. I always thought I was just like them, except I read a few more books and had a better-paying job.

It seemed queer that a woman like Arabella, a colored woman, could see them in such a cold way. The words felt like they were coming from someone else's mouth.

"They are something to be overcome, Wilton. They provide the fodder for racial hate and warfare and the demagogues who instigate both. They threaten the survival of mankind."

Her fists were clenched on the window sill. I didn't think she was looking at the crowds any longer. She was peering into a very intense vision which seemed to be her driving force.

"I think the time is drawing near for those of us fit to survive to do just that."

"You sound like some kind of revolutionary. You're not going to toss a bomb around anywhere, are you?"

My jest didn't break her somber mood. She took her hands and placed them on my cheeks.

"I told you that you were condemned to put up with

me. This is how I am, Wilton. A schoolmarmish intellectual. I wanted to tell you exactly how I feel, what's important to me. Because I thought you'd understand.''

Then she kissed me, hard and passionately. We pulled away from each other, breathless.

"I'm frightened of you," she said, burying her face in my chest. "You make me feel very weak. I have to be strong."

"You really want to change the world, don't you?"

Her naïvete and earnestness stunned me.

"Yes, I do."

"Where'd you get all these ideas?"

"You see that pile of books? Some are in English, others French, others German. I have my teachers here in this country as well."

It was hard to suppress the jealousy suddenly welling up in me.

"Teachers like Dr. Forbes?"

"Yes. He's really the one who opened up my eyes. I learned about Spencer from him. And Darwin and other pioneers. With Dr. Forbes I've learned so much. The work in which we're engaged is so vital. I wish I could tell you about it. I want you to know."

"Why don't you?"

"Dr. Forbes wants it a secret until we can publish the results of our experiments."

"You really admire him, don't you?"

"He's a genius, Wilton. One of the greatest scientific minds of our age. If only he'd publish some of his papers. The ones that didn't deal with mere anatomy. Then he would be accepted for the genius that he is. I am so privileged to be working with him. He's everything I said about the new breed of man. It was Forbes who took me in when my white classmates and negro brethren turned me away. It was he who made me feel like I was worth something. That I had something very special to contribute. I . . . am very grateful for that."

Arabella seemed so lonely. Her monologue came out

in a fury. Like she was marooned on a tropical isle and was talking to the first human she'd seen in decades.

I was sure I couldn't possibly understand how hard it must be for her. No one wanted her to succeed, for different reasons. Her vision of the future was similar to many I'd heard at lecture halls and on streetcorners. It made her feel important when nobody else would. If that was what gave her the will to go on, so be it.

The weight of her loneliness came down on me too. I wanted to lift that burden from her, for just a little while. And I wanted her to forget about Dr. William Forbes for at least an afternoon and think about me.

I said, "Let's go out to Laurel Hill and have a pic-nic. What do you say?"

It took a few moments for her brow to unfurl. Then she laughed and said, "We'll make a shocking sight. But I'd love to go."

"Let's go cause a scandal, then."

24

LAUREL HILL WAS the grandest cemetery in Philadelphia. On the eastern bank of the Schuylkill, its extensive grounds were covered with marble and granite shafts, stones, and mausoleums. I always thought it looked more like an abandoned city than a burial place.

We went through the Ridge Avenue entrance, passing under a building of brown stone with a corridor of columns like a Greek temple.

It was a big enough place for two people to lose themselves. We did just that.

The cemetery was divided into north, south, and central sections. We chose the northernmost part, hoping to avoid the Sabbath-day crowds.

We were lucky. There were few people about and none noticed the peculiar couple we made. Otherwise we might've been arrested for walking together in public.

On the streetcar there we'd got a few stares when Arabella asked me to hold her hand. I felt uncomfortable displaying my affection like that. I would have felt the same with a white girl. She told me to stop being stuffy, that we'd never see these people again. So we held hands like any other young couple.

Arabella and I had both decided without saying anything that we would behave normally this day. Her being colored and my being white would not make a difference in anything we said or did.

The easiest way to do that was to hide in this beautiful cemetery and shut out the rest of the world.

A chrysanthemum bush drew my eye after we'd walked around silently between the monuments. It was growing beside a set of tiny marble steps leading down an embankment. A large monument of a half-naked woman leaning on an urn stood nearby. A low wall stretched around the monument and down the embankment. It gave us partial cover from anyone else out on a stroll.

The sun was warm that midday. We basked in the light and heat. There was no talking. It was enough to be together, to hold her hand and watch her look at the flowers, the clouds skirting across the sky, the swarms of gnats swirling frantically.

To-day she wore no mourning dress. Instead she had on a gaily colored suit trimmed with yak-lace. Her skirt had three rows of lace flouncing which seemed to float like dandelion puffs over the ground. Ribbon bows, looped at her waist, accentuated the elegant bustle. On the left side of her jersey she'd pinned a bouquet of mums.

Arabella had never seemed so lovely as she was now. The light colored material of her suit offset her flawless, dark skin. Her lovely face was tucked daintily beneath a hat full of ribbons, bows, and dried flowers. I tried to restrain myself from kissing that face. I didn't try too hard.

Finally I said, "It's nice to get away, isn't it? To shut out everything and forget."

This time she was silent, waiting for me to say more. Now I was in the mood to talk.

"Like your dried flowers. I need to see pretty things too. I see enough ugliness."

I watched the clouds. I couldn't remember the last time I actually stopped to watch them move. It was amazing to see their motion. Like it was evidence of a secret world suddenly made visible.

Arabella put her hand on my shoulder and said, "I understand what it's like to be completely devoted to your work. What I can't understand is how you bear the work that you do."

"Police work? It's not that bad. Most of the time it's pretty boring, actually. I spend a lot of time standing guard at parades and baseball games. I roust dipsomaniacs and pickpockets off the street. And I keep corner loungers from loitering and annoying passersby. That's what most of my job entails. I haven't had to direct traffic more than a dozen times, thank heaven. Really sort of dull. But you get to meet lots of different people. And arrest them," I said with a smile.

"That's what I don't understand. How you can bear to deal with the dregs of humanity day after day?"

"You did it yourself, didn't you? Why'd you volunteer at the Magdalen Society? I thought you told me you'd given up on people like that a year ago."

She took a while to answer me, carefully preparing what she would say.

"I guess I never give up hope completely. I wanted to help them somehow. But it was the same with them as with the other lower sorts of people. They didn't want my help. They were suspicious of me, of anyone who wasn't in their 'sisterhood.' 'You don't understand what we is goin' through.' I used to hear that from them all the time. After a while I realized they were right and that I didn't *want* to understand."

"I know how you feel."

"Do you? From what I see you want to understand, to care. Why else would you worry about the disappearance of some colored prostitutes?"

It wasn't quite a rhetorical question. She was expecting a real answer.

I had to laugh. "You said we weren't going to discuss my police work to-day."

"But I want to know, Wilton. I want to know why you bothered with a case like that."

"What with them being whores and all that?"

"No. Why with colored women? And why with me? How is it that a policeman like you could care so little about color differences?"

I got the feeling she was testing me. The truth would have to satisfy her.

"I was the same as anybody else I guess. My mother subscribed to an abolitionist newspaper and maybe she influenced me. But I never thought I would have anything to say to a negro. Never really thought about them at all. Even in the war, when I was fighting for them, I didn't feel like we had anything in common. I was like a lot of people. I pretended they didn't exist, weren't important."

I leaned forward. The marble steps were killing my back. Remembering the past was uncomfortable too.

But I wanted to tell this girl. It had been so long since anyone had cared to listen.

"Then I got captured and sent to prison. It was wretched, Arabella. You have no idea what it was like. We became like savages there. We had to. It was like you said, a survival of the fittest. Except no one gave a damn about you surviving. I watched men get killed for their buttons. There was a group of scamps, we called them Raiders, who beat up and robbed, even killed, whoever they wanted, mostly greenhorns. They terrified most everybody else. We were too weak and my mess was too few to fight against them. As long as they didn't bother us, we didn't bother with them. Well, one night I was lying in my tent. All I could think of was how much I wanted to die. I tried to come up with ways I could end my life. The only one I could think of that would surefire work was to cross the dead-line. I was all set to go hop over the wooden barrier and get shot down. Then I heard scuffling outside. Just out of curiosity I went to see what was going on. I saw a bunch of those Raiders. They were beating a negro from the colored side of the camp, which wasn't far from where we pitched our tents. They had him on the ground and were really laying into him. I don't think he had anything they wanted. They were just beating him for the sport of it.''

I stopped and said, ''Aren't you going to ask me why I just stood there watching?''

''You already told me you were frightened of the Raiders.''

''That's true. The boys also didn't care too much for the negroes. We didn't get any exchanges because of them. The Union was more interested in protesting the South's treatment of colored troops than in getting us back home, they said. So there was no love lost. Maybe that's why I just stood there for a while. I was no better than anybody else. And I was frightened.

''Then something happened to me. I felt like someone was watching me just like I was watching them. Like the whole sky was one gigantic eye raising a bead on me. I felt like that eye could see into my head and my heart. That scared me more than the Raiders ever could. Because I knew what it was seeing. That's what got me up. I ran to where they were beating the negro. I didn't give them any warning. I just leaped on one of them and broke his arm. The others attacked me but by that time I had a broken bottle in my hand. It cut them up pretty bad before they scattered like hares. I was left with a few bruises and cuts and a negro at my feet, beaten senseless. I carried him back to his company. They didn't thank me or anything. I didn't expect them too. He was okay and I was satisfied with that. Then I went back to my tent and stayed up thinking on the eye watching me.''

Suddenly I had to bite into my lower lip to keep the tears back. ''It saw something in me I'd buried beneath my self-pity and despair. When I felt it watching I resurrected it. For a few moments I wasn't thinking on myself or my own pain. I wanted to stop someone else's suffering. I don't think I ever thought of dying after that. I saw how much work there was for me to do.''

Arabella gave me a kiss and said, ''I'm glad I met you,

Wilton McCleary.'' Even though she was smiling, the words came out sounding sad.

I went back to looking at the clouds, trying to hide my embarassment. I was breaking down in tears too much in front of this girl. Arabella was the kind of person that made you feel that comfortable and safe. She also had a way of making you feel strong, of bringing the best impulses out in you.

''Nobody else gives a damn for them, Arabella. They might not be the best sort of people. They might even be parasites like you say. But they got a right to live. Duffy can't just go around killing them at his leisure.''

''You're so sure Duffy has killed them?''

''He's as dirty as a dung beetle. Those papers we found prove it.''

''Why would he do such a thing? Just out of pure hate?''

''Sure. People have done even worse and not even out of pure hatred. All I got to do is find that warehouse. I'll bet my bottom dollar a few of the disappeared women will be waiting there for me.''

''Warehouse? What are you talking about?''

''Didn't I tell you? McNamee told me where they stashed the corpses. On Plume Street.''

The girl's jaw hung slack. It was a grim thing to think about. Nevertheless her squeamishness surprised me. ''You all right?'' I said.

''Yes, yes. I'm sorry. What else did McNamee say?''

''After a little persuasion he told me about going to the fence yesterday. A Jew who usually handles the valuables from the corpses he and Chew snatch. Apparently a negro had been in earlier that day with the jewels we found last night in Duffy's headquarters.''

''Goldie's jewels?'' she asked, tremulously.

I shook my head.

''Not Goldie's. Though she had them at the time of her death. The jewels belong to a girl named Josephine Martin. She's on my list of disappeared women.''

Arabella repeated her name as if she were reading a black-edged telegram. She stared at the clouds above us and said, "Do you think this girl is dead?"

"I'd bet my bottom dollar on it."

Her head began to shake in denial. To what, I didn't know. She put a gloved finger to her eye and wiped someting away.

"It's all right, Arabella. I'm tightening the noose on Duffy's neck. Soon I'll give it a good pull. There's no escape for him. Trust me."

"No escape," she repeated softly.

Her mood was disturbing me. Perhaps, I thought, I'm being too grim, too cold and calculating.

I didn't want her to think of me like that.

It was probably better, I decided, to take her mind off Duffy's fate. I tried to subtly change the subject.

"Before that happens I still have some questions, though."

"What kind of questions?"

I didn't bother pointing out to her we were talking about my work again. She seemed genuinely interested. So I went on, happy to voice some doubts I had.

"Oh, just some loose ends. Things that don't quite seem to fit. Like what Goldie Collins was doing with rope burns on her wrists. Did you ever notice anything like that when you were tending her?"

With a look of genuine bewilderment, she answered, "No."

"I got the feeling her hands were tied for some reason before she was killed. I could never make any sense out of it. So I forgot about it. A little thing. But big things come from little things."

"Still . . . there's no question that Sergeant Duffy killed Goldie, is there?"

Arabella didn't seem too convinced, though she wanted to be. I could feel it in the way her hand clasped mine. Her gloved fingers tensed, as if she were waiting for an ugly revelation.

Surprisingly, my answer did nothing to relieve her tension.

"No. Nor is there any question that he brained me to get Josephine Martin's jewelry back. If only there was more proof. The body-snatching ledger doesn't convince me."

"Why?"

"The handwriting in it. I'm sure it's not Duffy's. The hand is too fine for thugs like McNamee or Chew. I thought maybe it could be the coroner's. But McNamee told me last night that Brown didn't know anything about the resurrectionist business. Otherwise he would've wanted a cut."

"He must have been lying, Wilton! Remember what the morgue attendant told you? That Brown and Duffy had conferred over Goldie's body that very night?"

"Curious, huh? I don't know if I like that story anymore."

"Doesn't it just fit in with everything else? That Duffy had a hand in Goldie's death? And maybe many others?"

I had to shake my head. "Yes, but not logically. It's like a jigsaw puzzle piece that fits with the others but has a different design on it. Ah!" I cried out, exasperated. "I don't know what to think. But I know he's guilty, Arabella. You should have heard him. Anyway we have the other papers. The ones that *are* in his handwriting. That's all we need."

My mind went over the events of last night. I voiced my thoughts aloud.

"Levi Chew. He's what ties everything together. I'm sure of that. The link between the morgue, Duffy, the fence, Goldie, Josephine Martin, your Dr. Forbes and all the other medical college professors. If I get my hands on him he'll make sense of the whole business for me, I know it. I almost had him last night. Well, the next time I catch him he won't be running off so fast. Yes, he and I will have a long talk. I'd like to know why he hit Frank McNamee with a shovel. I know there's no honor among thieves but . . . And I'd also like to know what he was doing in Duffy's headquarters.''

"I already told you that, Wilton. He wanted to help me take care of Duffy."

"Are you sure? What would have happened if I hadn't showed up?''

The girl did not answer.

"He might've killed you. He almost killed McNamee last night, I think because he was afraid the Irishman would talk too much. There's something dirtier there, Arabella. I can smell it. It started really stinking when I found out Levi Chew was the one with Josephine Martin's jewelry."

"Perhaps Duffy told him to take it to the fence so he wouldn't have to. That way the sergeant wouldn't be linked with the jewelry."

"That's pretty good," I said admiringly. "But Duffy would be more clever than that. He would know that I might've seen the jewels at the ragpicker's shack. Or at least heard about them. It would have made more sense to destroy them instead of trying to pawn them for a few bucks. All that did was put me on to him even more. If the jewels were worth killing for once, why would he make it so easy to trace them to a fence?''

I shook my head in exasperation. Arabella kept her eyes averted, her hand clenching my own.

"Ah, hell. It hasn't made any sense from the beginning. Why should it now? Anyway, what does that matter? They're guilty, anyway. Of plenty."

"Who isn't?" Arabella said, as if inadvertently voicing a secret truth.

Without paying much attention to her, I went on with my train of thought.

"Sooner or later it catches up with you . . ."

Just then a couple walked by us on the embankment, the woman's skirt brushing against the brown grass. There were so many bows and ribbons on her she looked like a Christmas package. Tipping her parasol to cover her face, she whispered something to her escort, who began ogling us shamelessly.

As they both clucked their tongues I stood up, bristling with rage. I snarled a curse at them and took a threatening step forward. The two fops went white as fresh linen and scurried away.

Arabella just laughed. As soon as their backs were to us, I started laughing too.

"Am I that threatening?"

"I think you underestimate yourself," Arabella said, still giggling. "You're a little imposing. You have some rough edges here and there."

"What's wrong with the way I look?" I said, a little hurt.

"Don't get upset! I didn't mean that at all. It's just you have a very . . . dynamic presence. Confident, assured of your authority, and a little violent. You're also very sensitive, very . . . gentle. But when you're provoked, well, it unleashes that rage in you."

I smiled and said, "I got a mean streak, that's for sure. I don't know why."

"You fought in a war. That would certainly cultivate the violent side of your nature."

"Maybe. Or it could be because I'm around violent people all day long."

"I don't know if your environment has to affect you like that. You could always choose to be different."

"Remember what you told me? Survival of the fittest. Some people don't have the chance to make those kinds of choices."

"Well, you have. I'm glad you choose to be who you are."

"Whatever that is."

"Whatever it is, I . . ."

Her sentence stopped short. I wanted to hear the rest, but I couldn't goad her into saying more. She just shook her head and smiled sadly.

"Never mind. The day is getting to me. So beautiful. Fall always makes me melancholy."

Disappointed, I sulked a bit before I went along with her conversation.

"Me too. Those gray clouds. Profound somehow."

"Yes. They remind me of time. Endlessly changing, endlessly moving."

"I like that."

"It scares me. It makes me feel very lonely."

"Well," I said, embracing her, "you're not lonely today."

Her arms reached across my body to hug my side. She clung to my arm.

"I wish so much . . ."

"What?" I said.

She waited a few moments before she spoke again.

"I wish I hadn't met you sometimes."

"Why?"

"Because I'm afraid of myself . . . being hurt, I mean. Or hurting someone else. I wish that we were in that new world I was telling you about before. Where you could choose exactly who you wanted to . . . love."

My heart leaped into my throat. I felt paralyzed. She'd said it.

I wasn't going to go back now. I said, "You *can* choose who you want to love. And I choose to love *you*, Arabella."

The words were barely a whisper. An onslaught of emotion passed over me like the clouds above, somber, beautiful, and mysterious. I buried my face in her dark hair, inhaling the scent of her lavender toilet water. It threw my senses into confusion.

"Remember what you said earlier, Wilton?" Arabella said. "Some people don't have the chance to make those kinds of choices."

Then she kissed me, pressing my lips against my teeth. It was a savage, violent kiss.

When we were finished she lightly touched my cheek

and said, "Take me home now, please. I'm suddenly frightened. I want to go somewhere safe and hide for a while."

"What are you frightened of? Not me?"

"No, Wilton. I'm frightened of myself. Now may we go? Please?"

Arabella said nothing to me on our trip back into the city. We stayed in each other's arms, even on the streetcar. It didn't matter anymore what people thought about us being together like that.

We remained locked in that desperate embrace till we got to her door. Wrenching herself from me she ran up the marble stairs and slammed the door shut. The sound of her weeping buried itself deep into me. I decided the only way to drown out the sound was to get back to work.

The day was coming to an end. As dusk fell, I made my way to a certain broom shop. I was aching with pain and wanted to lash out at something. Or someone. I hoped for his sake that Moses Simon would be in a talkative mood.

25

I WAS BACK on Dana Street well after nightfall. The front
windows of the broom shop were darkened but I didn't
let that stop me. I followed the narrow tunnel to the back
court where I lost Chew that morning. Then I began trying
doors.

The broom shop must've been pretty expansive. I
thought I was at least a whole building away from it when
one door opened for me.

Feeble light flickered from around a wall. In the room
beyond, someone was singing a discordant tune. He
reached a crescendo by the time I rounded the corner.
Then he called to someone I couldn't see, "Hey, Bruno!
Where you goin'? You don't like my song, huh?"

My boot landed on something alive, crouching in the
darkness. From the squeal of pain I knew it was a cat.

The animal darted into the room while the man told it
to shut up.

"You afraid of the cockroaches now, Bruno? Eh? Get
to work, you! Earn a living."

Then the man looked up from his counter and saw me.

He was a middle-sized man with a long grimy beard
and snarled hair spilling off the sides of his otherwise bald
head. His suspenders were stretched to the limit to keep
his pantaloons up against a fat belly. Overall, he looked

not unlike Thomas Nast's version of Saint Nick. But his eyes were anything but jolly. They watched me with a gaze that held sharpness and suspicion in it.

"Eh? Whatta you want? Closed. Come back t'morra."

He didn't even try to hide the objects on the counter from me. Aside from a large pile of baubles there were a lot of weapons there: knuckle dusters, maces probably scavenged from beaten-up coppers, a few seventy-five-cent revolvers, and an assortment of Arkansas toothpicks, Bowie knives the size of meat cleavers.

No wonder he wasn't looking too scared of me.

Bruno the cat took a graceful leap and landed on the counter. Nearly unsettling the kerosene lamp perched there, he began navigating his way around the arsenal. Simon stroked the cat's mottled head and kept watching me. With his free hand he made a grab for one of the dime store revolvers.

I said, "Don't get the wrong idea. I'm here on business. I got something you might be interested in."

Curiosity stayed his hand. He let me fish something out of my vest pocket. I put it on the counter and slid it over to him.

He looked at the copper badge and snorted.

"That's a cute trick. I never seen that one before. Hah."

"You're Simon, aren't you?"

"What's it to ya? You want a broom, I got brooms. You wanna make trouble, I make trouble. Now get lost."

Bruno spotted something on the floor, in the shadowy part of the store. He pounced quickly, clawing at whatever it was. In another moment he brought back his prize to the fence.

"A big fat one, Bruno! Hah. Good boy."

Simon said to the cat, confidingly, "I got a real big roach right here, Bruno. You wanna take care of him for me?"

"Is this how you treat a friend?"

That made him snort with laughter.

"Friend? No copper's my friend. Hah. He's a funny man, Bruno."

My patience was wearing thin but I tried to keep it under control. I was tired of violence, at least for now. Simon was the kind of character who needed the soft touch. He was very gentle with the cat. I didn't think he would use any of those weapons on me.

"I don't think that's true, Simon. I know for a fact you're very good friends with a certain policeman by the name of Duffy. Who happens to be a friend of mine too."

"Duffy? Never heard of him."

I couldn't tell whether he was lying or not.

Those doubts I had at Laurel Hill were creeping up again.

"Listen, Simon. I got no beef with you. I don't care what you're buying or selling here. Or who you're buying or selling from. Except for one person."

Which wasn't exactly true. I didn't like to see so many weapons lying around. Especially ones that looked like they were stolen from police officers. Now that I knew where Simon was, I'd have to check up on him to cause trouble. But there was no need to let him know that right now.

"I don't know nobody. I sell brooms. You want a broom, I got brooms. But we're closed now. Right, Bruno? Hah."

I edged over to the desk and sat down on a corner, like Simon and I were old pals. Then I said, "Let me refresh your memory. There's a fella named Frank McNamee who sells to you now and then. Jewelry, clothes, that sort of thing. I hear the two of you do a pretty brisk business together."

There was no expression from the fence. Simon held Bruno so tightly the cat started struggling to get out of his grasp.

"He's growing roses now. A copper shot him last night in a cemetery where he was robbing bodies from their graves."

Simon shook his head and said something in a language I didn't understand. He was losing color steadily.

"I happened to be there too. I didn't shoot him. We just talked for a while. You wanna guess what we talked about?"

"That goddamn mick peached, eh? Hah. Oh, Bruno. This is bad. Very bad."

Simon tucked the cat under his chin.

I nodded and said, "He peached all right. I didn't get the chance to pinch him. But you'll do instead, I guess."

He held the cat to him like a mother protecting her child.

"No. Please. I ain't done nothin' wrong. This man bring me this, bring me that. I don't ask where it come from. Hah. I get all kinds here, mister. No. Don't pinch me. I got Bruno to take care of. What'll happen to him if I go inside?"

"That isn't my look-out. I got you pegged, Simon. You and the coroner and McNamee looted bodies like ghouls. That won't win you much sympathy. Even those weapons are enough to put you in the chokey for at least half a year."

"I bought 'em myself! They're for my own personal protection!"

All the swagger was gone now. He was just a tired and slightly addled old man.

"Look!" he said, flinging some greenbacks at me. "Look! Eighty-eight dollars! All for you! Just go 'way and leave me and Bruno alone!"

I knew a lot of fences. Some were fairly important and rich, doing business with York guns and grafters, moving goods from all over the Republic. Others were just prosperous shopkeepers who still had some pull with the coppers.

Simon was just an old man on the verge of dementia, with an animal for his only friend.

His meager attempt at bribery made me feel ashamed of myself.

"I don't want your money. Let's say we trade. You give me some information and I let you and Bruno enjoy the eighty-eight dollars in peace. Deal?"

"Okay, okay. Bruno, that sound good to you?"

The cat eyed me impassively.

"First off, I want a straight answer from you. Do you know a Sergeant Walter Duffy or not?"

"No. I swear on little Bruno's head here. I never heard of him. I know a Sergeant Wallis."

"Who's he?"

"The one I gotta pay off every month! Ain't that right, Bruno? Hah. He's no good, that copper. Barely make enough to keep Bruno in style."

The fence stroked Bruno's neck and smiled sadly, his face creased with years of oppressive loneliness.

I supposed it made sense he didn't know Duffy. The sergeant would always use a go-between to protect himself.

"What about Levi Chew? You know him?"

"Huh? What kinda name is that?"

"He's a negro." I described him to Simon.

"Yeah! We know him, eh Bruno? Been seein' him around a lot lately."

"How often?" I said, nearly stuttering with excitement.

"Oh three or four times these past two months."

"What kind of things does he bring in?"

"The usual stuff. Lots of clothes. Plenty of people around here who buy clothes secondhand. Got a need for that here. Lace pins, bangles, rings, leathers, combs, that kinda thing."

"You have any of that stuff still around?"

"Ah, no. Goes quick, don't it, Bruno? Hah. Lots of ladies around here, like pretty things. They want lace pins and leathers, I got lace pins and leathers. They want combs, I got combs."

"What about a lace pin, an earring, and a ring?"

I described Josephine Martin's jewelry to him.

"Did Chew bring that in, too?"

Simon stroked his cat's head. His brow stayed furrowed for a few moments.

"You didn't buy them, remember? You asked for too much."

That got a reaction from him.

"Who said that, eh? That no-good mick? Hah. He got some nerve, Bruno. I gave her good price."

I lost my ability to talk for quite some time. Finally I managed to exclaim, "Her?"

"That's right. Nigger gal. She liked Bruno, didn't she, boy? You liked her too. Nice lady."

"If you gave her a good price, why didn't she give you the jewels?"

"Good price, bad price. She don't care about price. She just wants to get rid of the stuff. Get it? I know this kind. Hah."

"She wanted to get rid of the jewels and she still didn't sell them to you?"

"No. That stupid mick came in just then."

"McNamee?"

"Yeah. He came in just then. She seen him before he saw her. We thought she was gonna drop dead. Right, Bruno? She walked out right quick with the stuff. And I didn't see her again. Too bad, eh, boy? Nice lady."

My head ached with a vengeance. I thought I'd had it all nice and simple.

Chew hadn't brought in Josephine Martin's possessions after all. I'd just made that assumption. Frank McNamee had never got around to mentioning the sex of the person. He might have if I hadn't interrupted him and let him get shot.

"This negress. Was she a fat gal? Really dark? With gold teeth? Scar on her right index finger?"

"No! No! This was nice gal. Pretty gal. Right, Bruno? I felt sorry for her, she was so pretty. And mourning too. Not too dark. Sorta in-between. Talked like a white gal, high-class. Nice gal."

I had to get out of there. I couldn't breathe all of a sudden.

I remembered that open grave from the night before. All I could think now was how much I wanted to be in it. To sleep and forget all about the description the fence gave me of the woman who tried to sell off Josephine Martin's jewelry. The woman who would know about her disappearance and the others.

The woman who was linked to Duffy, Chew, McNamee, and three ugly murders. Maybe more.

Arabella Cole.

26

AFTER I LEFT the fence I walked to my house. The distance was about two and a half miles. The streets were practically empty. It was a cold night, with the wind bracing to rip the leaves right off their branches I tried to calm myself by staring at the sky. Above I saw the moon surrounded by a halo-like nimbus. It drowned out the light of the other stars. There were some clouds encircling it like a spectral claw. It didn't take them long to blot out its light.

My own thoughts weren't very sanguine either.

The whole way I was thinking of one thing. And trying not to think of it at the same time.

There has to be a reasonable explanation, I thought.

Of course I must've known all the time that she was somehow involved. Why would Chew lead her right to Duffy's headquarters? And why would Duffy have been so interested in her? Just because she was poking her nose around, trying to find information about Goldie?

The fence had never said the person who tried to sell Josephine's belongings was a male or female. McNamee jumped to conclusions. So had I.

How many other times had I done the same thing during this investigation? How many times had I refused to see something that was right in front of me?

And yet, the information still didn't change the basic fact that Duffy killed those women. The ragpicker said he did it. Duffy was there that night to club me over the head and take the jewels back, leaving them in his headquarters. Of course he was the one who brained me. That explained why he, of all the coppers in the city, should show up there.

There was William Forbes's testimony as well. At least I could prove, through him, that Duffy was forcing the medical doctors to accept his stolen cadavers.

Finally there were the threats Duffy made to me and to Arabella. Hardly the behavior of an innocent party.

The more I thought on it, I realized how little I had after all the poking and prodding I'd done. Just some suspicion and hearsay. But suspicion would be enough. Duffy would have to give an account of himself. That would be sufficient for an indictment of some kind. It would make Heins and the Republicans happy.

There was still Heins to worry about. He wanted Duffy out of the way, no matter what it took. Duffy would pose too much of a threat to their machine taking over criminal operations in the Seventh Ward. I didn't care about that one way or the other. I wanted Duffy because he reminded me of the Raiders at Andersonville: he was an ignorant, bigoted bully who used his power to prey on others. Andersonville hadn't needed men like him. Neither did Philadelphia.

Aside from my noble reasons there was also the detective star. I still wanted it. No two ways about it.

I wasn't feeling compassionate or noble or anything like that. I felt nothing. I didn't want to admit that Arabella was involved in Duffy's game.

It was better for Mulholland not to know about her just yet. I needed to talk to her myself. I was still hoping she could make me trust her again, though trust was not that important to me. I loved her anyway, even now.

*   *   *

The first thing Chief Mulholland said to me when I walked into his office was, "You look like shit, Mc-Cleary."

I didn't have to bother telling him I felt like it too.

"You have something for me?" the chief asked.

His mood was phlegmatic. He had a sketch pad out and was scratching it with his pencil, making furious strokes.

"Are you all right?" I asked him.

"You asking me if I'm all right? The day before the election!" Then he broke the second commandment and said, "We're gonna be having some big trouble, Mc-Cleary. We're gonna need every man out on the streets keeping order. Otherwise we'll have a repeat of April last."

"Something tells me there'll be trouble even with all the men out. Maybe because of them."

"As if it weren't bad enough with all the drunken re-peaters. Now we'll have negroes to contend with. It's al-ready started, McCleary. Gangs of boys were out last night harassing negroes on the street. The trouble's just begun."

"You gonna have the reserves out in strength, I guess."

"You bet. We need their kind of muscle to-morrow. And to-night."

The night before an election was a policeman's worst nightmare. Aside from the drunkenness and huge crowds due to parades and last-minute rallies, there were crackers and guns going off till dawn. Fires and brawls both had a way of flaring up.

The Republican Club always had a bonfire, with a huge German band doing marches into the early hours. Every election any Republican victory was celebrated by firing a cannon from atop the headquarters.

Election day itself would be just as explosive.

"How much are negro votes going for?" I asked Mul-holland. "If I recall last year the Democrats handed out tickets good for one drink."

"The negroes have gotten smarter. They know the ward

heelers and businessmen'll pay them fifteen dollars to vote their way.''

That made sense. They were men whose livelihoods depended on the election. If you can call fleecing the city a livelihood.

Mulholland stopped his furious sketching and said, ''The trouble'll be in the Seventh Ward. We all know that. The Republicans are going to turn the negroes out. But I guarantee you they'll have trouble getting to the polls. A lot of men have a stake in keeping the Democrats where they are.''

''Don't you?''

''Well, McCleary, I've begun thinking how nice it would be to go to Paris for a good long while and study painting like I always wanted to. I say, muster out gracefully. Of course you'll still be in the ranks. I hear Stokley's gonna put William Heins in charge. I also hear you're his little golden boy.''

''I like being a copper. I do what I have to do to stay one.''

''I understand. And you are a damn good copper, McCleary.''

He turned his head from me in a dismissal. The chief was really preoccupied. I could understand why. It was a pretty fair bet that the Democrats were out by to-morrow. Even if he wasn't too concerned a lot of his friends would be. And he was expected to look out for their interests. That might mean pushing negroes around at the polls. What I knew about Mulholland made me think he wasn't relishing that duty.

A clamor came from outside. Another political club's band was marching down Chestnut Street. The bass drums practically shook the windows. Mulholland lowered his head to the desk and cupped his ears.

I decided to distract him.

''You might not like me so much after I tell you what I've found out.''

The chief wiped the charcoal off his fingertips and

leaned across his desk. His grim expression was a warning not to waste his time.

"This isn't about your disappeared colored gals, is it?"

"I think so. You told me to look into it, remember?"

"Sure, sure. But now we have an election to worry about. Everything else can wait."

"No," I said. My voice turned harsh and commanding. "This can't wait."

Taken aback by my insistence, Mulholland leaned into his chair and straightened his necktie. "All right then," he said.

"You asked me to investigate the disappearance of Josephine Martin. Along with the disappearance of some other colored women. I've been doing that. One of the missing named Goldie Collins wound up as a floater in the Delaware three days ago. I found out later she'd been trying to blackmail someone. With Josephine Martin's jewelry. The person she was blackmailing was Sergeant Walter Duffy."

Mulholland merely blinked before I continued.

"Duffy gave the jewelry to a ragpicker who witnessed Collins's death. Then he must've thought better of it. Because later that night, while I was questioning this ragpicker, we were attacked and he was killed. Whoever it was took Martin's jewelry. I found it two days ago in a grimy room in a St. Mary's tenement. A room belonging to Sergeant Duffy. In that same room I found numerous ledgers detailing a wide variety of criminal activities that the sergeant was involved in. From other informants I found out that Duffy was engaged in a body-snatching ring that . . ."

"What? Whatta you mean, body snatching?"

"Exactly what it sounds like. Two of his hirelings, one a negro mouth-piece of his named Levi Chew, and the coroner's wagon driver Frank McNamee have been digging up bodies from the Lebanon Colored Cemetery for months."

Mulholland squinted at me like a myopic. "That's outrageous!" was his only reply.

"Yeah. And it's also true. The negro fella sold the bodies to medical colleges for a stiff price. From what I gather Duffy's little gang soon cornered the market in the cadaver supply business. The doctors were forced to accept the cadavers or face exposure of their participation in body snatching."

"And you say Duffy was in charge of this operation?"

"Oh there's no question, sir. I found ledgers in his headquarters detailing his involvement. Account books really. They were pulling in the pieces. Not exactly in a big way. But when lumped together with all his other games, the gambling, prostitution, bunco, and so forth, it adds up. And that's not all."

"Do tell."

"These disappeared women, I believe, were abducted and murdered by Sergeant Duffy and Levi Chew. Their bodies were sold to medical universities."

"What purpose would he have in murdering these wretches?"

"Duffy belongs to a group called the Democratic Sons of Liberty. They're like the Ku Klux group down South. The ones who ran around with pillowcases on their heads and tormented freedmen and government officials."

"Yes, I remember."

"Well, Duffy's group—he's the Grand Master, by the way—is no different. They hate negroes and anyone who helps them. I think sheer maniacal hatred motivated the abduction and murder of these women. There's another explanation. Which you probably wouldn't like to hear."

"Go ahead. How much worse could this get?"

"From what I learned, Levi Chew used to supply the sergeant with colored whores, who he entertained in his headquarters. All of the girls except for Josephine Martin were streetwalkers, either in or out of the almshouse. It's possible that Duffy murdered them out of sheer blood lust during some sort of . . ." My upbringing made it hard for me even now to get the words out. ". . . sexual frenzy."

Mulholland was genuinely shocked. "Great God, man! Do you know what you're saying! It's absolutely loathsome! Diabolical!"

"Give me another explanation, sir. It would make me feel better too."

"I can't believe what you're saying, McCleary. Do you have any idea . . ."

"Yes, I do. Duffy made it very clear to me."

"He knows about your investigation?" the chief asked incredulously.

"Oh yes. But there's still more, sir."

I told him about the fracas in the cemetery. He'd heard some of it but I gave him the full story. Except the part where I shot the reserve copper, Uriah Strunk. It was better to give McNamee the credit for that one. Even though Strunk was a crooked murderer and had tried to kill me several times, I didn't think my colleagues would understand my reaction.

"You questioned this fence, I imagine?" Mulholland asked me when I was through.

"Oh yes," I said. "He corroborated McNamee. Chew had been there, with Martin's jewelry."

I was lying through my teeth. But I had to protect Arabella, for now.

"This could get really ugly, McCleary. A lot of important people are going to look bad. The physicians, the universities, Sergeant Duffy, the reserve officers, the coroner . . . Why not try for the mayor and a few clergymen? Just to round it out."

He was exasperated with me, like I was the cause of this whole trouble. Which was understandable, in a certain way. Nobody likes to face things they've been trying so hard to ignore.

"We have to handle this delicately, McCleary. You understand? Keep things quiet."

"Of course, sir."

"I need more proof. I need witnesses. As it stands,

without the corpus delicti, as it were, you don't have much.''

"It's enough though, isn't it, Chief?"

Mulholland ran a trembling hand through his hair.

"It's enough, McCleary. Bring him in. I wanna talk to him."

"Yes, sir."

I saluted and left the chief a little worse for wear.

It was Monday morning and I had some time on my hands to find Arabella and straighten out this whole mess. I wanted to believe she'd lied to me for a good reason.

Whatever her explanation was, as long as it made some sense, I'd believe it. I wanted to believe in her. And in us.

At the front desk I asked where Sergeant Duffy had got himself to. The desk sergeant checked a book and said, "Looks like he's down in the Seventh Ward to-day. There was some trouble there last night with the niggers."

"And Irishmen, from what I hear."

"Well, the niggers are causin' a lot of mischief with the election right around the corner. There's gonna be trouble, boy, I'm tellin' you. I heard there might be a regular invasion of them from Jersey. Mayor Fox is gonna station a whole mess of reserves at the Market Street ferry buildings to keep any niggers from Camden out of the city while the election's goin' on."

"What about all the Irishmen and Germans from Camden? He gonna try to keep them out too?"

"I don't know about that."

I walked outside onto Chestnut. The tourists were in front of the State House already. A parade of men was strutting by, banging drums and wearing fancy regalia. You would've thought they were marching off to war.

Elections could get like that. Especially this one. The way things were going, blood was going to be shed.

But I didn't have time to worry about that now. I had to find Duffy and locate the warehouse McNamee told me about. The one where the bodies were.

I got an impulse to pray. That I might find some bodies of the disappeared women there? Josephine's? Or that I might *not* find them? I wasn't sure which I wanted more.

I wished everyone would leave things buried, where they belonged. But I was digging around more than anyone.

Even though the things I found were too ugly, too corrupted, I couldn't finish digging yet. I was hoping I might uncover something, anything, that would keep this filth away from Arabella.

On my way to the Seventh Ward I kept praying.

That was a good thing to do, considering where I was going.

FINDING PLUME STREET was easy. Once I got to Barley
Street I just followed the smell.

I tried not to think too much on how close Plume was
to Twelfth and Pine, where Arabella lived.

Plume wasn't a street at all, but a back court. On either
side were rear tenements with laundry strung across the
alley like banners. Mostly to-day they were bedsheets and
ladies' unmentionables. A few men's drawers flapped in
the breeze alongside them.

There didn't seem to be a lot of activity among the
inhabitants. None of them was leaning out the windows,
chatting with people on the other side. No children scam-
pered around in the filth.

I understood why. All the ladies' undergarments probably indicated one or several brothels. When I heard a
parlor organ groaning out of one window I was pretty sure
I guessed right. Anyone respectable living in a place like
this wouldn't be able to afford a parlor organ.

I stood at the mouth of the alley and looked from east
to west. There was just enough room for a wagon to get
through. The west end held a row of backhouses. At the
east end large sacks of garbage were thrust against a brick
wall. A few decrepit doors ran along both sides of the
alley in both directions.

245

The garbage wasn't all in those sacks, by any means. Loose cobbles lay scattered here and there along with splintered wooden boards, piles of coal ash, and scraps of clothing and paper. Every item was covered with filth. You could fill a book with the diseases you'd catch if you touched anything there.

It took me about five minutes to try every door in the alley. They were all locked. Frustrated, I decided to go over them again and break through each one if I had to.

Heading to the east side I was about to kick my first door open when I heard a cat meowing right behind me.

He seemed a pleasant enough fellow, a black cat with a large patch of white on his neck. When he hopped over to me and nuzzled against my pantaloons I noticed he had only three legs. The fur clung to him in patches. A few scars, most likely from encounters with vermin, crisscrossed his lean body.

Poor creature, I thought. Trying to see how he lost the leg, I leaned over and reached to pet him. Pity made me forget about how dirty he was.

There was a leather collar on his scrawny neck. The collar was embossed with the cat's name: Tripod.

My friendly gesture scared him off. The cat hopped over to the sacks of garbage against the brick wall, turning back to watch me. I called to him in a low, gentle voice. All Tripod did was stare at me. Then I started meowing to him in my best cat voice. His face made a grimace and out came a raspy answer to me. Now that we were on speaking terms I thought the three-legged cat would be a bit more friendly. So I walked over to him.

As soon as I took a step Tripod disappeared behind a sack.

Then, a moment later, there was a noise, like a cabinet door being closed. The sound came from behind the sacks of garbage.

Now my curiosity was piqued. With a shrug, I began withdrawing the large pile of garbage-filled sacks from the wall, right where the cat disappeared.

After I removed two heavy and foul-smelling sacks I found the door, which was just a tiny metallic flap. Pushing my boot against it I saw it could open either way. There was a lot of space on the other side.

In no time at all I had the rest of the sacks removed. They were much lighter than they appeared to be.

Now I understood why they were piled up against the brick wall.

They were guards, of a sort, protecting a secret from discovery.

The door to the warehouse was set very low in the brick wall, just high enough for a man to enter if he bowed his head.

A rusted lock hung on the door handle.

I wasn't sure what to do next. If I shot the lock off the noise would call a lot of attention. And make it all too obvious to Chew or Duffy or whoever might show up later that they were discovered.

I could simply wait in the alley for one of them to come and unlock the warehouse door. That could take all day.

I had to get inside now.

If they found me out, so be it. There'd be some gunplay, no doubt. One way or the other I was going to settle things.

I ripped open one of the garbage sacks and pulled up a cluster of half-rotten cloth. I held the bundle on top of the lock. Then I put the barrel of my revolver into the bundle and fired. The lock blew off with a muffled sound. Acrid smoke leaked out of the barker and drifted up the narrow alley to the sky. I watched the windows up and down for any hint of discovery. No one took any notice. It was the kind of neighborhood where people minded their own business.

With the barker in hand, I opened the warehouse door.

The smell left no room for doubt. I was in a charnel house.

Tripod meowed at me, hopping around in a circle. His cracked bowl needed refilling. Beside the bowl was a rat carcass. Tripod served a very useful purpose. He kept the goods from being damaged.

I searched around for a lantern. The windows were boarded up or had their shutters drawn.

A kerosene lamp in need of a new wick stood on a trunk near the cat's feeding area. I lit it with a box of matches I found on the trunk. Then I closed the door.

The warehouse was actually the cellar of a house facing Tenth Street. A set of wooden steps led up to street level. With any luck Duffy or Chew would approach that way. The rear entrance would be more useful if they were transporting bodies at night.

I propped myself against a crumbling brick wall and scanned the room.

Twelve coffins sat atop wooden horses, arranged in two neat rows. I stepped over to one and lifted the smaller lid over the corpse's head.

The face was unfamiliar: a negro male, about forty years old at the time of his death. The top of the coffin creaked open and I saw how they kept the subjects preserved till delivery.

Around the naked body were heaps of ice. The bottom of the coffin was not solid but composed of numerous wooden boards with plenty of space between them for the melted water to drain to a compartment below. During the war coffins like these were used when a body had to make a long journey back home.

I closed the lid quickly. The ice wasn't entirely effective. The smell of corruption was powerful. I bit down hard on the insides of my cheeks to keep from throwing up.

Grimly, I held private viewings for the others.

Even though I knew what I would find the sight still sickened me. The human remains were laid out like a butcher's wares, stripped of every shred of dignity in life or death. Each time I slammed a coffin lid down I did it a little harder. The rage was growing in me.

I was looking for a face that matched the descriptions

of any of the disappeared women, especially Josephine Martin.

Only nine corpses were present. Four were men and the others were elderly or middle-aged women. None fit the descriptions of any of the almshouse streetwalkers on my list.

Disappointed, I finally accepted the fact that those creatures must've been picked to pieces by now in a university dissecting room. These husks would share the same fate.

Witnessing this violation brought the sting of tears to my eyes. Each one perhaps had grandchildren or children whose grief was still fresh. To think I would have to increase their grief by bringing this horrid business to light stoked my fury even more.

Well, I promised myself, this ends right here.

I looked around for somewhere to hide and realized there was not one place.

Except inside one of the coffins.

I wasn't in any hurry to climb into one. Instead I waited in the cold warehouse with the stolen dead. My hand rested on the lid of an empty coffin, ready if Duffy or Chew should enter. I'd have time to hide if they came from Tenth Street. If they decided to go by way of Plume Street then I would probably have to shoot it out with them.

I don't know how long I was standing there. Long enough that I started pacing back and forth to keep myself warm. The silence was overwhelming. A quiet room can get all the more silent when there is a dead body in it.

I went over the room several times, checking for any hidden caches of money, weapons, or writings. There was nothing but the trunk I found the lamp on. Inside were some vials and bottles of medicine. The labels were browned with age and I didn't know what half of them meant. There was one large bottle with a smell I recognized. The last time I smelled it was on my visit to the Pennsylvania Hospital.

Physicians often used it during surgical operations to

make the patient unconscious. Chloroform, they called it.

I wondered why there was such a large supply of chloroform. Everybody else in here except me was beyond pain.

Then I thought on the women I was looking for. The ones who weren't here. Like Josephine Martin.

Then I understood.

No wonder no one had heard her being abducted. The chloroform would put her under very quickly. All it would need would be a strong hand to keep the cloth clamped over her nostrils and mouth. The hand would hold the cloth in place until her body stopped struggling and slumped to the ground.

I could see it perfectly. The only thing I couldn't see was who held the cloth.

I closed the trunk and walked back to my coffin. Tripod weaved clumsily around my legs, eager for affection. We were well enough acquainted by now that he didn't mind my petting him.

Traffic noises from outside filtered through the windows and doors: the rattle of wheels against cobbles, the clatter of hooves and once, alarmingly, the gong of an ambulance.

I yanked the chain across my vest and out came my pocket watch. It was close to midday. I extinguished the lantern, wondering how long I would have to wait.

My answer was the sound of a key being inserted in the lock on the Tenth Street door.

Quickly I clambered in the coffin. As I pulled the lid down I shooed the cat away.

I wondered how many stolen corpses had been stashed right where I was. How many graves had Duffy and Chew and McNamee violated?

No matter. There would be no more resurrectionist jobs for them.

Cradling the barker in my hand, I propped up the smaller lid revealing the head and shoulders, used for viewings. Then I realized that it would look too obvious

for it to be open like that. Unless I wanted to be quickly
discovered I would have to remain shut in that coffin.

There were men coming down the stairs now. I let the
lid down and lay there in the darkness. The wooden slats
for the ice to melt through were no good for my back.
The quarters were cramped and they stank.

Duffy was talking.

"We gotta get rid of the things to-day, understand?"

"You been sayin' that, but you still ain't told me
why."

"The fella that shot you last night musta got McNamee
to peach. One of my boys heard him tell the chief all
about it this morning."

"So? They got important things t' do 'round here. Like
keepin' us niggers in line befo' to-morra."

"McCleary won't care about that. He wants my ass. He
even broke into my office in St. Mary's. Did I tell you
that?"

"No, boss! Shit. He dint take nothin' did he?"

Duffy laughed. There was no mirth in it.

"Nothin' I can't get back. When I find him."

My hand gripped the stock of my revolver, just for
reassurance.

"So, get to it," Duffy said. "I don't got much time."

"What we gonna do with them?"

"Put 'em in potter's field. We can dig them up later if
we have to. Just as long as McCleary finds nothing when
he gets here."

"That's gonna take some time, boss. We gots nine al-
togetha. And the wagon can only hold so many."

"I know, I know. So shut up and start loadin' 'em on.
The sooner we get rid of 'em the better."

"I wonder what be takin' him so long."

"McCleary? Yeah, I been wonderin' that too."

"What we gonna do with them coffins? You want me
to get rid of 'em too?"

"No. Hmm. Lemme think on it fer a minute . . . We
could use 'em later. I'll fix something with the fancy

house next door. They got a cellar. Maybe we can move them there for a spell.''

There was a creaking noise. Chew grunted with effort. Then came a dull, ugly sound like a fish slapping against a dock.

''Hurry up!'' Duffy said. ''Get that bag tied around it. I ain't got all day.''

''What you gotta do that's more important than this, huh?''

''Don't get cheeky with me, boy. I got work to do on my end, remember? Someone's gotta take care of the dab.''

It was a filthy word for her. There was no question in my mind who he meant.

''What you gonna do with her?''

''Sweat her. Nice and long. I got all night. And to-morrow if I hafta. But I'm gonna find out what they were doing last night.'' Duffy gave an ugly chuckle. The next sound was of a cylinder being spun.

In the darkness of the coffin I felt a surge of hope. Maybe Arabella wasn't mixed up with them after all.

She must have found out something about Duffy over the past few weeks. Something she was afraid to tell me, for whatever reason.

My admiration for Arabella increased again. She'd gone at it alone. Up against one of the most brutal and powerful men in the city.

Now she was in terrible danger. Duffy would not stop with the usual beatings. He had killed before. One more life snuffed out would make no difference to him.

''I'll take care of this end, boss.''

''Atta boy. You know where to find me if you need me.''

''You gonna be at the club all night?''

''Yeah. Don't worry. They know to keep their hands off you.''

I heard Duffy climbing the stairs back to the street. When the door slammed shut, Chew hissed out a harsh curse. Then I heard him drag the body out to the street. There was a horrible noise everytime it bumped against a step.

That's it, I thought. When he comes back I'll be ready for him.

I was all set to get out of my coffin when I heard the Plume Street door creak open. I stayed where I was.

Then I noticed the scraping sound coming from beneath me. I stopped breathing for a moment when I thought it might be coming from inside the coffin, beneath those wooden slats.

The second time I heard the sound I realized it came from outside. It was easy to guess the source.

Tripod the cat was clawing at the legs of the horse my coffin rested on.

Whoever came in from Plume Street made no sound. They took a few steps. Then I heard the trunk open.

Chew ran down the stairs just then.

"What you doin' here? That bastard what shot me last night found out about this place. He's liable to show any time!"

Tripod kept scraping. Then I heard his three paws pounce on something. It was right beside the coffin. Probably another rat.

Except this wasn't the kind of sound a rat makes. This was a metallic jangling.

My left hand, the one that was resting on my chest, moved slowly down the buttons of my vest.

A barrage of four-letter words ran through my brain.

Because my hand hadn't come across what should have been there: the watch chain that was usually strung across my vest.

It wasn't there because it must've fallen out when I climbed into the coffin. And now the cat was playing with it on the floor.

Just when I figured all this out, I realized that there was no longer anyone talking.

It happened very quickly.

I tried to push the lid up with my gun hand. It wouldn't budge.

A second later the smaller lid, the one right over my face, flew open.

The only thing I saw was the cloth. It covered my face, pushing me back in the coffin. I was trapped.

My brain tried to get my hand to pull the trigger of my barker. But my brain wasn't working so well all of a sudden. I tried holding my breath but there was a hand on my throat now. I gasped involuntarily.

No air went in my lungs. Just the chloroform.

Then the coffin lid seemed to close again.

28

IT WAS HARD to breathe in the tent. Lice were crawling all over me. Men were groaning with pain. Others, with no strength left to cry, were dying.

There'd just been a rainstorm. The hot damp air was choking me. Mosquitoes were a never-ending torment. I could hear them buzzing right next to my ear, looking for a fresh place to suck out my weak blood.

All around me lay sick and starving humanity. The stink of gangrene, vomit, and excrement was over-powering. After all the time I'd been there it was still maddening.

On this hot night I decided that I could take it no more. I thought on how nice it would be to lie down in the burial trench with my friends. How nice and quiet and cool.

The dead-line wasn't far away and I began walking toward it. As soon as I even touched the wooden boards marking it off I knew I was dead. Which didn't seem to bother me. All I wanted to do was escape.

I waded through sleeping prisoners of war till I reached my goal. Then I straddled the fence and leaped over to the other side, waiting for the shot.

But it didn't come.

I screamed, but no words came out. I tried jumping up

and down but the guards didn't seem to see me. I kept at it for a little while longer. Then I gave up.

Falling to my knees in the mud I began crying, completely hopeless. I screamed again, hoping someone would hear me this time.

I woke up in the coffin.

My mouth was contorted. No scream was coming out of it.

I tried to push open the lid but it was fastened shut. By what means I didn't know.

Nor did I know how long I'd been trapped in my grisly cage.

My arms and legs weren't bound. I touched my face and felt a hard growth of beard, the way it was in the morning.

Good God, I thought. Have I been out that long?

I started breathing quickly and nervously, my chest heaving with anxiety.

Stop it, I told myself. Don't waste your strength.

I did nothing but breathe slowly for a few moments. At least I was still breathing.

My heart stopped beating so quickly. Then it started up again.

Because I was thinking the inevitable thought. Where exactly was I?

Inside the coffin, of course. But where was the coffin?

I was afraid to open my eyes. They might see nothing but darkness. There might not be any light creeping through tiny cracks in the wood. And that would mean only one thing.

That I was buried alive with no escape.

My fingers ran over the wooden slats I rested on and the spaces between them. One hand strayed into the compartment below for melted water. It closed on metal.

My revolver.

Chew and whoever else had stuffed the chloroform in my face must not have seen the barker. It had slipped into the compartment below and remained hidden by my body.

I drew the barker out of the compartment. With the gun
in my hand I got the courage to open my eyes. If I saw
nothing but darkness, if I was buried alive, I could shoot
myself and not suffer an even worse death.

At first I thought I'd have to put that bullet in my head.

Then, as my eyes grew accustomed to the darkness I
saw a thin crack along the side of the coffin, where the
lid rested. It wasn't so much light as a lighter darkness.
But the darkness of the grave has no shades. It was
enough to keep the gun from my temple. Though the coffin was closed fast, there was just enough space for this
meager light to leak through.

Something landed right above my face, on the coffin.

Thump. There it went again.

By now my brain was working fairly well. I understood
what was happening.

Levi Chew was shoveling dirt on me.

I didn't have much time left.

With all my strength I shoved upward. But the lid
didn't fly open like I hoped.

I pounded right beside my head, and felt the lid aching
to give. The same was true when I kicked at the other
end.

They'd locked me in the thing.

I thought I heard Chew mutter a curse above my grave.
So he knew I was up and about. That didn't stop him
from shoveling more dirt on me.

I took my handkerchief out and held it to my right ear,
using my shoulder to keep it in place. My left hand covered my other ear.

With my gun hand I took the revolver and pointed it
at the spot where the lock was most likely to be. Then I
pulled the trigger.

The shot was still deafening, despite my makeshift ear
protection. Smoke filled the coffin and made it even harder to breathe.

With my ears still ringing and eyes stinging from the
smoke, I lashed out at the lid again. Dirt began spilling

on me. As I pushed harder, I saw the remains of the lock
Then I saw a wall of earth, and some sunlight.

I was free.

Before I lifted the coffin lid completely away, I stuck
my barker out and fired blindly. Then again and again
Only after the echoes of the shots faded did I realize my
screams were no longer silent.

The shovel slammed against the coffin lid after I'd fired
a third time. Chew wasn't sticking around anymore.

The rest was easy. Shoving upward I threw the lid open
and got quickly to my feet. The grave was shallow, only
about five feet deep.

I couldn't see too well at first. The sun was coming up
in the east. For whatever reason, I'd been in that coffin
for close to a day. What had happened in that time? I
wondered. Why hadn't they got rid of me sooner?

Whatever their reason was, I didn't care.

Clawing at the dirt in a frenzy, I clambered out of the
grave. When my arms reached all the way out, I grabbed
the grass like it was a life line.

I thanked the real resurrectionist for pulling me out of
another grave.

Then I spotted Chew's limping body, running away at
as fast a pace as he was able.

It wasn't going to be fast enough.

My joints ached as I dashed after him. The fresh air
sucked into me was the sweetest of tastes.

Negotiating my way through the steeplechase of
wooden grave markers, I came within shooting distance
of Chew. I shouted for him to stop, but he kept moving
toward his wagon.

With a final burst of speed, I caught up with him just
as he was climbing into the driver's seat. I dragged him
out and threw him to the ground.

There was a long, ugly knife in his hand. He stabbed
at my leg with it. The blade flew out of his hand when
shot him.

I was very careful about it. I didn't want to kill him.
Yet.

The ball went into his right shoulder, splintering his
bone.

He was crying in pain.

"Get up!" I shouted at him. Chew wasn't very attentive. A sharp kick in his side brought another moan out
of him. It also got him to his feet.

He was losing a good deal of blood. Which was fine
with me.

"Get in the back of the wagon and lie down. If you
move an inch I'll make sure you don't move anymore
after that. Understand?"

I wasn't going to stand around potter's field and sweat
Chew. Especially not now. I didn't want him bleeding to
death. He had to live and tell a jury all about Sergeant
Duffy.

And whoever else had been in the warehouse. The one
who stuffed the chloroform in my face.

I didn't want to think on who that person might be now.
I was starving and my nerves were shaky.

I grabbed the reins and started the horse moving south,
toward the Seventh Ward. Duffy told Chew that he could
be found at the club. With any luck, Arabella would be
with him at Keble Street. The three of us would have
some talking to do.

As we headed back, I suddenly realized that it was
Tuesday morning, election day. I'd missed the usual spec-
tacular Republican parade last night. Heins would be disappointed. Well, he'd get over it. Especially when he
heard I was bringing Duffy in. Whatever Chew and Duffy
told in court, it would be enough to discredit the Democrats for quite some time.

But I didn't care about that now. All I wanted was for
someone to pay for what I'd seen at the warehouse. And
for some other things that I was going to make Duffy tell
me about. I was hoping he'd be difficult. Because I was
going to enjoy making him talk.

First I had to get Chew to a physician. The best bet was the Pennsylvania Hospital. It was on the way. That morning I was supposed to stand guard at the State House. Mulholland would have to do without me.

The closer we got to the hospital the more I heard what I took to be thunder. But the skies were clear.

Then I realized it wasn't thunder at all. It was gunfire.

The usual election riots had started. But this election would be different. And deadly.

29

I WAS DELAYED at the hospital. There were more cases than usual. Rows and rows of miserable, bleeding, weeping people, mostly colored, were lined up waiting to see a doctor. By the time I brought Levi Chew in he was unconscious.

I showed my star to a nurse and asked him what was going on in the Seventh Ward.

The nurse wiped his bloody hands on an already soiled apron and said, "From what I hear the police are trying to keep the negroes away from the polling stations. Those two over there were beaten by a mob before they even got to the window to give their names. That young woman's husband was attacked on the front door of their house on South Street."

"Any reason?"

"Reason? A mob doesn't need a reason."

I thanked him and left special instructions that Chew should not be discharged without my permission.

Then I took a walk down Eighth Street. I could see a huge crowd of people at the corner of Lombard Street. The ones closest to me appeared to be watching something. At first I thought it was a parade.

Then I heard the shots, volleys of them. Muskets and pistols.

I started running toward them.

Suddenly the crowd headed down Eighth to South Street, toward the First District polling station.

At the corner where the mob had been the street was ripped apart. Half the cobblestones were torn right out. They were in the hands of the rioting crowd.

There were other signs of riot. Aside from the demolished street I saw a few demolished colored bodies which still moved, albeit agonizingly slow.

A colored mob was forming around the bodies. Some quickly lifted the men and women and bore them off in different directions. Then a few of them took notice of me. They picked up cobblestones themselves and heaved them at me.

I didn't try to convince them I wasn't a part of the white mob. I ran off down Eighth Street. They pursued. Gunfire popped into the air behind my back.

Up and down each street there were the same scenes. White thugs fresh out of the saloon were kicking and beating any colored man or woman in easy reach. Heavy objects rained down on them from the windows above. They in turn sent cobblestones through every window they could break. A few had guns but most were armed only with their fists or broken bottles.

Taking cover behind an ash can, I took out the small paper container that held extra cartridges for my revolver. I kept my eyes on the street. Half a square down I saw five men trying to kick in the door of a residence. They were after a colored man I'd just seen run inside.

They busted their way in shortly. In a few seconds they had the man, a middle-aged negro dressed rather nattily, no doubt to celebrate his first chance at voting in a major election.

He wasn't celebrating now. In fact, he was pleading for his life. So was his wife who was leaning out the front window, screaming.

I pinned my star on the lapel of my frock coat. No sense in hiding the fact I was a policeman.

I stood up from behind the ash can. The sound of shattering glass came at me from all sides. Shouts and curses issued from a square down, where the main crowd was. Behind me I heard some colored men round the corner.

The five rioters near me had their prey on the ground. Their boots sunk into him with ugly little sounds. The man tried to protect his head, but it was already bleeding.

While I watched like an idiot I remembered our late President's words, that our nation would have a new birth of freedom. What I saw before me was a hideous abortion instead. It made me tremble with anger and shame.

I shouted for the men to stop what they were doing. They told me to go and fornicate myself.

So I shot one, in his left leg. He sunk to the ground, clawing at his wounded thigh and screaming at the large amount of blood that started pouring out. I walked closer and barked another one in the arm. The ones who weren't shot already saw I wasn't going to stop. As I pulled back the hammer for a third time, they scurried away, carrying their wounded.

The colored man's face was to the pavement and his tears mingled with the blood pouring down from numerous head wounds. I gave him a quick check and saw it was nothing too serious.

Taking my handkerchief out, I began wiping the blood from his eyes.

"Thank you," he muttered between sobs.

His wife and son were on the front doorstep by now.

"Oh my God!" his wife screamed. "William! Is he hurt bad?"

"No ma'am. But I'd get those head wounds cleaned up. Cuts and bruises. No bones broken, I think."

The boy stared at me with wonder.

"You're a policeman?" he asked incredulously.

"Yeah. Special Officer McCleary's my name."

"Why'd you help my father?"

"Because he needed my help. Now look, people, why

don't you go back indoors until we get these maniacs under control?''

"Are you kidding?'' the wife asked, bringing her husband up the steps. "The police are the ones making it happen.''

I remembered Mulholland's words. The coppers were going to "prevent trouble by making sure everyone did what he was supposed to do.'' Which meant keeping the negroes from voting by the usual means of the club.

Except this time the Irish Democrats in the ward were getting a little too riled up. There was a seething hatred in the air.

I knew just where the fire had started. And who was fanning the flames.

"Listen,'' I said. "What's your name?''

"Devers,'' the young man said. "Ben Devers.''

"Well, Ben, do your ma and pa a favor and keep them inside. And yourself. Lock your door and draw the curtains. I don't want any of you folks getting hurt worse. Understand?''

I turned to go and Ben Devers said to me, his voice choking, "Thank you, Mr. McCleary. I won't forget what you did for my father.''

I nodded and ran to the crowd on South Street.

The scene was one of total chaos. The only thing close to it I remembered was the wild disordered shooting that took place that day eight years ago at Cemetery Ridge. The day I was captured by the Rebels.

Men, white and black, ran through the street like wild animals, screaming and hurling stones, beating on anyone left alone and vulnerable. The curse-laced brogues of Irish Democrats clashed with the quick-tongued oaths of negro Republicans. They snarled at one another like dogs. When their curses and stones weren't enough, the few who had pistols and muskets opened fire at anything moving that wasn't their color.

There was nothing I could do here. The gunfire was making it hard for me to think. My body quivered every time I heard a shot. I wasn't in Philadelphia anymore, but back at Gettysburg, hearing the first volley tearing into our ranks, wondering how long it would be before a minié ball struck me down.

I did the same thing I'd done that day. I ran. But this time my running was not full of panic, but of purpose. This was a battle I wouldn't retreat from.

I weaved my way through the rioting crowds, sliding through pools of blood and shattered glass. I backtracked a square and made a left down Keble Street, to the Democratic Sons of Liberty Club.

I got there just in time to see a mob of colored voters charge a line of policemen barricading a polling booth. The reserve coppers were backed by a host of supporters, mostly the men I'd seen at the meeting three days before.

The two crowds clashed with a ravenous fury. Every copper had his club out. Maces rained down on the negroes' heads, cracking skulls right and left. But there were more negro heads than there were clubs. Soon the reserve coppers were being overpowered and thrashed. They retreated into the club and took up positions at the second story windows. Meanwhile the colored mob was busy trying to storm the entrance. They kicked at the door and tore up Keble Street for fresh ammunition. In no time the cobbles were whistling through the air, sent right to the windows where the coppers perched, hurling curses, bottles, and occasionally, a shot.

I wasn't sure what to do. If I tried getting into the D.S.O.L. club I'd have to wade through the colored mob. That would be something very close to suicide.

But I had to get in there. Duffy was inside, I knew it. And so, I feared, was Arabella.

With all this insanity going on, Duffy would have the perfect chance to get anything he wanted from her. Even her life.

The rain of bricks and cobbles went on for about ten minutes. I searched vainly for another entrance. Finally, I decided to charge the front door and run the gauntlet of negroes.

I started off toward the rear of the mob when I heard a familiar voice cry, "Hold it, McCleary!"

It was Chief Mulholland with a host of coppers. They charged the colored men and drew their fire.

Mulholland grabbed my arm, shouting, "How long you been here?"

"About fifteen minutes. Enough to see everything."

I told him about the police barring negroes from the poll station. And the brutal result.

"Well, we got about thirty officers here and I think we can quell the disturbance."

"Whatta you mean, Chief? This is no disturbance. It's a full-scale riot!"

"I know that McCleary! I'm talking about the fun and games going on right here, in Keble Street. The mayor's just called in the United States Marines. They're going to march into the city and restore order. Or so we hope. The two mobs equal about a thousand men. The Marines'll have their work cut out for them."

The chief watched the progress of his officers. Their guns were very persuasive.

"They got orders to arrest the ringleaders." Then he added, seeing my expression, "On both sides. That order applies to you, McCleary. He's in the club, isn't he?"

"Yes, sir. I think so."

"Well, what the hell are you waiting for? Pinch him."

He didn't need to say it a second time.

The door to the club was already partially battered down. Looking at the windows above I noticed there were no longer any coppers leaning out. Most likely they had escaped or joined the crowd below to wreak more havoc.

While the blue bellies and the negroes clashed, I ran to the door and kicked it all the way in. Furniture fell to the floor, the remnants of a hastily wrought barricade.

The saloon and billiards rooms were empty. It took me a minute to find the flight of stairs leading up. I stumbled through an arsenal of bottles on my way to the second floor.

The din of warfare was waning outside. The coppers probably had the negroes pinched or on the run by now. Inside the club there was no noise except when I kicked a bottle out of my way.

There were a lot of doors in the hallway I came to. It was going to take me a long time to work my way through them all.

Arabella saved me the trouble. She started screaming just then.

I followed the clamor to a door halfway down the hall.

My mind was having a hard time doing its job. The only thing I was aware of was the revolver in my hand.

I had just enough sense left to try the knob to see if the door was locked or not. It wasn't. The knob twisted with ease and my boot kicked the door wide open.

The first thing I saw was Arabella, bound to a chair in the middle of the room. Her mourning dress lay at her feet. Duffy was working on her undergarments. So far he had a shoulder exposed. Ugly bruises covered her brown skin.

Blood leaked from both sides of her mouth when she cried my name.

Duffy was staring at me too. I saw the gleam of brass knuckle dusters on his clenched fists.

Rage swept over me like a wave of volcanic fire. I threw my revolver across the room and sprung at Duffy with my bare hands.

Arabella kept screaming as I flung myself into Duffy's rock-hard chest. The knuckle dusters grazed my jaw. Even with a light blow, it felt like my jaw was pulverized. I flew backward into Arabella, knocking her on her side.

Scrambling to my feet I dodged a few cumbersome blows from Duffy. Then my experience as a pugilist in Andersonville paid off.

Without thinking, I grabbed Duffy by the shoulders and gave him a backheel. At the same time I let loose one hand and slammed it into his throat. With a choking sound, Duffy fell to his feet. I hit a few roasters on his rib, with little effect. One of Duffy's fists crashed into my bread basket. I leaned back, holding on to my stomach like it was about to pop.

Before he could get up I landed a braincrasher that stretched him out on the floor. I thought I had him with that one.

But Sergeant Duffy wasn't finished yet. I stood over him, coughing up a bit of blood. Between deep breaths I said, "Get up you son of a bitch! Get up!"

To hell with the jury, with Heins, with the detective position, with everything. I just wanted to kill this murdering bastard with my bare hands.

Duffy wouldn't get up. Instead he flashed a smile at me. I was concentrating on the gaps in his ivories. Then some drops of sweat and blood dripped into my eyes. When they cleared I saw he had a barker in his hand. He pulled back the hammer.

I heard the shot and closed my eyes.

I must've waited at least two or three seconds. No bullet was that slow.

Opening my eyes I saw Duffy slumped on the floor. Just another "thing" now. Except the resurrectionists wouldn't have been able to use him. His head was too damaged from the ball that came out of my revolver.

The barker was smoking in Arabella's trembling hand.

When I'd knocked her over she must have fallen within inches of it. In her struggle to free her hands she'd lacerated both wrists.

Now I took the revolver from her and returned it to the holster. Then I untied her legs. Cut loose, she clung to me, her body heaving with sobs. I buried my face in her hair, quieting her down with little kisses. The whole time I kept whispering, "It's all right, honey. It's all right now."

But I didn't believe that.

Not after what I'd seen to-day.

30

AFTER THE SHOOTING died down outside I emerged with
Arabella, clothed in my suit jacket. The story I told Mulholland went something like this: Duffy had kidnapped
the last of his victims and was in the process of torturing
her when a stray ball fired from outside killed him as he
stood by a window. The chief and I decided that was a
good story and that the latter part was fit to print.

R.I.P. Sergeant Walter Duffy.

I took Arabella to the Pennsylvania Hospital where I
used a little pull to get a physician to take a look at her.
While she was being examined I wandered over to Levi
Chew's ward.

On the way there I felt the way I usually do when
something stupendous happens. That is, I felt nothing at
all. Some people might go into hysterics, some might curl
up in a corner and stay there. I just went on doing what
I usually did. From all outward appearances I looked normal. But inside I was different. I'd taken my emotions
and stashed them away for a while.

The timing was good because at this point I wasn't sure
how to feel.

Duffy was dead and without him Chew wasn't that important. Heins would lose his chance at bargaining with
Duffy to keep the whole mess out of court. That bargain,

I'm sure, would have included certain concessions to the new machine. Duffy could've been allowed control of certain businesses, but the lion's share of the Seventh Ward would pass into the hands of the Republicans victors.

Now with Duffy gone that transition wouldn't be so smooth. A lot of small-time guns and grafters were going to try filling up the gap in authority. That would keep the new police force busy in the Seventh Ward for quite some time, busy doing something other than taking scale and meddling as Duffy had.

More importantly, my chances of finding out the fates of Josephine Martin and the other disappeared girls were blown to smithereens. Without Duffy to help me, I might never know what happened. Maybe that was a good thing. I wasn't sure I wanted to know how their miserable lives had ended in even greater misery.

The Martin girl's parents would want to know, however. For their sake, I hoped Chew would be willing to talk. With any luck he might have played a part in her murder. I could probably sweat a confession out of him. Then I'd have the satisfaction of watching Levi Chew hang.

That would be a consolation, at the very least.

When I went to Chew's ward they told me he wasn't there any longer.

It took a lot of effort to keep the profanity out of my words.

"What do you mean he's been discharged?" I shouted at the doctor.

"Well," the man said, flinching, "I suppose I'm not quite sure whether he was discharged or not. But I did see the man you describe exiting the hospital some time ago."

"Who gave him the permission to do that?"

"I'm sure I don't know. I can tell you he was accompanied by a physician, if that's any help."

"Who?" My echo bounced back before I got my answer.

The doctor seemed reluctant to get a colleague into trouble.

"I can't say the doctor was going along willingly."

"You mean Chew was threatening him? Did he have a weapon? Think, damnit!"

"I didn't see a weapon. But that doesn't mean there wasn't one. Plenty of surgical instruments are lying about. Enough to do some damage. That's the only explanation I have for the doctor going along."

"So Chew had a knife on him?"

"Quite possibly, yes."

"And forced the doctor to go with him?"

"That must be the case. Otherwise I'm sure he wouldn't have gone away with such a dangerous prisoner."

"Who are we talking about here? What's the name of this doctor?"

"Forbes. William Forbes."

By the time he got the Christian name out I was already running back to Arabella.

The doctor was just bandaging her shoulder when I burst in.

"Arabella! You must come with me at once!"

"What is it, Wilton?" she said, trying to fix her dress.

"No time to get decent! Move it!"

I dragged her out of there and onto Spruce Street. An ambulance driver was idling at the corner, his horse's nose deep in the feed bag.

"I need a ride," I told the young man, showing him my star. "Police business."

"I'm supposed to stay right here!" he protested. "An alarm could come in any moment. I can't just go dashing around the city!"

"How'd you like to change your story for five cans?" I said, fishing out the last bit of money I had on me.

His answer was to step down and pull the feed bag off his complacent horse. Then he got back up, grabbed the reins, and said, "Where to, Officer?"

I turned to Arabella who was still trying to pin her jersey together. She stopped altogether when I said, "Where does Forbes live, Arabella?"

"Why would you want to go there, Wilton?"

"Chew escaped from the hospital. I think he might have taken Forbes hostage."

"Is he in danger?" she asked, sinking her nails into my arm.

"I don't know. The sooner we get there, the sooner we'll know. Now where does he live?"

The address was in Society Hill, not far away.

"226 Pine Street," I told the driver.

On the way there, a journey of seven squares, Arabella and I had a chance to talk.

The first thing I asked her was what she'd been doing in the D.S.O.L. club, being tortured by Duffy.

She shook her beautiful head and covered her face with her hands. From behind her mask of elegant fingers, she said, "He was a maniac, Wilton. Just like you thought. He said he'd been watching me for days, ever since Chew happened to see me with you at the morgue. Watching my every move. And having McNamee and Chew watch me when he couldn't."

"Why?"

"Because he wanted me! Like he wanted the others, your disappeared girls! The ones he probably killed! Do you understand, now? Do I have to tell you more?"

"Yes. I want to hear all of it."

"Chew told me some things about him, Wilton. About his taste in women, a taste he could never tell his friends at the club about. Because he was ashamed and humiliated by it. He, the Grand Master, the leader in a new war against my race, hungered for colored women. Funny, isn't it?"

For a moment she broke into hysterical laughter without any joy in it. "He was obsessed, Wilton. With a vile, horrid mania. I found out to-day what he must have done to all those other girls. Beatings. Violation. He came at me like a rabid beast. Right before you broke the door down, Duffy had just finished telling me about what he was going to do to my body. After I was dead.''

She burst into tears again, covering her lovely face with gloved hands.

I kept running my hand up and down her back, very softly. The words were hard for her to get out. I didn't want to cause her any more pain than I had to. But I had to know the whole truth.

''Wasn't he also interested in you because you were looking into Goldie's death? Behind my back?''

''You're right. I was trying to find evidence to link Goldie with Duffy, as you suggested. I found out a great deal from Levi Chew. But I don't think Duffy cared what I knew. He wanted to demonstrate his hatred to me by violating me in every way, in life and death. Thank God you came before he could do either.''

''What about the jewels, Arabella? The ones Goldie had on her when she died?''

''Jewels?''

''The ones we found in Duffy's headquarters. You had them, tried to sell them to a fence.''

The girl began to tremble more than usual. Quickly she averted her eyes from mine and stared straight ahead along Pine Street.

''I don't know what you mean.''

''I talked to Simon, the fence. He told me you were there to see him. You sure you don't remember that, Arabella?''

''Look, Wilton! There's the doctor's home! And there's a wagon out front!''

I saw it too. The wagon was the same one I rode from potter's field.

As we pulled up, I helped Arabella down and told the driver we wouldn't be needing him.

Then the two of us walked to the stately row home.

It was an ancient building, over a hundred years old. Forbes kept it looking brand-new. The black paint on the shutters and cornices was nice and shiny. There were three stories of brick, marked off from each other by plain strips of stone. On the roof three dormers poked out along with a chimney. This was the house of a prosperous man.

We walked up the granite steps, our hands on the elegant iron rails. The arched doorway barred our entry. When I was about to try the knocker, Arabella said, "Don't bother."

She took out a long key from the pocket of her dress and fitted it into the lock. The freshly varnished door opened inward.

It was very silent in the house, the kind of eerie silence I'd experienced the day before among the dead.

Arabella, standing behind me, whispered which room lay where. I had my Smith and Wesson out, with all the chambers full of lead.

"That's the study there," she said, indicating a door which stood ajar.

We walked into an expansive room, darkly furnished with a mahogany desk and chairs upholstered in red velvet. The floor was covered with a magnificent Turkish carpet of deep, rich reds and greens. I got a good look at it because as soon as I walked in I tripped over an edge that was slightly out of place.

A three-sided book stand, intricately carved, stood beside the doctor's desk chair, which resembled something the Pope might sit on in the Vatican. I looked at the books but they were written in Latin.

Shelves ran along each wall, showcasing a gruesome collection of skulls.

"This is part of Morton's old American Golgotha," Arabella told me. I remembered the doctor mentioning it. Now I had a whole room full of skulls grinning at me. I didn't care for their sense of humor.

The curtains didn't want to be drawn back. The doctor had somehow fixed them in place, not wanting, for whatever reason, sunlight to penetrate his sanctum.

"Put the gas on, Arabella, I want some light in here."

She headed for a lamp by the entrance. Soon the gaslight had the whole room illuminated.

Now I had a chance to make a thorough study of the place. My study didn't last long.

Not after I went to smooth out the carpet I tripped over.

I saw it wasn't the only thing that made me trip. There was something slick on the darkly varnished floor. Something that, when I rubbed it on my fingertips, looked a whole lot like blood.

We were standing in a corner of the study, to the right of the gaslight at the entrance. A case of skulls grinned at me as I asked Arabella, "What's your professional opinion on this?"

She examined the stains on my fingers. Then she gulped and said, "I think it's blood."

"I *know* it is."

Arabella started getting hysterical.

"Oh my God! William! What have they done to him?"

I tried to hold her, to calm her down, but she struggled in my grasp.

"It's all my fault!" she cried. "I never should have listened to you!"

She kept trying to break free from me. I pushed her into a corner and held her there till she started lashing out at me with rather sharp heels.

I stumbled back a few steps. Then I saw it.

When Arabella pushed me away this time I'd once again upset the already crooked rug. The corner flap was folded over now, just enough for us to see what lay below.

It looked like the outline of a door.

"What's that, Arabella?" I nearly shouted at her.

Her eyes were wild now, full of fear.

"I never saw it before, Wilton! I swear to God!"

"Well, let's take a look."

I motioned for her to stay in the corner as I drew the flap further back enough to uncover the whole door. It wasn't too large, about three feet square. A brass ring was set in the middle, in a circular depression, to prevent detection once the carpet was drawn over it.

I took the ring and pulled. The door came up quite easily.

We both stared at the set of wooden steps leading down into darkness.

Pushing the door all the way back I gestured into the black emptiness with my barker.

"Ready?" I said.

"No," Arabella said. "I'm afraid."

"So am I."

I put a foot on the moldy carpet covering the first step. Then we went down into the pit.

31

THE LIGHT FROM above got us to the end of the stairs. After that we couldn't see a thing.

"Feel around for a lamp or candle or something," I told her.

Her teeth were clattering against each other. It was cold down there, all right. But the cold wasn't what was bothering us. An echo coursed through the dark tunnel. The sound was like a night wind moaning outside a window, or the cry of a lost and wandering ghost. It seemed to give the darkness a voice.

We walked in the direction of the sound, pressed against each other. Now my teeth were clattering too.

We went on for another forty or fifty feet or so. The passageway seemed straight but it was hard to tell with no light. Our shoes shuffled quietly over a floor that was sometimes earthen and other times covered with boards.

There was a sudden turn in the way. That was our first glimpse of the light. I wasn't sure how far we'd gone under the house. I thought we might be well into the back court.

The moans were getting louder. I couldn't console myself with a pleasant explanation for them any longer. There wasn't any wind. This was no underground cavern with scores of air passages.

277

The moaning was human. The cries were heartrending. I felt disgust, fear, and pity all at once.

We got closer to the source of the light. My revolver pointed the way, though it was little comfort. I had the feeling it couldn't help us here.

"There's something there, Wilton! Something lying in our way!"

Her voice was a harsh whisper.

I saw it.

Whoever it was lay right before an entrance to a well-lit room beyond. I heard someone talking there.

Leaning over the body I could see the hands pretty well. The patches of white and brown skin left no room for doubt.

It was Levi Chew.

There was a deep fissure in his neck, still oozing blood.

Before I could get up I heard Dr. Forbes say, "Put the gun down, Mr. McCleary, and get up slowly."

I raised my head and saw him silhouetted in the doorway. He was dressed the same as I saw him last, in a sable frock suit. Except he had a new article, not usually part of a gentleman's wardrobe.

It was a carbine, pointed at my head.

I dropped my revolver on Chew's lifeless body.

"Now get up and walk toward me," the doctor said impassively. He took a few careful steps backward.

When I was through the doorway he called to Arabella.

"Pick up the gun, my dear, and bring it in here."

I felt her moving behind me. Then she walked into the room and stood between us, shivering.

"Arabella, listen to me now. I want you to point that gun at him and if he makes a move I want you to shoot him. We're too close now. Do you understand?"

She turned to look at me. Her eyes held the hint of an apology. Then her lips grew taut. She said, "Yes, William. Whatever you say."

"Good."

He turned his back to me and walked further back into

the room, where the meager flame of the lamp couldn't penetrate.

The darkness enveloped him, except for his free hand. It floated there like a luminescent spirit hand—the kind you see at seances.

At that moment I felt rather close to the spirit world.

Forbes's voice came out of the shadow.

"This does complicate things somewhat. I wasn't quite ready to bring you in on this stage of the project."

Arabella moved over to a large roll-top desk, where the kerosene lamp was running out of wick. With the gun still leveled at my mid-section, she calmly adjusted the hemp. Suddenly the flame grew brighter.

I could see most of Forbes now. He was standing against a tattered curtain divider. Whatever was on the other side stank. I watched Arabella's nose wrinkle with disgust.

At least that was some kind of emotion, I thought. I had enough time to stare at the face that had seemed beautiful to me just a few moments before. Now I could see a cruelty there that had been previously invisible. Her hand still held the revolver on me with frigid nonchalance.

Finally, she said, "What stage are you talking about, William?" There wasn't a tremor in her voice.

"The next necessary stage, my dear. I think you know. In fact, I am very much convinced you have known for quite some time. Isn't that right?"

The challenge didn't provoke her. Still calm, she said, "Why don't you tell me about it? I want to hear it from you."

She looked at me instead of him this time. There was hatred in her eyes. As if I were the one responsible for this.

Forbes turned to me as well and said, "I think we're not being very polite to our friend, Arabella. Mr. Mc-Cleary, you remember that day we talked at the college? I recall we discussed, albeit briefly, the subject of race and intelligence. I've begun studies in that area that I never would have dreamed before . . . I met this charming young lady. New directions, Mr. McCleary.''

"To where?" I said.

I got no answer from him.

Arabella was sorting through the roll-top desk. She sat on the edge, quite casually, and picked up papers at random. Behind her was a slate resting on an easel. A table of some kind was written on it. I had no idea what the figures represented.

"What are you doing, Arabella?"

Forbes stepped out of the shadow, his carbine swerving for an instant from me to her. I tried taking a step forward.

The sound of my sole on the damp earth floor warned him. The carbine came back to rest haphazardly a few feet from my idea pot.

The doctor repeated his question, almost harshly now.

"I'm looking at your research notes, William."

The papers were crunched in her grip.

"You have more than one subject listed here, William. You told me there was only supposed to be one living subject."

"And you understood the necessity, Arabella. Didn't you?"

"I . . ." she hesitated, catching her breath. "When you spoke to me about it I thought I understood. It seemed to make sense."

"That was before you saw it face to face, wasn't it?"

They were both startled to hear my voice.

Her eyes suddenly turned to mine. Deep lines furrowed her brow. There was something I saw in her face, something that I'd been afraid was gone for good.

It was there now. It made me feel a little less like a fool.

"It was the only way," she said. "I thought it was . . . How could we ever hope to understand how intelligence operated? How else could we hope to find its source?"

She turned away from Forbes as if to shut him out, speaking only to me. Her words sounded like pleas.

"It was our goal, Wilton, to pinpoint the precise spot in the brain from which intelligence stems. Dr. Forbes and I had been studying the brains of cadavers for over a year . . ."

Interrupting her, Forbes said, "I knew that my old teacher Morton was wrong. It has nothing to do with the size of your brain. If that were the case elephants would be solving calculus quicker than I . . ."

"Then he hit on a brilliant idea, something never done before. He told me it was possible to operate on a person's brain while he was still alive."

It sounded like a recitation, a chant—something that used to make sense in the past but no longer had any meaning now. A faith that she had never bothered to question.

"Impossible," I said. "You'd have to crack their skull open. The shock would kill them."

"Not impossible, Mr. McCleary. I've discovered the brain has no nerve endings. There would be no pain. And for the initial surgery to reach the brain we would administer a large dose of ether to the patient. Then, after we reached the brain, with the patient conscious, we could begin our experiments."

"What kind of experiments?" I asked, without really wanting to know.

"Removal of tissue. To see which parts corresponded with memory, intelligence, language, and so forth."

Arabellla nodded automatically. The motion was insistent. But the gesture of agreement seemed more like a denial—of something inside her own head.

"No one knows where those parts are," I said.

"Precisely. It would be a trial and error process. That is why we selected a subject who was . . . dispensable."

"Goldie Collins," I said, turning to Arabella with disgust.

"We needed someone alive on the operating table to test our theory," she told me, her mouth quivering.

"But why? What use is information like that?"

"The applications would be endless, Wilton. We might be able to cure insanity, paralysis, epilepsy, amnesia, a host of ailments."

"We were explorers. Isn't that right Arabella? We were blazing a trail, just like I told you."

"I thought . . ." she said, "that it would alleviate so much suffering."

Her voice shook with a last attempt at justification.

I didn't notice at the time her use of the past tense.

All I could think of was how angry, how betrayed I felt.

"You sick fool," I said. "You think this is some kind of noble adventure, don't you?"

Forbes was now right beside her. His free arm encircled her hunched shoulders.

Though he tried to sound encouraging, Forbes's next words came out like a threat.

"Tell him, my dear."

She looked from him to me. Beneath her dark jersey I saw her bosom swell but not relax. With Forbes's arm around her like that I fancied she was some sort of grotesque marionette. When she opened her mouth I wasn't sure whose words were really coming out, her own or the ones she'd been fed. It didn't matter much anyway.

"We were on the brink of the greatest medical discovery of the age! I was! A negro woman! Don't you understand, Wilton? This was my chance! My chance to redeem myself and my race! For us to take our place in history, where we belong!"

"By butchering a woman? Of your own race?"

"It doesn't matter what race she was! She was a whore. A stupid brute. I got to know her plenty well at the Magdalen Society, heard the filth coming out of her mouth. I experienced her ferocity and ignorance, firsthand. When William convinced me we needed a human subject, I thought, Why not her? Of use to no one. Now we could put her to use."

She turned her face to Forbes, who nodded at her. She was an apt pupil.

I slumped against the dank brick wall behind me. I kept looking into her eyes, trying to tell myself that I saw something there that might not mean complete defeat.

Between making excuses for her and hating her, I said, with all the bitterness I could muster, "You're no Prometheus. You're just a cold-hearted, murderous bitch."

The kerosene flame was burning in a desultory way. It turned Arabella's skin the color of a sunset. I watched her hands as they held the numerous sheets of paper from the roll-top.

Those delicate hands seemed to tremble now. Maybe I was just noticing the flickering of the lamp light on them.

Arabella had to clear her throat before she said, "I don't understand."

I wasn't sure what she meant.

She said it again.

"Is that so, Arabella?"

Forbes was quite close to her now. So was that carbine. The girl was aware of both but not afraid of either. If she was, she hid her fear very well. I realized how good Arabella was at hiding things.

"Yes," she said cautiously. "What exactly is the meaning of these figures here? The headings don't make sense to me."

"Those columns each represent a subject. And those figures indicate the amount of time it took before each succumbed during various . . . administrations."

The girl craned her neck. I could see the muscles of her neck stretched very taut.

"Subjects succumbing?" she asked, a little hoarse.

"Yes. I administered a variety of . . . well, you can see it there."

"It's in Latin, William. I don't think Mr. McCleary reads Latin."

I shook my head ever so slightly.

The locks of Forbes's hair were turning glossy with sweat.

"How about this one?" she said.

"The English would be . . ." He paused as if searching for the right word.

Then he said in a monotone, "I suppose scourging would be the best translation."

"And this one?"

There was just a hint of hysteria in her tone now.

"That . . . uh . . . would be burning."

All three of us heard it then.

The sounds.

The ones I'd thought Levi Chew had groaned as he bled to death in the crumbling passageway.

Forbes's words had brought them back, like revenants.

They were pitiful, heart-wrenching. Something welled up in my throat.

Forbes, for the first time, lost his cool. Turning to the tattered cloth he screamed, "Shut up! Shut up, goddamn you all! I told you what would happen if I heard one word from you didn't I?" Saliva sprayed from his mouth. He turned back at us, shaking with rage. Or fear.

Then, once again, he was calm.

"Ah, well. No use now, I suppose."

He ran a tremulous hand through his hair and said, "Why don't you go over there and draw the partition, Arabella?"

Forbes looked excited now. Like a child showing off a new toy.

"I want you to see . . . and understand."

With the notes still clenched in her trembling hand, the girl moved slowly across the room. When she drew the curtain the stench grew worse. And so did the cries.

We could see their source now.

The low-ceilinged room went back about twenty rods further. There was nothing to distinguish it from the study where we were.

Nothing except the twin rows of cells.

The iron bars looked rather new. I stepped closer to see what lay behind them. The vile miasma was worse than a carcass on a hot day.

In all I counted six cells.

From behind the new iron bars, weeping came. And voices.

"Help me," one said. It sounded barely human, like an animal's imitation of speech. My guts contracted inside me.

Another voice croaked from a cell. It said, between sobs, "Some water, for the love of God. Some water. Please, Jesus, please."

Dr. Forbes stood before us now, alternating the carbine from Arabella to me. His face remained placid.

"All that work over Sergeant Duffy for nothing. Oh well."

Even though Arabella had the revolver I lunged at her. The barrel, pointed right at my chest, made me stop in my tracks.

"What did you know about this?" I nearly screamed at her.

She shook her head, her features sunken. The color was draining out of her bit by bit.

"I knew nothing of this, Wilton. I swear to you. Sweet Jesus, William."

"You understand now, don't you?"

"Oh yes. I understand completely now."

I was watching her when she said that. And I was close enough to feel rather than see something drain out of her. It left very little behind.

I moved over to the nearest cell, feeling one gun barrel follow me. I wasn't sure about the other one.

Peering into the shadowy, reeking cage I saw a woman. She was lying against the wall, weeping. It was the same one who asked for help. This one still had some strength left in her. And some hope.

The kerosene lamp made it easy enough to see her face. It was one I recognized despite the pitiful toll taken by starvation. Looking at her naked body I saw that hunger had been the least of her tortures.

"Josephine?" I called to the withered creature.

The girl stumbled to her knees. She reached the bars of her cage, gripping them feebly.

Her swollen eyes blinked at me as her cracked and scabbed lips curled downward.

"Papa? Is that you?"

I reached my hand to hers, ignoring the stench. Something trickled from my eyes down my face. It stung.

"They're not dead," I whispered.

Forbes had heard me.

"Of course not, Mr. McCleary. We need them alive."

I whirled around, screaming with rage, "What are you doing to them?"

Arabella made a choking sound. I could see a few of her teeth biting down on her lower lip. The blood wasn't long in coming.

At that moment I wanted to inflict every kind of torture Forbes could come up with on her. For lying, for being lied to, for believing it all.

I didn't know which of them to hate more.

"They're all here, aren't they, Forbes? All eight of them!"

"Yes, they're all here," the doctor said quite plainly. He acted like the horror around him was completely natural.

"They are subjects," he said, as if that explained everything. "Arabella understands. Don't you?"

Arabella stood there, immobile, biting down on her lip. She made no reply except a noise that sounded something like a hiccup.

"You better control yourself, my dear."

Forbes pulled a handkerchief from his coat pocket and held it to her face. He pressed himself close to her, laying the gun against her bosom so it propped up her chin.

Then he took the papers from her hands.

For a terrible moment, I thought he was going to kill

her. The worst part was I almost wanted it to happen.

Arabella said, barely loud enough to hear, "I understand, William. We have to do what is necessary."

The doctor took the rifle from her face and said, "That's . . . right."

I tried to imagine how she must have worshipped him. The one person who made her feel the way she wanted to feel, like she was worth something.

She got what she'd wanted, but the price had been high. There wasn't much of her left now.

Just enough to make her afraid of Forbes.

She kept that gun trained on me.

"This," Forbes said, holding up the papers, "has been a great burden to me. To think that all this toil might never bear fruit, that the world might not see the results of my labors. That's the nightmare of every creator, every discoverer. Wouldn't you agree, Mr. McCleary?"

All I could do was shake my head and ask, "Why?"

It was a silly question. But I had the feeling he was about to kill me. I wanted him to keep talking.

"So you're curious?" Forbes said, chuckling.

Curiosity suddenly seemed like something dirty and full of corruption.

I was fascinated by this corruption. And that fascination made me feel sick and full of guilt, like I was somehow in complicity with this creature.

I put my hand around the iron bars of Josephine's cell. I felt like I was in the cage there with them.

Forbes began to talk. His words were like ticks of a clock, ticking my life away.

32

"BUT THEN AGAIN," Forbes said. "Perhaps we'd better kill you right now and get it over with. What do you think, Arabella?"

Very slowly and cautiously she answered, "I think Mr. McCleary deserves to hear all about it. Don't you, William? Let him know just how much you duped him, how perfectly you made an ass out of him. Wouldn't you like to do that before you kill him?"

Arabella had recovered some of her coolness. She wouldn't look at me. I seemed as invisible to her as the women in the cages were to Forbes.

There was no emotion in her face for me to decipher. That blankness terrified me more than anything else could. It reminded me of her mentor.

"I want to hear it too, William," she said. "I want to hear all about it."

"Why not?" Forbes said, leaning against one of the new sets of iron bars. His eyes glanced at the row of cells with the pride of a lord overlooking his manor.

"For years, I've been experimenting on the cadavers of negroes. Ever since the death of my mentor, Dr. Samuel George Morton. Like him, I've tried to define precisely what determines intelligence. And I've tried to prove what Morton and other great scientists knew in their hearts but could not undeniably prove. That negroes are the intellectual, cultural, and moral inferiors of whites."

Arabella raised her head, still betraying no emotion.

"Does that sound like a worthy enterprise, Arabella?" I asked.

"She won't answer you, McCleary. She knows I never thought of her as one of them. Didn't you, Arabella?"

The girl wouldn't answer him either.

"She's being demure, I think. There's no need to be reticent, my dear. Don't you think I realized you knew ... or at least suspected what exactly was the nature of our work? How many times did we talk about the bitterness you felt when they rejected you, shunned you? Didn't we agree that the inferior must be overcome? All I'm saying now is that if I could prove that negroes, as a race, are inferior then ... we could speed up the process of evolution."

Arabella's soulless voice said, "Yes, William. I can see that now."

With a glimmer of triumph, Forbes said, "That is why I knew you were never one of them! But"—he turned back to me now—"I had to prove all this scientifically, not with Morton's crude methods. Thus I needed many cadavers, you see. Many, many of them. Potter's field, the morgue, the almshouse, the penitentiaries—these couldn't supply the amount I needed. So I began to appropriate my own subjects. With the help of Levi Chew, who had tried selling me a resurrected corpse years before, I decided to pursue the business whole-hog. It was like the old days in medical school, I tell you! The two of us out there in the dead of night, prying our prize out of the cold earth! How I savored those moments."

He paused to look dotingly on Arabella who stared at the cages, transfixed.

"Then Miss Cole matriculated into the college. I was intrigued by her brain to say the least. I wanted to study her. Then I conceived the idea of having her assist me in my research. Of course I didn't tell her the full extent of it, or the eventual goal I sought. But she was so eager, so desirous to please and be accepted, that I couldn't help but tender a sort of . . . affection for her. She assisted me with the dissection of many cadavers. I didn't hide from her the fact that many of them were resurrected. She was a scientist. She understood the necessity of procuring the maximum number of subjects.''

He brandished the papers at me, the ones describing in cold detail how he tortured these women.

"You see these?" he said, with a smile creasing his coldly handsome face. "This is but a portion of the statistics we gathered. Other papers contained measurements of cranial capacity, brain size, anomalies, and so forth. By this time I told Arabella we were engaged in the discovery of the source of intelligence. I let her believe that because by now she was quite useful to me, exceptionally loyal and sworn to secrecy. She understood the importance of our work. That if people were to find out the exact conditions of our experiments that there would be misunderstanding and censure. And then all our work would be wasted. Isn't that right, my dear?"

"Of course, William. That would have been too great a risk."

Her words held just a tinge of sarcasm.

Forbes looked confused. I threw him off by saying, "When did you decide to start torturing the living instead of the dead?"

The pleasure he took in describing his crimes was uncanny. I'd never seen someone so empty of even hateful emotion.

"Serendipity brought this current stage of the project to fruition. You see, our friend Chew was beginning to enjoy the lavish salary I paid him, throwing it away in gambling hells. His increased income came to the attention of our dear friend Sergeant Walter Duffy. Chew was, I think he called it, 'in the toils' of Duffy, a paid informant of the police for many years. The sergeant began to follow Levi and surprised him one night while he loaded some corpses into our warehouse on Plume Street.''

"So Duffy started taking a piece of that business, right? And you had to withdraw because the coppers might sniff you out."

"Something like that. I couldn't have Chew deliver too many corpses to me. Nor could I be seen too often around Plume Street. How I hated that sergeant, Mr. McCleary! Thanks to him my project was in severe danger. Not just because of his usurping the resurrectionist business. Now he'd brought in that McNamee fellow who knew me and Arabella from the numerous deliveries he made from the morgue. It was impossible for us to be seen around Chew any longer. We resorted to a great deal of subterfuge, eventually deciding that it was less conspicuous for him to meet Arabella. She became my courier to Chew."

The doctor began pacing around the room, leaning against the cages, with his carbine trained on my heart. He kept his eyes on Arabella, who was still pointing my revolver at me.

She was walling herself up in her own private cell. I could see it in her cold, impassive face. It looked ugly now. I got the feeling she could just as easily shoot both of us. That way she could pretend this had never happened.

Forbes was acting confident. He rubbed his back against the iron bars, not even noticing the whimpering of the captives.

"Arabella was quite indispensable. I have to admit she was becoming more and more intriguing to me. I wondered what it would be like to have her around all the time, whenever I wanted her."

The two of them raised their heads to look at each other. Arabella was squinting as if she didn't comprehend his words. Or didn't want to.

"I began to . . ." He chuckled as she stared at him. For the first time, he seemed embarrassed. "I began to think on her a great deal. Think on . . . well, I had certain ideas that kept flitting through my brain. The ideas became very distracting. Then one day I arrived at the decision to circumvent Duffy by acquiring live subjects. It seemed like such a natural decision. And it banished those distracting thoughts for the nonce. This cellar down here was constructed by an abolitionist to hide runaway slaves in the old days. I thought it would make a wonderful accommodation for the new subjects. Then I could continue my experiments with a great deal more privacy, without being restricted by any . . . silly conventions of our age. I could devote myself to a thorough, scientific study.''

''A thorough, scientific torturing of innocent women?''

''Not so innocent, Mr. McCleary! I only selected, with the help of Levi, the lowest, most degraded women. That way, I was sure, there would be no inquiries made as to their disappearance. Chew abducted them from their places of employment and secreted them to this house, where he assisted me in certain . . .''

I didn't want to give him the pleasure of reciting his tortures again.

''So you kidnapped eight whores?'' I said, interrupting him.

''Yes, and we wiped away any trace of them. Chew knew a receiver of stolen goods referred to him by McNamee. The same one to whom they brought clothes and baubles salvaged from the dead. Now I had Chew bring him clothes salvaged from the living.''

''Then Chew got his hands on Josephine Martin. That was a mistake, Forbes. She had parents, that one. Parents that loved her. They were respectable enough to make us listen to their problem.''

There was a weeping sound behind me. Josephine must have been listening the whole time. I grasped her hand again and only now did I notice the rope tied tightly around one wrist. Looking closer into the cell I saw the rope tied in loops around a brass ring set in the wall.

''What in hell do you have them tied up for?'' I cried. ''Isn't caging them bad enough?''

Forbes cleared his throat and said, "All part of the study."

He abruptly changed the subject. "You're right, of course. I suppose kid—I mean, acquiring that subject was risky. But I needed to have someone who wasn't a prostitute. That one," he indicated Josephine, "was the beginning of a new group who would be left alone, by which the other group could be measured."

"So you were planning to get more?"

"Oh yes."

"Like Goldie Collins?"

"That one was different. Arabella chose her. I only said we needed a live subject, like she told you. I was beginning to get those distracting thoughts again. Something told me they might go away if Arabella and I could work together. All I wanted was to share some of my work with her. The important part of it."

"By lying to her and using her."

"What she did, she did willingly. To help me."

Arabella began backing away from us, ever so slightly. Forbes's words were acting like a repellent.

I knew how she felt.

As I watched her, I remembered wanting to go to war. I thought it would be romantic, heroic. Hell, I thought it would be fun. It had been easy to think that.

Then I actually did go to war. I saw what it was really like. And at night when I couldn't see, I could still smell the death and fear.

I could see that same pain of recognition written all over her now.

Forbes was too busy reliving his past triumphs.

"Chew lured the woman away from her situation in a mill somewhere. And brought her to me."

It all made sense now. The rope burns on her wrists. Her knowledge of Josephine Martin. What had she said to her killer? She was going to tell everything she knew about what he did to her and the others.

"You damn fool," I said to myself. "All the time you were thinking it was Duffy."

"That's exactly what I wanted you to believe. Chew made a big mistake letting Goldie escape. He always had a weakness for that creature. Wednesday last he let her out of the cage with the ropes still on her."

"To rape her?"

"A vulgar expression. But Goldie was a little strong for him. She tore free from the ropes and overpowered him."

"After grabbing some of Josephine's jewelry that Chew had lying around, waiting to be fenced."

"The whore tried blackmailing me. I sent Chew to silence her."

"And dispose of her body?"

Forbes took a deep breath of the putrid air and said, "I thought it would be better if Goldie's body weren't lying around too long. The fewer people to see it and possibly recognize it the better. Spiriting it away from the morgue provided a little obfuscation. Enough to intrigue you, I might add."

"Where did he take the body, Forbes?"

Bored, the physician said, "Dumped it further up the river, I imagine. And made sure it didn't float this time."

I backed away from him slowly, instinctively drawing closer to Arabella. She was listening attentively, staring at the revolver in her hands.

Forbes followed me till he was leaning against Josephine's cage.

"It's too bad," I said, "that Chew botched things up by bribing the ragpicker with Josephine's things."

"It should've worked," the doctor said defensively, "he was supposed to tell anyone that he'd seen Duffy do the killing."

"But then you saw how important it was to not have Josephine's jewelry in circulation. So you sent him back that night to do the job right. And plant a badge from Duffy's club for me to find."

And, I realized, he arrived just as Gus was about to tell me the real killer's identity.

The ragpicker's last words came back to me now: "The nigger . . ."

"A pity he didn't kill you too, when he had the chance," Forbes said. "Anyway, we'd bribed the morgue attendant, who told you the story we wanted you to hear."

I shook my head in admiration for him. And dismay for me.

"You played me like an expert. I'll give you that. Even at the College, with all that stuff about burking and resurrectionist work. You didn't even care by then about your body-snatching business, did you? You just fancied the idea of ruining another man's life."

"A life that had ruined many others, I assure you."

That he bothered to justify himself at all was enough to make me laugh.

It was bitter laughter, directed at me more than him.

I saw now how much I'd been lying to myself.

Out of my own stupidity, greed, or whatever, I might have enabled this horror Forbes contrived to continue. Only by sheer chance had I stumbled on the truth that had been staring me in the face the whole time.

Now that I saw the truth I was powerless to do anything about it. Arabella would have to be the one to act. But whether she'd shoot me, Forbes, herself or all three was anyone's guess.

With Forbes raising a bead on me with his carbine, all I could do was stand there and listen to him.

I didn't try to ignore the wails of the captive, tortured souls behind those iron bars. I let their moans and weeping reach into me and grip my heart. Somehow I felt responsible for their pain.

I decided to distract Forbes for a while longer. I needed to get the truth into the open. If I had ignored the truth for my own ends before, I wasn't going to do it anymore.

That thought had been like a terrible secret I'd been

dying to admit to someone. I felt strangely relieved.

Arabella had backed away from us into a shadowy corner of the room. I watched the darkness envelop her. When her spine ran up against the wall she made a sound that was like a gasp. I couldn't see her face, or any other part of her except the hand that held my revolver.

She wasn't pointing the gun at me anymore. The barrel began to hesitantly change directions, aiming itself at her instead.

I swallowed audibly, wondering if it mattered to me anymore if she did it or not.

Forbes wasn't paying much attention to her. His eyes were drawn to the women in their cages. I couldn't read his expression. Perhaps because it was so much like that of a dead man's.

I decided to keep his attention focused on me. It was better that he didn't look too closely at Arabella. If she was going to shoot herself it might be the distraction I needed. The harshness of that thought did not concern me just then.

"I guess Goldie gave you the perfect opportunity to frame Duffy, take him out like you always wanted to. After all, he made the perfect killer. A sadistic thug with a taste for colored whores. With him out of the picture you were free to go on with your experiments without his interference."

"That was the plan. Arabella and I discussed the matter at some length, didn't we dear?"

I moved between the two of them so he couldn't see her.

She answered him with a choking sound that might have been a sob.

"I'm sure it was easy to manipulate her," I said. "You had her fear of being caught for Goldie's kidnapping and murder. A fear you planted in her."

"I had to. She knew nothing about Goldie's kidnapping, of course. Didn't even know she'd disappeared. It took several weeks for Chew and I to plan it after Arabella told me about the whore, that she would be the perfect subject. Does that shock you, McCleary? That she would do something so contrary to your petty morality?''

Even though I spoke to him, the words were for Arabella.

''I think she would've done just about anything for you, Forbes. She was in the toils. If there'd been someone else she could've trusted . . . But there was only you. With the way she worshipped you, it would've been easy to plant any idea you wanted to in her brain. You made it easy for her to feel estranged from everyone, especially her own people. Once you had her believing some kinds of human life were worth more than others, it wasn't such a stretch to have her pick a low colored whore for those experiments of yours.''

I took a threatening step toward him. The carbine stopped my advance.

''Except you left some things out, didn't you? Some crucial information. Like what your experiments were really going to be about. I think you knew what would happen if she found that out. Arabella couldn't quite be fashioned in your image, could she?''

Forbes made an impatient, dismissive gesture.

''She could've come around in time. But then the whore escaped. I wasn't ready to tell Arabella the full extent of my . . . research here.''

''So you told her some lies about Goldie, didn't you?''

''Levi and I told her that Duffy had killed the whore while attempting to rape her. Chew, having procured the whore for the sergeant, was around at the time. Duffy forced Chew to dispose of the body. Arabella believed us. We had spoken about Sergeant Duffy before, and she well knew he was no friend of her people. It was also no secret that he had prevented us from resurrecting corpses for months. The three of us decided that Duffy's heinous crime should not go undiscovered.''

''And you also put a scare into her, didn't you? That maybe her association with Goldie might come out—that the police might even discover what you'd been planning.''

''Yes, we did imply that as a sort of incentive. Arabella was eager to see justice done to the sergeant. Weren't you, dear?''

The doctor chuckled as he tried peering into the shadowy corner where Arabella had fled to.

''You played upon her fear and guilt so well it must've been easy to convince her to go to St. Mary's Street that night. I'll bet it was that morning when I saw you at the hospital, that you decided to plant evidence in Duffy's headquarters. Chew knew all about that place, since he was the one who supplied his boss with colored whores. I think that was the one part of Arabella's story that had any truth in it. Chew hated Duffy with as much of a passion as Duffy hated all negroes. Chew must've seen this as the chance of a lifetime. He was fed up with being someone's creature. Of course he didn't know he was your creature, did he, Forbes? Because you gave him a sense of power, letting him assist you with your experiment.'' I was beginning to hate that word. I put all the venom I could into it.

''You had another creature, too. Maybe she told you what I told her—that other colored women had been disappearing. I'll bet you made her believe it was Duffy again. Hell, I had myself believing it. I guess that makes me your third creature.''

''I'm so glad,'' Forbes said, a queer glimmer lighting up his eyes. ''So glad that someone appreciates the irony of having two negroes assist me.''

For the first time since we'd entered his private hell the doctor burst out laughing.

His laughter stopped when I asked him, ''Why did you have her followed?''

''For my own reasons.''

He glared at me, a baleful look in his eye.

''Maybe because you were afraid. Is that it? Maybe you

were asking yourself why Arabella was spending so much time with me?''

It was clear to me now that Duffy had been wondering the same thing. The reason he'd been watching Arabella and having her followed by Chew was to figure out what she had to do with me. Chew would've been glad to keep her spotted for his supposed boss and for his real one at the same time.

There had been no nefarious scheme behind Duffy's surveillance. He'd just been suspicious first and foremost of me, and anyone I happened to associate with. All the time he'd known who the real enemy was.

Forbes had manipulated us all.

The doctor's arms grew tighter around his carbine. Arabella, just beside me, held my revolver in a neutral position, waiting.

Clearing his throat, Forbes said, ''The way she talked about you made me suspect things. I had to start questioning her loyalty. I didn't like doing that.''

I changed the subject, not quite ready for a pill in my neck.

''I wondered what was in that bundle Arabella handed to you Saturday last. It must've been Josephine Martin's jewelry. Except you told her they were Goldie's. You should've been more careful.''

Forbes shrugged.

''A minor oversight. Those baubles were getting tiresome. She should've gotten rid of them for me that morning, while you were napping in the lecture hall.''

''Except McNamee came in and surprised her. She saw him from the street and didn't want him drawing any conclusions. Everything worked out all right though. You gave the jewelry to Levi Chew, who was more capable. By the time I showed up at Duffy's headquarters Chew'd planted the evidence very convincingly. But I wonder why you had him bring Arabella along.''

The doctor shifted slightly and said, ''Bait.''

''Yes. And I came, didn't I?''

Forbes gave a modest shrug.

"It was perfect, doctor. Except one thing. The ledger describing the resurrectionist business. The one that listed the girls Duffy abducted and murdered, and the swag he fenced."

Forbes raised his eyes questioningly.

"I knew right away that Duffy didn't keep those ledgers. The penmanship was way too elaborate for the late sergeant."

"Well, no matter. It didn't deter you from chasing after Duffy, did it?"

Maybe he hadn't underestimated me after all. I'd wanted to believe Duffy was guilty, no matter what the evidence was.

"Naturally it didn't. He was no paragon of virture. It was easy for you to hate him, wasn't it? Just as I hated him."

"You're right. Duffy was easy to hate. He was involved in the resurrectionist business, and no mistake about that. But he wasn't a murderer." I pointed an accusing finger at him and said, "The murderer was you, Forbes."

"No, I'm afraid you're wrong there. Levi took care of all that for me."

"Then you took care of him."

"Yes, I knew he'd become a liability after you captured him. When I saw him at the hospital this morning I knew it was time to silence him, permanently."

"But who would do your dirty work for you then?"

"Dirty work? I was hoping that Arabella and I might finally co-operate fully on the project. I was counting on her standing up to Duffy's interrogation. Chew told me she'd been arrested and taken to the D.S.O.L. club. Duffy was eager to learn why the two of you broke into his sanctum sanctorum. In a way, Arabella saved your life, temporarily. You see, I didn't want to bury you alive while she was in Duffy's hands. I thought Duffy might be willing to make an exchange. The girl for you. I knew from my negro friend how much the sergeant wanted you for the same kind of treatment he planned to give my Arabella. But I changed my mind after sleeping on it. I decided to have Chew kill Duffy instead as I saw how the day was turning out. It would have fit right in with the general rioting.''

"That was his next job after burying me alive?''

"Yes.''

"What about Arabella?''

"I prayed this whole morning that she would be safe.''

"Prayed? To whom? Or what?''

Forbes snickered and said, "A figure of speech. Well!'' He shuffled the carbine again, moving toward me. I backed up right against Arabella, who had used this time to gather together something inside her. From the way she curled her lips I thought it might be disgust or rage. Whether they were for herself or for him was a question I couldn't answer. I wished she would, and pretty damn soon.

Forbes was standing directly in front of Josephine Martin's cage. From the way he was looking at me I knew my time was up.

"So now, back to business, eh?'' My calm demeanor was transparent, even to me.

"Yes.''

"You can continue with the important work you've begun.'' The sarcasm didn't do much good either. I was scared to death and he knew it. From the way he was grinning at me I could see he thoroughly enjoyed my fear.

"That's right,'' he said.

My voice was quaking. I had trouble getting the words out. "I want . . . to know . . . why.'' I flung an arm toward the cells, the roll-top desk, Arabella, everything.

A fatuous smile creased his handsome face.

"There doesn't have to be any meaning, Mr. McCleary,'' he told me, in a suddenly gruff voice. "I do it because I can.''

My vision seemed to contract. All I could see was the mouth of that carbine.

Then a hand reached beyond the bars and knocked his arm, just as he fired the shot. There was a loud crack from the carbine and a great deal of smoke. The ball burrowed into the ceiling.

Josephine Martin had saved my life.

Forbes tossed the gun away. There wasn't enough time to reload. Instead he screamed at Arabella, "Shoot him, damn it! Kill him, kill him!"

The girl did nothing at first.

Forbes tried pleading with her.

"You kill him or he'll ruin you! And me! Do you want to rot inside a penitentiary for the rest of your life? Give me that gun, you silly bitch!"

Arabella stared at me from behind the barrel of my revolver.

She must've seen something in my eyes, something past the fear and anger and horror. A feeling that I had once had for her that was not quite dead.

Her trembling hand extended the barker toward me. I gripped the stock.

Forbes called on a God he didn't know to damn me. Then, regaining control of himself, he straightened his necktie and said, "Well, I suppose this means I'm under arrest."

I said, "Not a chance."

Then I shot him to death. I didn't stop until all seven chambers were empty.

It didn't take me long to find the keys for the cages. The women, stumbling out of their cells, clawed at each other for meager protection and followed me through the long, dark passageway. I had to carry Arabella myself. A part of her, like these other women, had been destroyed. I couldn't decide whether that meant I should pity her.

Once the two of us were up the stairs and into the study, I helped Josephine Martin climb into the large open space.

I kissed her forehead lightly and murmured my thanks. She couldn't hear me, I don't think.

Then I helped the other women out. When all of us were out of the cellar, I went to the curtains and tore them off the windows.

We stood together in the warming glow of the afternoon.

I WASN'T AT all surprised when the papers refused to report on it. The resurrectionist business jeopardized the careers of half the physicians in Philadelphia. Discrediting Duffy would make the police force look mighty bad too. The new Mayor Stokley was interested in beefing up the force's reputation. The disappeared girls . . . well, nobody was interested in what happened to a few colored whores. Josephine Martin's family, after a long talk with me, decided to let it drop. They moved down South, I think, where the mother was from. North Carolina, maybe. A new start, they said. Josephine was already recovering. Since Forbes had selected her to remain a standard by which the rest were measured, she had escaped the sort of torment reserved for the other women. But the memories of those horrible weeks wouldn't be erased so easily. I hoped she could find something, or someone, who could help her forget.

With the election over the Democrats were scrambling to squeeze the last bit of profit they could out of their government jobs, before the Republicans took over and did the exact same thing. The riot that Tuesday had only been suppressed by the intervention of the Marines. Two hundred shots were fired. Six people were killed.

Mulholland instructed me to hand over the books and

ledgers detailing Duffy's criminal activities that I'd stolen
from his headquarters. Heins wanted them, too. They held
the kind of knowledge that simply couldn't be put to any
good use.

One cool November night I made a fire out of them all.
They burned quite nicely, but slowly. The ink gave off a
peculiar stench.

While I crouched at the fire there, Arabella came and
lay beside me.

Ever since we got out of Forbes's house I'd kept her
with me. She couldn't take care of herself. The second or
third day she got a hell of a fever and was sick for many
days.

I wasn't about to forget what she'd done to Goldie Collins, or tried to do. Nor could I forget that she'd gone to
the fence with Josephine Martin's jewelry. It didn't matter
to me that she'd believed Forbes when he told her the
baubles had belonged to Goldie. I think perhaps there was
some part of her that didn't believe him and went along
anyway, because Forbes made it easy for her to think that
good and evil were irrelevant distinctions.

What I'd seen that day changed the way I felt about
her for good. If some part of me still loved her, as I knew
it did, then it was only because of the horror I'd seen
contorting her face that day. The horror that comes with
the realization that there is a hell, and you and only you
have put yourself there.

Forbes had made it all seem attractive, covering its hid-
eousness with a patchwork fantasy tailored to match Arabella's deepest yearnings and aspirations.

I was no different. Forbes had constructed a fantasy for
me, too.

My dream was to bring down a man I'd convicted,
tried, and executed before I even knew the whole truth
about him.

In a way, Forbes had been right. Duffy was an evil man
who deserved a violent end to his own violent life. And
I, Wilton McCleary, had played god and judged him.

Now before the embers I asked for forgiveness. Not because I'd struggled against an evil man like Duffy. But because, during my struggle, I hadn't recognized how much like him I'd become.

I had no right to judge Arabella for being seduced by Forbes.

Any punishment I might've wanted for her had already been meted out. Every day I saw hatred, loathing, fear, and anguish in her eyes. She would sit at the window, stare out into the street, and weep. We did not talk to each other.

Somehow I thought Arabella might be relied upon to punish herself.

But I didn't want her to recreate the torture of those women in her own life. That would accomplish nothing.

Arabella agreed. When her fever broke she told me that she wanted to leave Philadelphia and leave her medical, scientific life.

She said there was some need down South for educated negroes. Ones who could teach the freedmen.

"So I can earn forgiveness," she told me. "From the ones I said were not fit for survival. I want to prove myself wrong. I want to see if I can't make them fit. And myself too."

That night before the fire, when she crawled over to me, was the first time in days she'd moved from the convalescent bed I'd set up for her.

I saw something glint in the orange glow and heard a snipping sound. She had some scissors and I was frightened, at first, that she was cutting off those tresses of lovely hair. But she had cut just a curl, which she pressed into my hand.

"Put it in a secret place," she told me. "Where you can always find it."

We sat before the fire there and hoped all our personal evil could be consumed in it. I was shocked to hear her voice after so many days of silence. She told me a story about a bird. A legend from Egypt, she said. This bird they call a phoenix would die in a pillar of fire only to emerge reborn from the flames.

"That's what we hoped for during the war," I told her. "Look how it's turned out."

She knew what I meant. The riot against the negroes on election Tuesday, the hideous experiments of Forbes, Duffy's hatred, and evils to match them in the conquered South.

The two of us didn't have a chance. Not before, or now.

Arabella knew that. It didn't stop her from kissing me. Then she said, "See how long it's taking those books to burn?" she said.

"A long time," I said.

"But they will burn. Eventually."

I pulled her to me to savor a last embrace as we watched the fire die down.

By the morning the books had turned into a fine, powdery ash.

Afterword

THE *PHILADELPHIA LEDGER* ran this headline for the December 5, 1882 edition:

PROF W. S. FORBES
DEMONSTRATOR OF ANATOMY
IN JEFFERSON MEDICAL COLLEGE
ARRESTED FOR COMPLICITY IN
GRAVE ROBBING OF LEBANON CEMETERY

An expressman named Frank McNamee, his employee "Dutch" Pillet, and Levi Chew, a stable worker in Lombard Street, were arraigned the next day, charged with robbing graves. A fourth man, Chew's brother George, was arraigned with them. He was the superintendent of the Lebanon Cemetery.

For months black leaders had suspected sinister goings-on at the cemetery. The arrests were finally made by concerned black citizens and a party of reporters from the *Press*, a paper long-since defunct. With them was a Pinkerton operative by the name of William Henderson. Since it took reporters and a private detective to put an end to the body-snatching, one is led to believe the police were not interested.

McNamee, Chew, and the others were caught pulling

out of the cemetery. In their wagon lay six colored bodies. (The newspapers were always careful to specify such racial distinctions). All of the bodies were nude and appeared to be recently buried.

In court, Louis N. Megargee, the city editor of the *Press*, testified that he saw the grave robbers leave Lebanon Cemetery the previous March with another haul of six bodies. It was an easy thing for him to trace the wagon: it had McNamee's name painted on it. McNamee had a key that fit two doors at Jefferson Medical College. A clerk there, who was also arrested, paid the expressman three dollars per "subject."

Several people came forth to identify the bodies, including the undertaker who'd just prepared them for burial a few days before.

Frank McNamee was employed to haul the U.S. mail. As a sideline he also transported bodies from prisons and the House of Correction. In court he gave a price list for his services: $3 for hauling the corpse of a prisoner, $8 for one from the almshouse. The city paid him $6 to haul bodies to the morgue.

Levi Chew happened to know Dr. Forbes and was able to furnish him with bodies on request, for the price of $1 per corpse. Later he upped his price to $3. Their business relationship lasted about three years. During that time, Chew averaged three per week from the cemetery for four to five months per year.

The papers do not recount how McNamee and Chew got together.

Dr. Forbes was careful to calm their fears of discovery. He read the law to Chew, informing him that he "wouldn't get in any trouble." The most they would do, he said, is discharge his brother.

Three months later, Dr. Forbes was acquitted, largely due to the support given him in court by one of the most eminent physicians in the nation, Samuel Agnew. Agnew, perhaps the greatest surgeon of the day and one concerned with the progress of medical science, was the subject of

Thomas Eakins's famous painting *The Agnew Clinic*. Agnew felt passionately about the need for fresh corpses (no matter where they came from) to further the study of anatomy. However, he wasn't concerned with some other recent discoveries in medicine, namely Lister's program of antisepsis. Years later, when Agnew was called in to care for President Garfield (after he was shot by the infamous Guiteau), he caused more damage to the President than the bullet did by poking his unsterilized fingers around in the wounds.

There is no record of the fate of McNamee, Chew, and their accomplices.

The other major event in this novel, the election riot of 1871, also unfortunately really happened. It was the last serious race riot in the history of Philadelphia and occurred pretty much the way I describe it. One black man was hacked to death while others were shot, stabbed, or stoned.

Octavius Catto's death by an assassin was the greatest tragedy of the riot. Catto was a civil rights leader and the principal at the Institute for Colored Youth, the high school for black children. His murderer was apprehended years later and acquitted by an all-white jury. There was an accomplice to the crime who also escaped punishment. He was referred to only as Sergeant Duffy.

While researching *The Resurrectionist*, I came across two volumes that were invaluable in recreating the atmosphere of racial tension that permeates this story. The first was W.E.B. DuBois's classic, groundbreaking *The Philadelphia Negro: A Social Study* (Philadelphia, 1899). A more recent book, *Roots of Violence in Black Philadelphia, 1860-1900*, by Roger Lane (Harvard University Press, 1986), provided a wealth of information on the nineteenth-century Philadelphia underworld, and how its tentacles ensnared a disenfranchised people—a people to whom the victorious North made many promises and kept few.

The reason I decided to fuse the riot and the body-snatching incidents (despite their historical disparity) is self-evident. They both dealt with racist violence. But the story is not the trite one of white oppressor versus black victim. Chew and his brother, both black men, played a leading part in violating the graves of their brethren. I find it ironic that it took criminals to break the barrier of prejudice. Their partners were white men, something that was almost unheard of back then, when even criminal gangs of different colors never mixed. That they preyed on their own race for the sake of money is both tragic and somehow reassuring. We at least know our collective lowest common denominator: greed.

You have already noticed, I'm sure, that neither Forbes nor Duffy escape punishment in my revised account of the events. I told it the way it *should have* happened. Unfortunately, justice back then was more of an anomaly than I make it seem. As a creator I feel the need to bring order to a past which was so disordered. My story is not just a history but also a wish—that justice might have a place in the future where it never did in that long-gone past.